PRAISE FOR LEXI BLAKE AND MASTERS AND MERCENARIES

"I can always trust Lexi Blake's Dom̲.̲ ̲.̲.̲.̲ ̲.̲.̲.̲.̲ ̲.̲e̲a̲v̲e̲ ̲me breathless...and in love. If you want sensual, exciting BDSM wrapped in an awesome love story, then look for a Lexi Blake book."

~Cherise Sinclair USA Today Bestselling author

"Lexi Blake's MASTERS AND MERCENARIES series is beautifully written and deliciously hot. She's got a real way with both action and sex. I also love the way Blake writes her gorgeous Dom heroes--they make me want to do bad, bad things. Her heroines are intelligent and gutsy ladies whose taste for submission definitely does not make them dish rags. Can't wait for the next book!"

~Angela Knight, New York Times bestselling author

"A Dom is Forever is action packed, both in the bedroom and out. Expect agents, spies, guns, killing and lots of kink as Liam goes after the mysterious Mr. Black and finds his past and his future… The action and espionage keep this story moving along quickly while the sex and kink provides a totally different type of interest. Everything is very well balanced and flows together wonderfully."

~A Night Owl "Top Pick", Terri, Night Owl Erotica

"A Dom Is Forever is everything that is good in erotic romance. The story was fast-paced and suspenseful, the characters were flawed but made me root for them every step of the way, and the hotness factor was off the charts mostly due to a bad boy Dom with a penchant for dirty talk."

~Rho, The Romance Reviews

"A good read that kept me on my toes, guessing until the big reveal, and thinking survival skills should be a must for all men."

~Chris, Night Owl Reviews

Submission is Not Enough

OTHER BOOKS BY LEXI BLAKE

EROTIC ROMANCE

Masters and Mercenaries
The Dom Who Loved Me
The Men With The Golden Cuffs
A Dom is Forever
On Her Master's Secret Service
Sanctum: A Masters and Mercenaries Novella
Love and Let Die
Unconditional: A Masters and Mercenaries Novella
Dungeon Royale
Dungeon Games: A Masters and Mercenaries Novella
A View to a Thrill
Cherished: A Masters and Mercenaries Novella
You Only Love Twice
Luscious: Masters and Mercenaries~Topped
Adored: A Masters and Mercenaries Novella
Master No
Just One Taste: Masters and Mercenaries~Topped 2
From Sanctum with Love
Devoted: A Masters and Mercenaries Novella
Dominance Never Dies
Dominance Never Dies
Submission is Not Enough
Perfectly Paired: Masters and Mercenaries~Topped 3, Coming
November 29, 2016
For His Eyes Only, Coming February 2017
Treasured, Coming April 25, 2017

Lawless
Ruthless, Coming August 9, 2016
Satisfaction, Coming January 3, 2017

Submission is Not Enough

Masters and Mercenaries, Book 12
Lexi Blake

Submission is Not Enough
Masters and Mercenaries, Book 12
Lexi Blake

Published by DLZ Entertainment LLC

Copyright 2016 DLZ Entertainment LLC
Edited by Chloe Vale
ISBN: 978-1-937608-54-5

McKay-Taggart logo design by Charity Hendry

This is a work of fiction. Names, places, characters and incidents are the product of the author's imagination and are fictitious. Any resemblance to actual persons, living or dead, events or establishments is solely coincidental.

Sign up for Lexi Blake's newsletter
and be entered to win a $25 gift certificate
to the bookseller of your choice.

Join us for news, fun, and exclusive content
including free short stories.

There's a new contest every month!

Go to www.LexiBlake.net to subscribe.

ACKNOWLEDGMENTS

Thanks to my team and to all the readers who have followed the Masters and Mercenaries series since it all began five years ago. I hoped the series would make it for five books so being here at book twelve is amazing to me. I thank you all for the support and I hope you'll come with me on many more adventures!

PROLOGUE

Grand Cayman

"Kill her."

Theo heard the words of his CO, but he hesitated. His heart was thumping in his chest, but it was an oddly pleasant rhythm. Adrenaline flooded his system, making him hyper-aware of everything going on around him.

He'd done the impossible, gotten through all the security to save his boss. Tennessee Smith had been his full-time boss at one point and now he was also a friend. The ex-CIA agent had recruited him out of the Navy and then led him straight to McKay-Taggart and this mission.

Unfortunately it had gone haywire and Ten had been captured, and now looked worse for the wear. It was up to Theo to get him out and save the mission.

If he could pull this off, no one would look at him like the littlest Taggart ever again. He wouldn't be in the shadow of Ian or Sean. He wouldn't merely be Case's baby brother. He was well aware of the fact that while there were only a few minutes between him and his older brother, everyone considered Case to be the badass. Theo was the sweet one, the one everyone worried might not be fully capable of handling himself in the field without big brothers looking out for him.

He didn't want to be the sweet one. He wanted Erin to look at him like she did Case. Like he was competent and not just some himbo she'd allowed into her bed. Some kid she would dump when she found a real man.

Fuck, he loved her and he was going to prove to her that he was worthy.

But first he had to decide if he was going to follow Tennessee Smith's order.

Hope McDonald was some kind of crazy scientist, and it was obvious she was the reason for Ten's extremely bad day. He'd been captured by her father, and it looked like the senator had been doing some experiments of his own. In torture. Ten could barely walk. He'd begged Theo to run and take the rest of the team with him, but Taggarts didn't leave their men behind. Even when they were surly and difficult.

Still, standing there and aiming right at the blonde's head, he had to wonder how far he could go. "She doesn't have a gun."

"That bitch doesn't need one." Ten's lips were dry, his voice cracking out of his mouth.

Dr. McDonald's well-manicured hands came up. "Theo won't kill me. He's a gentleman. You should move. Father's men will attack from behind and the Chinese will come up the road."

Theo stared at her, knowing precious seconds were flying by. She was an odd duck. It was obvious she'd had a thing for him back in Dallas. Was that why she was helping him out now? He'd never done a thing to encourage her. Since the moment he'd seen Erin, he hadn't looked at another woman. He'd known that crazy redhead was the only one for him. "Why would you tell us anything?"

"Because it won't change the outcome. I would like for us to work together, Theodore. I find you fascinating. Even more now that I've read your records. Mr. Smith was a good subject, but you will be a masterpiece. You should hurry. They're almost here."

"Kill her," Ten insisted.

The moment seemed almost stuck, as though he wasn't sure what he should do. He'd had a few moments like this, when he'd known somehow the outcome depended on his own choice. The world seemed to slow and he knew whatever he did next would change things.

In the end, he had to follow his conscience. He put an arm around Ten Smith and started to drag him out into the night. They had an army of MSS agents after them and all of the senator's mercenaries. "I can't shoot an unarmed woman, Ten. You can fire me later, but I can't."

As they exited Ten's torture chamber, he seemed to perk up a bit. "Faith. Tell me Faith left the island."

Brody Carter stepped out from where he'd been clinging to the shadows. The massive Aussie was part of the team Theo was in charge of. Dressed in black from head to toe, he somehow managed to blend into the night. "I'll take him. And Faith is safe and sound back at the vehicles with Hutch and Erin."

The Aussie chucked Ten over his shoulder with a thud.

"Why is Faith with Erin?" Ten managed with a huff. "The last I heard she never wanted to talk to any of us again."

"I needed her intel." Theo touched his earpiece. There would be time enough for a full debrief later. "We're on the move."

His communications specialist's voice came over the comm device in his ear. Hutch's voice was steady over the line. "You've got trouble heading your way, Theo. Your girl just took off. She and Faith are on their way to rendezvous. I'm coming after them."

Theo felt his stomach drop. Cool. He needed to stay cool, but the idea of Erin charging in made him anything but.

Brody stopped beside him. He'd certainly heard the news.

"What's wrong?" Ten tried to twist his body up.

"Are you kidding me?" He didn't wait for Hutch's reply. Greg Hutchins might joke around, but never during an op. If Hutch said Erin had lost her damn mind and decided to no longer follow orders, then she was on her way and apparently bringing a civilian with her. He had to deal with it. Oh, there would be hell to pay when they were done and it would all come out of her sweet ass, but he had to keep it together for now. Later she would get a spanking that would make even her masochistic self cry. "Fuck. Erin and Faith are on their way in. Hutch is firing up the van and coming after them. It looks like we're going to have to squeeze into one vehicle. I'm going to have her ass."

Gunfire splattered through the air. It was hard to figure out where it was coming from sometimes. It seemed to come from every direction.

Would Erin walk into the middle of a kill zone? Was he putting them all in a position to be slaughtered?

Deep breath, Taggart. Your brother wouldn't have made you second in command if he didn't believe in you. You can do this. You can save Ten and your team and when it's all done, you'll get the girl.

Because he knew the girl was pulling away from him. He wasn't sure why, but despite the fact that she spent every night in his bed, she was still afraid. Not of him, but of what they could be.

If he showed her he was strong enough, he could put it all to rest.

"I've got a line coming in from the north," a feminine voice said. Desiree Brooks was former MI6 and cool under pressure. Despite the cracking gunfire around them, Des's voice was cool and calm.

"We need to fall back." Her partner, Nikolai Markovic, wasn't as calm. His Russian accent normally wasn't as thick, and now he sounded like he barely spoke English. "Des, get down. Down! Damn it, Taggart. We're about to be surrounded."

And he was terrified for his lover. The Brit and the Russian were from Damon Knight's team. From the moment they'd gotten to the Caymans for the mission it had been obvious their closeness wasn't simply cover.

Or maybe he just knew what a man in love looked like and he damn straight knew how shitty it was to have his woman in the field. Sometimes he cursed the fact that he couldn't have fallen for a simpler woman than his Erin. His fucking warrior goddess who was going to throw herself into battle if he couldn't get them out of here.

"I'm going to need you to stand for a minute, Ten. Or at least sit. Keep your head down. Des, Nick, what's going on?" Brody had to practically yell because the night had exploded around them.

The few lights that had been on blinked out and they were surrounded by darkness. *Thank you, Hutch.* The kid could work miracles. Ten flattened himself against the building and he seemed like he was going to stay upright. Theo forced himself to focus. Erin had to have seen something he couldn't. It was the only real reason she would disobey a direct order. He watched, his eyes settling in as Nick backed up toward them.

"We've got incoming," Nick shouted back.

It was going to be all right. They would retreat. They had the package and they would lose whoever pursued them in the jungle. They would go straight for the building he'd found Ten in. The senator would be worried about his daughter. Hell, talking to the doc might even slow them down. This was still going to work. He felt it. "We'll let them come in and sneak out when they raid the building. They can't see us here. And Hutch just cut the power. We've got the cover of night on our side."

He fell back as lights ahead split the darkness and he could hear the thud of tires rolling over the pavement. "Get back."

At least they were all together. They would stay in a tight formation and move toward the road where Erin or Hutch could pick them up. He only saw one set of lights at this point, though he was sure there would be more coming. A few minutes and they would be gone and the senator could look all he liked. He would have Ten and put him on a plane as soon as he could. Then the rest would break up and sneak away without another problem.

He was about to give the signal to move when Des broke off from the group.

"I can cause some chaos," Des said. "Get ready to run toward the back. We can go up the trail to where we left the cars."

He leaned forward, ready to order her back into formation.

Before he could get the words out of his mouth, Des moved around the side of the building. There was no way to miss the way Nick tensed. Theo nearly shouted, but it would only have served to give away their position. Two quick shots pinged ahead of him and then he watched as the vehicle that had been coming their way flipped and rolled. The sound of metal gnarling and gears crashing filled the night. The SUV crashed into the building to its right and Theo could feel the ground shudder under his boots.

"Let's get out of here." Des turned and started back.

The lecture would have to wait, but she was going to find out that he didn't play that way. They'd walked in with a plan and that was to stick together. Damon was going to get a hard earful about his people from Theo. But it wasn't happening now. He readied himself to move, visualizing the steps.

A single shot split the air and Des stopped. Even in the low light, Theo could see the way her skin paled and the bloom of blood on her forehead. Des hit her knees and then slumped forward.

He heard another volley of gunshots to the west. Before the true horror of Des's death could sink in, he realized they were about to be pinned down. Someone was coming up behind them.

Theo bit back bile and followed his instincts. He reached out and grabbed at Nick before he could get to Des's body.

The big Russian pulled at him and for a second, Theo thought he might lose that battle. Thank god for Brody. Brody gripped Nick's arm and held him tight.

"You can't go out there. They've got a sniper." He couldn't quite believe what he'd seen. Des had been standing right there. He needed to get to her, needed to pull her back to safety. If he allowed Nick to run out there, he would be gone, too.

"She could be alive," Nick insisted, his voice tortured.

Not likely, but Theo understood. They didn't leave men behind. Never. He couldn't walk away from her, couldn't be the one to abandon a teammate.

"Give me a second. Let's see if we can take out the sniper." He needed to figure out where he was. They were protected behind the wall, but there would be another car coming and then they would likely be completely outnumbered.

He had to do this with careful forethought, unlike this clusterfuck of a mission he'd embarked on. He could see it now. Erin was going to be the one to have his ass. She'd begged him to call back to his brother, to see if there was any intel at all Ian and the team at home were hearing.

But he'd known what Big Tag would do and he'd been determined to show his big brothers that he was as good as they were.

And now Des was probably dead.

"We have to move." Erin ran up the street and his heart nearly stopped.

It could have been Erin. She would have thought to create some chaos, too. It could have been Erin lying dead in the street.

Fuck, he loved her. He should have listened to her because she was smart and infinitely competent and he wondered if she would ever be able to love a man who couldn't command her both in and out of the bedroom.

He shoved that shit down because he had work to do. Hutch wasn't far behind her.

"I take it we have guests coming we didn't expect." It was the only reason she would have disobeyed orders. Erin was disciplined and years of military service had ingrained a deep respect for her commanding officers into her personality.

He craved that respect from her.

She turned and cursed under her breath. "You could say that. And more than just unfriendlies."

Hutch slid in beside her, going down on his knees. "Expect Faith to be right behind me. She had to have seen Des fall. It was Des, right. Shit. On your left, Argent."

Hutch popped off a few rounds and Erin laid down some cover fire herself. Trouble was heading their way in the form of Faith McDonald. Ten's girlfriend was making her way to them.

So now Ten would beat the shit out of him once he could function again. It was all going to hell and it was his fault.

"Not losing you, too, Nick. Get it together, mate." Brody's hard words brought him back to reality.

"We have to get to her." They didn't leave their people. It was a lesson engraved on his freaking soul. It had been there from birth, he thought sometimes. Case wouldn't have left him. And then the Navy. His team would have died before leaving a man behind. And Ian and Sean. They would be so ashamed of him.

"She's gone," Erin argued. "That was a headshot. We get the fuck out of here before we lose someone else. Nick, I need you to remember your goddamn training."

Somewhere in the background he heard Ten saying something, but all he could think about was the fact that Erin was here and they were about to be surrounded. He wouldn't have another shot to get to Des. He couldn't allow Nick to do it. Nick would be far too emotional. It had to be him. He would do it for Nick because if anything ever happened to Erin, he would need someone to bring him her body.

God, he couldn't be the one who got Erin killed. He couldn't.

He'd worked so hard to convince her she was safe with him and now…he was doing it all wrong. Cool. Calm. Get to Des. Bring her back. Get out.

He could still do this. He could make this happen.

"No. You don't. She's dead." Ten's voice cut through his thoughts. The night had gone quiet around them. Ten was protecting Faith, obviously using every bit of what little energy he had left to force her not to run out and try to treat Des. Faith was a doctor who took her oaths seriously. She was also Ten's woman and she was going to find out Ten took that damn seriously. "Erin's right. That was a headshot. The Chinese don't miss. We have to leave now."

Theo could see Des. She was barely out of reach. Maybe if he got low, he could crawl and drag her back to relative safety. "I can't leave her body. We don't leave men behind."

Ten managed a few steps, enough that he could glare at Theo. "Cut the naïve bullshit, Taggart. If you take a step out from behind that wall, we're all dead. Des proved that. This is a clusterfuck situation and I assure you that we leave men behind when they're corpses and getting them back would produce more corpses. You've been in charge up until now. I'm back and we fucking retreat. Do you understand me?"

Bile threatened again. She was standing right there. Erin. Listening to him being dressed down because he'd fucked up entirely and Des was dead. She was dead. His first command and this is how it turned out. He'd been worried about his brothers? Erin wouldn't forgive him. "Yes, sir. This is my fault, sir."

"There's time for recriminations later. Let's get our people to safety now." Ten's hand found Faith's. He was solid. Even after everything he'd been through, Ten stood tall and made the hard call without hesitation. "Markovic, we're leaving."

The Russian stood. He looked blank, like a mask of nothingness had fallen over his face. "Yes, sir."

Nick wouldn't forget or forgive.

Would he be able to look any of them in the eyes again? All his life he'd wanted to do one thing. He'd wanted to be a soldier and now he wasn't sure he would be able to find a team who could trust him again.

Ten moved out. "Stay behind me."

The horror of the evening sat in his gut, but he had to finish the mission before he dealt with the fallout. Before he had to look at the woman he loved and know she couldn't trust him in the field. And if she couldn't trust him in the field, she would never truly trust him anywhere else. He had to get her to safety before he dealt with the fact that he'd gotten a teammate killed. "Can you walk? Brody, take our six."

Ten walked stiffly ahead of him. "I'll make it and if I don't, you better leave me the fuck behind and get Faith the hell out of here. We're going to have a long talk about bringing her on this clusterfuck of an operation."

"Why wouldn't you be able to walk?" Faith clung to his hand as they started to make their way toward the back of the building.

"Later, Doc. Move now or your father's men are going to cut us all down. They won't be able to tell who you are. They'll put a bullet in you with the rest of us. And watch your back. Your sister is still in that building."

Erin moved close to him. He could feel the brush of her body against his as they crept along the wall.

"I can handle it," Faith replied.

There was another volley of gunfire, but it was obvious the enemy had lost them in the shadows. The fire was to the north and they were moving south and west.

"Keep your head down," Ten commanded. "I think we got most of them, but I promise reinforcements are on the way. We need to move and quickly. You're lucky you came up the back or they would have torn you apart."

Brody brought up the rear, keeping his eyes on Nick. "They've got a sniper somewhere. That shot at Des didn't come from the ground."

Theo took point. Yes, he'd lost command, but he damn well was going to be the one to lead them out. He wasn't letting Tennessee take a bullet. If there was a bullet coming for them, it was damn straight going through him first.

"He's likely on the roof of the main house." Ten's voice was a low, pained growl. "It's well within range and if I had planned a meeting with MSS, I damn well would have had cover. It would have been easy to switch positions and start picking us off. Where are the vehicles?"

"Erin had me park on the side of the building," Faith replied.

"Good girl. More cover." Ten moved closer to the edge. He stopped, breathing in for a second.

Theo whispered, unable to hold it in a second longer. Everything had gone to hell. "Tennessee, I'm so sorry. I didn't know about the handoff. I didn't think about snipers or any of this."

Ten frowned at him from the shadows. "No. You were thinking about being the hero in front of your girl and showing big brother that you can handle yourself. Expect to be scrubbing the floors at McKay-Taggart with your fucking tongue after this."

"Ten, he was trying to save you," Faith argued quietly.

There was no defense. Ten was right. He wouldn't have a job after this. He likely wouldn't have a girl, either. And he fucking deserved to lose it all. "Don't. He's right. I fucked up and now Des is dead."

Ten shoved off the wall. "Suck it up, buttercup. You can deal with the ramifications of your decision making when we're all off this fucking island. The op is over. We get the hell out. I'm not losing anyone else. Am I understood?"

Theo understood everything. He understood that he was the reason Des was dead and Nick would mourn for the rest of his life. Shame washed through him, but he had to find a way to get through the next few moments. He would deal with all of it later.

Ten moved another few feet, his body obviously struggling. Theo was going to have to force the issue. He knew Ten didn't trust him, but it didn't matter.

Ten stopped, slumping against the wall. "I'm going to need someone else to take the front. I can't move fast enough."

Thank god. At least he was going to be reasonable. They were rapidly running out of time.

"What's wrong?" Faith asked as Theo started to move.

"Later, Doc." Ten reached out and gripped Theo's arm, his eyes shining in the gloom. "If I fall, you leave me. That's an order. You get her out of here. You get them all out of here. I am not worth this. Do you understand me?"

He understood. He wasn't losing another single man. He was going to get them all home safely. No matter what.

The lights blinked on and Theo bit back a curse. They had to move and now.

"Shit." Ten cursed behind him and Theo could feel him hitting the ground. "Down. The shooters are behind the front wall, but they'll figure out that we're retreating so they will come over that wall and enter the compound. I want you to stay low and close to me."

Theo's knees jarred as he followed Ten's excellent instincts. They needed to make themselves as small a target as possible. The shooters likely didn't know exactly where they were and they would be nervous, too. He needed to use their hesitation to his team's advantage.

"I got her back." Erin was behind Faith and he wished like hell she was behind him. He couldn't protect her. She wouldn't allow it. "When we get out in the open, head for the van. It's got the most cover. I'll drive since I know the road. Hutch can follow in the Jeep and Brody can keep everyone off our ass from the back."

"I will join him. I will do my job." Nick's voice was cold.

How would he ever look Nick in the face again?

"Brody, pop up and give us some cover," Ten commanded. "We go on three."

Theo let everything else go. He was the point. He was the gatekeeper and he wasn't going to fuck up again. Three. He took a deep breath. Two. He was a rock. He wouldn't let anything get through to his people. One. Go time.

"Go," Ten said.

Theo stepped out. It was as though time slowed down and he could think in this place. It was a good headspace to be in. He let go of everything except the job at hand. His senses seemed to heighten as he raised his weapon. The tango rolled out from his cover and he heard the shot sound a mere second before he aimed and fired his own. Two to the chest. Nice and easy.

He was the far better shot. He waited a second for more, but it appeared the tango had been alone. Excellent. He'd been in front and he wouldn't have a chance to signal to his team where they were going.

He turned back, looking to his team. "We're clear. Go."

He couldn't get a deep breath. Something was off and his chest

23

felt weird. Pressure. He felt an odd pressure in his chest. They needed to move, but he couldn't quite. He reached down with his free hand. Why was he wet?

"No!" Erin was staring at him. The world seemed to narrow down to her face as she ran toward him.

Vaguely he heard the pop of more gunfire, but he was falling.

Someone was screaming. Something about hope. He wasn't wet. He was bleeding. Fucker hadn't been as bad a shot as he'd thought.

He felt someone dragging him, his body a useless thing now. It had done its job. It had stopped the bullet from hitting Ten or god, Erin. His whole body ached, but there was some comfort in that. He looked up at the sky. The stars were so fucking bright here.

Just for a second he wished they were here for a different reason. He wished he could bring her here and stay in one of the beach bungalows. It would be their honeymoon, but they wouldn't be alone. He'd spent too many years without his brothers, and Erin had never truly had a family to love her. They would get married on the beach and then spend a week playing and fishing and being together.

They would sit under the stars and know they had a future. Hell, maybe one day he would convince her to have a kid or two. They would bring their children here, tiny boys and girls who would never truly understand that their parents had begun their lives here.

Was he dying?

"Hope, please. Please. You know you can save him. Open this fucking door."

He wasn't sure who was talking. Faith, maybe. All he could see was Erin.

"You have to go, baby," he said. She was hauling his ass back to cover, but he couldn't allow it. "Have to leave me."

She didn't say a word, merely kept moving. That was his Erin. She was a slender woman, but so fucking strong. She had walls built of concrete around her and so damn high it felt like he'd never breach them. Oh, but when he'd gotten inside he'd found what he'd expected. Sweet. Soft. Loving. All for him.

Would she remember him? Would she remember that he'd been the one to get Des killed, or would she remember he'd stepped into a bullet for them? For her? It would all be okay if Erin lived. Hell, it might be better. His brothers might not be ashamed of him. She might remember him as something other than a fuckup.

His vision sort of focused but it wasn't Erin looking at him. Faith's eyes stared down.

"It's bad, Doc." He didn't recognize his own voice. It seemed to rattle out of his chest. Where had Erin gone? Had she run? Had Ten gotten her out? God, he hoped so. *Run, baby. Be safe.* God, he wanted her to be happy. He wanted her to find a man worthy of her who would love her and protect her and teach her it was all right to open up. She had so fucking much to give. He was always so possessive of her, but now, in the moment, he realized it would be okay. His love was larger than the singular possession of her body. He loved her soul and it would need someone. He would praise that man, be grateful to him.

Because he realized that moment that it wouldn't be him.

Something warm touched him, holding his hand.

His girl. Fuck, but she was pretty. So little time. They'd wasted it in the beginning. He wished he could go back to that first day. He would look her in the eyes and tell her there would never be another woman for him. Not ever.

If he had to go, at least it was with her holding his hand. He loved that curly red hair and the way her skin was brushed with freckles. She hated them, but he could spend a lifetime counting them and kissing them.

"We need to move. They're coming over the wall." Brody was somewhere behind him, reminding Theo that Erin was still in danger.

"I can't move him," Faith said.

He opened his mouth to tell them all to run, but a shudder went through him as he tried to breathe. He could barely breathe. It hurt and Erin's hand clung so tightly to his that he was sure she would crush him. Such small hands to hold all that strength.

Faith was talking. It was something about his lung. Definitely his lung. It was all kinds of fucked up. Couldn't breathe. Pain flared through him, but he needed to talk. He'd promised Ten and now he needed reciprocity.

"Get Erin out of here, Ten." A cough rattled through him.

Erin's face loomed over his, his ferocious warrior. His queen. He so wished he'd been her king. "Don't. Don't you dare do this, Theo. You promised me."

He'd promised her a lot of things. He'd promised to be better for her. He'd promised to give her everything he had. He'd manipulated their last assignment to get himself in her bed. This assignment. It had started out in Africa and they'd been posing as a D/s couple. He, the Master, and she the bratty, lovable sub. He'd used his position to force her to finally see him, to let him in. Months he'd had to work on her and now he saw it in her eyes. She cared for him.

He wasn't going to keep all his promises, but he'd kept one.

He touched her face, memorizing it with his fingertips. He knew every inch of her body, but he always found something new to love about her. "I did. Promised I'd love you until I died. Kept it, baby. Kept it."

Faith's hand closed on his chest, making him groan. She didn't seem to understand that he was done. "I need something plastic."

"They're coming." Nick stood over him, his eyes not unkind as he looked down. But there was a gravity to them. Nick knew what Faith did not.

"I'll get the van started." Hutch nodded to him, their eyes meeting in silent promise. Hutch would watch over her. Hutch had been his friend for years. He would watch Erin, make sure she was all right.

He had seconds left. Oh, his body might go on for a few moments more, but she had to leave. He stared at Erin. His love. His joy. Did she know how much joy she'd brought him? "Let Case take care of you. He won't…he won't know what to do. Took care of me so long, he doesn't know what to do with himself. Now go, baby. I'm done."

He let his head roll back. He felt a bit stronger than he wanted her to know. Faith's hand on his chest made it easier for him to breathe. He might make it long enough to have one of the senator's men shoot him in the head. But Erin would live. His team would live.

He was going to miss his brothers, but she was everything. They would take care of her. He had not a single doubt in his head.

His brothers would watch out for the love of his life. She would be family to them, a Taggart if not in name then by the force of his love.

"No. You promised." Erin held his hand to her chest and he felt something wet hit his face.

She was crying. For him.

"Such a pretty girl." He didn't want her to cry. "Don't cry. You never cry."

"Don't do this to me." Her jaw was set in a stubborn line. "You don't get to do this, Taggart."

"Erin, ask Tag…" He could barely speak. He had to tell her, had to ask this one thing of her. "Fuck, ask Tag to forgive me."

Her head shook. "No. No. You tell him yourself."

"Love you, baby. Forever." He went still. They were out of time. He was too weak, but he could make one last sacrifice for her. She would stay with him. She would die with him. They all would.

"Theo? Theo?" Erin's voice became panicked and she tried to shake him.

He wanted to hold on to her forever, but he let his body go limp. Right before he gave in to the darkness, he felt her warmth. She'd loved him.

That meant she could love someone else, someone better. It meant she could move on and find the life she deserved and his family would stand beside her.

She wasn't alone. He'd done that one thing for her.

It was so odd that he wasn't angry, wasn't sad. All he could feel as his strength drained was an overwhelming grace.

He'd been loved. By his brother, Case. He couldn't have asked for more. He'd been blessed again when he'd found Ian and Sean and taken his place in this weird and wonderful family.

And Erin. His stubborn girl. She'd loved him and he'd given her a home and a family.

It was a good fucking life to be loved. It was all a man could hope for.

He tried to tell her again, to tell her he would love her forever, that if there was any way, some odd place where souls could meet in the after, he would find a way to wait for her, to watch over her.

But the darkness came, its warmth flowing around him.

Theo Taggart died with one prayer—that she would live and be happy.

He came to in a cold white room, nausea rolling through his system.

It was too bright, too much for his eyes to handle.

He was going to throw up.

Something cool washed over him, as though calming water rushed through his veins.

"The anti-nausea drug I gave you should be working right about now," a soft voice said. "Sorry. I thought you would sleep longer. I should have known you were strong as a bull. How do you feel?"

Disoriented. So fucking confused. Where was he? What the hell had happened? He tried to sit up but strong hands pressed him down.

"Don't try to move," the feminine voice said. "You've recently had some serious surgery. I was able to stabilize you back in the Caymans, but we had to come to Havana to perform the real miracle. You almost didn't make it."

"Make it?" His lips felt so dry, his throat parched. Why did everything hurt? "Why are you holding me down?"

"Don't mind Robert. He's only doing as I asked. If you'll be still, he'll let you go. You have to understand that the bindings are there for your protection. You can't struggle against them or you'll undo all my good work."

Bindings? He tried to move his legs and sure enough something stopped him. He was trapped. His wrists were held to the bed. Was he in some kind of hospital?

"Where am I?" Intel. He needed intel. That's what his brother had taught him.

He had a brother. His mind was foggy, but he was pretty sure he had a brother.

Shouldn't he know?

"I think he's fine now, Robert." A woman's face came into view. She was blonde, her hair in a chic bob. So unlike Erin.

Erin. Case. Brothers. He had brothers. Case and Ian and Sean. The memories came rolling back and that made him feel more awake than anything. She'd been crying.

Was he alive? How had he managed that? He was in Cuba? Had Ten gotten him on a plane? Where was Erin? Faith was a doctor. Had she managed to save him?

"We're going to stay here briefly and then I've got a lovely new home for us. I know you don't remember much. You're probably frightened, but the injuries you went through were grave. You'll likely never get your memory back. It's all right. You're here with me now. And your brother. Robert was worried."

A man he'd never met before smiled down at him. "I know it seems weird. I went through the same thing. I couldn't remember either. It's going to be okay. You're here with your family and we're going to take care of you."

Every word hurt, but there had been some kind of mistake. "I don't know what's happening. My name is Theo Taggart. I need to contact my brother, Ian. He's in Dallas. He'll come and get me."

Her smile faded. "That was fast. You must metabolize drugs quickly. Robert, could you help me?"

The big guy disappeared and a chill went through Theo.

Hope. He was staring at Hope McDonald. It hadn't been Faith who saved him. It had been Hope, who he'd chosen not to kill.

"Dr. McDonald, I need to call my brother. He'll be happy you saved me. I think you'll find he won't come after you if you call him and let him come get me."

She put a hand on his head, smoothing his hair back. "Your brother is certain you're dead. He won't come after you and he likely won't care about me since it was my father he blamed. As my father is now deceased, I think your family will go back to Texas to mourn. I'm sorry. I thought the drug would work. I can see you need more. Robert doesn't require as much as you obviously do. I'll have to ensure you get enough on a daily basis or my therapy won't work."

"Therapy?"

"Don't worry about it." She turned away. "Thank you, Robert."

"Of course." The big guy with brown hair and a ready smile looked down at him. "Don't worry, Tom. You're going to be okay."

"My name is Theo." He started to struggle because she had a hypodermic needle in her hand and he couldn't let her poison him. Shit. He didn't want to die like this. It had been all right when Erin was here, but now it was wrong.

He wanted her. Above his brothers. He wanted Erin here with him.

"Here you go. This will help you, Tomas," Hope McDonald said. "When you wake up again, you're going to feel so much better. We'll be in a new home and you'll have your whole new life. Here with me. Where you belong. I knew it from the moment I saw you."

He felt the drugs when they hit his system. The world seemed to go fuzzy. What the hell had she given him?

He heard her whispering against his ear. "No more fighting, love. No more."

But he did fight. He fought the sleep threatening to take him over.

And he fought to keep a single vision in his brain. A vision of her. A vision of Erin.

He would never forget her. Never.

CHAPTER ONE

Dallas, TX
Eighteen months later

He raised his weapon, putting the young lady's forehead securely in his sights. It wasn't something he enjoyed doing, but he understood the need. Cash was required and it wasn't like Mother could get a job. Her work was far too important and it was up to him to ensure their survival. For him and his brothers.

So he would kill the girl if he had to. He told himself that over and over again. He hadn't been able to force himself to do it before. Hopefully he wouldn't have to now.

"Place the money in the bag," he said in Spanish.

Tears rolled down her cheeks as she rushed to do his will. His arm was steady, but in that moment she changed. Somehow she morphed right before his eyes, her hair lightening to a natural red and her skin turning ivory with the sweetest dusting of freckles.

"You don't want to do this, Theo," she said. This girl wasn't crying. She was a woman and not a girl at all. She wasn't afraid of him. Her clear green eyes were steady on him.

He didn't want to kill her. Oh, no. He wanted something entirely different from her.

Pain flared through him, threatening to split his skull. His name was Tomas and he didn't know the woman in front of him. He didn't fucking know her so why did she constantly show up in his dreams? Why did she appear like a ghost he couldn't quite rid himself of and screw everything up? She couldn't be here. Not now.

If he fucked up they would all pay. They would pay in pain that only seemed never ending.

"Theo, come back to me. Come home, baby."

Every word sent another spike through his skull. Come home? He was home. He'd never had another home. The blood was starting to pound through him. He needed that money. Mother made it clear. When her orders weren't followed he lost more. He lost days. Nights. He started over again.

He lost those brief moments when he thought he remembered other brothers.

"Theo? Theo, are you with us?"

The voice was deeper, but familiar. The redhead was speaking with a masculine voice, but it didn't matter. Just her face made his head hurt. What the fuck was her name? Pain. Her name was pain and trying wouldn't help anyone.

"Hey, princess? You not getting enough sleep?"

"He's fine. Leave him alone."

Why was he always stuck between two worlds? Between the one where he knew his place and found some form of peace and this one, where odd voices called to him.

There was only one way. Mother had told him what to do. Stop the voices. Give in. Stay in his place. Peace was there.

He lifted the gun and fired directly into the beautiful redhead's face.

Theo came awake with a shudder.

God, when would it end? When would he stop killing the woman he was supposed to love?

"Well, Princess Theo? You want me to grab you a blankie? I think they have some in the nursery."

He forced himself to sit up properly. The room was dark and the slightest bit cold. He was sitting in a chair and surrounded by people who were around some kind of table.

McKay-Taggart. He was at McKay-Taggart and he was in the conference room and he was Theo Taggart.

A hand covered his, soft skin making his body come alive. "Are you all right, babe?"

He had the sudden instinct to turn his hand over, offering up his palm so he could tangle their fingers together. So he could hold on to her like a lifeline. Erin. Pretty Erin, who apparently lived in his house and…god, she'd had his child and he couldn't remember her past the fact that he often murdered her in his dreams so the pain would stop.

He moved his hand away, turning back to the man who was his oldest brother. Ian.

Sometimes he wished they all wore nametags.

"Sorry. I'm fine. I drifted off." He sat up and looked around the table. It was something he'd done every single day for the last six weeks. Since he'd been rescued from Mother…Hope McDonald's experiments, he'd had to retrain his brain in a number of ways and one was to constantly remind himself of where he was and who was around him.

Adam Miles. Computer junkie. He was sitting in front of his laptop, running the visual portion of this meeting.

Nick Markovic. He was Russian, though he was based in London. He'd come to the company after he left Russia's foreign intelligence and that was also known as SVR. So many initials to remember when it came to the agencies around the globe. Nick looked like he always wanted to murder someone, and that someone might be Theo. He got the feeling the Russian didn't like him.

Liam O'Donnell. Irishman. Everyone here seemed to look up to the man.

Charlotte Taggart. She could be hard to look at. It was the red hair. It was close to hers. Charlotte was married to Ian and she was pregnant with their baby. Their third, he thought. He wasn't good around kids.

Case Taggart. Brother. Twin. He used to look a lot like Case. He was easy to remember most of the time. He lived in Case's apartment. Not his own home. He hadn't even walked into it. He hadn't met his own son. He wasn't ready. Not even close.

He didn't look her way. He tried not to because when he looked at her he remembered how he often made the choice to kill her.

Erin. Thinking the name didn't hurt so much anymore. Erin Argent.

"Is he doing that thing again?" Ian stood at the head of the table. The most sarcastic of his brothers. All around asshole and never-ending pain in Theo's butt. Ian wouldn't back off. Even Case left him alone most of the time. Not Ian. Ian poked and prodded and made him want to explode.

"You know what Kai said." Charlotte shot Ian a look that could freeze fire. Ian called his wife Charlie, but it seemed like everyone else used her full name.

Ian's eyes narrowed. "Kai's taking too long, but we can discuss that later." He turned his gaze back to Theo. "You manage to get through everyone? Know all our names?"

"Leave him alone, Ian, or we're going to have a long talk you won't like." Erin didn't seem to be intimidated by big brother.

He wanted to get on with the meeting so he could go back to Case's place and play video games with Robert. He felt better around Robert, easier. They didn't have to talk about what happened. They could simply be. "I'm good, boss. We were talking about Hutch. What have we found?"

"Nick, if you don't mind." Ian nodded the Russian's way.

Nick Markovic sat back, looking at the screen. It showed a map that apparently tracked the movements of a man named Greg Hutchins. Hutch. Theo did remember him, although according to Case they had a longer history. Hutch had been in the base with him. It's what they called home. Base. At the base they each had their own cells. Hutch had been across from him at first, but then Mother moved him because Hutch irritated him and when he got irritated he tried to get out.

Sometimes he could see the man sitting in front of a computer, a smile on his face and something red dangling between his lips.

Red Vine. Candy. Hutch used to like candy. Mother cured him of that.

He let the image float through his brain, not trying to catch it. That was what Kai said he was doing wrong. The pain came when he tried to force himself to remember. Memories would come and go as they pleased and Theo should ride the wave, not attempt to dominate it.

A sudden vision slammed into him.

Erin Argent on her knees, her thighs spread wide and not a stitch of clothes covering her glorious body. She looked up at him, her lips curling slightly. *You wanted something from me, Master?*

The memory slipped away, but only from his brain. His dick was suddenly hard and aching. The damn thing hadn't worked the entire time he'd been with Moth…McDonald, and now it perked up like a puppy eager to play every time Erin walked in a room.

He wanted her and he didn't trust himself to have her.

"I tracked Hutchins from the Turkish border where he entered Europe under press credentials," Nick said. "Apparently he posed as a photographer working on a story about the immigrant crisis on the Turkish-Syrian border."

"It was one of our covers." Theo sat up a bit straighter. This he did remember. It made him feel like he was worth something. Too often he sat in a chair with nothing at all to add. "After we made the deal with the doctor in Africa, McDonald wanted to ensure we had a route out if we needed it. She tried to have more than one contingency plan at all times. If we headed into Europe, we would use the press credentials. If we needed to go to Asia, we would pose as a small medical team connected to Doctors Without Borders. She never left us without choices."

Nick's icy eyes pinned him. "Of course not. You were her prized pupil."

"Experiment." Erin stared right back at the Russian. "He wasn't a pupil, Nick. He was an experiment in torture. Do you have a problem with this assignment?"

Nick shook his head, sitting back in his seat. "Not at all. Finding Mr. Hutchins is extremely important. Especially when I believe finding him might lead to finding Dr. McDonald. That is the goal, is it not? That's what everyone wants? You do know we're not the only ones looking for her. I had to deal with several agencies who are also interested in Dr. McDonald. I've managed to keep Mr. Hutchins off their radar so far, but I can't imagine it will last. He's been quite aggressive."

"Our CIA contacts assure me they're not interested in Hutch,"

Ian said. "You read the debrief from Ezra Fain? Excuse me. He's one of those assholes with fifty-two different names. I believe he's going by both Beckett Kent and Mr. White as well these days. You know it makes me miss Ten. Well, when he lets me miss him. Asshole's buying a place here and wants to like socialize and shit. What's up with that?"

"It's called growing and maturing, and he and Faith want to set down some roots," Charlotte shot back. "He's coming home to his family."

"Freaking family is too big already," Ian said with a shake of his head. "And sometimes the puppies get off their leashes. So we tracked him crossing the border. Do we have any idea where Hutch is now? Have we checked the candy shops?"

"I found him on the Deep Web," Adam said.

"Deep Web?" He knew about the Internet, though he hadn't been trained on computers the way Hutch had been. It was precisely why they'd stolen Hutch. Mother had needed his skills.

Liam turned to him. "You don't remember? I don't understand how it works. You remember how to drive a car but not something like the Deep Web?"

He could brush his teeth, but he couldn't remember that he hated certain brands of toothpaste. He'd known instinctively how to get to the McKay-Taggart building from his brother's apartment. He'd gotten behind the wheel and found himself pulling into the lot, likely because he hadn't been thinking about it at all. He'd been listening to the radio.

But he couldn't remember what the house he'd bought for he and Erin looked like.

He couldn't remember how she liked to be kissed or what it felt like to sleep beside her.

"He remembers everything," Case insisted. "It's all under a heavy veil right now. Kai assures us one day Theo's going to get his memory back. For now we have to remind him."

Kai Ferguson. His therapist. The man he spent most of his time with and who was certain he could pierce that veil over his brain. Theo wasn't at all certain.

"The Deep Web is the part of the web we can't see on the surface," Adam explained. "Think of the web as an ocean. Most of us live on the surface. That's where you can buy socks and download movies and order pizza online."

He liked pizza. A solid week of eating nothing but pizza had taught him that he liked pepperoni and sausage and that Canadian bacon was weird and gross and vegetables had no place on a pie. "All right. So the Dark Web is what's underneath and Hutch is there?"

"Yes. You can't reach the Dark Web through conventional browsers. Google can only find about four percent of what's actually out there," Adam explained. "To find the rest you have to know where to look. I found Hutch on a site for black hat hackers. I tried to get close, but he made me and I lost him. He'll have changed his profile and servers. I'll keep trying."

"Physically I believe he's somewhere in Germany," Nick said. "He entered the EU on the press passport. Once there he has freedom of movement, but I suspect he wanted technology and top-notch access to the Internet. Germany is perfect."

"Lots of places in Europe have good Internet," Erin pointed out.

Nick shook his head. "Ah, but Greg Hutchins took several years of German while he was in school and scored high on his CIA test for the language. His father was in the Air Force and he spent seven years of his childhood outside Ramstein. He'll go where he'll feel comfortable."

"He would feel comfortable in his own freaking home." Ian huffed, a deeply annoyed sound. "Although after I find him and drag him back he'll find his home is now a freaking cell until I deprogram the little fucker."

Charlotte got to her feet and moved in behind him, putting her arms around him and hugging her body to his. The comfort he took from her was obvious in the way he leaned back and how his hand moved over hers, bringing it up to cover his chest. "We'll find him."

Ian nodded. "That's what Nick's here for."

"I'm trying," Adam said quietly.

Nick shook his head. "You're too similar to him. I don't think we'll find him through a computer, though I will need your help. I think he's trying to set himself up to make some cash."

"You think he's trying to take over where Chelsea left off." Erin was stiff beside him as though she'd seen the intimacy between Ian and Charlotte and realized how different it was between them.

They'd had a baby, but she was a complete stranger to him.

"Chelsea Weston. She was the Broker at one point in time." He sat up at night reading the files on the people he should know. His brothers had given him file after file filled with information he'd known before. Chelsea was Charlotte's sister and married to Simon Weston, another operative at the company. For years she'd been a commanding online presence, brokering information she found for money and power. Now she worked for the CIA. "You think Hutch is setting himself up as an information broker? Why would he do that?"

"Power. Money. Insulation." Case counted out the reasons. "He knows what it did for Chelsea and Charlotte, and he has some connections I don't think he ever really let go of. Hutch was a black hat when Ten found him. He was into some pretty dark stuff. I think he's going back to what he knows. Nick, how are you going to catch him?"

Nick picked up the coffee mug in front of him. "First I need Adam to use his facial recognition software. I've got the dates I believe he would have traveled on. I've talked to some friends at Interpol and they're willing to get me CCTV footage from the *Hauptbahnhofs*. We'll start with the major cities. Munich first. It's the southernmost. I'll work my way north. From there I'll use my contacts and find out what name he's using. I'll find him. Don't doubt it."

"And then?" Liam asked.

"Then we have a decision to make," Nick replied. "Do you want me to bring him home or should I watch him? He's smart and resourceful and he's extremely angry. I think he could find her before anyone else."

"We bring him home," Erin said resolutely.

But Theo already knew what the others were thinking. "If Hutch is looking for her, should we sit back and watch and wait? He could lead us to her."

"I'll find her." Adam slammed down the top of the laptop. "We don't need Hutch. Chelsea and I are on it. Bring him home. That's the only choice."

But it wasn't. Theo could see that clearly. Maybe it was because he couldn't remember actually giving a shit about anything, but he could see plainly that the best plan of action was to wait and watch Hutch. If he had connections in the black hat world, he might be their best bet to find Hope McDonald. It made sense to use whatever assets they had to assess, find, and eradicate the target.

It wasn't like Hutch wanted to come home. If he did he would be here right now.

Would he have run if he'd had the chance? Theo had been surrounded by his brothers and Kai for days. He'd been locked in a room when they couldn't be with him. He hadn't been allowed to be alone, hadn't been allowed the chance to run.

Was he still thinking about it? Was he thinking about how peaceful his life could be if he simply started over again? It wasn't like he remembered any of these people and yet they looked at him with expectation in their eyes.

Erin looked at him and he could see how much he disappointed her. Would he disappoint the boy, too? Would it be better to walk away and let her find a better man to raise their child with?

Ian slammed a hand on the table, his decision obviously made. "Find him, Nick. Do whatever you have to. Do we have anything on McDonald?"

"Her last known location was Malaysia," Liam stated, his Irish accent lilting. "She's been using a shell corporation that was connected to her father's old accounts to clean the money they stole. From what I can tell she's got a couple million in capital, but that won't last long the way she likes to run through it. There is something that's worrying me."

Charlotte sat back down, and Ian's gaze sharpened on Liam. "What is it?"

From what he could tell, everyone at McKay-Taggart listened to Liam O'Donnell's instincts. Even now they were all leaning in, waiting for whatever the Irishman was going to say. Wouldn't it be nice to be so trusted?

"She had a secondary site in Malaysia. One as complex and well-staffed as the place in Argentina. Theo and his friends weren't the first experiments, from what I can tell," Liam explained.

That was news to Theo. A chill went up his spine. He'd only ever known Robert and Victor. His brothers. Victor was dead. He'd been killed in the fight that had rescued Theo and Robert. There had only been the three of them. That was the extent of his family.

Not his family. Of the experiments.

"Why would you think she had other men?" He asked the question, his whole body tensing at the idea.

You're special, Tomas. You're my greatest work.

He shivered and told himself it was because it was cold.

"The men on the ground found evidence of several inhabitants other than the doc and her ground staff. There were seven cells in the compound, much like the ones Theo described. They all appeared to have been used. We found some records and I think she'd kept up that base for a good while. You'll find it all in Ten's report. He and Ezra led the team into the compound." Liam turned his gaze to Theo. "Would Dr. McDonald leave for periods of time?"

"If she did, he wouldn't remember," Ian shot back.

But he did remember a little. "She would leave us with Tony for training. We would still take our meds, but we got a break from the therapy. It was hard to tell days and nights. We wouldn't go outside often unless we were casing a site. We had sleep periods. She would leave for a few. Maybe five or six. That was usually when we would run a job."

When he would shove a gun in a girl's face and demand money. When he became the monster he used to hunt.

He wasn't sure exactly how many times he'd robbed banks or individuals. He got images in weird flashes at times and sometimes he dreamed and he knew he was reliving some of the things he'd done. Like he knew the girl in the dream who'd become Erin had been real and she'd been alive when he'd left her. One of the things he could clearly remember was his feeling of elation as he and Robert and Victor had raced out of that bank with their biggest haul ever. Adrenaline had rushed through his system and he'd felt free for a moment. He'd felt powerful.

It was awesome that the only pieces of himself he could remember was what a complete shitbag he was.

Nick was staring at him.

"You have something to say to me?" He was sick of not being in on the joke. The Russian obviously hated him and he had zero idea why.

"I have nothing to say to you." His accent had thickened, eyes dark with distaste. "As far as I am concerned, you're not here at all."

The rage that seemed to always be simmering below the surface bubbled over. Yeah, that felt good. He liked that. It was better than feeling hollow. He burst out of his seat and was practically on top of the asshole. "You want to see how real I am? I can show you."

He wanted a fight. He wanted to punch that asshole right in the fucking face. For a second, the Russian's countenance dissolved and he could see Tony there. Tony. He'd been the one to break bones and burn flesh. The left side of his face was fucked up because of Tony. Tony liked to call himself the dog trainer.

He could see himself doing it. He would smash his fist through Tony's face. He could see the red of the blood and hear the way the bones would crunch. When he did that, he would be free.

He felt his whole body hauled back, feet scrambling to find purchase.

"He got strong while he was gone," Ian was saying as he gripped Theo's waist and forced him back over the table.

When had he gone over the table? His head ached and all he could remember was that he'd been about to kill Tony.

Except Tony was dead. He'd died weeks ago.

He started to turn, to try to explain why he'd freaked out on Nick, who had to have been scared out of his mind that a raging lunatic had been coming his way.

The Russian hadn't moved. He sat back watching the scene play out as though none of it mattered to him. He frowned, but it wasn't a frightened thing. If Theo had to guess, he would say the Russian was almost disappointed.

"Relax, brother. I don't want to have to sedate you." Ian kept a tight grip.

"You should do as he says." Case was standing over him as though waiting for him to flip his shit again. "Big brother has a plan in place. We've got tranquilizer guns stashed around the office just in case."

"I like to call it Operation Sleepytime." Ian forced him to his seat, but Theo was already coming down.

"I call it Operation You're An Asshole," Adam replied.

Ian grinned down at him. "I might have tested it out on Adam."

"That shit hurts, you know." Adam huffed as he started to pack up his laptop. "I take it our meeting is over. I'll get on the facial recognition Nick asked for. Unless we're about to kill Nick. Are we about to kill Nick?"

"I'm thinking about it." Erin eyed the Russian.

Why was that woman so hot when she was mean? She seriously looked like she was ready to take the man out even though he outweighed her by at least a hundred pounds of pure muscle. She was also willing to kill him despite the fact that Theo had been the one to attack.

What the hell had he done that someone that beautiful was so loyal to him? Had she loved him because he'd been handsome? He'd seen pictures of himself.

He wasn't handsome anymore. He wasn't whole anymore.

"Ease off, Argent. You know this is hard on him, too." Ian had backed off, but not by much.

"I can make it easy and send him back to London," Erin replied.

"You know he's the best tracker we've got right now and he's got skin in this game." Ian seemed to realize the crisis had passed and moved back to his own seat at the head of the table. He shoved a weary hand over his head. "How would you feel if I told you to sit this one out? Because I want to, Erin. I want to order you to concentrate on your personal life for once and let cooler heads deal with McDonald. How do you feel about that?"

Erin chuckled, but there was no humor in the sound. "Personal life? You think I have one of those, Tag? I'm a single mom. I have no life at all. I have a man who can't look at me without his head hurting and a bunch of dates with a shrink. So no, I'm not leaving this case. The only joy I have in life is the fact that I'm going to find that bitch and make her pay."

"Yes," Nick said, his voice silky and deep. "You see, we do have much in common, Erin. We should work together, not be fighting. We worked beautifully together once. Do you remember how we took down the senator? Two shots in perfect synch. That was pure pleasure."

Now he wanted to close his hands around the Russian's throat for a different reason. He wasn't stupid. That voice the asshole was using wasn't a friendly tone. Pleasure. Fucking pleasure?

Before he knew what he was doing, Case was shoving him back into his seat with a growl. "Do you need a time-out?"

Because he was a fucking child.

The Russian stood up, smoothing down his perfectly tailored suit. "There you go, sweetheart. You say he can't look at you, but the moment another man does, he goes crazy. I would say that is hope. He might not remember much, but he knows what belongs to him. That's as primal a memory as a man can have. As for taking me off the case, if you try I will simply work on my own and then you will not have my intelligence. I'll find her and kill her myself. Should I send you a postcard when I'm done?"

Charlotte moved toward the doors. "Not at all, Nick. Why don't we find you an office for while you're here?"

"That would be nice. I have much work to do and I need to call back to London," Nick said as they walked out of the conference room.

"Are you okay?" Erin asked. "You have to ignore him. He's an asshole. He was born in Russia so it comes naturally."

From what he could tell, Erin thought everyone was an asshole. She was surly and at times unfeminine. So why did he feel something every time she walked into a room? Oh, sure that weird feeling was followed by a nasty kick to his brain pan thanks to the doc's torture therapy, but there was always an instant where he felt something akin to joy.

"I'm fine." He couldn't forget that he tended to go blind with rage. He'd proven it twice in a five-minute time span. He took a deep breath, trying to banish the anger. He could hurt her, had hurt her a hundred times in his dreams. Hurt her. Hurt the kid. He didn't turn her way.

She sighed, a deeply frustrated sound. "Of course. Well, I guess I'll see you at Kai's this afternoon. We have a session. Unless you don't even want to see me there anymore."

He didn't. Not really. He wanted to pretend she didn't exist. "I'll be there."

Because Case would force him. Because he saw the disappointment in everyone's eyes when he came up with excuses about why he couldn't go to couples therapy. He didn't even know he was part of a fucking couple, damn it.

He wished she'd just been a girl in a bar. He wanted to go back to that second when he'd seen her and she'd smiled and he'd thought one good thing had happened to him. He could take her hand and buy her a beer and laugh a little. And then he could take her to bed.

If he remembered how to have sex. His dick seemed to, but only when she was in the room. Or in his head. Which was always.

"Come on, then, darlin'," Liam said in his smooth Irish accent. "Let's get the boys and meet Avery in the park. She's got a nice picnic for us. It'll be good to get outside for a bit."

He didn't like the way the Irishman put a hand on Erin's elbow, hated how proprietary he was with her. Case put a hand out as though giving him the signal to stay still. To sit.

He was always someone's dog.

The door closed and he was alone with his brothers. The biological ones. The ones who seemed so tired all the time.

"He's been her partner since she joined the company," Case said, slumping back into his chair. "Liam is like her big brother. He wouldn't touch her with a ten-foot pole, but he will touch you if you hurt her."

He'd already hurt her enough. "It's fine. She can do whatever she wants. I'm not going to stop her."

Case's eyes rolled. "What she wants is for you to try. Can't you see that? It's been six weeks and you still haven't met TJ. He's here in this office in day care and you don't even stop by to look in on him."

"Kai doesn't think it's a good idea." He went to the only crutch he had. He hated those sessions with Kai, but they came in handy sometimes.

"Kai didn't think it was a good idea in the beginning," Case shot back. "Now he thinks you're being too cautious and I want to know why. You have a kid, man. Why won't you spend time with him?"

"Case, will you give us a moment?" Ian asked.

Case pushed his chair back. "Sure. Why not? It's not like he's going to listen to me. I've got a meeting with Mike about the Houston job. We leave in a week. He's going to have to stay with you while I'm gone."

"Or I could stay on my own." He was sick of being treated like a freaking kid. He was a man. At least he looked like one in the mirror.

Case didn't even answer, merely strode out the door, letting it thud closed behind him.

But it wasn't like he was alone. The main conference room had glass walls and he could feel everyone looking at him. They would avert their stares if they saw him looking, but he knew what they were doing. Pitying him. Or in Nick's case, hating him for some reason.

"What did I do to the Russian dude?"

"Never mind about that." Ian sat down beside him. "You have to forgive Case. He doesn't understand. He's never been through what you've gone through, and all he sees is that he's losing his brother all over again."

"I'm still here."

"Are you? Tell me you're not thinking about walking away."

Theo was silent for a moment. "Sometimes I think it might be better for everyone. I do get why Hutch did it."

Ian sat back, his shoulders up around his neck. "I yell about it, but I understand it, too. It's hard to make the transition after something like that happens. I do get that."

Now that he was alone with Ian that terrible numbness seeped into his system again. He was supposed to feel something for this man. He was supposed to feel something, anything at all. Yet most of what he felt was rage, and even that came in moments of blindness, as though there was some other Theo inside him and he was pissed. "He needed space. I think eventually he'll come back."

"I know you think about walking, but you can't. You get that, right?"

"Because I have a kid." It was all about the kid he didn't know, didn't remember creating.

"Because you love Erin," Ian insisted quietly. "I know how hard the kid thing is. I do. Women don't get it. They get knocked up and suddenly they're a mom. She can feel the baby move and she has a connection. You don't feel that."

"No. I don't." He didn't feel anything at all.

"And you never will if you don't allow yourself to meet him.

45

Charlie's pregnant and she's so excited, and all I can think of is all the things that can go wrong. I look at what happened to you and wonder what the hell kind of world I'm bringing another kid into. Do I have that right? And the minute I hold that kid in my hands none of those questions will matter because he's going to be my son and all that matters is loving him. You need to meet your son. I know Kai wants to slowly reintegrate you, but I think you should be sleeping with your wife. You should be in the home you bought for her, sleeping beside her and letting her help you rebuild your life."

He shook his head. "You don't understand."

"Not entirely, but I do know that deep down the man who loved Erin is still there. It's the only reason I'm not kicking Nick out. He did you a favor. He showed you what's still inside you."

A raging beast? "I don't know. I can't be around her without something in me aching."

"I'm not ready to give up on you and I don't think Case and Erin could handle you walking away. The pain associated with Erin is all about her name, isn't it?"

He wasn't sure of anything. "I don't know."

"Robert said you watched her in the bar. He said you didn't have any trouble at all until you found out her name."

The entire conversation was making him anxious. "I have some trouble with her all around, okay? When I think about her, when I try to remember, I end up hurting her in my head. I have no intentions of hurting her. I'm not going to hurt anyone else."

Ian leaned toward him. "Good, because you will not be allowed to hurt her. Not ever, brother. Know this. Understand this. You never put a ring on her finger, but she's my sister and you're my brother. I won't let you hurt her because I love her first and foremost, and after that I won't allow you to hurt her because I love you. So you are safe, Theo. Erin…she's stronger than you think. I know you don't remember this, but she kind of put you on your ass the first time you met. Don't think she can't take care of herself."

The first time they'd met.

How had he met her? Why had she put him on his ass?

His head started aching and he groaned from the pain.

Ian sat back up. "Stop. Don't even try. God, I'm sorry, Theo. This was exactly what I'm trying to avoid. You have to stop thinking. You have to let it all happen. Stop trying to remember her and let her be the girl in the bar. Come to the club. I'll pair you with a nice sub and you can get back in the groove."

"I don't want a nice sub." He wanted her. It welled deep inside him. He wouldn't accept anyone but her.

And he couldn't have her.

"Okay, I'll pick a bitchy, bratty sub who'll make your life hell." Ian's lips lifted. "You've tried it Kai's way. Try it mine. You're good with muscle memory. That means you'll know how to work a flogger or a whip. Come to Sanctum and try it. One night. It's all I ask. You don't have to have sex with the sub. As a matter of fact, you likely won't, but you can find your place again. You can find your power and help her find hers. Can you do that for me, Theo?"

The club. Sanctum. His brothers were invested in the D/s lifestyle. Dominance. Submission. He couldn't say it didn't call to him. Sometimes when he dreamed of her she was tied up, her face relaxed and peaceful, and he knew deep in his soul that he'd been the one to give her that peace. He'd been the one to bring her there. His Dominance fed her soul and her submission lit his world up.

Could he find some peace with another woman? One he simply dominated? One he didn't have a deep, dark past with?

"I don't want to hurt her." He knew that above all other things.

"You won't. I promise."

"Then I'll come." But he had to get through a session with her today. Some days were too long to bear.

CHAPTER TWO

Erin had to fight back those stupid, useless tears that always, always seemed to be at the surface these days. Even as she cuddled her boy, she could feel them starting to well.

"Do you want some more chicken?" Avery was sitting on the same large blanket she'd set out at the beginning of this picnic she'd arranged for the boys. Her son, Aidan, was giggling madly a hundred feet away as his father pushed him on a swing.

TJ wasn't big enough to sit in the toddler swings yet, but he loved to do that pre-crawl thing where he got to all fours and bounced around. She kissed the top of his dusty blond hair. "No, but thank you. It was delicious."

She was sure it had been, though everything tasted like ashes in her mouth.

Theo had pulled away again today. He couldn't stand her touch, couldn't look at her for more than a second or two.

What was she doing? It hurt to see him every day and know he wasn't interested in her.

It was like time had twisted and they were in the reality they always should have been in. She was too old for him, too hard and cynical. He should have been with a sweet young thing who would have looked up to him like he was the sun in the sky, who wouldn't have wasted time fighting with him.

He could have that now. Was she selfish for keeping it from him? He'd been through so much. Didn't he deserve the life he wanted?

"Li told me Theo nearly killed Nick today."

She sighed. "He rages out from time to time. Something will set him off and he doesn't even remember that he attacked someone."

"What set him off this time?"

That was easy. "Nick's an asshole. I don't get what women see in him."

"He's ridiculously handsome," Avery pointed out. "And he's got the bad boy thing going on. I have to admit, I might have a thing for tall, dark, and handsome European bad boys."

"Reformed bad boys, me darlin', and Nick meant to fuck with Theo. He said some fairly salacious things to Erin and it brought out Theo's inner caveman." Liam lowered his big body to the ground, setting Aidan down next to TJ. The two boys immediately started babbling and giggling at each other.

At least her son was happy. Some days that was all she had to hold on to. "Salacious? I didn't think anything he said was dirty. He was talking about taking out Senator McDonald. That was like the best."

Liam frowned her way. Of all the people at McKay-Taggart, Liam O'Donnell was the only one who could make her feel like a dumbass. He was the big brother she wished she'd had, kind and protective and willing to offer advice over a beer. His wife was the single best woman Erin had ever met. They'd taken her into their family and she would be forever grateful for them.

Some women would have been angry that their husbands had taken on a female partner, but Avery simply invited her over for dinner and made her feel welcome.

The first time she'd ever felt welcome in her life.

She looked back at Liam, giving him a latitude she gave few people. "Okay, I said something dumb. What?"

"You seriously didn't understand that man was flirting with you?" Liam asked, his Irish accent going deep. One day he would

49

use that on a daughter and it would work.

Like it did on her. She felt herself flush under his gaze. "He was talking about killing McDonald. It *was* pure pleasure."

Avery's eyes widened. "He called it that?"

"Aye, love, and he talked about what perfect synch they'd been in at the time," Liam replied with a grave nod.

"Jeez. No wonder Theo almost killed him." Avery turned her way with a brilliant smile. "See. That's a good thing."

But it wasn't. She couldn't see how it was. "Like I said, he does it from time to time and Nick had already said something kind of nasty to him. I don't think it had anything to do with me."

"Then you didn't see the death stare he gave me as I escorted you out." Liam laid back, his body forming a wall his son couldn't get through. Aidan liked to toddle off. Since the kid had learned to walk, he would roam far and wide, never once thinking something bad could happen to him because his parents were always there to snatch him up and away from trouble.

"If he was jealous, then I don't know why." She was so tired. Somehow she'd thought getting Theo back would be the real struggle. Oh, she'd told Case and Ian all the right things, but deep down she'd thought the minute he saw her again he'd fall into her arms. "I'm thinking about telling Kai we should stop the sessions together. It's not getting us anywhere."

A single brow arched over Liam's left eye and she realized she was in trouble again. "Oh, really now? That boy chased after you forever and you give him what? A whole six weeks? That's all he's worth?"

"I think what Liam's trying to say…" Avery began.

Li put a hand out to stop her. "I'm saying exactly what I mean, love. Ain't no pussyfooting around that one. She's got to have it said hard and true. You're failing him because you doubt yourself. It was easier when he wasn't around, was it?"

She hated this. Life had been so much easier when she didn't give a shit about the people around her. Oh, she'd cared about the guys in her unit, but not a one of them would have called her to task about her love life. She hadn't had a fucking love life. She'd had some one-night stands when she couldn't take it anymore. She'd had some play partners in clubs because not a one of them was looking for a relationship.

Not a one of them until Theo.

And none of her COs treated her like this. Like they cared about her happiness so much they were willing to make things uncomfortable for them all.

In the beginning she'd thought they were all unholy, nosy dicks, but slowly, so slowly, she'd figured out this was what a family was supposed to look like.

This was the time when the pre-Theo-and-TJ Erin would have walked away. Now it was the time she fought with her family, knowing they wouldn't leave her no matter how obnoxious she got. "It wasn't easy, Li. Losing Theo was the worst thing that's ever happened to me, and that is saying something. I missed him every single day and I still do because he's not Theo. I don't know who he is."

"Then walk away. I'm sure he'd prefer that at this point. It's obvious he's uncomfortable with you and he has no idea what to do with the fact that he's got a kid. So let him go. Tell him it's all right and tell Team Taggart to stop busting his balls."

Avery leaned back against Liam as Aidan started to try to climb up his father. "I could set you up. I've been thinking about it a lot. I actually think you and Nick could work. Why don't you ask him out for a drink?"

Her whole body shuddered at the idea. "No. I'm not going to do that."

"Then how about Deke?" Avery's face lit up like that was the best idea ever. "He's looking for a play partner and I think you would get along well. He's a nice man."

What the hell was this? They were trying to set her up?

"And I know Big Tag's talking to Theo about finding a sub to play with," Liam said as though they were talking about the weather and not ripping her fucking heart out.

"I'll kill her." She could see herself doing it.

"Now, there's my partner." Li's hand slid over Avery's.

"Yes, there she is." Avery gave her husband a wink.

Damn it. She hated it when they caught her like this. She should have known something was up the second Avery wasn't arguing for true love. "Fine. I'm a jealous hag, but seriously, I can't handle watching him with some pretty sub. I can't do it. If that's Tag's suggestion then I'll stay away altogether."

Or walk away. Could she stay here and watch Theo fall for some young sub who didn't have scars or a boatload of baggage on her back? Could she watch him collar another woman?

Her gut twisted at the thought. She was stuck because this was her family and it was TJ's, too. If Theo wanted another woman, she couldn't simply walk away. And she couldn't lay down and fade because her son needed her.

She had to face the fact that if Theo didn't want her, she would have to move on.

What had Li accused her of? Giving him six weeks when he'd chased her for a year. When he'd poured his heart and soul into wooing her.

Did he deserve the same from her?

"I'm the sub." It hit her smack in the face. Big Tag wouldn't pair Theo with some random sub. For all his grouchiness, no one believed in love and family more than the big guy. "He's tricking Theo and you two are setting me up. Did you plan this before or after the meeting? Wait, it had to be before."

"I always said you were a smart one," Li conceded. "We've been talking about it for a while now. Kai knows. He's worried he's put himself in a box. He thought keeping you separate was best in the beginning, but now he thinks Theo sees it as a crutch. But he's also worried that if he tries to force Theo…"

"He'll be a stubborn bastard because he's got all those Taggart genes and no amount of freaky drugs can possibly wipe those out." She leaned back and watched as TJ sat on his diapered bottom and gummed the hell out of his teething ring.

He deserved better than a mom who gave up because she'd never been sure she was worthy of any of this. A mom who let his father go because she was a little older than he was, not as bright and shiny.

This Theo wasn't bright and shiny anymore. He was dark and that killed her.

Her son looked up and smiled. Tears pierced her eyes because that was Theo's smile right there. That was his light in her child.

He'd shown her the way out of darkness once. It was time to

man up and be what he needed her to be.

"I'll do it. I suppose we're not telling him." She reached out and cupped her baby's head. So soft. So sweet. He deserved everything she had and so did his father. Even if it hurt like hell.

"I think it's best," Li offered. "Let's talk plan of action because I know you don't like going into a mission without a plan."

Making shit up as you went was for suckers who expected to fail. A good plan of attack was the only way to go. A plan *A*, plan *B*, and plan *everything's fucked up, let's blow it all to hell*. She hoped she didn't need that last one, but she would have it in her back pocket all the same.

"I'll have to start this afternoon. Maybe I've played this all wrong. For six weeks I've sat by and wrung my hands and hoped he'd come to his senses. I've tried to play the sweet, supportive wife."

Avery's lips curled up in a grin. "But that wasn't what attracted Theo in the first place."

No. No, it hadn't been. "I think I'll call Kai. It's time for something different."

She wasn't going down without a hell of a fight and a good soldier knew a great fight sometimes involved surrounding the enemy and making sure he never got entrenched. Keep him on his feet. Never let him relax.

Yeah, she could do that.

She started to talk to Avery and Li about how to bring that man down.

And lift him back up.

CHAPTER THREE

Theo sat back and wondered where she was. He was going to think of her as "she" for a while. Even thinking her name hurt at times so it was best to refer to her as well, her.

The redhead. His wife in all but a legal sense. He wasn't sure if that made it better or worse. If they'd actually gotten married, he would have a legal obligation to her.

Of course, they'd had a kid. Didn't he have that obligation? His head hurt again, but not from Mother's training. His head hurt because he couldn't feel anything for a kid he'd helped create.

"While we're waiting, why don't you tell me how you're getting along with the rest of the office." Kai Ferguson watched him from behind his elegant desk. He was all laid back, but it didn't fool Theo. They weren't here to shoot the shit. They were here because Theo was a walking, talking time bomb waiting to go off and Kai was the bomb squad.

"It's going fine."

Kai let that sit for a moment. It was one of those things Theo was sure he'd been taught in shrink school. Let a moment play out until it became uncomfortable for the subject and he let loose with information he would rather not actually share. These things were somewhat like interrogations. If you got the subject in a room and stared for long enough, some of them would actually start talking to fill in the awkward space. They couldn't handle the silence. A couple of Navy SEALs staring at them, standing at attention like they were waiting there for an order, and all the Agency dude had to do was offer the unlucky guy a way out and he would scramble to take it.

Like that time in Iraq when he… It was right there, the memory of that day. He could see himself, but the vision was almost blurry. He needed to think harder. See better.

The pain flared through his head, a lighting bolt jarring his thoughts.

"Take a deep breath and let go." Kai's voice was almost melodic, deep, and without the sense of panic Theo felt. "One breath in and then out. Allow the memory to float away."

He dragged a breath in and tried to shove the damn memory out.

"Stop fighting, Theo. Let your mind go blank. Concentrate on your breathing. Feel it. Take it in and consider it. Think about how it fills your lungs, about whether the air is hot or cold."

He took a long breath and tried, really tried to consider the air, but that was so douchey and stupid, so he followed the other order and let his mind go blank. Let it drift while he breathed in and out and let the sound of Kai's voice fade away. He was still talking but a vision took the place of memory.

A vision of her. It wasn't memory. He knew that because it didn't hurt and there wasn't the deep-seated need to hold it and force it to the forefront. This was good, old-fashioned daydreaming, and that didn't send his nerves into overdrive.

He didn't think of her name. He let that go. He thought about her eyes turning up and her mouth curling slightly, enough to let him know she was happy to be where she was. She started out wearing a white tank top, but he let that drift off as she bit into her plump bottom lip and winked his way. Her breasts came into view. Perky and sweet, with tight nipples he could suck on. She held out her hand and there was suddenly a sunny bedroom behind them. No darkness for his girl. He would take her in the light and see all of her.

The better to lick and taste every inch of her. He wouldn't miss a single bite.

"There, that seems to be better." Kai's voice broke through.

Theo opened his eyes. It wasn't better. It had been better and then he remembered he was in here with Kai. Maybe it was for the best. At some point he would have remembered her name and the vision would have gone dark.

Everything went dark.

"How are you getting along with Nikolai?"

Theo felt himself frown. "He's a dick. Do you know why he doesn't like me?"

Kai crossed one leg over the other and sat back, giving Theo that look that let him know he was considering exactly how much to tell him.

Theo was sick of that look. He got it from everyone. "If you don't tell me I'll ask him myself. I'm sick of being the only one who doesn't know."

"I'm sorry. I assumed you read the reports from your last mission."

"The one in the Caymans? Yeah, I read it. I know how I screwed up."

"Ah, but I suppose Big Tag didn't write up the relationships. Desiree Brooks was Nick's lover."

Shit. Heat flashed through him. Embarrassment. Shame. He wasn't sure which. Maybe both. No wonder the Russian couldn't stand to look at him. He was the reason Des was dead. "Well, I understand why he hates me."

"I wouldn't call it hate. I would say he's conflicted," Kai corrected. "You have to understand he was there that night. He watched you both die. He attended the service we had for you. He didn't hate you then. I don't think he does now, but your return has brought out the fact that he won't get the same ending. We found Des's body. He took her home to England. I believe there was a nasty fight with her family and he wasn't allowed to attend her funeral. They didn't know about what she did, you see. They blamed Nick for getting her involved in something dangerous."

"But she was MI6 for years." Despite the fact that those files contained the horrors of a night he couldn't remember, he'd read them all numerous times. It was like reading over someone else's debrief. He could pick out the mistakes.

If he'd been in charge, he would know where to place the blame. On himself.

"And those records are classified," Kai continued. "They thought she was a secretary. When Nick tried to explain, they shut him down and shut him out. I don't believe he intends you any malice or I would have advised Big Tag to leave him out of this op. I think he needs this. Give him some space. Concentrate on what you need. I take it Ian talked to you about coming to Sanctum tonight."

He felt his whole body go rigid. The idea was tantalizing and yet repulsive. Tantalizing because he wanted what D/s could give him. He might not remember his training, but Ian was right. His body remembered how good it felt to dominate a woman, to know that she trusted him with her body and her pleasure. It would be a place he could go and feel like he belonged. Not the Theo he used to be. The Theo he was now.

He wanted it so badly, but there was a part of him that couldn't imagine playing with some sub he didn't know.

He forced himself to breathe again. The walls were closing in.

"I'm going. I'll give it a try." He wasn't sure what made him more nauseous—the idea of being alone or the idea of touching someone who wasn't her.

He had to try. He had to try something, anything. He was in a rut and Ian was right. He didn't have to fuck the girl. He merely had to service her D/s needs and see where that went.

"I'm glad." Kai leaned forward. "I think it could be good for you."

"You don't think it's going to hurt her…Erin." He said the name with a tight jaw. "I don't mean to hurt her. I know she wants this family thing, but I don't know that I can give it to her. But I also know I promised her a lot. I can't remember it. Can't remember her. I know that sounds lame, but I know I owe her and I don't want to bring her more pain. She's had enough."

"I think it could help Erin move on, too."

"But she doesn't play anymore." His whole body went stiff in the chair. "I heard she doesn't go to Sanctum now. She has a child. Shouldn't she be at home watching her kid?"

Kai's brow rose high over his left eye. "Seriously? You're going to shame her for having a sex life?"

He knew he shouldn't, but he didn't like the idea of her running around a freaking sex club. It bugged him on a primal level. Who would be watching out for her? Was she trusting some Dom who would use her body and not give a shit about her needs? Would he care that she had a kid and needed more than an incidental orgasm?

Fuck. He shouldn't think about those damn questions at all. He shouldn't think about her. He needed to concentrate on himself and getting better, and he wasn't sure he could do that when her very name brought him pain.

His whole soul ached but that part of him was broken. The piece of him that had loved her was severed and broken and couldn't be made whole again.

This was why Hutch had run. A part of Hutch was broken and he couldn't handle the fact that he would always know a piece of his soul was gone.

Theo had to let it all go. Wasn't that what everyone kept telling him? He had to let go of that ridiculous primitive possessiveness that tended to take over the minute she walked in a room. He wasn't going to do anything about it, didn't deserve her. So he had to get used to the fact that she would eventually be with someone else. Shouldn't he want her to be happy?

"Sorry. I get this feeling deep down when it comes to her." This was the place to be honest, so he gave Kai what he could. "I have no intentions of acting on it. Of course she should have a full life. She should date. That would be good for her."

Kai nodded. "Excellent. I was hoping you would feel that way. It's become obvious to me that you no longer have sexual feelings for Erin. I still believe you should attempt to form some kind of a friendship for the sake of your son."

"I didn't say that." Not have sexual feelings for her? All he could think about was how she would look naked.

"Didn't say what?"

"I didn't say I...never mind. You're right. We should try to be friends." He needed to stop thinking about her sexually.

"Theo, if you still have feelings for her, why won't you try?" Kai asked. "Is it because of the pain? Because I've been thinking about that."

"It's not the pain. Well, it is and it isn't. Can you imagine what it would be like if you woke up one day and couldn't remember anything of your life? You could remember how to do things. How to type. How to spell. How to speak. But can't remember your name or what you did for the last twenty plus years of your life. And then someone tells you this is your family, but you can't remember them, you can't feel them. I don't feel anything for my own brothers."

"And Erin?"

The pain flared at the mention of her name. He winced. "I feel pain every time I try to remember how we met or when we first made love. Everyone tells me I was passionately in love with this woman, but she's a stranger to me. I'm attracted to her. I am. She's the only woman I seem to be attracted to, but at night when I dream about her...I do terrible things, Kai. Things I can't imagine the old Theo would have even thought of. I hurt her because Mother programmed me to."

"I thought we were going to stop calling her that."

"Sorry. Habit. I'm nothing but a group of habits now and every one of them was force-fed to me by Hope McDonald. I want to reach out to her, to Erin." He took a deep breath, letting the pain play out in his head before continuing. "But I can't because I know I'll hurt her in the end, and I don't mean emotional bullshit. I'm talking physical harm."

"I think you would be surprised. Erin can take care of herself. You know she handled you pretty well the first time you met."

The first time they'd met. He should remember. Had they been at a party? Or had it been his first day of work? Had he taken one look at her and known he wanted her? He was supposed to love her. Case had told him that baby they'd made hadn't truly been an accident. That baby had come out of love and had brought them all hope when they were down. He had to remember and everything would be all right.

His vision went blurry with pain. It thrummed through him, starting in his head and threatening to take over every muscle of his body.

"Theo, stop thinking about it," Kai's voice said. "Calm down and stop. I need you to stop trying to remember."

Somewhere in the distance he heard the door opening, heard her voice calling out. She was here. How was she here?

Her face was right there. Right in front of him. Erin. She was here with him and she was everything that was wrong. He was dreaming again and there was only one way to stop it.

He reached out to wrap his hands around her throat.

"Theo!" Kai yelled.

And then the beautiful vision of Erin rolled her green eyes, reared back her fist, and popped him right in the face.

Pure pain blossomed over him and he fell backward, hitting the floor with a thud.

Erin stood over him, a frown on her face as she looked to the doc. "Seriously? You thought I was threatened by that?" She held a hand out to him. "Weak move, Taggart. You need more training. Come on. Let's get the huggy shit over with so we can get on with our days."

He stared up at her. What the hell? Since that first moment in the bar, she'd been nothing but sweet and patient with him. The woman he'd met in Africa would never hit a man, much less damn near break his nose. The woman he knew practically babied him any chance she got. It was one of the horrible ironies. She treated him like a prince and he killed her in his dreams. In his dreams and up until now, she'd seemed so fragile, her eyes haunting him at every turn.

Now she looked pissed and he was surprised how much that did something for him.

"You hit me." He was still shocked she'd done it.

"Yeah, well, that's what you get when you half ass a strangulation attempt, buddy. You get my fist in your face. And I pulled that punch because I know you're all weak and shit."

"I'm not weak." But he reached for her hand and let her haul him up. Yeah, he needed to rethink her fragile status. And when had she started talking to him like that?

She gave him a once-over that let him know she didn't buy a word of what he was saying. There was an arrogant set to her lips that made him want to cross the space between them, shove her pretty ass up against the wall, and show her exactly how not-weak he was. "Sure thing, Littlest Tag. Now what do you say we get through our therapy for the day? I have things to do."

"First of all, I'm not the littlest freaking Taggart. Not by a long shot. There are babies everywhere. Maybe the girls don't count, but I would definitely say that…" He'd almost said *our baby*. Our baby is the littlest Tag. It had been right there on the edge of his tongue. He turned away from her and got back to his seat. "It doesn't matter. You're right. We should get through the therapy so we can get back to whatever we need to do."

Like going to the club and meeting this sub Ian wanted to introduce him to.

His stomach turned at the idea because she was right there. She was easing into the seat next to him.

He'd tried to strangle her not moments before.

He was going to do whatever it took to not hurt the mother of his…of a child.

Erin sank into the chair next to him. "Sorry about your nose. I don't think it's broken. Like I said I pulled my punch, but you should know I'm not pussyfooting around you anymore. I've been careful because I felt bad for you and shit, but you're kind of an asshole and I'm just going to be me now. I get it. You don't want a kid."

"I never said that." Why was she being so difficult?

She shrugged. "Whatever. You show no interest in him and that's okay. I would have had him whether or not you wanted him, so no harm, no foul. We can stop these sessions if you want."

"I don't think that's a good idea," Kai began.

"Hey, I never said any of this. Can we slow down for a second?" He wasn't sure why he wasn't jumping at the chance to quit these sessions. He dreamed about her after these sessions. If he stopped them maybe he wouldn't anymore.

Maybe he wouldn't see her anymore.

He couldn't. He couldn't stand the fucking thought that he wouldn't see her again.

What the hell was wrong with him? He needed to tell her that he wanted to end the sessions, too. That he didn't consider the child his and he didn't know her and it wouldn't ever work.

"Could we get started?" He sat back, unwilling to move even an inch away from her.

Kai had his notepad in hand. "Yes, but I think we should try something different today. I've been considering this and we've talked around the past, but not directly about it. Are you interested in learning about your history, Theo? In a way I think might not hurt you?"

He could learn about his past with her? It was stupid. He should be asking about his childhood and his military service, and all he wanted was to know about her.

"I want to know how we met."

Kai's lips curled up, and Theo wondered if he hadn't fallen into a trap. "I want her to tell you, but it's a story. Nothing more. It's like the files you've been reading. You can distance yourself. This is a story about how she met a man who ended up becoming her lover. It's nothing more than a story, and I don't want you to try to remember any of it. Listen to her. Put yourself in the man's place, but simply listen and let it flow over you. You can relearn your history. Not as memory but as stories. Do you understand?"

Stories about her. Yeah, he could do that. "All right. I'm willing to try."

Kai looked toward her. "Can you do that for him? Tell him about how you met? It needs to be detailed, so he can sink into the story. He might start to understand if you can do that for him."

She bit her bottom lip and for a moment he thought she might reject the idea entirely. He waited for her and realized he wanted to hear that damn story more than he'd wanted anything in a long time. Maybe ever. His memory was shit so it could be ever.

"All right, but I'm going to warn you. He might not come off so great in my version of the tale. He was kind of an asshole."

He wasn't sure he liked her thinking of him as an asshole. "That's okay. I want to hear it."

She leaned forward and began her story.

Their story.

* * * *

62

Dallas, TX
Three years before

Erin thought about slamming the phone down and never calling back again. She'd thought he would be happy, but once again her father had proven her utterly and completely wrong. Maybe he hadn't understood.

"It's a security job. I'm working with Ian Taggart, Dad. He's legendary in the Green Berets."

There was a huff over the line. "He was a CIA butt kisser and he left to make money. You left because you couldn't handle it. I believe I told you it was a mistake for you to join up."

Ten years. She'd spent ten years in the damn Army, but he acted like she'd washed out of basic. She'd moved up the ranks and done a damn fine job. "I left because it was leave or murder my fucking CO because he was a misogynist pig who didn't like it when a woman said no."

There was a slight pause on the line and she could practically see her father rolling his eyes. "This is why women shouldn't serve. I think I told you that, too. You're a distraction to the real soldiers. You should have paid more attention to your marriage than your career and then you would have saved us all a lot of trouble. You know you got a good man in hot water the way you left."

Because she hadn't been willing to let his sexual harassment go? Tears pierced her eyes as she finally acknowledged she was never going to please her father. Nothing she did was good enough because she wasn't a boy. Her three brothers could murder people and as long as they were in the right branch of the military, moving up properly, her father wouldn't bat an eyelash. But she'd always been told she wasn't enough.

Not enough of a woman to keep a husband. Not enough of a soldier to be admired.

It wasn't her fault the military didn't accept women in Special Forces training. She'd gone counterintelligence and she'd been damn good. Unfortunately, her father thought counterintelligence was some kind of place for over-privileged brainiacs. Her father didn't like brainiacs. He'd always said hyper-intelligent people couldn't be trusted. She'd likely been the first kid in his history whose genius-level IQ test had disappointed her parent. The general hadn't approved of her being accelerated through school and hadn't offered to pay for college. He'd thought it was a waste of time when what she should do was get married.

Her mom was MIA and had been since she was a kid.

"I was wondering if you wanted to come visit me." She got to her point because talking to him about her job was apparently not the way to go. "I heard you're coming out to Dallas in a few weeks. You could stay with me. I've got a two-bedroom."

"I've got a place to stay. I don't think I'm going to have time to see you. I've got that reunion thing, you know."

She felt her jaw go tight. She should have known. She'd called because she knew his yearly fishing trip with the guys from his old unit was coming up and they always started out in Dallas, where two of them lived, and then moved up to Lake Texoma for a fishing weekend.

She wouldn't get that. There was no old unit for her to go back to. Not anymore. They all looked at her the way her dad did. Or even if they didn't, she wouldn't bug them. Most of her old unit was still military, and she'd known she was leaving them behind when she'd chosen to get out of the fight.

Of course, she'd be nowhere if Ian Taggart hadn't shown up on her doorstep with a job and a place to be. He'd asked for a meeting the day after the Army had given her CO a slap on the wrist and told her to suck it up. She'd been ready to shove it all up someone's ass and then Big Tag had told her he had a way out for her. He'd told her she wasn't the only good soldier who'd run up against politics and power and gotten her ass handed to her because of it. It happened all the time. To women and men.

Six months later she was in Dallas and had a new purpose. Sure her partner was a Euro weirdo, but his wife was all kinds of awesome, and honestly, Liam O'Donnell might be smarter than she gave him credit for. The office was nice and the pay was way better than the Army. She liked taking down douchebag corporate spies. They were way less clever than they thought they were.

And there was Sanctum. She fucking loved Sanctum. Sometimes she thought her life hadn't truly begun before she'd found Sanctum. She'd been married for three years and not once had she felt like a sexual creature. Walking the floor of Sanctum had changed all of that.

"Have fun." She avoided calling him Dad again.

"You know Hank is getting hell because he's your brother. He's working under your old CO and he's catching hell for your shenanigans."

"Well, tell Hank to fuck the major and everything should be fine. After all, that's where I went wrong. If Hank spreads his legs, it should go well for him. And Dad, fuck you, too." She slammed the phone down.

"Now that seemed like an unpleasant conversation." Liam O'Donnell was standing in her doorway, leaning against the jamb. He wasn't an unattractive man, but somehow he came across as an authoritative figure, and not the kind of man she might try to boff. Not that she would. He had a wife who was twenty kinds of awesome. And she didn't do married guys, as the major had discovered.

She'd been the wife in that scenario. She wasn't putting another woman through that kind of pain.

"It was nothing. My father is coming into town. I thought I would set up a meeting because of the bio connection. Turns out to not be as strong as you would think. So hey, I'll spend that weekend hanging at Sanctum. No trouble."

"Your birthday?"

She wished he didn't know that. "Not a big deal. Last year I spent it listening in on some dipshits who thought they would bomb the US embassy in Singapore. All in all, getting some impact play in will be a better way to spend the day."

Maybe she would even give in and have sex. She'd held back because she was still getting a lay of the land, so to speak. She'd played a bit with Kai but always knew he had an eye for someone else. Lately she'd been bottoming for a homicide detective she had a lot in common with. Detective Heath Neilson was good with a flogger and gave her what she needed for the most part, but she hadn't slept with him. They'd been playing for the better part of a month and she knew the time was coming that she had to make a decision.

She wasn't sure which way to go. She knew she should give in and take what she could. It had been over a year, and a girl needed to get a little something something, but still she held back. She wasn't sure why. Erin liked the detective. He simply didn't move her. Not that anyone moved her, but the older she got the more she wondered what it would feel like to have that spark.

"I don't think that's going to be a problem." Liam walked into her office. "We're having a party for you this weekend at Sean's new place. I believe you'll find he's serving up a decadent pot roast with potatoes and carrots followed by Italian Cream Cake."

Her favorites. She wasn't sure she liked how her heart twisted at the thought. No one made her favorites. She'd been lucky her brothers loved pot roast. Of course, she'd always been told by her father that she ate far too much of it. "How did you know?"

He shrugged slightly. "You talked to Avery and she listened. Do you remember her asking about your favorite foods? She's got a list now. I think you'll be happy with your presents, too."

She was not going to fucking cry. Not at all. She wasn't going to tell the man that it had been years and years since anyone had recognized her birthday, had bought her a present. Her father hadn't believed in them. Not for her or her brothers. Their birthdays had been marked with a trip to the gun range at an appropriate age, and tests on weaponry every year thereafter.

"You don't have to do that. It's cool."

He lowered himself into the chair in front of her desk. "I think you'll find my wife enjoys a good party. After all, look what's going on here today. Damn, but that smells good."

She breathed in and sighed. "What is that man cooking? When they told me they were having a baby shower, I thought it would be cake and punch you would probably spike."

Li winked her direction. "Oh, I've already spiked the punch, love. Ain't Irish without a bit of whiskey. And Sean doesn't believe in desserts. He's a pushy busybody, but Grace knows that well. She announced she was throwing Alex and Eve a baby shower and would buy some chips and dips and stuff, and Little Tag's food-snob heart couldn't handle it."

Now there was a woman who knew how to handle her man. "So now we're getting all kinds of good stuff. Did I say thank you to Avery for going shopping with me? I'm afraid I don't know much about buying baby stuff. I've got some nephews but I don't see them often."

"I get the feeling you don't see a lot of your family at all, and for good reason."

Because they were douche nozzles and she'd never once fit in. Because she didn't go home for holidays anymore since her ex-husband was still welcome. He'd cheated on her, but he was an Army buddy of her brother's and that meant more than blood to him. "Hey, it's all cool."

Li's eyes narrowed. "One of these days, you're going to want to talk and you should know I'll be ready. Or Avery. You're part of our family now, Erin."

Take one bullet for a dude. "It wasn't a big deal, Li. You're my partner. I saw he had a gun."

"And you jumped in front of me," Li pointed out.

It had been their second assignment together. It had been a nothing job, but at the end the asshole who'd sold his company's new software design to a rival had taken exception to getting caught. Unluckily for her, asshole corporate spy had been packing and tried to take his anger out on her partner. She'd seen him going for a piece and jumped Li to get him out of the way. Now she had another scar on her shoulder and apparently a friend for life.

He was like an overgrown Irish bulldog. Did Ireland have bulldogs? Maybe if she let him take the next bullet he would stop acting like her big brother.

Wouldn't that hurt?

"Hey, gorgeous." Avery stepped into the office.

This was what she got here. At any time of the day, someone would stop in and want to chat. She wasn't sure how much she liked it. It was easier to deal with at Sanctum. At Sanctum she had her place. She could let those walls drop because she was a sub at Sanctum. Here she was Erin, and she wasn't sure she could handle all the mushy crap these people did.

Even if she kind of craved it.

She'd learned that the world kicked a girl when she asked for too much. She could like Li and Avery all right, but she couldn't let them in.

Li stood up and walked to his wife. "I'll let you get back to work. The party's in twenty minutes. Let's hope Ian's back by then. Could you make sure we've got restraints ready?"

Avery's eyes widened. "Restraints? I thought this was going to be a kid-friendly party."

Apparently Avery hadn't heard the news. "Oh, it's not fun restraints. It's 'we've got a spy in our midst' restraints. Turns out mousy Phoebe is some kind of plant."

"What are your thoughts on that?" Liam asked. "Big Tag is thinking she works for The Collective."

Erin had been pondering the situation all morning. "I don't know about that. If I had to bet I would say she's Agency. She's perfect, man. I didn't see her and I worked counter for years. She's been flawlessly trained. From what Adam's said, she hasn't touched a single system she shouldn't have. She's been dug in like a tick, waiting for something. The Collective would want more than that. But the Agency, well, they like to play some deep games."

Li nodded. "That's what I was thinking, too. I was wondering if Ten Smith might not want someone watching Big Tag to make sure he doesn't get into something he shouldn't."

"We get into shit we shouldn't all the time." It was one of the best things about McKay-Taggart.

"That's me point." He took his wife's hand. "I've got me own test for Miss Phoebe. I don't think she's the hardened operative Big Tag imagines she is. If you don't mind leaving some restraints in the conference room, I would appreciate it. The last time he called he was stopping for ice cream and then coming this way. Phoebe's drugged so it should be easy to get her down."

Like it wouldn't have been if she'd been awake. "Will do, boss."

Thirty minutes later she was sipping on some punch she'd stolen and wondering about Phoebe. She hadn't been allowed to interrogate her. That was kind of a bummer. It had been a long time since she'd been allowed to torture the info out of someone. Apparently, despite the whole spy thing, PTSD Jesse still wanted some of that, so Erin was relegated to hanging with a bunch of women she had no idea how to connect with.

There was gorgeous Grace, with her hunky food-snob hubby, and Charlotte Taggart, who looked like she could throw down with some torture herself. There was Serena Dean-Miles, who probably did a shit ton of laundry since she was married to two dudes. No idea how she handled that one. Except Adam was practically a chick, so maybe it was okay. Then there was Eve. She was cool and precise. Super smart, but she didn't try to hide it all behind a wall of tough-chick attitude. She would bet Eve McKay never tried to hide how smart she was from anyone.

But then Eve McKay hadn't been raised by a man who didn't value her in any way.

Grace announced they would be opening presents in a few minutes and Erin took that as her cue to sneak away. It was too weird. She'd helped in restraining a prisoner not half an hour earlier and now she was surrounded by babies and being served appetizers. Grace had promised something called tenderloin bruschetta would be out in a few minutes, but Erin needed a time-out.

She snuck back to her office and closed the door. Sometimes she wondered if this was the right place for her. She liked the job and all but these people…

They would make her soft. They would make her want what they had. Family. Home. Peace.

She'd learned a long time ago that none of that was for her.

She sank into her chair and stared at the monitor for a moment. What was she doing? She should have taken the real mercenary job she'd been offered. Guy Ferland didn't have the same problems with sending women into combat the Army had. He would have put her on the front lines and then…what? She could play soldier and wait for a bullet to take her out and hope that dying in the line of duty was enough to please her daddy?

Shit. She had some serious fucking issues.

The ground shook slightly and Erin got to her feet. What the hell had that been? She stopped and listened. It sounded like a chopper had buzzed the building. Fucking news crews. Didn't they know how damn dangerous that was?

"Erin!"

Was that Li? She opened her office door in time to see Li running down the hall, followed by Jesse, who was carrying Phoebe. She'd come out of her drugged stupor okay it seemed. So Big Tag had a light hand with the tranquilizers.

"What?" Erin asked Li. She was still surprised they'd brought a spy back to the office. "What the hell is she still doing here? Don't we have a shallow grave for her or something? I thought she'd be fertilizing Big Tag's trees by now."

Phoebe struggled in Jesse's arms. "You have to let me go. He won't play around."

"Who?" Jesse looked down at her, his face more fierce than Erin could remember the kid ever looking. "Tell me who the hell is about to burst in those doors, Phoebe."

"You have to let me go," Phoebe pleaded.

Something was happening and it didn't look like it was good. Erin looked over at Li, whose jaw was tightly set.

"Erin, can you lock her in?" Jesse asked.

Were her people on the way? Had Erin been wrong? Surely the Agency wouldn't come for her in broad daylight? That wasn't how they worked. They would burn her if she got made and move on. She opened the door. The sooner they got spy girl out of the way, the better they could deal with the situation. "Of course. Throw the princess in there. I promise she'll have nowhere to go."

"Don't do this, Jesse. Please let me talk to him," Phoebe begged.

Jesse dumped her on Erin's couch and walked away, locking the door after him. It was a dick move. She kind of totally respected him for it. Hadn't known the kid had it in him.

"What the fuck is going on?" Li asked.

Jesse checked the knob again, ensuring it would stay locked. "I think the Agency is about to attack the office."

Fuck all. The day was about to get interesting. Who the hell was Harry Potter-loving Phoebe Graham that the Agency would risk Big Tag's wrath like this? Her brain was working overtime. They wouldn't do this for a mere asset. No. She was someone important.

"The bloody Agency?" Li's voice went deep. "Are you telling me that a Special Forces unit working for the CIA is about to walk into the office?"

Jesse reached for the SIG Sauer in his shoulder holster. "I'm afraid they aren't going to walk in. I think they're going to try to take Phoebe without giving themselves away, and I won't let it happen."

Okay, so PTSD had gone insane. "Dude, we can't attack an American military unit."

"I'm not attacking. I'm defending." Jesse strode down the hall and into the main office. It was quiet at the time. Everyone was in the back either working or getting their party on. "Get the doors locked."

Li was moving to the office doors as all hell broke loose. Erin watched in equal parts horror and excitement as a booted foot kicked open the doors. There had to be seven or eight of them, all clad in black from head to toe. They were serious about protecting their identities. Each soldier was wearing a black balaclava and tactical goggles.

Damn it had been too long since she'd been in a room full of dudes trying to take her out. That got her heart pumping. It thudded in her chest and made her feel alive. She stared at the one who'd kicked in the door. Six foot three and broad as the day was long. She couldn't tell a damn thing about him, but he was hot.

Her father was wrong. She wasn't the distraction. They were. Big gorgeous soldiers who tossed a flashbang her way.

This was going to be so much fun.

"Bloody fucking hell!" Li yelled before tackling her.

She hit the floor as the world exploded around her. Did Li honestly think this was her first rodeo? The big Irishman hit hard and her bones ached, but the rest of her was already coming to life. Nothing like a goddamn explosion to perk up her day. Even the smoke was kind of welcome. The acrid, awful scent reminding her of the good old days when every day was a fight she wasn't sure she could win. Her ears were ringing and she might have blown an eardrum, but this was a fight she was ready for.

Li yelled something her way, but she couldn't quite hear it. She was certain it was something like *be careful*, but careful was for pussies. This was a knock-down, drag-out and Jesse was fucking right. They thought they could come into her home? They thought they could roll a fucking flashbang her way?

"Are you okay?" The big guy who'd kicked in the door was standing over her. He shouted the words and held a hand out.

Aw, the kid hadn't wanted to hurt the girl, had he? She gave him her biggest and best doe eyes and reached up as though the poor little woman couldn't manage to stand on her own.

"Let's get you out of here." He got down close so she could hear him. "Run back to your office, sweetheart. As soon as we get our target, we'll be gone. I don't want you hurt."

Smoke was wafting through the room, but she could see he had the most perfectly sculpted lips she'd ever seen on a man. She kind of wanted to pull his face down and lick that fat bottom lip and offer to do him on the conference table.

Perhaps the adrenaline rush of battle made her react differently than it did others. She was sure the resident shrink would tell her she was a total perv for getting hot as hell the minute combat broke out, but Kai was also a perv, so it was okay.

The minute his hands touched hers and she got the advantage, she flipped him on his back, perfectly satisfied with the way his big, hot body bounced off the floor. It was grand chaos all around her and now she'd caught one of them. He'd broken formation to save the girl from the big bad smoke, and now he was going to pay the price.

God, she hoped he was as hot as he seemed. He was Agency, so he was probably ex-Special Forces. She was envisioning a hot silver fox who might want to play with a slightly younger woman.

He frowned up at her as she got fully to her feet. Yeah, now they were going to play. His legs kicked up and his body twisted and he was on his feet again in a show of pure masculine strength.

That did something for her too.

"Tennessee Smith!" Jesse shouted out the name.

Her combatant grimaced as though knowing he'd been caught. She couldn't see his eyes but she could practically feel them rolling.

She glanced to her left and realized she had to stop playing with the pretty man. Anger flared through her system as she saw Li being forced to his knees, a fucking M4A1 pointed at his head.

It was one thing to play some war games and another thing entirely to point a gun at her partner's head. No one got away with that.

Erin kicked out, catching Hottie Solider in the gut. He held his ground, but didn't counter attack.

In the background, she could hear something about finding someone. Probably Phoebe, who apparently was either in possession of way better intel than Erin had given her credit for or she was awesome in the sack because this was some serious overkill. She couldn't pay too much attention to that though. She had to take out the guy—who likely wouldn't date her after she dropped his ass in the middle of a mission—and then kill the dude who was threatening her partner.

She coughed as smoke hit her lungs and her tango leapt on the opportunity. He grabbed her wrist, twisting her around so he could haul her against his body.

"Calm down, wild cat," he whispered in her ear. "Like I said, this is all over in a few minutes and then I'll leave you to your day."

She shoved back and broke his hold with ease, putting her elbow right into his solar plexus. Despite all the gear he was wearing, there was no body armor to impede her. He immediately let go and was back on his ass.

He was still treating her like a civilian, giving her a couple of inches of rope she firmly intended to tie him up with. She glanced to her left and Li was still there. It was time to forget about her horniness and save her partner. He needed some chaos.

She turned to run at Li's guy, since hers seemed unwilling to hurt her, so she maintained the advantage. He would be slow and try to be careful with her. She wasn't going to give the dude with a gun to Li's head the same courtesy.

He was looking away. She could get in behind him and knock him to the side, then Li would be free to deball the dude. She was almost there when her whole body went flying. She hit the hardwoods with a jarring *thwack* and wished like hell Big Tag believed in carpet. That had hurt.

A massive body pressed her into the ground. "I said stay down, Red. I swear to god if you hit me one more time I'm not responsible for my actions. Fucking shitass job."

She squirmed underneath him, trying to bring her leg up. All around them chaos was going on. Jesse was saying no to someone and there was yelling she was starting to be able to hear pretty clearly, but all that mattered right now was flipping Hottie over and getting her partner off his knees.

"Get off me."

"Do you want me to handcuff you?" His voice was low and

against her ear, the warmth of his breath making her shiver.

"Do you want me to cut off your balls and shove them down your throat?" They were probably big if that was his cock rubbing against her ass and not an extra weapon. She moved against him and heard him groan. Yep. That was a big dick she should probably be offended by, but it was good to know the heat of battle didn't work only on her.

"Please stop squirming like that. It's disconcerting. I'm sorry. I get a little excited when it comes to a mission. I think it's all the damn adrenaline, but I'm disturbed because you're married to my brother."

She stopped. Who the hell was he? Oh, no. No. No. It must have been the red hair, the smoke, and the fact that he hadn't been expecting another red-haired female operative. "I'm not Charlotte Taggart, you infant."

It was one of the baby Taggarts, and now she was the one who felt like throwing up. They were practically teenagers. There went all her daydreams. He was maybe twenty-four. Maybe.

"Get off me." She wasn't going to ever admit he'd gotten her hot.

"When the op is done," he whispered in her ear. "When you're safe. And if you're not my sister-in-law then who are you? And I really am sorry about...I'm not the type of man who would molest a woman. I won't hurt you. I promise."

Did he think she was some kind of shrinking violet? "I *will* hurt you and the name's Erin. Are you Case or Theo?"

He went still above her and then cursed. "Damn it. They're going to fire me. Fuck."

"They won't shoot!" Jesse yelled.

She felt the Taggart on top of her tense as the yelling continued. He covered her body with his, protecting her head as she watched two pairs of boots scuffling in front of her. She couldn't tell who it was, couldn't see much of anything since the man on top of her was a mountain she couldn't quite move.

"Let my people up or I will blow this motherfucker's head off his shoulders. And I don't want to do that. I don't even have plastic down. My wife has a strict edict that when I blow some dude's head off, I have the courtesy to put some plastic down. You're going to get my wife pissed at me."

Thank god. Big Tag was here. Boss might be pissed she'd gotten put on her belly by baby brother, though. Damn. She was supposed to be tougher than that.

"It's going to be okay, sweetheart," he promised in her ear. "Like I said, I won't hurt you."

But he had. He'd made her look like an idiot in front of the boss. He'd made her feel something and then taken it all away.

"You know I think this is all going to work out. If they don't kill each other. My boss and your boss, that is," he said with a chuckle. "I'll buy the beers tonight. How about that? And you can teach me that elbow move. I have zero idea how you managed to get out of my grip."

He was offering her a date in the middle of what still might be a gun battle. Damn but that was her kind of guy.

Except he was younger than her and related to her boss, and from what she'd seen he was perfect and shiny and had a flawless military record. Just like her father would love. The same kind of man she'd married before. The kind she couldn't possibly please.

"I would be happy to show you again." She went still underneath him because apparently Charlotte had shown up and she was pregnant. No way was she causing any chaos now. Everyone needed cool heads.

She lay under him as he started to give her a play by play and wished she hadn't come into work that day.

CHAPTER FOUR

Dallas, TX
Present day

Theo frowned her way as she finished the story by telling him then Ten and Tag punched each other a bunch and everyone had cake. "Are you serious? You didn't like me because I was younger than you?"

She shrugged. She'd told the story like it had happened. No more coddling him. It didn't work, hadn't worked, and she was done. "You were an asshole and then I found out you were a super-young asshole who probably lived with his mother in a basement or some shit."

"I did not live with my mother," he shot back. "I haven't lived with my mother since I joined the freaking Navy. And by the way, I'm not that much younger than you, and apparently I was quite a gentleman during a difficult time."

She had to stop the tears that threatened. She couldn't give over to wild emotion, couldn't jump him and beg him to remember more. Beg him to remember that he loved her, that he was the only man in the world who'd ever fucking loved her with his whole heart. She couldn't do that because they were finally making progress and it had all come because there was no expectation on him.

He was relaxed and he'd listened to her story with rapt attention, as though he'd been so interested in the outcome. Like he hadn't lived it.

Tell him a story, Kai had told her on the phone earlier today. *Like it's nothing more than you telling it to a stranger.*

In order to take pressure off Theo. When he tried too hard to remember it hurt him. That bitch had planted bombs in his head and she was walking across a field of landmines every time she tried to talk to him.

But there it was. He was looking at her like the old Theo for the first time since he'd come home. He was rolling those gorgeous blue eyes and huffing in righteous indignation. "Obviously I was in a bad situation. I couldn't go against my CO, but I also wasn't going to hurt you. You had me at a distinct disadvantage, so I don't think that proves anything. Once I got you down, you stayed down."

Oh, she had. She'd been pinned under his hot bod and she would give almost anything to get back there. "I made the logical decision that fighting you wouldn't help anything. Besides, Jesse had gone feral and that's all the chaos anyone needs. You should totally understand that part of the story."

"That's rude." He'd gone the sweetest shade of pink.

It was actually kind of fun to remind him of what a bitch she could be. She'd been so careful around him. This felt so much more like them. "And yet still true, buddy."

Not lover. Not babe. Buddy. Erin was going to be friends with Theo for now.

Theo stopped, his whole body going tight. "You're older than me."

Naturally that was what he stuck on. "Yes, I am."

His eyes closed. "I remembered my mother. My real mother. Remember is the wrong word. I knew. I knew that I moved out when I left for the Navy." The flush to his face turned red. "But I can't remember where I grew up or what my mother looked like."

"Let it go, Theo." Kai's tone held a note of warning and he'd lost his relaxed posture. He sat up in his chair as though waiting for the explosion.

He didn't have to wait for long.

Theo slapped the side of his head. "Fuck. It's right there. It's right fucking there. I can almost taste it."

Her heart ached and she couldn't stop herself. She reached out for him. "Baby, it's fine. Let it go. If it's there, it will be there later. It's not time for you to remember yet."

Her voice had gone soft and she tried all the tricks Kai had taught her in the beginning. She tried to soothe him. Tried to touch him and ease him back from the edge. She couldn't tell him never to remember. She had to put it off, to give him hope that it would happen one day.

"Let it go, baby," she said, trying to put her arms around him.

He shoved her away. She hadn't been ready for the move so it caught her off guard and sent her flying back to Kai's desk. She hit it hard and winced as she slid to the floor.

Theo stood over her, his face going white. "I can't do this. I can't fucking do this. I'm done, Kai."

He strode out the door.

Erin watched him, tears making the world blurry. So close. She'd gotten so damn close.

Kai was suddenly in front of her, offering her a hand up. "He didn't mean any of that. He's said those same words about a hundred times to me and he always comes back."

She let Kai help her up. "At some point he will walk away. If we can't get through to him, can't make him understand that this is his home, he'll leave."

He would leave and not look back. He might send her child support, but he wouldn't be in their lives. Her back ached and she stared at the door he'd walked out of. For a moment she'd thought she had him.

Wasn't that kind of their story?

"I know you don't like this word, but I need you to be patient with him," Kai said.

She hated the word. She wasn't a patient person and yet she'd had to learn it for her son. He brought it out in her. That tiny kid had become her whole world and she'd found reserves of patience she'd never known had existed. She stretched and forced herself not to run after Theo.

Faith was another quality she'd had to cling to lately.

She sighed and sat back down because their time wasn't quite up yet. "You know if you'd told me three years ago that I could put up with a screaming kid with an ear infection and not kill myself, I would have laughed at you."

Kai smiled slightly. "You know it's not a bad analogy."

"A couple of months back TJ wakes up in the middle of the night screaming his head off. I already wasn't sleeping well and Case was off working. Naturally it's a Saturday night so I have to go to the ER. Do you know what it's like to sit in the middle of a cesspool with a screaming kid for five hours before they even bother to get you back to a room? Apparently gang violence trumps earaches."

"I don't know but I can imagine it's awful."

"I'm sitting there and I'm so tired I can barely stand and I want it all to stop and I actually think about how much better everything would be if I'd never met him. Theo, that is. I have the thought that if I could wish him out of existence, then at least I wouldn't be here with a squalling kid and nothing in my life."

"Erin, you have to know that everyone thinks things like that when they're tired."

She held a hand up. "And that was when I looked down at this screaming baby and knew I wouldn't change a thing. The pain I felt, the annoyance, the lack of peace, they're all because I have a life and I have this little soul that someone thought I could raise. And I finally realized I wasn't my dad. I wasn't my mom and my childhood hadn't wrecked me because Theo had found me and put me back together. I felt pain because I had love and that was worth it. So I took a deep breath and held my baby close and we got through it." She could still remember how well she'd slept after the antibiotics had kicked in and TJ had fallen asleep on top of her. It had been the best sleep because she'd earned it. "Tell me I'm going to get through this, too."

Kai reached out, offering her his hand. "One way or another."

She took it, squeezing and gaining strength. Kai was her friend, but he was also someone she admired and trusted for his skill. "But I still might end up alone."

His expression softened. "Even if he did remember, if it had never happened, there's no guarantee that you don't end up alone.

He could have died some other way. The two of you could have grown apart. I worried that Theo wasn't strong enough for you."

"What is that supposed to mean?"

He took a step back and moved around to his desk again. "It means before he died you continually tested him. I worry that might have gone on past what he could stand. In some ways, it was TJ who forced your growth and if Theo had been around, it wouldn't have happened the same way."

Because Theo would have taken care of TJ. He wouldn't have forced her into a position where she had to figure herself out. She could have remained the old, insecure and hard Erin because TJ would have had a loving parent.

How would they have survived? When TJ got an ear infection, would she have rolled over and let Theo handle it? Would she have ever truly figured out how much she loved her son if she hadn't been left alone with him? Would she have figured out how much she loved Theo if he hadn't died?

If there was one thing she'd learned since she'd come to McKay-Taggart it was to step back and look at things differently. When she thought about it her training had began all those years ago when she'd found herself in counterintelligence. They'd taught her to look and think about things from the other perspective. Yes, it had been the perspective of terrorists and traitors, but when she'd gotten here, she'd learned that not everything was shitty. Some things, once embraced and taken to heart, could actually be good. Life was only as good as she made it.

She could weep and rail at fate or she could believe that things happened for a reason.

"I'm still going to kill that bitch." The truth was she'd made her decision long before. She'd made the decision to live fully the moment she'd decided to be TJ's mom. He couldn't have a mother who lived in the past. He needed a mom who fought for their future. Maybe it could have been different at one point, but she wouldn't change the woman she was today.

The things she'd gone through, they'd made her realize that she loved her son and Theo.

And they'd made her realize that she kind of loved herself, too.

So many years and only now could she admit that she deserved his love. Any love.

"I think that is a healthy way to think given the circumstances," Kai admitted.

Yeah, he was the perfect therapist for her. "So I'm concentrating on the positive. Our boy had a breakthrough."

"He did. Next time he starts to lose it like that, punch him again. He responds well to you that way. I don't think he quite understands the new Erin. Somewhere deep down, he still responds to the you he knew."

Luckily, there was still enough of the old Erin to go around. "That's a promise, doc."

* * * *

Theo stumbled out of Kai's office and into the lobby. He couldn't drive like this. He couldn't even walk until he'd calmed down. Could he make it over to Sanctum? Kai's office was in a building beside the club. If it was open, he could hide in the locker room until he'd calmed down. But that was a big if.

Kori was sitting at her desk. She looked up from her laptop. "Women's room. There's a nice chaise in there you can rest on and I recently restocked the granola bars."

"Ladies' room?" His head was pounding.

"Way better than the men's." She turned back to her computer. "There's some aspirin in there and some chilled sodas. Caffeine helps with headaches sometimes, or so I've heard. But if you throw up, do it in the toilet. I do not get paid to clean up after you."

He walked toward the women's bathroom. He could use something to eat. Sometimes focusing on eating or drinking helped him get through an episode.

If Kori had hurried around her desk and tried to help him, he would have run as fast as he could. Something about her no-nonsense advice had soothed him.

My poor Tomas. Let me help you. Let me make it better for you.

He shuddered, hating the sound of that voice in his head. He heard it every time a woman started in on him with soft hands and eyes and promises of making things better.

He'd liked it better when Erin had punched him in the face.

"Hey, buddy. Want a granola bar?"

Theo let the door slam behind him. He wasn't alone in the women's room and he wasn't the only guy. Robert sat on the chaise lounge, a bottle of water in one hand and a granola bar in the other. Kori had been right. This was nicer than the men's room. The men's room was nothing but a neatly kept bathroom with two urinals, a stall, and a couple of sinks. This was like a freaking spa. There was an overstuffed chaise that looked comfy, a rack full of magazines, and to his left, the marbled sink contained trays of all sorts of feminine needs. There were samples of makeup, perfumes, hair products. The music piping in wasn't music at all. It was more like soothing forest sounds.

"You should try the lavender spray. Very relaxing. If you open the second drawer, she's got eye masks."

"What the hell are you doing in the women's bathroom?" Theo had to ask. His friend looked incongruous sitting there in his gym clothes amidst the frilly feminine décor.

"I'm chilling while I wait for my appointment with Kai. And I'm in here because it's nice and I like it, and if you have a problem with it go to the men's room. Also, I am not hanging out here to find a girlfriend. I was told not to do that anymore, so now I only come for the granola bars and the fine, fine scent of lavender."

So he was pissing off everyone today. "Sorry, man. I wasn't expecting anyone in here."

"The good news is I'm the last appointment today. Apparently sessions with me take a lot out of Kai, so he schedules me last. In ten minutes I'll be gone and this will be all yours." He stood and moved to the small fridge, opening it and grabbing a red can. He offered it to Theo. "Here, you look like you could use the caffeine. It helps with the headaches. Probably precisely why Mother kept us away from it."

No caffeine. No liquor. No sugar. His body was the doc's weapon and she wanted him finely calibrated. Daily workouts lasted two hours. Enforced sleep cycles. Always, always take your vitamins.

He took a long swig of the soda, trying to banish the thoughts. "Sorry. I was being a dick."

"Bad session?" Rob moved over, offering him half the chaise.

Yep, he was hiding in a frilly bathroom, a crazy ex-mercenary his only solace. "It didn't start out that way."

"Were you with her? Joint session?" Rob was one of the few people who would never say her name around him. Probably because he was the only one who knew how much it could hurt.

"Yeah, but it was going pretty well. She was cool this time."

"No more tears?"

That was the problem. She always seemed on the verge of tears when he was around. Or she was pleading with him to come see their son. "No, she was kind of a bitch. I don't know. I felt closer to her today than I have since I met her. And then I tried to kill her."

Rob chuckled. "Has anyone told you you're kind of fucked up?"

Only every single person who met him. "She told me how we met. It wasn't like the other times. She wasn't trying to get me to remember. It was a story. That's all. I think she's got a skewed view though. I came off the tiniest bit douchey."

Rob opened his granola bar. "Douchey?"

"Apparently we met during a pretty illegal raid of my brother's company. She took exception to our invasion. We swooped in via chopper and hit the office. I threw a flashbang her way."

Rob grinned, as though they were talking about a football game and not real life, but then that had kind of been Kai's point. "Seriously? Damn, man. This was when you were with the CIA?"

It was only history. Only information written in a file somewhere. He'd been a Navy SEAL and then he'd worked for the Agency under a man named Tennessee Smith. When he looked at it from an academic standpoint, he was okay with it. "Yeah. Ten had his sister embedded with McKay-Taggart and he thought Big Tag was going to murder her or something. It all worked out, but the point is the way she tells the story I got my ass kicked and then hit on her after tackling her. And I had a hard-on."

"That surprises you?" Rob asked. "You like have a hard-on any time she walks in the room."

"Yeah, awesome. I also get a blinding headache when I think about her, so it all evens out." He'd been so close. It killed him. "When she told the story I remembered some things about my life."

Robert nodded. "Ah, and that's why you're in here holding your skull like it's going to crack open."

"Pretty much." Shame washed over him. For a moment he'd been so happy. He'd loved hearing her story, adored the husky tone of her voice as she'd laid it out for him. For a second he'd felt normal. And then he'd felt soft hands on his flesh and he'd shoved her away as fast as he could. He'd seen her eyes as she'd hit the desk. "I think I need to leave."

Rob nodded. "Awesome. I've been wanting to do that, too. We should take off now. We can find a homeless shelter some place where no one knows who we are and no one gives a flying fuck if we live or die, and we can rob banks for a living because it's all we know how to do."

Asshole. "I'm not joking. I'm going to hurt her."

"It's been six weeks, man." Rob leaned back with a sigh. "You were tortured for way longer than that. Shouldn't you at least give yourself some time to heal before you blow everything up?"

"Do I need time?" It was what he thought about constantly.

Rob stared at him. "It's all we have so yes, we fucking need it. I've been quiet this whole time, but I have to say if you want to walk out, please tell your brother that I'll take your place. You might remember some facts every now and then but I have nothing. No name. No family. No one waiting for me."

"Just because they haven't found you yet doesn't mean they won't." Adam was trying to figure out who Robert was in real life. He'd come up with nothing so far.

"I don't care," Rob shot back. "That's the crazy thing. I no longer give a shit. I like this place. I like figuring out the foods I enjoy and playing games, and damn I would do almost anything to be you."

Did Rob think he had it good? "So you can disappoint everyone around you? You think that's easy?"

"You're not disappointing them, man. They give a shit about you. They care. You've got a chip on your shoulder about pleasing people or you would see that. It's what Kai would call an intrinsic part of your personality, but it's fucking with you right now. You've got people who love you but you're so afraid of hurting them that you're willing to walk away. *That* will hurt them."

"And if I kill her?" He wasn't thinking through all the ramifications.

"I don't think she'll let you. Beyond that, I don't actually think you would do it. Look, I remember our time with Mother way better than you do."

There were reasons for that. "Because she tortured me more."

Rob sat back, his shoulders slumping. When he spoke again there was a weariness to his voice. "Because my mind wasn't as strong as yours and it soaked the drug in. I didn't fight the way you did. I didn't require extra drugs and therapy. She wiped my mind and it didn't come back. So I know what happened. I have a working knowledge of most of the last two years of my life and a whole lot of that included you, brother."

Rob had always been the good boy to his problem child. Still, despite the therapy, Theo knew Rob meant well. The minute he'd had a chance to run with Theo, he'd taken it. "So tell me why you think I won't actually kill her."

Rob turned, obviously happy with the chance to explain. "Because you refused to hurt the women. It was exactly what got you in trouble. Do you remember the job in Colombia?"

"Vaguely. I know we pulled it off. It was a good day."

"Victor was running point."

He'd hated Victor. He'd known he was supposed to show loyalty to his brother, but he'd found the man distasteful. Victor genuinely enjoyed hurting women. Not in a fun, everyone-gets-off way. In a bleeding, pleading, dying way. "So Tony was in charge."

Tony hadn't liked him, hadn't trusted him at all. When Mother was away, Tony would play. Evil games. Games that left Tomas hurt and bleeding, and then he would give out some of the drugs and there would be no talking.

"They tested you," Rob explained. "You were ordered to kill the teller. You refused. He tried to force you to kill and you refused. Mother attempted to get you to hurt numerous prisoners and you refused. Time and time again."

He didn't remember. He couldn't remember. Sometimes he thought all he could remember was pain. His whole life had been pain.

Except for a second he'd had a flash of Case tossing a football his way and he'd known it wasn't imagination. It had been memory, and he'd smelled the honeysuckle that had grown wild through the trailer park. He'd heard the whooshing sound of the football as it hit his hands and his brother calling a play that no NFL fan would ever remember. He'd felt the last light of sun on his face and known that they were waiting on the bus that would take them to Great Lakes.

He'd known he'd never lived in that trailer again.

"I want to remember my life."

Rob took a deep breath and sat back again, his eyes turning away. "I know, but I worry you're going to fuck up the life you could have now by trying to find the one that no longer exists. You spend your every day going over files and reading about the past. You could be going out with her. You could be going to family dinners and having fun."

"We have fun."

Robert shook his head sadly. "We play video games and try to forget that we were tortured. I need you to understand that the minute Kai says I'm good to go, I'm asking your brother for a job and I'm getting an apartment and I'm going to figure out who the hell I am now, and I'm going to move on."

"You don't understand. I know you don't remember and there's no record of how she caught you, but I know how I got fucked. I did it. I made the call. I fucked up so many lives that night because I was an arrogant shit who thought I knew better than everyone else."

"You can't know why you did the things you did," Robert insisted. "You're not in the moment. You're looking back on it."

"I know I should have called it in the minute the leader of the op got kidnapped. I have it on the highest authority that if I'd done that, none of what happened later would have happened." It hurt knowing how roughly he'd screwed everyone over, but not quite remembering why he'd done it. He found himself the villain of the piece but could ascribe no motivation beyond the fact that he'd been arrogant and foolish and he'd cost an agent her life and a son his father.

"You can't know that. Perhaps you do call it in and Smith is killed by MSS."

He'd gone over it a million times. "They wouldn't have killed him. He was too valuable an asset. Besides, he had a double planted in their organization. She would have gotten him out, so I got Des killed for no reason and by not following his direct order, I got tortured and turned into the good doc's trained monkey."

Every time he read the file, he stopped at that page. Ten Smith's written debrief included all the dark shit. He'd noted that he'd ordered Theo Taggart to murder an unarmed woman because he felt that she was too dangerous to be left alive. Theo Taggart had known better and refused the order.

Fucking idiot. He'd had her in his sights according to the documentation. He'd had a gun on her, pointed at her head, and he'd been too weak to pull the trigger.

The room was quiet for a moment.

"Have you thought about what would have happened if you had killed her?" Rob asked.

Every single day. "I would have saved myself a shit ton of pain."

"You would be dead. She wouldn't have been able to save you. I would be dead. I would have been left in a cell to starve to death. So I know you probably will sit here and feel sorry for yourself, but I'm glad you didn't kill her. Maybe you would rather be in the ground than have to fight to get your life back, but I won't ever feel that way." He stood up. "My session is starting soon. I'll see you at home, brother."

Rob shoved his uneaten granola bar in his pocket and strode out the door with his water in hand.

Theo looked around. Rob had no trouble accepting the bounty offered to him. Why couldn't he do the same?

He groaned and laid back. Was Rob right? Was he incapable of truly hurting her? It didn't feel like it. Somewhere out there she was nursing an aching back because he'd shoved her away so hard. She'd only offered him comfort and he couldn't take it.

He stared up at the ceiling. Someone had painted a sun and stars up there. It was stupid because even he knew you didn't get the sun and stars. You got one or the other. No one got both.

He could try to figure out why he felt connected to Erin. He forced himself to think her name even as the pain washed over him. He could try to work things out with her or he could go with Big Tag's plan and take a sub tonight.

He couldn't do both. Despite her attitude today, he knew it would hurt her to see him with another woman.

He wanted it so badly. Not to have sex, but to be out of himself for a while, to be the Master and not the dipshit who'd screwed everything up and fucked up everyone's lives. He wanted one person in the world he could give to without this heavy sense of guilt.

He sat up. He couldn't run away. That was all talk. Besides, Big Tag had a tracer device embedded under the skin of his left bicep. The better to not lose his puppy again, as his asshole brother had said. Unless he wanted to dig it out, if he ran his brothers would be all over his ass, and they had their own forms of torture.

He was stuck here and he had no idea what to do.

He could sit her down and tell her he couldn't love her again. He could offer to pay child support and attempt to integrate into her life in a friendly way.

Or he could try. He could go back to session with her tomorrow and try to connect.

He wasn't sure if it would work. Hell, if he was honest with himself, he wasn't certain he wanted it to work.

What Robert didn't understand, couldn't possibly, was that he was free. Yes, he'd been through something horrible and he had no memory of his past, but Robert also didn't have this crushing sense of letting everyone down because he couldn't possibly feel for them what they felt for him.

They loved a ghost, a Theo he couldn't possibly be again.

So what did he fucking choose? The sun or the stars? Comfort or honor?

Was that all he had for her now? He wasn't sure he was capable of feeling love anymore. He'd been hollowed out, all the good things about Theo Taggart scooped up and tossed in the trash. He walked. He talked. He felt pain and guilt and seemingly nothing else. The minute he started to feel something for her, he was rewarded with an ache and the knowledge that he was empty inside.

Could he find even the smallest place where he could simply be? Where guilt didn't weigh him down? Did he deserve that place?

He stared up at the picture and wondered what the hell he was going to do.

CHAPTER FIVE

Theo sighed as he tied the laces of his leathers. "This is bullshit. He's ignored me all day and now he won't even walk into the damn locker room so I can have a two-minute conversation with him? Are you serious?"

Case leaned against the locker beside his. "You know big brother can be stubborn. And he wasn't ignoring you. He had a meeting with some clients earlier this afternoon. It wasn't something he could walk out of so he could solve the problem of your cowardice."

Theo felt his eyes narrow. "I'm not being a coward."

"You agreed to try a session with a sub. She's been informed and a contract written. She's eager to meet you. Since she's not the one running away, I would say you're a coward for not telling her to her face that you've changed your mind."

He wasn't going to punch his brother. He told himself that a couple of times before reaching for his vest. "I don't even know the girl. I don't see how she's going to be disappointed. And I get that Ian was working. He's not working now. He could take two seconds to walk in here so I don't have to put on leathers I have no intention of wearing all night."

"So you're going home?" Case asked. "Looking forward to another big night of Xbox and beer?"

It wasn't a bad way to spend the evening. At least he couldn't hurt anyone if he was sitting on his brother's couch. Theo settled the vest over his chest and slammed the locker door shut. "You have a problem with it? Because let me tell you I can move out anytime you like."

Blue eyes rolled his way. "I wish you wouldn't take everything with the harshest meaning possible. I'm worried about you. Nothing more."

But there was something more. Case had to be annoyed with him. He was a damn newlywed. He'd married Mia Lawless a few weeks back and he was sure having two crazed weirdoes with PTSD and blank memories hanging around had done nothing for his marriage.

"Look, I thought about it for a long time today. I know what Ian's trying to do. I get it. I'm not ready." He'd tried to envision himself working with some nameless, faceless sub. Every single time that blank face turned into green eyes and freckles and a mouth made to kiss. Her. "I'm supposed to take things slow."

"Slow, yes. Never moving at all is what you're doing, Theo."

Theo turned on his heels. All around him the locker room was starting to fill up with men getting ready to play for the night. They laughed and joked with each other, perfectly comfortable with their roles. He wasn't sure which were which, but he knew some of the men here were subs. They didn't submit in the locker room. They flipped off their Dom counterparts and talked about work because in here they were simply friends.

That would all change once they hit the dungeon floor. Once they were on the dungeon floor, they would leave behind their daily roles, their cares and personas. They would become Doms and submissives and they would know their places. They would relax and find pleasure in their partners.

He would go back to an apartment that wasn't his and play games he didn't care about.

"Why are you doing this, man? It's so obvious to me that you want to try," Case said, his voice low. "Why won't you let yourself try?"

"I could hurt the sub."

"I tested you on everything. You passed with flying colors when you let go and simply followed your instincts. You won't hurt the sub."

"Fine. I'll hurt her."

Case frowned for a moment. "Are you talking about Erin? Sorry. Of course you are. Uhm, you're not going to hurt her. She's already here and she's planning on finding her own play partner."

His hands fisted at his side. That was a kick in the gut. A massive, brutal kick in the gut. "Who?"

Case took a step back, his hands coming up. "Dude, you look crazy right now. Tone that shit down. You've made it clear you don't think a relationship between you and Erin can work. Did you think she'd wait around forever? It's already been almost two years for her. She's gotten the message. She's ready to try something new."

Someone new.

Fuck and fuck. He'd been ready to turn down something he needed to spare her feelings, but apparently there were no more feelings to be spared. Maybe she'd finally figured out that he wasn't the man she'd loved before. He was merely wearing his skin.

"Fine. Let's go and meet the sub." He wasn't sure how he would handle it if he saw her on the dungeon floor. Something ached inside him at the thought. Was this what they would come to? Would they nod each other's way as they passed by holding the hands of their new partners?

He knew he shouldn't care, but he did. He simply didn't know why. Was it a habit he hadn't quite forgotten?

He stopped before they made it out of the locker room. "Did I really love her?"

His brother would know. According to everything he'd learned about himself, he'd been close to his twin. He was sure they hadn't sat around talking about their feelings and shit, but shouldn't Case know if he'd been in love?

Case's face went tight with emotion. "You loved her so much I was jealous. Not because I didn't want to lose my brother, but I wanted to feel what you felt. I wanted to find a woman who made me better than I'd been before."

"Did you? Did Mia make you better?" His sunny sister-in-law always had a smile on her face.

Case nodded. "She does. But I almost screwed everything up. I almost lost her. Do you know how I got her back? I took your advice."

"I gave you advice? I didn't think Mia came around until after I'd gone missing."

"No, but you have to know you were always there for me," Case said solemnly. "I know that sounds silly, but I would ask what you would have done. And when you were first trying to chase Er…her…you would call her and leave her voice mails about your day. You had to because she wouldn't answer your calls, but I learned later on that those messages wore her down. They made her understand how you felt. So I did it with Mia and six months of pouring my heart out to her phone did the trick."

He'd done that? What would he have talked to her about?

He chased her. Pursued her. Wanted her so desperately he was willing to accept the fact that she wouldn't answer when he called but he would still leave messages about how he'd hoped she had a good day.

There it was. A tendril of memory he knew was truth.

He let it go. If he tried to follow it he would end up in a ball of pain on the floor and nothing would get done all night. He would fuck up the evening for everyone.

He had to talk to Ian. There was no getting around it. Even if he decided he couldn't partner with a sub, he did need to explain why. He needed to tell the sub it wasn't a rejection.

He might need to find his ex and ask her not to play with anyone else until they'd had more time.

Did he have the right to ask that of her when he wasn't sure he could ever be with her again?

Why was everything so fucking hard?

He strode out of the locker room, leaving behind the laughter and entering Sanctum.

His brother's club. He'd been told this was the second version of the club, the first having been blown all to hell by one of his former team members. Ian had laughingly told him that he and Case had been the only reason everyone inside hadn't died because they'd rammed the bomb with Case's truck.

What a hell of a time that had probably been. His former self had been a badass and for all the right reasons. He'd been a man willing to sacrifice for others.

Who the hell was he now?

Thumping industrial music greeted him as he walked to the stairs that led to the second floor and the lounge and playroom. More exotic play occurred on the third floor and there were several privacy rooms he would likely never use with the woman he was about to meet.

"Ian's in the bar with the sub and the man who's representing her in your negotiations." Case pointed toward the bar area.

Damn it. He would have to explain to another fucking Dom, who would probably get pissy with him for rejecting his reject. She was probably a former sub he wanted to send off into the leather sunset with another Dom so he didn't have to deal with her anymore. He would get a lot of pomp and circumstance and then anger when he explained he wasn't going to help him out.

He got to the top of the stairs and looked over at the bar. He could see his brother's back. No way to miss Ian. He was the biggest dude in the place, and there was Charlotte sitting in a chair as he stood. When he decided to sit, he would take her chair and either pull her down to his lap or she would sink gracefully to his side and place her head in his lap.

On the other side of the table was Liam O'Donnell. His wife was sitting across from Charlotte wearing a pretty corset and laughing at something.

"Why is O'Donnell here?"

Case stared ahead. "He's representing the sub."

Damn. He'd thought O'Donnell was a one sub Dom. His instincts must have gotten shot. He hadn't thought O'Donnell would have a couple of subs on his string along with his wife. Who was the sad-sack sub who played second fiddle...

Ian moved to his left and he saw her. *Her*. She was on her knees, smiling at something Charlotte had said. His *her*. With red hair and freckles he wanted to kiss and breasts he could hold in his palm.

The implication hit him hard and fast.

Case's hand was suddenly on his chest. "Don't you fucking dare. He's not here as her Dom. He's here as the man she respects most in this club. They've never once played together. Not once. He's the godfather of your child, so you chill out right this second and you think this through."

Think it through. She was sitting right there. How the hell could he think when she was on her knees waiting for some fucking Dom? "He's negotiating with her new Dom?"

"He's negotiating with you, brother."

He stopped, staring at her. She wore a forest green corset and what looked like black boy shorts. Her fire-red hair fell around her shoulders and she looked softer and younger than she did at work. She so often wore it in a severe bun and made sure her clothes were utilitarian and hid her sweet curves.

"I can't even say her name."

Case put a hand on his shoulder. "You don't even know her name yet. She's not Erin in this club. She's a sub named Red. You will call her Red. You will think of her as Red. Your relationship exists in this club alone and it does not include a past or a future."

No past. No future. Simply a woman he wanted more than he did his next breath.

Red.

He thought the word, playing it around in his head as he stared her way. No pain. No memory. Just a sense of pure anticipation flowed through his veins. Oh, it had a destination. His cock.

Ian turned and Theo realized his big brother was kind of an asshole. Not that he hadn't known that about two minutes after he'd met the man, but he wasn't foolish enough to think this hadn't been Ian's plan all along. He'd said he wanted to try something different and then he hadn't given Theo an out.

"So you had an off site? And couldn't answer your phone?" He had to play this cool. She was a girl in a club and he didn't know her. It was the only way this could work. If he rushed in, he would be all over her and she would be Erin again.

Deep breath. Let the pain go.

Ian shrugged, one massive shoulder moving up and down negligently. "You know how it goes with picky clients."

Yeah, he did. His brother typically put them on their asses and moved on to less annoying clients. This had been one long play to get him here, to force him into a position where he could almost taste her.

Fuck, if this worked, he might be able to taste her.

"You could have told me." He moved to join the group. He wasn't going to do what he wanted to do, which was scoop her up and take her to one of the privacy rooms and start exploring.

Red shifted on her pillow. They were scattered around the bar area for subs to relax on. The woman who was so competent and independent during the day seemed perfectly comfortable lounging like a sleek cat on her big fluffy pillow. She leaned to one side, her long legs curling behind her. Her eyes were down in submission, but for a moment she looked up and he could see the heat there.

She wanted him, too. She wanted this. She'd plotted and planned with Ian and that did something for him. For so long she'd gone without and she sought to end her lack of physical affection with him.

Could he give her what she needed? He had once. By all accounts, he'd given her everything. He wondered if she knew what had been shoved in the bottom of the backpack she'd sent to him when he'd first come home. As Case explained, it had been his favorite. He'd carried it all around the world and she had kept it after his death. She'd brought it home and enshrined it.

When he'd come home and gone to Case's to stay, she'd sent it over, stuffed to the brim with socks and boxers and his clothes. At the bottom had been a book it looked like he'd been reading, a crossword magazine that had been half filled out, and a diamond ring. An engagement ring.

Had he meant to ask her while they'd been out in the islands?

Ian stepped in front of him, blocking his view. "This won't work if you can't stop thinking about it."

It. His past. All the things he couldn't remember. All the things he'd lost.

He let it go. "Her name is Red?"

Ian nodded slowly. "Yes. It's the only name you will call her in this club and she will call you Sir or Master Theo."

"And I can't see her outside the club?" He wasn't sure how he felt about that.

"Outside the club she has to be who she is during the day. She can't give up her identity."

Because she had to think of more than pleasure. She had to think of her kid. This was all she could give him. He intended to take it. "You're comfortable giving me back my Master rights?"

"Yes, Theo. You've passed every test. Could you stop being afraid for five minutes and try to enjoy yourself? Could you stop thinking about all the ways you'll hurt everyone around you and think about how you could please them? I know you're here as a Dom, but you understand what that means in this club."

It ultimately meant serving his sub. It was the odd thing about his brother's brand of D/s. The sub served the Dom. The Dom served the sub. The Dom's happiness and pleasure was the utmost goal of the submissive. The sub's happiness and pleasure was the ultimate concern of the Dominant.

When he thought about it that way, it was kind of like a marriage.

He couldn't get on one knee and offer her the ring he'd found in his backpack, but he could do this.

He moved around his brother, walking up to her. Her head was down and he knelt beside her. He reached out to tilt her chin up. Those green eyes opened and stared up at him as though waiting for him to reject her. It was there in the stubborn tilt of her chin, in the hollow way she looked through him.

How hard had this been on her? How many times had she been rejected before? Told she wasn't traditionally beautiful, wasn't perfectly feminine?

"I came here to explain to you why I couldn't do this," he said quietly.

She started to pull away.

He let his eyes go hard. "You will allow me to finish. I was told you had some training. Was your last Dom so lax he didn't teach you to respect a Dom who's speaking to you with kindness and politeness?"

Oh, he loved how she flushed. He had her because her last Dom had been him. He watched as she obviously found her patience, biting that full bottom lip before allowing her eyes to go soft again.

"My last Dom trained me well. He was a good man."

She'd loved him. Loved him so much that she'd had his child and kept his clothes and closed off the part of herself that had belonged to him.

"I'm not him."

She looked down but didn't move. "I realize that, Sir. It's all right. If you'll allow me, I'll get back to the locker room."

"I don't allow you. Like I said, I came here to explain all the reasons why I can't top you. And I forget all of them now. I had reasons that had to do with not wanting to hurt another woman."

Her eyes came back up and the sweetest smile curled her lips. "I don't think she'll mind, Sir."

"She is far more complex than I gave her credit for." He'd never suspected that she would do this. It was inventive and sexy and he needed to see her as more than the woman from his nightmares. She'd been everything to him and now he saw her through the filter Moth...Hope McDonald wanted him to see her through. "Would you like to play with me, Red? I hope you say yes because you are the most beautiful woman I've seen."

She flushed again, but he suspected it was for a different reason. For a second he saw a sheen of tears cover her eyes, but then she seemed to shake it off.

"Yes, Sir. I would love to play with you."

Then it was time to let the negotiations begin.

* * * *

She reached up and allowed Theo to draw her to her feet.

Master Theo. He was Master Theo in this place. She had to remember that at all times. For the last thirty minutes while they'd negotiated the terms of their contract, he'd seemed more relaxed and settled than she'd seen him since he'd returned. She wasn't about to screw with that. Not for anything.

But she was so having a long talk with Li. Did he have to drag out the contract negotiations when it came to the weird stuff? She caught his grin when Master Theo had blushed. They were giving him shit, but then that was pretty normal for these guys.

When he'd looked down at her and asked her to play with him...for a second it was like the old Theo had shown up. He'd told her how beautiful she was and she'd believed him. He was the only person in the world who could make her believe it.

"Now that we know I'm not going to pee on you, would you like to walk a bit and watch some scenes, perhaps?" Master Theo asked politely.

Yes, Li and Ian had fun with this negotiation. She wanted to go to the privacy rooms and ride him like a stallion, but patience was the word of the day. "I would love to, Sir."

Sir. He was back to being Sir. She remembered the first time she'd called him Master. The first time she'd submitted to him. It had been in Africa.

No. Let it go in here. In this place she was discovering the new Theo and not longing for the one who had died. In this place, she was looking to the present, enjoying the moment with the handsomest Dom she'd ever seen.

He helped her to her feet and she expected him to let go of her hand. He seemed so hesitant to touch her, but this time his fingers entwined with hers. He turned to lead her out of the bar, not bothering to look back at his brother.

"You'll walk her to her car?" Li asked, calling out.

"I'll take care of her," he said, but his shoulders had gone stiff.

This was the part when she would normally try to soothe him, try to coax him back to his previous good mood. It hadn't worked for six weeks. For six weeks when she'd laid hands on him and tried to ease him, that was precisely when he would walk out. It was killing her to not know why he could no longer accept her comfort, but she had to go with what seemed to work on him.

"Are you a jealous ass, Sir?"

He stopped and his eyes flared as he turned on her. "What did you say?"

Oh, yeah, now she had his attention. The masochist inside her flamed to life. She'd been carefully banked since Theo died, as she would only ever accept him as her partner again. She'd had fun in the years before Theo, but she wouldn't play with anyone else. Had he stayed gone, she likely would have lived out her life in widowhood, her sexuality carefully packed away with her heart.

But he was here and she didn't have to pretend when it came to this part.

"I asked if Sir was a jealous ass because he seemed to get upset that I had a friend negotiate for me. It was explained to Sir that my relationship with Master Liam is strictly familial in nature. He acts as the big brother I always wanted. So that means Sir either can't stand the thought of me being around any male but him, which is selfish as shit when you think about it. Or Sir thinks I'm a liar and I'm actually sleeping with my partner and cheating on the best woman I've ever met. Which is it?"

"Are you always such a mouthy brat?"

"Always." She was an honest one, too.

His shoulders eased down and a self-deprecating chuckle came from his mouth as his hands found her waist and he drew her close. For the first time in forever her body brushed against his and every cell seemed to leap back to life. Her skin heated and she could feel her nipples tighten. Only this man could ever do it for her.

"I think I'll have to do something about that," he said, staring down at her. His hands moved over her shoulders, running down her arms. "I am a jealous ass. And no, I don't think you're lying to me. I can't imagine that he wouldn't want you."

"Then you have very little imagination, Sir. I assure you he's perfectly happy with his wife. He doesn't look at other women. I thought it would be easier to have someone negotiate for me. I thought it would give you some time to settle your mind around the thought of playing with me."

"Somehow I suspect this was all carefully crafted to manipulate me to the exact place you wanted."

Thin ice. It was everywhere. If she stepped the wrong way, she plunged them both back into the chilly waters they'd been swimming in for weeks. "I don't think of it as manipulation. I think of it as getting what I wanted. You as my Dom. Your hand guiding me. Your hand disciplining me. Your hand as the only one on my body."

All true. She simply wouldn't mention that she was desperate to have him hold their son, to have him wake up next to her in the house he'd bought for them, to grow old with him.

Sex. Red was going to concentrate on sex because there wasn't so much pressure that way. Red would offer Master Theo pleasure and harmony and peace, and sometimes that came in the form of a tart tongue and letting him smack her ass.

Yes, she would get pleasure and harmony and peace, too.

"You say potato. I say topping from the bottom," he said with a grin on his face. "If you do it again, you'll find yourself over my knee."

Unfortunately, that was pretty much where she wanted to be. This was how it had been for them. Play. Fun. Some people took the D/s relationship super seriously, but for her and Theo it had always been a way to seek pleasure and let off steam in a healthy, consensual way.

How would it change now that he truly needed the control? Before, it had been a fun game. Now, he needed this, needed to be the top. Could she truly submit?

"Yes, Sir. I'm sorry for cursing, Sir."

He frowned. "Don't think I hate your smart mouth. And don't hold back on me. I'll be disappointed if I don't get a chance to slap that pretty ass."

Warmth spread through her. Yes, he was still in there somewhere. She simply had to find him.

His hands came up as though he couldn't quite make himself stop touching her. He smoothed back her hair, letting his fingers play in it. "Have I told you how pretty you are?"

So many times she'd started to believe it. "Once tonight, Sir. I appreciated it."

"I'm going to kiss you before the night is over. I'm going to spank you and then you're going to sit on my lap and let me kiss you. We'll watch some scenes and then finish with some impact play and I'll kiss you."

It was the Dom's way of asking for permission. He would tell her what he would do and then it was up to her to agree or to call an end to the play. She wasn't about to do that. "Yes, Sir. That sounds like a lovely way to spend an evening."

He reached for her hand again. "Come on. I think I heard that someone was doing a suspension scene. Let's go watch."

She followed him, her hand warm in his, but her mind had flown back. Back before TJ. Before Theo died. Before Africa.

To their first kiss.

CHAPTER SIX

Dallas, TX
Two and a half years before

Erin slammed the door to her office. This was utterly ridiculous and she wasn't putting up with it. It had to be some kind of a damn joke. There was not a file sitting on her desk with the contents of her next job laid out all *Mission: Impossible* style. That stupid file didn't include the fact that she was going undercover for what might be six damn months of her life as freaking Theo Taggart's submissive.

It wasn't happening. It was some kind of a sick joke and she knew exactly who was responsible. Her boss was an asshole.

She strode down the hall, stopping at Li's office. Luckily the door was open. She'd learned the hard way that sometimes her partner had his wife up to the office for some afternoon fun that involved seeing way too much of Avery naked. Today, it was just Li, staring at his computer screen.

"Do you know where Big Tag is?"

"He's meeting with some Hollywood types this morning. Apparently one of his childhood friends is now a reality TV producer. Why do you…" Li grimaced. "Got that assignment, huh? If it's any consolation, I told him you would be upset."

Upset didn't begin to cover it. According to that report, she was going to spend the next few months working and living in Africa, befriending a woman named Faith McDonald. Doctor Faith ran a clinic in Liberia. She was some kind of do-gooder, but her father was the real target. This was a long game meant to get Tennessee Smith into Senator McDonald's Caribbean compound so he could prove the senator had ties to an organization known as The Collective. Ten Smith was sure the senator had been the one to get him burned with the CIA and he was out for blood.

She totally understood revenge. She got that sometimes blood needed to be shed. Africa? She could live there and work there. No problem.

Theo Taggart was a problem. A big, gorgeous Viking god of a problem.

She'd managed to hold him off the whole time they'd been in Dubai. She'd even tried to convince him that she had a thing for that walking, talking venereal disease Kash Kamdar, who'd actually turned out to be a pretty decent guy. Oh, she had zero interest in sleeping with the man. How the hell could she when all she could think about was a ridiculously young, sunny piece of man meat?

It had taken everything she had not to go to Theo in Dubai when he'd made it so plain he would welcome her in his bed. Now she was supposed to pretend to be his sub for months at a time? In the middle of a dangerous mission? When they had only the two of them to hold on to?

Yeah, it was a fucking romance novel Serena would write. It was also a disaster in the making.

"I'm not doing it." She wasn't going to let Big Tag manipulate her. He thought he was so sly, but she saw right through him. This was all about putting her in a position where she had to give Theo a shot.

She wasn't going to make a complete fool of herself. She wasn't sure what the hell that kid thought he was doing, but she wasn't going to play along.

"You're going to refuse the assignment?" Li frowned as though he hadn't thought that scenario through. Li always thought everything through.

And that told her something. "This was your idea."

He put a hand up. "You're the only one who can do it. Everyone else has kiddos. You can't expect them to leave their babies for months at a time."

He wasn't understanding her. "I'm more than happy to go. It's not the assignment I have a problem with."

He sighed. "You have to work with him sometime, love. He's here now. He's not going away."

Because he was the boss's brother. It hurt her heart, but she might have to think about quitting. She couldn't win this battle. Blood always won out. Well, unless it was her blood and then anyone else won. She turned and saw the one person who might be able to save her. Big Tag was walking down the hall with Alex, probably headed toward the main conference room at the front of the building. She marched down the hall, calling out to him.

"Boss, you can't be serious."

Big Tag stopped, his broad shoulders taking up most of the hallway. "I'm never serious."

She practically shuddered with relief. Maybe she could keep her job. "Thank god. I was hoping it was a joke."

Alex sighed, sending Big Tag a nasty look before turning back to her. "It's not a joke, Erin. You can pick up your tickets with Grace. You and Theo are set to fly out early Thursday. You have a meeting with the security head of the hospital on Monday, so rest up. It's a long flight and you've got a half a day's layover in Frankfurt. Grace gave you a nice long layover so you don't miss that flight to Monrovia. Also, since your cover is that you're an ex-military, down-on-her-luck girl looking for work, we put you in coach. I'm really sorry."

She felt herself flush.

A snort issued forth from her ever-sympathetic boss. "But we made sure Theo's got the seat right beside you. After all, a Master always looks after his precious submissive."

If only the idea was truly distasteful to her, she could probably handle the job. The trouble was the idea of Theo Taggart topping her made her whole body tighten in anticipation. Damn it. She was not going to be his fool.

She gave Big Tag her full attention, her body straightening as it would when she'd been in the military. He was her CO and maybe if she showed him some respect, he would do the same for her. "Send someone else with me. Send me in with Case or Hutch or Michael Malone. I understand that I'm the only female operative who can handle this mission. Hell, I believe in this mission. I want to take out Senator McDonald as much as anyone, but I don't think Theo is ready."

Big Tag's eyes narrowed and she wondered if she hadn't made a mistake. "In what way? Is his SEAL training not sufficient? Was his time as a CIA operative too short for your liking? Or is there something else you would like to tell me? Has he harassed you?"

It was her chance. All she had to do was explain to Ian the multitudinous ways his brother had crossed the line. The little ass wouldn't take a hint. He'd asked her out and she'd turned him down. So he'd asked her again the next day. She'd told him to fuck off. The trouble was, she liked hanging out with his group. They were fun, so she ended up actually spending time with him. He'd backed off and they'd kind of become friends. Sort of. They had a few beers together. Talked some shit. Every now and then he would get this dumb wistful look on his face and ask her out again.

It was getting harder and harder to say no.

She could lay out all the shit his brother did. He'd taken to calling her lately and when she wouldn't answer, he would leave long voice mails asking about her day. Between that and the continual way he asked her out, she could easily call him a stalker and say he was sexually harassing her.

Except he wasn't. Maybe in some men it would be, but Theo wasn't aggressive. He didn't push her. His voice mails weren't threatening. They were…sweet.

She couldn't do it. "No, Sir. You know he's actually very kind. I don't know how to handle it. I would be more comfortable with Hutch."

Big Tag crossed his arms over his massive chest. "Hutch is incapable of looking like he's in love with you and he has zero training in D/s. Faith McDonald has been in the lifestyle for longer than you have."

"Longer than Theo, too." From what she understood, he'd only started training in the last few weeks.

"But Theo has been training day and night," Tag explained.

"Theo is perfectly prepared for this mission and you're the right operative to get close to Faith McDonald. You'll be her personal bodyguard and you can bond over giggling and tea and whatever girls bond over."

He was such an ass. She flipped him off since the whole respect thing definitely didn't work on Big Tag when he wasn't wearing a set of leathers. "I'll take care of Faith. I actually kind of admire her. She's smart and seems to be trying to do good in the world."

Tag shook his head her way. "Don't go into this expecting a lifetime friendship. She's the target. Talk to her. Convince her to come to Dallas with you so she can meet a new Master. She's single right now, but the word is she always indulges during her off time. Get her back here with you and Ten will handle the rest."

It was exactly the kind of mission she would be good at. She was ready to show them all how good she could be out in the field. She would likely be bouncing up and down at the shot if it hadn't been for one thing.

"And Theo?"

"Don't sleep with him. It's just your cover. Sometimes operatives don't use their covers to get a little something something." Ian scratched his head. "Alex and I went undercover once and we did not sleep together."

"He tried but I wanted someone a little more tender," Alex snarked. "Li used to go undercover with Karina and he's never once slept with her. Then there was that first mission we sent Jesse on at the strip club."

Ian cleared his throat pointedly.

"JoJo, Eboni, and Misty Rose weren't his partners," Alex pointed out. "Simon was. Si swears up and down they've never cuddled. Not once. So you're safe, Erin."

They weren't going to help her. It was obvious she hadn't been selected for this op because they thought she was smart and could handle the job. She'd been chosen because Big Tag was trying to give his baby brother an in. She wasn't about to let them know how much that hurt.

"You're all jackholes, you know that, right? And Liberia? Really? I left the damn Army so I didn't have to spend all my time in the world's shit holes." She turned and started back toward her office. "Simon gets to go to Venice. Li's biggest op was in London. I get fucking West Africa."

"Don't forget the Ebola," Tag called out. "You're welcome."

She didn't turn back. She walked right past Li's office without a glance.

She had a decision to make. It might be time to pack it up. It was awesome here, but she wasn't some toy they could toss around. Erin stepped into her office, closing the door behind her and shutting them all out. *Deep breath. Don't fucking cry. Don't let the happy, shiny people with their babies and husband and wives see the dipshit divorcee who couldn't even stay in the Army cry.*

"You honestly don't want to work with me?"

She went still. Damn it. Had he been freaking following her? She'd closed the door and he was on the wrong side. Erin took another deep breath and forced herself to turn around. "I don't think it's a good idea."

He was leaning against her desk, his muscled chest molded against the material of his T-shirt. "Why? You don't think I would take care of you?"

She clung to the one thing she could. "The fact that you would think I need taking care of is why it's a bad idea."

His face fell. "I don't understand how giving a shit about you makes me the bad guy. I really don't. I'm not trying to play you or manipulate you. Could you please explain it to me? We have fun. We laugh together. Why can't we do this thing together, too?"

Because I want you so fucking bad I can taste it. Nope, she couldn't tell him that. "You don't respect me as an operative."

"Of course I do," he shot back. "Are you kidding me? You worked counter for years. Look, Erin, I'm a great shot. I'm excellent in the field when it comes to taking someone out, but I've never done what you have. You're smart. You know how people think. I wouldn't want to do this mission with anyone but you because I think you'll figure Faith McDonald out quickly. You'll be the one to reel her in, not me. I'm arm candy. I'm there because you need a Dominant partner."

Why did he always have to say the right things? "I don't think it's a good idea."

"Why? Why did you run to my brother and try to get me kicked off this op? I would never do that to you. I would face you and tell you what I thought and give you the damn option to go to Tag together as a united front."

"Would you?"

His jaw tightened. "If I seriously thought you couldn't stand me, yes, I would. I would do it for you and I would do it for me. I would do it because I don't want a partner I can't trust. I thought I could trust you. I would let you watch my back in a heartbeat. I know how good you are."

She stared at him. This man always knew exactly what to say to her. It didn't mean he was being honest. It didn't mean he would still want her five minutes after he'd had her. She knew what she was like in bed. It had been told to her many times over.

Frigid. Unfeminine.

"I know you're an excellent soldier," she explained. "I respect your talents, but unless you're willing to give up this foolish pursuit thing, we're never going to be able to work together."

His eyes closed briefly and when he opened them there was pure frustration there. "Why? I don't get it. Again, I need you to explain it. I'm not crazy, Erin. We have chemistry. You're the single most beautiful woman I've ever met and I don't think you're repulsed by me. I'll give up. You don't want me. I'm okay with that. Not really. It kicks me in the balls because I've never wanted a woman the way I want you, but I care about you. I don't want to make you uncomfortable. Tell me why. Friend to friend."

Damn it. Why couldn't he get nasty? He wasn't the first dude to decide he wanted to sleep with her. He was the first who didn't either walk away when she said no or get nasty when she kept saying no. He was standing there looking at her with big, sexy puppy eyes and asking her what he'd done wrong. She wanted to kick his ass out, to tell him she didn't give a damn what he needed to know.

"I don't believe you," she said quietly. "Look, you're a sweet kid, but I'm not looking for romance. I did the marriage thing once before. I'm not doing it again. Tell me something, you want to hit the sheets and work this out between us and then go back to being friends?"

She wasn't sure she would actually do it, but she was interested in seeing how he would handle the offer. It would tell her everything she needed to know. She was fairly certain given the way they'd met that fucking her would be a balm to his wounded masculine ego. She'd given him a hard time. There were a ton of guys out there who would see banging her as a way to get back at her.

He sighed, a sad sound. He moved toward her and invaded her space. "I would in a heartbeat if I thought you meant that. Not the stupid, get-each-other-out-of-our-systems crap. I don't want you out of my system. I like you there. You're funny and tough and you make me want to be better. I'm not a kid, Erin. I haven't been for a long time. I might be optimistic, maybe more optimistic than I should be, but I figured out why. You need me this way. You need some damn sunshine in your life because you think it's all gloom and doom, and maybe it has been until now, but I swear I won't let you stay in the dark. You're too vibrant, too smart, too amazing to stay in the dark. I could love you."

His hand cupped her face and her heart nearly stopped. Who the hell was he? Why would he say those things to her? She could feel the tears welling in her eyes. "You don't have to spout this crap to me. I don't know who's writing your material, but he goes overboard. I told you. I'm offering you a weekend in bed. Free and clear. No mushy shit needed. We'll do it and then maybe we can work together."

She suddenly knew that she would do it. If he took her up on the offer, she would take him in, soak in every second she could have with him, and then move on at the end of forty-eight hours secure in the knowledge that he was like everyone else. Maybe he would be a better lay, but he would be like all the other men in her life. Temporary.

He stared down at her and for the briefest second, she thought he was going to kiss her. It would be electric because he was right about one thing. They did have chemistry. It was completely unlike anything she'd ever felt before. That was exactly why she couldn't bring herself to trust it. Not for a second.

She knew the truth about herself. She might have a toned body, but she wasn't lovely and beautiful like Charlotte Taggart. She wasn't some bombshell to tempt a man. There was no smooth, delicate femininity to her like there was in Eve McKay and Phoebe

Murdoch. She was one of the guys and no man wanted that. Not for long term.

But she could have him for a couple of nights, maybe even pretend he was truly into her.

He leaned over and kissed her forehead. When he stepped back, there was a look of grim resolve on his face. "I'll tell my brother to send Case with you. He'll watch out for you. He won't expect anything but a good work partnership. I'll give him a crash course in D/s, but you're going to have to cover for his flaws."

He was leaving? He took a step back.

"You'll talk to Ian?" The words felt weird coming out of her mouth. She was getting exactly what she wanted.

He nodded, but his face was flushed and he wouldn't look her in the eyes. "Yeah, I thought it would be a good way for us to spend some real time together, but you're not ready."

"I told you I would spend time with you." In bed.

Now he looked at her and the saddest smile tilted his lips up. "Yes, you would take what you want and not get a damn thing you need, girl. I don't want to be that man. I think you've had far too many of those men in your life. You need more time? You need to hide away for a little while longer? Okay. I'll be here. But it's going to be Case watching out for you. I don't trust anyone else." He turned and started to go. "I'll work the op from this side. I'll be your contact and make sure you have all the support you need."

"I don't understand you." She stared as he put his hand on the door. It was perverse. She should be thrilled. Everything she wanted was being handed right to her and the boy toy was backing off. She could spend months away from him. Sure, he was sending her with someone she wouldn't touch with a ten-foot pole, but they were all kind of like that. It was no biggie. She'd gone way longer without sex. Come to think of it, she hadn't actually had any since she'd come to McKay-Taggart. A long dry spell, and there was zero end in sight and all because she couldn't get that sweet idiot out of her head.

What if he wasn't lying? What if by some weird turn of fate he did want a sarcastic, unfeminine, older woman with small boobs? There was no accounting for taste with some men. What if he meant everything he said?

Was she so far gone that she let a man like him walk away because her ex-husband had told her she wasn't worth fucking? Because her father had never seen her value? Didn't she owe it to herself to try?

She reached out before he'd managed to open the door and put a hand on his arm. He turned and she could tell he was far more upset than he'd allowed her to see. His jaw was tight, fine lines appearing around his mouth. She so rarely saw him when he wasn't smiling and happy. She'd put that look on his face.

He frowned, his brows rising as he turned and put his back to the door. "What is it?"

"Hush." She wanted to look at him, really freaking look at him. All she'd seen so far was his youth and beauty, and somewhere in her brain that meant he was perfect, but no one had a perfect life. How much pain did that smile hide? According to what she'd learned about him, his father had left and he and Case had watched their mother disintegrate under the pressure and loss.

Yet all she'd truly seen was his beauty. She hadn't considered that she could hurt him.

"Tell me you're real." She couldn't force herself to step back. Now that she was so close to him, so close to spending months and months without seeing him, she knew she couldn't. Somehow in trying to distance herself from him, she'd still gotten in way too deep.

His hands came up, cupping her waist. "I'm real, baby. I'm not ever going to play mind games with you. I'm going to be honest. I want you and not only in bed. I want you for selfish reasons. I think you're good for me. I don't want you simply because I think you're gorgeous. I like you. You make me laugh. You put me on my ass when I need it. I've never known a woman like you."

If he wasn't real, the universe sucked even harder than she thought it did. If he wasn't real, she wasn't sure she wanted to ever know.

She went up on her toes. God, she loved how much bigger he was. She wasn't a petite thing and yet she only managed to come up to right under Theo's chin. It took extra effort to bring her lips to his.

Heat sparked through her the second she brushed her lips

against his. His mouth was sensual and sexy, and she'd dreamed of it every night since the first time they'd met. This was what she needed. She didn't need to push him away. That was fighting her nature. It was a much better idea to bring him close and enjoy him for a while. It wouldn't last forever. No matter what he said, he wouldn't stick around. He would get tired of her sarcasm, bored with her ways. It was what happened.

But why shouldn't she enjoy him while he was here? She would watch for the signs and dump him before he had the chance to dump her.

She felt the second he took over, his hands coming up and dragging her body against his. His mouth dominated hers, lips moving in pure carnality. He was a massive predator and he wanted to eat her up. Her breasts crushed to his chest as he picked her up, drawing her body higher so he didn't have to lean over. He turned around, putting her back against the door. His tongue invaded, sliding against hers.

She'd never loved making out. It was easiest to get to the fucking and get off as fast as possible. Everything else was weird and awkward. Not so with him. Naturally, he was the one who could make her forget about everything. She didn't feel ungainly. She felt like a woman for once in her life.

Like she did when she was playing. Except they weren't playing.

Over and over again he took her mouth, his tongue dragging over her bottom lip. His big leg slid between hers until she was riding it.

Every cell in her body felt electrified. She gripped his shoulders, but it was so obvious she wasn't in control anymore. This was Theo's game and he seemed to know how to play her to perfection.

"Do you know how long I've waited for this?" His words rumbled against her lips.

"A couple of weeks."

"For fucking ever." He moved against her.

She gasped because he'd placed her perfectly. His big thigh was between her legs and she was tilted so her clit rubbed against him. So long. She'd waited forever for this, too. One damn kiss and suddenly she didn't feel so frigid anymore. She knew she should slow down, move off of him and maintain some semblance of sanity, but her body wasn't listening.

Her body wanted something it hadn't had in a long time. Her hips rolled as he kissed her again, tongues playing. She rubbed herself hard against that muscled thigh.

"That's what I want. I want you so hot for me, you'll do anything. Take it, baby. Take this one. I want you to come because you're rubbing against me like a pretty cat in heat."

She felt like she was. Somehow he affected her in ways no one else on the damn planet could. Somewhere in the back of her mind, she knew it was the middle of the day and there was a whole office right behind that door. They were all out there going about their daily business, and any moment someone could knock and need something.

And she would tell them they could damn well wait because she was busy fucking Theo. Well, his thigh, kind of. It didn't matter because it felt so good. She held on to him as he steadied his big body and let her have at it.

Over and over she moved against him, her pussy wet and ready. She would care about her clothes later. Nothing mattered but the pursuit of pleasure.

The orgasm burst over her and when she would have shouted out, he covered her mouth with his and drank down her cries.

Her whole body was weak and sated as he eased her down. If he wanted, she was ready to turn around and let him do her on her desk. Why had they waited? They should have done this that first day. They should do this every day until they were totally sick of each other and then they might stand a chance of being friends.

He kissed her again and then stepped back. There was a smug look on his face, but it did nothing to diminish how attractive he was. "I want you to think about that every single day you have to put up with Case. He doesn't shower often, by the way."

"Case?" Why the hell were they talking about Case?

He leaned over, kissing her again. "Case. My brother. The one who's going to Africa with you."

She shook her head. "I don't want Case."

"Precisely why I feel comfortable sending him with you."

Damn it. He was an ass and he was going to make her say it. "Just come with me, Theo. We'll do this thing and figure it all out later. Okay?"

He was suddenly in her space again. "No. Not okay. First off, you have to prove to me that you can respect me enough to actually look like you would obey me in a club, much less out in the field. Don't think for a second that makes me in charge. This is our op and we'll handle it our way, but in front of Faith McDonald, I have to look like the Dom at almost all times. And Erin, if we do give this a shot, you should know damn well that I *will* be the Dom in the bedroom. Do I make myself clear?"

Every word said in that dark, delicious tone made her want to pounce. He liked to talk way too much. She put her hands on his waist, loving the way his muscular body felt. "Good. Fine. We're going to Africa. I'll be the sub. We'll work everything out. Let's fuck."

He stopped and frowned down at her. "Not a chance. Not until I actually believe you want to give this a real try. It's all right. I'll kiss you and get you off absolutely any time you like, but I'm not going to let you use me for sex."

She rolled her eyes. "You know you sound like a shrinking violet virgin."

He stepped back and she could see plainly he wasn't unmoved by the experience. His dick was straining against his jeans, but he put his hands up. "Put me down all you like but I won't be something you use and toss aside. I'm the man for you, Erin Argent. I'm going to prove it to you."

"You could prove it now." She had zero idea what had crawled into his silky undies and died.

"All I would prove is that I can fuck you and you'll put me in the same place you put all the others. I'm going to love you. That's the plan. I'll kiss you and hold you every night. I'll touch you and we'll play. But you're not getting little Theo until I trust that you have good intentions toward me."

She growled his way, letting him know how frustrated she was. Of all the men in the world, she got the girl. "You've watched way too many rom coms, Taggart. If you're not going to throw down with me, get out of my office so I can get ready. We've got an op, you know. Maybe you can sit around and write our names in a notebook with hearts and shit, but I have to prep."

His lips curled up right before he leaned over and kissed her again. "Fine. I'll let you prep and I'll make sure we're comfortable. Luckily, I memorized Ian's credit card. I went in and upgraded us. First class, baby. He'll kick my ass later, but we'll have fun. And I'm not lying, Erin. You're not getting in my boxers until I think you're serious."

She shook her head. Where had all her good intentions gone? It no longer was even in the back of her mind to get another partner. One kiss, an orgasm, and she was all about the boy. Damn it. "I'm serious about getting in your boxers, Taggart."

He winked. "Dinner tonight. I'll come by after five and we'll go over our cover. Stay out of trouble."

He opened the door and walked his hot ass out into the hallway.

"Dude, what is wrong with you?" she heard someone say. It sounded a lot like Hutch. "Put that thing away. There's like kids and shit here. Go take a cold shower or something."

She laughed at the thought of poor Theo walking around with a hard-on.

And she wasn't going to be able to stay out of trouble. Not in any way.

CHAPTER SEVEN

Dallas, TX
Present day

"Hey, are you still with me?" Master Theo whispered in her ear.

Erin nodded, forcing herself back to reality. All evening she'd been watching scenes and thinking about him. It wasn't fair. She needed to be in the moment, but her mind couldn't help but run back to all their firsts together. "Of course, Sir, but it's getting late. I have to be back in an hour."

Back to TJ, who was being watched at home by Kori and Kai. Kai was anxious to hear about how the evening had gone, but had thought it was best to let Theo ease into his role. He would insist on walking her to her car and if she'd brought TJ, he would have been confronted with reality. So for now, she would find a sitter on her nights here.

And pray that they found enough of the old Theo that he could learn to love his son.

He stepped back, his hand tugging hers along. In the hours they'd spent watching scenes and talking, he'd always had a hand on her body. He'd tangled their fingers together or stood behind her, his hands on her shoulders or hips. They'd watched the suspension scene and then moved on to a violet wand tutorial.

Now they were finishing up the night with some whip play. Nick was showing his proficiency with a four-foot whip on one of the waitresses from Top. There was an odd disconnect between the two, though Lucy seemed to find her subspace. Maybe it was more about Nick, who hadn't relaxed even once. He was technically fine, but it was obvious he wasn't enjoying himself. He was servicing the sub and would likely take no pleasure from her.

She knew because she'd been Nick. She knew what it meant to walk through her days like a zombie because she couldn't bring herself to feel anything but numb. TJ had saved her from that fate. And then Theo had returned.

No matter what happened between them, she wasn't going backward. If he couldn't love her again, she would still be happy he was alive and grateful for every single day she had with him.

"Are you all right?" He stopped at the outer edges of the crowd.

She forced a smile on her face. Despite the fact that he'd touched her all night, they'd had a disconnect, too. They were awkward and hadn't talked a lot about anything beyond the lifestyle.

Patience.

"I'm good, Sir."

"I still have forty-five minutes before I have to let you go to the locker room."

Sometimes he sounded like a pouty boy. "What would you like to do, Sir? I'm ready for anything."

He strode down the stairs and back into the lounge, but he kept to the sides, obviously trying to avoid the group in the middle. His family. Her friends. He selected a couch at the far edge of the lounge, sitting down and tugging her onto his lap. "I told you how I wanted to end the evening."

With a kiss and a spanking. Her body heated in anticipation. She wanted that, too, but she was worried they would be like Nick and Lucy. Two people on the same stage with knowledge of their parts and no real heat between them. It would kill her.

His arm went around her waist, tugging her close. "Tell me how you got started in the lifestyle."

Ah, the original question between new play partners. Vanilla people would ask about jobs and schools. Not so in the kink world. "I went to a couple of clubs because I was curious but it wasn't until here that I got serious about it. Well, not in this club, but in the original Sanctum. This one is new."

"Because the first one blew up," he said seriously.

"Yep, a complete ass decided that the way to kill Jesse was to blow up a perfectly nice club. It made Big Tag pissy for a long time, but it worked out in the end. This place is ridiculously nice. Most dungeons are in some dude's basement."

His hand moved over her knee. "You've been in some dude's basement? I thought you were trained here."

Such a jealous ass. "I was, but some of the Doms I played with back then had private dungeons, too. I would go there for sessions."

"I don't know that was safe for you."

"Every Dom I ever played with after I joined McKay-Taggart was vetted by Ian, and I always let my friends know where I was going and when to expect me back." She liked to think of it as her serial killer protocols. "I wasn't going to be kidnapped and kept in a cage. Though I played with a cop who actually had a cage in his dungeon. He was into puppy play and some of his bitches were bad, if you know what I mean."

Master Theo didn't seem to see the humor. "Were you serious about him?"

"I was only ever serious about one man in my life."

"But you were married," he insisted.

Wow. She hadn't mentioned that to him. She'd totally avoided talking to him about her first marriage. "How did you know that?"

"I might have read your file," he allowed. "Not here. Outside the club. So you weren't serious about your husband?"

Such an arrogant man. "Maybe he was the one I was serious about."

The hand on her knee tightened. "Don't tease me about that. I can handle everything but that."

She sobered a bit. "I got married because he asked me and I thought it was time. We were both military. It's how we met. One of my brothers brought him home when they were on leave. I kind of fell in with him. I thought that meant we had similar goals. What it meant for him was that I would quit and stay home. I'm not really that kind of girl and it all fell apart after a couple of deployments. He found his perfect military wife and I think they have a couple of kids now. From what I understand she's good at looking the other way when he fucks around, so they're a perfect match."

"And the other man?" His voice had gone so quiet she barely heard the question.

She'd promised him honesty. "Was the love of my life, but I want to talk about you tonight."

A groan went through him. "Do you honestly think this can work? We're sitting here talking like I'm not him."

This was something he needed to understand. "You're not. You won't be again. I'm not waiting around for you to hit your head and suddenly remember everything. But I'm also not willing to give up, so I think we should enjoy this time we have together. I think we shouldn't put pressure on you."

"No, you take all the pressure so I don't have to."

"Don't. You want me to not tease you. I want to spend time with you that doesn't end in you feeling guilty. Please stay here with me. No past. No future. Nothing but the here and now. Can you do that?"

His hand began to move over her again. "I can try."

She wanted so badly to push past his guilt. "I believe you promised that you would kiss me when I sat on your lap."

"I promised I would do more than kiss you." His voice had gone deep.

Her body tightened. "You did, Sir. As this is our first evening together, you wouldn't want to disappoint your brand new sub. I've heard she can be mean sometimes."

"She better not be. She better be a good girl while we're playing or she won't get what she wants."

She was working so damn hard to get what she wanted. It was difficult. It was easier to tell herself she didn't deserve it and let it go, but there was no way she could do that now. This was the man who'd taught her she was worthy.

"I can be a good girl."

"How far are you willing to go tonight?" Master Theo asked. "I would really like to see your breasts. I'd like for you to take off that corset, let me spank you, and then cuddle for whatever time we have left. I want to play with your nipples. Just my hands."

"Master Theo, my body is yours. I made that plain. I have a safe word, but don't expect me to use it." She slid off his lap and presented her back to him. "You're going to have to unlace me. Charlotte tied it pretty tightly."

She heard him sigh and felt him move in behind her. His fingers brushed over her shoulders, pushing her hair out of the way, and she held back a shiver of pleasure.

"How is it that I remember so easily how to do this?" His hands moved down and started to work her laces even as he kissed her neck. "I don't even have to think about it to know I've done it a hundred times. I know we're sticking to the here and now, but I've done this for you before, haven't I? I've unlaced your corset and I've kissed you while I did it."

Oh, so many times. Her Theo had loved to undress her like he was unwrapping a present. "You've freed my breasts, Sir. You've undressed me and held me and made me ready for your kiss and your cock. It's why my body is yours. I signed that contract with no times or dates. You can do with me as you will because I trust you. Not the you that was. The you that's still deep inside. The soul of you no one can touch because it belongs to me, Sir. You're mine and I'm yours. Body. Soul. You remember because it's as natural as breathing for you to get me naked and hold me close. Stop trying. Just let us be, Theo. We'll find our way. We did before and we'll do it again."

He tugged at her laces and she could breathe more easily. He'd always been damn good at getting her out of her clothes quickly. His lips brushed up her neck and then she felt his tongue rimming the shell of her ear. "Tell me how I fucked you."

He'd made love to her in a way that could only be described as fucking. It had been hard and long and so good she'd never been able to forget the way he'd felt when he moved inside her. Hours he would spend touching her, lavishing her with his never-ending affection, prepping her for the hard drive of his cock. "With determination. With power. With dominance and always with my pleasure in mind. You were the best lover I ever had and I can't wait until you touch me again."

"You make me feel like I'm ten feet tall, Red," he whispered in her ear as her corset wriggled loose. "When you talk like that I want to be the man you knew."

"Just be you, Sir. I don't need anything else." She felt the corset stretch and held her hands up, allowing him to draw it over her head. Cool air chilled her skin, but it did nothing to lessen the heat she felt about him. She was ready to get on her knees and do anything he asked of her.

"Turn around and let me see you."

She turned for him, pivoting on the four-inch heels she only ever wore in this club. The heels still didn't make her as tall as Theo. She let her shoulders fall back, her breasts upthrust and presented to him like the gift he'd once called them. He'd told her she was beautiful and she was going to do her best to see herself the way he saw her.

Strong. Beautiful. Worthy.

He stared at her, but she didn't cringe. She went still, allowing him to look his fill. He'd enjoyed looking at her, studying her like she was a work of art. Her skin felt alive under his gaze.

"Do you have any idea how gorgeous you are?"

Only because he'd told her so very often. She'd never once felt beautiful before him. He'd been right. She'd been good for him and that had made her understand exactly how lovable she was. "Thank you, Sir. You make me feel that way."

He sat back down on the couch, his eyes hot as he looked up at her. "Tell me you need this because god knows I do. I don't know why, but this feels right. I feel more settled than I have since I came home, but I don't want to hurt you."

He was sliding back into guilt and she wasn't about to let that happen. "If you hurt me, Sir, I'll hurt you back. You seem to think I'm some fragile thing. If that's what you're looking for, I suggest you find a cowering flower of a sub because I'm not your girl."

His eyes hardened and he reached out, tugging her down and over his lap. "You are my girl. I signed the paperwork that states it's true."

She forced herself to relax, but there he was. Her Theo had always seemed so laid back. Losing his memory and being taken down to the core of his being was a revelation. He was a possessive caveman. She could handle that. "All I'm saying, Sir, is if you hurt me I'll take your balls off and serve them to you for dinner. Stop feeling guilty or get off the dungeon floor. There's no place for it here."

The first slap came down in a hard arc, the shock of it sending a shudder through her body. "You want to be a brat? I'll show you how I handle a brat."

Unfortunately, being a brat kind of came naturally to her, which was good because it dovetailed nicely with her inner masochist. His hand started to rain fire on her backside and she bit back a squeal of pure delight. It hurt, yes, but something about the pain felt so damn good. She was sure Kai had some explanation about her childhood or some shit. She didn't think so. When she got too stressed out, she used a sadistick on her own skin to force herself to relax. Some people liked yoga. She liked a sting followed by the roll of sensation that pulsed outward from the pain. Like it was doing now.

Pure fire and then the fine chill of awareness. It made her skin come alive and her whole body relax as the chemicals started to course through her brain. Dopamine. Adrenaline. She wasn't sure which. She only knew it felt like heaven.

He slapped at her cheeks, one and then the other. "You like this. You enjoy this. It makes you hot."

He didn't need memory to figure that out. He could likely tell from the flush of her skin and the way her body was already softening up for him, getting warm and wet.

"I love it." The words came out on a gasp as he spanked her again. His big hand held the heat against her flesh. "I didn't know I could be sensual until the first time I got spanked. It woke me up, made me want something I'd never had before."

He smacked her again, twice in rapid procession. "It made you want to submit?"

"It made me want to give over. It wasn't really about the Dom. Not until…" She let the thoughts drift away as she held on to his muscled calf. "It was about being able to let go. I never let go until I found the lifestyle. It's important to have a place where you can let go and simply be."

It was one of those things she'd learned as she'd gotten older. Everyone needed this. Some found it in books or by playing games online. Some found it when they worked out, pushing their bodies to the point where nothing mattered but the next mile, the next rep, the next breath.

She found it by giving over. She found that piece of herself she denied in the real world, that piece that wanted to be of service to someone, to be praised and prized. It was a part of herself she'd learned to suppress, but here she'd been given the gift of valuing it again. Of truly accepting all of who she was.

Tears pressed out of her eyes, falling to the floor below. And yes, she'd been given this as well. Years she'd gone without the solace of tears. They'd been wrong, a sign of pure weakness.

Theo flipped her over and she found herself on his lap again. He manhandled her with ease, showing no signs of strain as he wrapped a strong arm around her. He stared at her for a moment.

"Such a pretty girl. You shouldn't cry."

If only he knew the last time he'd said those words to her. He'd been dying. She closed her eyes, willing the memory away. So much of Theo was simmering below the surface, but it fled when she tried to catch it. She took a deep breath and smiled up at him. "I never used to cry. My father didn't like it. Then there was the military. It was good for me for the most part, but it could be harsh. I didn't learn to cry until I came here."

His fingers brushed over her cheeks. "You're beautiful when you cry. I changed my mind. I don't want to do this."

Her jaw went tight. He hadn't kissed her. He didn't want to kiss her? She hadn't thought of that. She'd thought the minute he had the chance, he would get his hands on her and they could both find a measure of relief. She'd thought he would want her at least physically.

She'd had a baby. Her body wasn't the same. Sure she'd dropped most of the weight, but her boobs sagged more now. They'd had a baby hanging off them for almost seven months. Her milk had only recently dried up as she'd weaned him. She had stretch marks.

If Theo had changed during his time away, so had she.

She went stiff in his arms and wished she had something to cover up in. "All right, Sir."

He stood up, hefting her easily. "I want more than a kiss. I want some privacy. I know we said we would take it slow, but you also told me to follow my instincts. Every instinct I have tells me to take you somewhere private. It tells me to mark you as mine so no one thinks twice. So they know you're mine. That's what my instinct says."

She nearly sobbed in relief. Erin bit back a cry and managed to nod, her arm going around his neck to steady herself as he started toward the stairs. "You should follow your instincts. Mine tell me to submit to my Master. Here and now."

She relaxed against him. Now was all they had and she was going to enjoy it.

CHAPTER EIGHT

T heo took the stairs as quickly as he could. He knew where he was going, but he wasn't going to think about it. For the first time since he'd gotten home, he didn't care about his past or figuring out who he'd been. He wanted. He wanted something and that felt good.

She'd been right. There wasn't a place for guilt here.

He strode up the stairs, her weight comforting in his arms. Yeah, he wasn't going to think about that either. He was going to enjoy it, not wonder why his body remembered her when his mind would not.

"Hey, is everything okay?"

Damn it. Case was standing at the top of the stairs, obviously having come out of the privacy rooms. His wife was at his side, her face flushed. Mia had sex hair. Good for them. Red was about to have sex hair, too. Lots of messy sex hair. "Everything's great. Night."

Case put a hand on his shoulder. "Whoa. I thought you were going to take this slow, brother."

"If you don't get your hand off him right this second, Taggart, I am going to ensure that you never have children," Red said, her eyes narrowing on his brother. "You won't be able to cock block anyone because you won't have a damn cock. Am I clear?"

Case's hands came up immediately, as though he knew that tone and was not going there. "Trying to help."

"Three is clean and has plenty of condoms. We're taking a monitor turn up here. I checked all the rooms." Mia grinned at him. She actually was helpful. "Have fun and we'll see you at home."

He didn't bother to look back. Case could give him a lecture later. He wasn't waiting anymore. He'd waited forever. Even when he couldn't remember her face, he'd known she was there. He'd felt her, or rather he'd felt her absence.

Could he truly be with a woman whose name he couldn't think without hurting her?

It didn't matter. He wasn't making those decisions tonight. He was enjoying her. His sub. He was bringing her pleasure and he probably should do a good job of it because his sub was fucking mean.

And fragile. He'd seen the moment she'd thought he was rejecting her. He'd watch her skin flush and her body start to turn in on itself. She was such a mix of strength and need. It was intoxicating. He wanted so badly to be the man who gave her what she needed.

Affection. Pleasure. Comfort.

Love—he wasn't thinking that word tonight. Nope. Pleasure was way better.

He kicked out lightly at the partially open door number three. It looked like Mia had done her job. The room was perfectly clean, the lighting soft and romantic. The best thing about this room though was the complete lack of any of his friends or family being here.

It was him and her, and that was exactly what he wanted. No Ian. No Li. No Kai asking them hundreds of questions. Him and her and the night.

He tossed her on the bed and stood back, looking down at her. "Tell me why you thought I was rejecting you."

The instant she hit the bed, she was up on her knees. So graceful. So deadly. What the hell was this woman like out in the field? She moved like a predator, but the look on her face was pure sarcasm. "Uhm, your words. That's what sealed it for me. 'I don't want to do this' is generally considered a rejection."

Somehow she managed to put an unsaid "dumbass" on the end of her sentences. Not all of them. She'd been perfectly sweet most of the night, but she could turn it on when she wanted to. "I didn't mean that. When I said the words, I watched you change. Why? You're good at slapping people down. I wouldn't have said that until today."

"Because I've been careful around you," she admitted.

"Why? You think I'm delicate?"

Her lips curled up. "I don't think you're delicate. I think I'm a lot to take, but I'm starting to believe I was wrong. You like me rough."

"I like you a lot." More than he could ever tell her. "I'm more comfortable with this particular version of you. Now tell me why you thought I was rejecting you."

Her eyes rolled and a groan came from her pretty mouth. "God, Taggart. What does a girl have to do to get fucked around here?"

He loved her bratty, but he wasn't about to take that. "Turn around. Hands and knees."

Her eyes went wide. "The…Master Theo, I apologize."

She thought she could turn those big doe eyes on him and everything would be all right? "Every second adds to your punishment. I said I'm comfortable with your brattiness. I won't, however, allow you to disrespect me. I don't know what I used to be like, but I'm the man you deal with now and you will either put that ass in the air or call it a night. And take off the shorts. We're alone. That means you're naked."

It was obvious she had to pull her patience around her. She took a long breath before pushing off the bed and shoving her tiny leather boy shorts off her hips. In a single graceful move, she was back on the bed, her ass in the air.

It was still pink from the earlier spanking. He didn't intend to make this a long session, but he couldn't allow her to talk to him like that. Even if he was comfortable with it. Even if it was kind of adorable. He found a nice cane in the armoire and tested it against his palm, letting the sound ring out. It was all part of the play. He wanted her to think about what he was going to do. The cane was thin and round, flexible. It would hurt, but depending on how he wielded it, it wouldn't leave a real mark.

Though the thought of her feeling it all day tomorrow did something for him.

He moved to the bed, anticipation thrumming through him. This was what he'd needed from the second he'd come home. He'd needed to pull off all his outer layers and get down to the primal part of him, to the part that needed her. The part that didn't mourn the loss of their past or rage at what had been taken from him. The part that had seen her across a room and known deep down that she was his.

He let the emotion flow through him, not trying to catch it or pull it apart to understand it. He didn't have to do that. Finally, he understood what Kai had been trying to get him to do all along.

Relax. Everything important was right here with him and he wasn't going to lose it if he didn't force the memories back.

Why struggle to remember when all the beauty he needed in the world was right here? He studied her, her gorgeous heart-shaped ass presented to him like the gift it was. His girl was built on slender lines, athletic and yet still feminine.

"You do understand that you're killing me," she said under her breath.

It was time to teach her a lesson. He brought the cane down, the sound whooshing through the air and landing with a satisfying smack. "What did you say to me?"

Her whole body shook. "I said you're killing me, Sir."

Such a brat. He brought the cane down again, the sound as deeply satisfying as the way her skin went hot pink and the breath seemed to shudder out of her body. "You don't get to pick the time and place. I do. You don't get to decide when I'm ready to fuck you. I wanted to spend time looking at you. I enjoy looking at you. It makes me happy."

A third strike brought a gasp from her mouth. "I'm sorry, Sir. I was eager."

"Get those knees wider apart. I'll see how eager you are." He tapped the cane between her spread thighs, showing her how wide he wanted them.

He wanted to be able to see her pussy. Such a pretty pussy. She wasn't lying. She was eager. His brother probably should be happy he'd backed off. She wasn't one to take sex casually. When she wanted some cock, she could be aggressive about it. Like that time in Germany…

He pulled the cane back again, letting it go. It took a lot to do it. He wanted to chase the memory. For a single second he'd seen her in a white bikini against a sea of green. She'd been with another woman, Faith, perhaps. Something about a camera and taking a picture and then he'd seen the look on her face and he'd known she was going to jump him.

Pain hit him fast and hard. He wasn't going to ruin this. Not this. He could fuck up tomorrow. He was going to give them one goddamn good night.

"Look at that." He was pleased that his voice came out even and solid. The pain was bad, but he could handle it. He would handle it for her. For Red. He brushed his hand along her backside. "It seems you are eager."

"You have no idea, Sir. It's been a long time for me."

"It's been a long time for me, too."

"Yes, but you don't remember most of it."

He stopped, a little shocked. And then he couldn't stop the burst of laughter. It was so fucked up. It was funny. He couldn't remember most of it. He tossed the cane aside. Play was done. He wanted to be with her. He jumped on the bed, rolling with her. "Seriously? You joke about that?"

She winced, but her arms went around his neck. "I have a dark sense of humor, Sir. You'll have to get used to it."

"I think I can handle it." He brushed back her hair, loving the intimacy of being able to hold her and touch her. It felt right. He felt centered and more real than he had in weeks. "Tell me why you thought I was rejecting you."

"I don't look the same way I did before."

He frowned down at her. "I don't either, baby. I've seen pictures of myself before that fucker carved up half my face."

She reached up and brushed her fingers along the nasty scar that split the left side of his face and had almost taken his eye. "This? This is nothing, Sir. You were too pretty before. I like this better. You look more manly this way. I was actually surprised I went for the male-model-looking dude. This is way more my type."

That made him feel good and she was avoiding the question.

"How do you not look the same?"

Her eyes glanced away. "My breasts aren't as firm as they were and I've got stretch marks."

Because of the baby. Because of his baby. He got to his knees, looking down at her. Her legs were spread, but he didn't move to make her more comfortable. He liked her like this. Open and vulnerable and trusting. He had the feeling this woman wouldn't allow herself to be like this with many people. Apparently she wasn't like this with anyone but him. There were faint, silvery lines on her gently curved belly. He traced them with his fingers. "Are you talking about these little things? They're nothing, baby. They're beautiful like the rest of you."

Her body relaxed beneath his. "I'm glad you think so, Sir. I think you're beautiful, too. You're the most beautiful man I've ever seen and the scar is incredibly sexy. I don't like to think about how you got it, but it's lovely to me because it means you survived."

Survival. Sometimes that had been all he had. One more day. He had more now and Robert was right. He was wasting them by wallowing in what had happened. This was happening now. She was here. She was open and waiting for his touch.

She was his prize for coming through hell alive.

He tossed off his vest, dragging his palm over her chest. "Do you know what I want to do to you?"

"Everything," she replied with a breathless whisper.

She knew him well. "Everything."

He dropped down, covering her body with his. Her lips were as soft as they seemed, her mouth flowering open for him. His cock was hard as hell, but he wanted so badly to take his time with her. To learn her. To explore every inch of her soft skin and find out if she tasted as good as she looked. They still had time.

He kissed her, his tongue foraging deep. Any thought he had about the future or the past flew away. There was only this moment and this woman. They didn't need names. They knew each other instinctively.

Her hands touched his back as she wound herself around his body. His leathers were still between them, but he needed them for now. His cock was a greedy bastard who wanted inside her as soon as possible.

But his mind wanted even more.

He kissed his way down her neck, noting the sweet smattering of freckles that dotted her cheeks. He would kiss every single one of them. Perhaps next time they wouldn't waste hours on watching scenes. He would haul her up here and spend every second he had with her naked and wrapped around him.

Best fucking therapy in the world.

Somehow he knew it had always been like this. It was nothing more than a thought that played through his brain as he kissed her breasts. They'd been incendiary. Oh, she'd fought it, but the minute he'd finally gotten his hands on her, they'd exploded.

He moved down her body, his target in sight. He could smell the spicy scent of her arousal. The spanking had gotten her hot and wet.

Or maybe it had been him. Maybe the thought of finally, finally coming home was what had made her so ready for him.

It didn't matter. Nothing mattered except that he loved how she smelled. Milk and honey and sex. The fucking promised land.

"Did your last Master ask you to keep this pretty pussy so well groomed?" He had to stare for a moment. Her sex was perfect. Pouty and smooth, glistening with arousal. He could see the way her clitoris was already begging for affection. It poked out of its hood, a pearl to play with.

"He was very exacting. He liked to be able to eat my pussy at any time. He wanted me to think about him every time I shaved or touched myself because this part of my body belonged to him."

"Every part of your body belongs to me." But he was particularly interested in this part. He inhaled her, taking in her scent without a single reservation. She was right. There was no place for guilt here, and there would be no place for doubt or insecurity.

"Yes," she whispered back. "Every part of me belongs to you. Please kiss me. Kiss me there. It's been so long."

"You like this? You like it when a man eats you up like the finest meal of his life?" He stopped. "You like it when I do it."

"Only you," she replied. "You're the only one who ever…did that to me."

He didn't even begin to comprehend how her other lovers had let her down, but he wasn't going to do it. In this he needed no reminders. He leaned over and dragged his tongue across her pussy.

Her body bowed beneath him as she gasped.

He pushed her thighs apart and settled himself in. "Don't make me stop. I don't want to stop but I will if you can't stay still. I told you. This is my time. I won't be rushed and I won't allow you to take something I'm not ready to give you yet."

"Yes, Sir. I'm sorry. It felt so good. I'll be still. I'll hold on and let you have your treat, Sir." Her hands drifted up and she reached for the slats of the headboard.

He didn't need to question why this made him feel good. He'd spent so much time trying to figure out why the lifestyle used to call to him, but this needed no explanation. This was the single most beautiful woman he'd ever seen, spreading herself wide, trusting him with her pleasure.

He wasn't about to let her down.

He settled in, putting his mouth over her pussy and delving inside. She tasted perfect, exactly what he thought she'd be. His mind might not remember, but his body knew her. Knew how to lick her and suck her. Knew how to make her squirm underneath him. He ran his tongue over her labia, reveling in how soft it was, how easily he could move because she was so slick and wet.

His cock was going to ease right inside her. He was going to fit inside like he'd never left her. Like they'd never once been apart.

He had to make it good for her because there was zero chance he was going to last once he got in there. She was so hot, he would go off like a bomb detonating the minute he touched her.

He moved up, sucking her clit between his teeth gently. A shudder went through her. "That's right. I've got you right where I want you. Tell me what you need."

"You. I need you so badly. Please, Sir."

He gave her clit a lick, nothing that would send her over the edge. "What part of me do you need, baby?"

How could he have not thought of this? He could call her Red or baby all day and not feel a single bit of pain. He could be with her. He might have to find some work-arounds, but he didn't have to let anything keep him away from the woman he wanted. This worked. They could have this.

"Your cock," she said without hesitation. "I need your cock."

And she would get it. "First, I want you to come for me. I need to hear you and I want to taste you on my tongue. You come all over my tongue and I'll give you my cock."

He would have to leave her after that. He would walk her to her car and kiss her good-bye, and that bugged him. He should have all night with her.

Next time, perhaps she could get an overnight babysitter.

He forced the issue out of his mind and concentrated on what was good. Her. Her scent and taste and the sounds she made while taking her pleasure.

He felt the moment she went over the edge. There was a fine shaking through her body and a cry as she came.

Theo pushed himself up. No time. There was no more fucking time to wait and he didn't have to. His hands went to the ties on his leathers, ready to free his aching cock. He could fall on her and pound away because she was so ready for him.

Her arms were open, prepared to welcome him.

The knocking on the door stopped Theo in his tracks.

She shook her head. "Don't. Whoever it is, they'll go away. If they don't, I can shoot them."

He went back to the annoying knot at the front of his leathers. Condom. He needed a condom. He should have pulled one out before, but he'd been too interested in getting her naked. It was all he'd been thinking about.

There was another knock, louder this time, and then his brother's voice.

"I'm sorry, you two," Ian said through the door.

"Good, then go the fuck away." He got to his feet because the condom wasn't going to magically appear in his hand. It might also be a good idea to make sure the damn door was locked.

"I can't," Ian shouted. "I need Erin. Kori and Kai had some trouble out at her house."

Her whole face flushed and she couldn't get off that bed fast enough. She was on her feet and running for the bathroom, where she grabbed one of the robes hanging there. She didn't even look back at him before throwing open the door.

"TJ? Is TJ okay?" Erin asked, pure fear in her voice.

Her son. Of course.

His son. The one he didn't feel anything for. The one who wasn't quite his because he belonged to the Theo who no longer existed. It was precisely why seeing her only in the club had made sense.

Her skin had paled, going from the prettiest pink to a pasty white as she looked up at Ian. The lines around her mouth tightened and she'd gone from hot lover to scared mom in a second.

He wasn't sure he could handle the scared mom.

Ian held up a hand. "TJ's fine, but I need you to get dressed. The police are out at your place. Someone tried to break in. Kai fought him off, but he got away. There was some broken glass though, and TJ caught some of it."

She bit back a cry at the thought of her baby being hurt.

Ian put a hand on her shoulder. "Stop. He's fine. He didn't even require a single stitch, but the police can't leave until they talk to you."

Ian was doing *his* job. He should be the one trying to comfort her. It should be his hand on her shoulder right before he maneuvered her into his arms and promised her everything was going to be okay.

The trouble was he knew it wouldn't. The world wasn't a place where things could be made better with a hug or a promise.

She was shaking her head. "Someone tried to break into my place? It doesn't make sense. I live in a decent neighborhood. It's a nice, solid, middle-class neighborhood and I have a killer alarm system."

"They managed to disable the system," Ian said. "No idea how. I'll get Adam on it ASAP."

She turned to him. "I'll get dressed and meet you downstairs."

His stomach turned. How had he gone from aroused as hell to this terrible feeling in the pit of his stomach? Everything had gone so perfectly, and he had the feeling it was all about to go to hell. Still, he had to give her something. "Of course. I'll walk you to your car."

"What?" Her head shook as though she couldn't quite understand what he'd said.

Ian moved between them. "I'm afraid I've got something to talk to Theo about so he can't head home with you. The night's perfectly fucked up and the team's downstairs in the conference room."

"But our baby was hurt." Her wide eyes turned his way, pleading plain in them.

"Ian says he's fine. Didn't even need stitches." He knew what she wanted. She wanted him to suddenly be a fucking father, but he couldn't do it. He couldn't pretend something he didn't feel. It was even worse than that. He was jealous of the kid, jealous that she would drop him and run after the baby. It wasn't fair. He knew that. The kid needed her, but the resentment was right there. It festered inside him. He needed her, too. He'd had one night with her and it was already going to hell. One night and he hadn't found the peace he'd needed, hadn't gotten inside her. He knew what he wanted and it looked like he wasn't going to get it.

He felt for the kid. Poor little guy had a shitty fucking father. He really was a selfish piece of shit.

He'd needed to not be Theo Taggart for a night, and now he realized he might never truly be him again. She'd lied. This had all been one long play to get back the man she'd loved.

He wasn't that man.

"Theo, someone broke into our house." The words came out on a desperate gasp, as though she couldn't quite understand that she had to say them at all. "Someone hurt our child. I need you to come with me. I need you to help me."

Ian's jaw was tight as he spoke. "I'm sorry, Erin. I need him downstairs. Li is waiting for you. I'll fill you in tomorrow on the new intel. It appears Hope McDonald has finally resurfaced."

Her eyes remained steady on him, piercing him in a way no knife could. "Nothing is more important than our son. I know you're afraid of meeting him, but I need you to come with me now. I'm so tired of doing this alone. Please come with me."

And let her figure out how utterly incapable he was of being the man she wanted him to be? How would she take it when he didn't want to hold the kid?

He moved toward her, cupping her shoulders. How had he felt so close to her mere moments before? Now he was simply trying to hold on. "I need to go with Ian. I need to find out what's happening with Hope McDonald. She's still a huge threat to us. And the baby."

"He can give us a briefing later. Right now you need to take care of me and TJ."

He couldn't. He just couldn't. If she knew he couldn't care about the kid, couldn't be the dad she thought he would magically be, she would completely walk away. It was better for her to think he was a dick than to think he was so empty he couldn't love his own child. He stepped back. "I'm staying here. Li will go with you. I'll send you a text when I know something more. Maybe I can come by after the meeting and make sure you don't need anything."

By then the kid would probably be asleep. Could he stay with her and be gone before the kid woke up? That might work. At least for a while.

She stepped back, breaking the contact entirely. "Don't bother. I'll take care of him. Alone. Like I always have."

She turned and walked out the door, never looking back.

"Well, that went well," Ian said, a grim look on his face.

Theo watched her walk away and wondered if she would ever look at him the same way again.

CHAPTER NINE

"He's scared, you know," Li said as he took the Walnut Hill exit, turning right toward her neighborhood.

It was an older neighborhood with gorgeous trees. The houses had been built in the sixties and seventies, comfortable ranch houses and small bungalows. They were starter houses. Theo had bought this one on Timberview Lane without even consulting her. It had been a grand gesture. At one point, he'd been good at those.

This is just the beginning, baby. One day I'll get us something even nicer, but we can start here. We can be happy here.

Now she couldn't even get him to check and see if his son was okay.

"He's being a coward," Avery said under her breath.

Thank god she had Avery. Ian had done nothing but enable Theo.

"Now, love, you know we've talked about this," Li began.

Avery shook her head. "I understand your position, but it's cowardice. He has a responsibility. Even if he wasn't acting as TJ's dad, he signed a contract with her tonight. He's being a shitty Dom."

Damn straight, but she wasn't going to let anyone know how much she hurt. He'd gutted her. She'd been so certain after how they'd connected tonight that he would get it, would understand how much she needed him. All this time and she'd been alone. Oh, she'd had friends, but no one could love TJ the way his parents would.

How would she ever explain to her son that his dad wouldn't even meet him?

"It's fine. The contract was for the club only. He's not my Dom in the outside world." She needed to see her baby. God, had there actually been a moment when she'd been angry she was pregnant? In those first few days, she'd denied it. She'd been so mad that Theo was gone and she was going to be some kind of sad-ass single mom.

TJ was the best thing that had ever happened to her. Tears clouded the world around her.

Was the world this cruel? Was she going to have to choose between the only man she'd ever loved and her son? There was no question. She would make the decision every mother had to make, but it seemed so unfair.

He'd wanted her. He'd needed her. She'd seen it in his eyes. It had been there in how he couldn't keep his hands off her, how he'd tried all night long. They'd almost been there.

None of it would work if he couldn't accept their son.

Not merely accept. Love. He had to love TJ or it couldn't work. She wouldn't allow her son to be brought up with a cold and distant father. Better to let Theo go and allow Li and Case and Ian and Sean to be his male role models.

"It's not fine," Li said with a long sigh. "But I don't know what to do about it. I know you won't understand this, but men view children differently than women, and he simply doesn't understand yet. He needs time."

"Is there actually a meeting occurring?" She wouldn't put it past Ian to give his brother a way out if he thought he needed one. He would cover for Theo as much as he possibly could.

Li nodded, glancing at her in the rearview mirror. "Yes, she's surfaced. Nick got word that she showed up in France. He's got boots on the ground already, trying to trace her."

She knew she should be more interested, but at the moment, she couldn't work up the will. TJ was more important. After she'd ensured her baby was fine, she could think about the Hope situation. "Well, it's good to know he didn't make something up to save

Theo."

"Ian wants this to work as much as any of us do," Li replied. "He blames himself for Theo's death."

"Because he sent him out in the field?"

Li's hands tightened on the steering wheel. "Because he knew damn well you should have been in charge. I even argued with him about it. Alex and I had separate conversations with him about that mission and Ten wanted you as his second. Ian insisted that he wouldn't allow the mission to go through without Theo in command."

A long sigh went through her. Well, she'd known at the time. "Yeah, I suspected that. You know, Theo's his brother. He prefers him over me. I'm not going to bitch about it."

Avery turned in her seat. "It wasn't like that. You have to know why Ian did it."

"Because blood is thicker than water." Again, something she'd always known. Couldn't Li make this car move faster? Up ahead she could see the hint of blue lights from the police cars.

"No, because he was trying desperately for you to see Theo as an equal." Li slowed down as they approached the house. "He thought it would never work between the two of you if you couldn't respect Theo in the field. Because the two of you work together, he wanted Theo to gain the same experience. He wasn't putting you down. He was trying to avoid a problem that might have come up later. Don't ever think Ian doesn't know how valuable you are. Or me. It might have been brought up that with the new recruits we've brought in, the more experienced operatives should pair up and train them. I explained to Ian that if I lost my partner, he would lose me."

Li had gone to bat to keep her as his partner? She wouldn't have expected that. "You shouldn't risk your job for me."

Avery reached for her hand. "You're part of our family. I wouldn't want anyone else watching his back out there. We love you, Erin. This is all going to be okay. You'll see. Let's go and check on TJ. You'll feel better once you make sure he's okay. I'll make us all some tea."

Avery had spent too much time in Europe. "Top mine with some bourbon and you've got a deal."

The car stopped and she could see Kai standing in the yard,

talking to a uniformed officer. Erin opened the door and sprinted toward the house. Only one thing mattered. Getting her baby in her arms.

The door was propped open and she ran inside.

Kori was pacing, holding a crying TJ in her arms, his tiny body in a pair of footie pajamas. Kori's eyes flared as she turned and saw her. "Thank god. He had a scare, Erin. I think he needs Mama."

She drew him into her arms, holding him close and rocking him. His chubby arms reached around her, hugging her as much as they could. "Oh, baby, Mama's here. It's okay, my baby boy. It's all right."

He was okay. She could breathe again. His cries died down and he settled into her arms as though he'd been waiting to be right where he was. He sniffled and then sighed against her, obviously exhausted. She could start to ask the questions she needed to. "What happened?"

"We were watching a movie about an hour ago," Kai said as he walked in with the officer. "TJ was asleep and I got up to get a bottle of water. That's when I saw the security system was off."

"I turned it on the minute you left," Kori promised. "I know I did."

She nodded Kori's way. If she said she did then she had. "It's okay. What happened?"

"I tried to turn it back on, but it was dead," Kai explained.

Avery and Liam walked in, Avery coming to stand beside Erin. She leaned over and kissed the top of TJ's head.

"The rest of the house had power." Kori put an arm around Kai and he hauled her close. It looked like they'd all had a rough night. "I didn't notice a thing until Kai started giving me all those weird hand signals."

Kai sighed. "I didn't want to yell out to keep quiet when there might be someone in the house. It tends to let the person in the house know we're on to him."

Poor Kori, surrounded by ex-military. Erin was sure their ways were strange to the screenwriter. "What happened then?"

"I moved down the hallway and that's when I saw him. He was coming out of TJ's room. I about had a heart attack." Kai squeezed Kori close.

"He was in TJ's room? How did he get in?" The answer hit her quickly. She was thinking like a freaked out mom when TJ needed her to think like an operative. How would she get in without being seen? "He came in through the window of the back room."

It was the only reasonable explanation. The front and back doors would lead through the living room and then Kori and Kai would have seen the intruder. The master bedroom was split, so that would again lead past the living room. On the other side of the house there was a bathroom and two bedrooms, one of which served as an office.

The police officer nodded. "Yes, ma'am. We found evidence that after taking down the security system, he took the window apart. It's why we think he was a professional of some kind. It looks like he used a knife to cut through the glue and then pulled the window pane out."

Oh, she was getting such an upgrade in the morning. But then she'd never really expected professional criminals to come after her. It was an oversight. She'd gotten soft.

"I'll put the team on it," Liam assured her.

McKay-Taggart had a whole team dedicated to security systems and home and business safety. She was sure Remy Guidry and his boys would be at her place bright and early tomorrow. "Whatever it costs." They wouldn't charge her for their expertise, but changing out her windows for high-security glass would cost a pretty penny. "What was he doing in my son's room and do we have the fucker in custody? I would love to have a talk with him."

Kai's face fell. "I caught him walking out. He had a gun and I wasn't carrying. I didn't think I needed to. I'm so sorry. He took a shot at me and when I tried to rush him, the gun went off again. The bullet hit the window in TJ's room and that's how he got cut."

"I called the cops and got TJ out of there while he and Kai were fighting," Kori explained.

Kori was a civilian. How much had it cost her to run into a room where the bullets were flying? She'd run in and saved a baby who wasn't her own. Erin let the tears roll as she hugged her friends. Theo hadn't wanted to come, but she wasn't alone. She was surrounded by people who loved her. Brave, amazing people.

"Thank you both. Thank you so much." TJ wriggled in her arms but he didn't cry again. He simply yawned and looked so much like his dad it hurt. "I'm so glad he didn't tag you, Kai. You should have let him go."

"I didn't know TJ was okay. I thought he'd hurt him at the time. I was quite angry," Kai admitted. "I'm apparently out of practice. He choked me out. I came to and he was gone."

"He went back out the window, I think," Kori said. "But I checked and all that was wrong with TJ was he had a cut on his forearm. I still had the EMTs examine him."

"Ma'am, this seems to be a robbery gone wrong." The police officer had already put away his notebook.

Li slid a look her way.

She knew what he wanted. Privacy. Maybe it was a robbery gone wrong, but maybe it was something else. Something they should handle in the family. She fully intended to figure out what that massive ass had done in her child's room. But maybe she should thin the crowd before she brought out that card. It was obvious the police hadn't figured out she had a camera in her son's room, aimed at his crib. It wasn't tied to the security system. It should have caught everything the man had done to TJ.

She held a hand out to the police officer. "Thank you so much for coming out, Officer. I'm grateful and I'll help out in any way I can."

He shook her hand and then passed her his card. "Dr. Ferguson gave us an excellent description of the subject. We'll do what we can and get back to you in the morning. Is someone staying with you tonight, ma'am?"

Li took that one. "She'll stay with us tonight. We'll take her and my godson home and they'll stay there until the house is perfectly secure again."

Well, she'd known the minute she heard someone had broken in that she wouldn't be staying home tonight. She should be staying with Theo, but at least she had somewhere to go. "We'll be good. Thank you, Officer."

He nodded and within ten minutes, they were alone again.

Kori slipped her hand into Kai's. "Is there anything we can do before we head home? Do you need anything?"

Kai's eyes narrowed. "Oh, I'm going nowhere until I figure out what Erin's doing. You know something you didn't want the cops to know. What is it?"

Li already knew. "Where's your laptop? Or do you want to watch it on your phone?"

She bounced TJ gently. "It's in the office. Pray he didn't take it, but I would have gotten a notification on my phone if the feed had been interrupted." She looked at Kai and Kori. "I've got a small camera set up directly facing TJ's crib. It feeds into my laptop, phone, and a small monitor I keep by my bed."

Li jogged down the hallway toward the office.

"I'll make that tea." Avery started toward the kitchen. "It looks like we're going to need it."

Why the hell had that man been in her baby's room? The fact that he'd been walking out of TJ's room didn't feel like a coincidence to her. Not on the same night that Hope McDonald managed to surface. That man wasn't lost and looking for loot. He'd come to do something to her son.

And she was going to find him and kill him.

Liam strode back in, her laptop in his hands. "The man was definitely a pro. The job he did on that window was damn near flawless. I'll figure out how he took out your security system, but right now I want to know what he was doing in that room and how long he was there."

"I took his pajamas off," Kori said, her face tight with tension. "I said I did it to change his diaper, but I wanted to make sure he hadn't…you know."

So maybe Kori wasn't so naïve. She'd learned some good paranoia from the people around her. Erin had been planning on going over every inch of her son's skin as soon as possible. "No needle marks?"

Kori nodded. "Absolutely nothing but where the glass cut him. I was very thorough, Erin. I even checked between his toes. The EMTs said they saw absolutely nothing that made them think TJ was having a pharmacological reaction to a drug."

Erin shuddered at the thought, but it was her fear. She needed to see that tape. If that man had done something to her kid, she would make him pay in the most painful way possible.

They all followed Li into her small dining room. He turned the laptop around, pulling up the feed to TJ's room. It was working perfectly, showing his empty crib, all the lights on and the glass that had shattered with the intruder's gunshot.

God, her son could have been shot. It had been a mistake according to Kai, a shot that had gone off during the fight.

What the hell was going on?

"Do you remember what time this whole shit storm started?" Erin asked Kai.

"It was roughly an hour ago," Kai replied.

Avery strode out of the kitchen with a glass in her hand. "Kentucky's finest."

Thank god. She needed it. She downed the shot. She'd avoided alcohol completely at the club, so a little indulgence wouldn't hurt. Especially since her car was back at Sanctum and she was sleeping at Li and Avery's. "Thank you. Hit play, Li. Let's figure out what this asshole was doing."

The video rolled and Erin watched as TJ slept, his rump in the air. It was the cutest thing. He'd been doing it ever since he'd been able to flip over. He would turn and put that baby butt in the air and sleep like that.

The night vision showed a shadow move across the head of the bed and then there he was. Erin held TJ close as she watched the intruder look down at her sleeping baby.

He leaned over and what he did next chilled Erin to her bones.

CHAPTER TEN

"That was pretty shitty," Ian groused as the door slammed and Erin walked away, going off to check on her son. "You could sound like you give a shit about the kid. You know he's your son, right. Do I need to get a test for you or something? You want your Maury Povich moment?"

He should have known all that support from his brother was just for show. He should have known it because he fucking didn't deserve support. He deserved the scorn. He'd broken trust with her.

"I know I'm his biological dad, damn it."

"You don't act like it."

"Because I don't feel like it. Can you not understand that? Can you not get that I'm different? I don't remember fucking anything. I can't even remember that we're brothers but I'm just expected to accept some kid I don't know? I don't feel anything for him, Ian." He had to make someone understand what a shit he was. "That's not true. You know what I feel? Irritated that he's the reason she's not here with me. Upset that I want her so badly and I'll never come first with her. I don't remember ever wanting a kid at all and now he's the thing that's coming between me and the one woman I need."

Ian turned and sighed. "Is that what your problem is?"

"My problem?"

"Why you won't meet your son."

How did he make Ian understand? "If I meet him, she's going to want me to…I don't know…suddenly be some kind of happy dad or something. She's going to want to see something I can't give her. She's going to figure out how fucked up I am."

Ian put a hand on his shoulder. "Everyone knows how fucked up you are, brother. And you're not saying anything I didn't think before Charlie had our girls. You think you're the first man to worry that a child is going to fuck up his marriage? Welcome to parenthood. We don't have the same experience women do. They become mothers pretty much the first time that sucker kicks them from the inside. She gets nine months to get used to sharing her life with this kid and we sit back and pray we survive."

He shook his head because Ian was oversimplifying. "It's not the same. I don't even remember why I loved her."

"Don't you? I think you remember more than you're willing to admit. Tell me you weren't more comfortable with her tonight. Both when she was being submissive and when she was giving you hell."

Somehow he'd responded to both of those Erins. Even earlier in the day when she'd been super sarcastic, it had felt like he'd known her. The submissive Red had felt familiar. The one he didn't get was the woman who coddled him. It bugged him. It reminded him of things he would rather not think about.

The passionate Red and sarcastic coworker, yeah, he could handle her. He wanted to handle her hard-core. He would have if that crazy bitch hadn't reared her head again.

"I'm attracted to her, yes, but I don't remember our lives together and I can't see the kid as anything but a problem." He wished it weren't true. He wished he could hear that he had a son and magically want nothing more than to be his father.

"Because you won't sit down and hold him," Ian insisted. "Because you're being a coward. Look, I get it, but your time is almost up. She's only going to wait for so long and at some point she's going to pull some rough shit on you. I'm not sure if it's going to be to walk away or to put your ass in a corner. Either way, you're not going to like it and how you deal with it is going to decide the rest of your relationship with her. So think long and hard about this, Theo."

Did Ian think he thought about anything else? He thought all day about how he could lose her. About whether he deserved her at all.

"Did I love her?" He'd asked Case, but now he wanted Ian's take.

Ian stood in front of him, a serious look on his face. "You loved her so much I consider her my sister-in-law despite the fact you never married her. I honor her because I love my brother and she was the love of his life. Not because she was the mother of his child. I would help her. I would love my nephew, but it would be different. Erin is my sister because you loved her."

It was as sacred a vow as Ian Taggart could make.

Had he loved her that much? The ring he'd found would seem to prove that theory. Should he take that as evidence? Should he honor who he used to be and throw himself in?

How could he do that when he could still hurt her?

"I'll think about it." Was she hating him right at this moment? She was likely in Liam's car being driven home to deal with her problems. That had been a cowardly move on his part. He owed her protection and he hadn't given it. He'd allowed Liam and Avery to act as her family. He was supposed to be the one she turned to. He'd been the one to turn her away.

He could still see how upset she'd been at him for staying behind.

"Come on." Ian turned away with a long-suffering sigh. "We do need to talk about the fact that Hope McDonald's shown up again. Nick got some intel earlier this evening. He says it's significant."

He followed Ian out of the room. God, how had it all gone to hell? One minute he'd been so close and the next he was back in purgatory.

The answer was clear. Hope McDonald. The bane of his existence.

"Where did she surface? Does she have her other followers with her?" He called them followers but they were victims. Victims like him and Robert. Victims with their minds wiped and their loyalty stolen.

The heavy thud of industrial music had stopped, replaced with quiet. Sanctum was closing up for the night. Ian's boots rang against the metal of the stairs. "I'm not sure. I spent more time on the phone with Derek than I did talking to Nick. I had to prioritize my nephew."

His son. TJ. Theo Jr. "Is he really all right?"

"According to Kai, but I'm sure Erin will let us know. I suspect she's going to stay with Li tonight and tomorrow we'll send the boys out to secure her house. Bear and Boomer are going to stay there tonight to watch over the place until we can get the glass reset and figure out what happened with the security system."

He followed Ian down the final set of stairs. To his left a few of the subs were cleaning the lounge area.

A vision of her laughing with a group of subs flashed through his brain. She was standing with Charlotte and Avery and Serena. She wasn't dressed in fet wear, but she wasn't wearing her typical utilitarian pants and plain button-down either. She was in a stunning emerald cocktail dress, her hair up but with the sweetest tendrils flowing around the graceful curve of her neck. She laughed at something Charlotte said and then the women held up shot glasses and slammed them back with a holler.

Someday that would be their wedding.

"You lost again?"

Ian's question made him shake his head and come back to reality.

"Whose wedding was held here?" He needed to know it had been real and not something his brain was making up to fill in the empty places.

Ian frowned. "We've never had a wedding here but we've done some collaring ceremonies and a couple of receptions."

"She was wearing a green dress."

Ian's lips curled up. "Ah, that was Jesse and Phoebe's wedding. She was a bridesmaid. After the ceremony we came back here for the party. If I recall you hit on her pretty hard and she shut you down. She might have actually punched you in the face that night. She gets mean when she drinks too much tequila, but at the time I thought it was progress. Back then Erin was a little like the playground bully. She hit the people she cared about, ignored the ones she didn't. I don't think she was hugged much as a child."

He didn't like her being referred to as a bully. She wasn't like that. "I read your report on her as an operative. She's competent and smart."

"She's brilliant with amazing instincts," Ian agreed.

"She was better than me in the field. Why would a woman like her ever want me?"

Ian wagged a finger his way. "Because she wasn't very smart, brother. Women get weird ideas in their heads and we have to jump on the chance. If you want that woman, your best bet is doing anything you can to stay close to her. You don't even have to wear her down. You already managed that. I don't think you're taking proper advantage of the situation. Dude, you died like right in front of her. That's going to buy so many Sundays where you don't have to run errands or go to church or do anything but sit in your chair with a beer in hand, watching whatever sport happens to be on that day. Also, I bet you could get a real increase in the amount of blowjobs offered. Don't expect that to last though. They get super embarrassed when they have to go to the doc for jaw pain. Yeah, stick to the football plan. Every time she asks you to go grocery shopping on Sunday, kind of put your hand to your heart and wince a little as you agree. It'll work every time."

His brother was such an ass. "I can't even call her Erin without a pain going through my head."

Ian stared for a moment. "You hid that one well."

Theo touched his hand to his head. "That didn't hurt. Erin. Erin." He winced as the pain shot through him. "Maybe it's because I'm overthinking."

"Or it's because nothing that woman did to you is permanent and you're going to come out of this."

"You believe that?" He wasn't sure he did.

Ian nodded. "I do. You're a Taggart. She can't beat you. She can't break you. She sure as fuck can't remake you. You relax and let nature take its course. You were meant to be with Erin. The biggest obstacle you face right now is her worry and your fear. When you both let go and let yourselves be, you'll find your way home. But you have to try, Theo. You can't keep sitting in Case's apartment playing video games and hiding from the world. Say her name. Take the goddamn pain because there's something amazing on the other side. Now stop reliving your love affair. We've got a meeting to attend and a crazy, creepy doctor to take down. Can we do that without you weeping or bursting into some mangina song?"

He shot his brother the finger. That was Ian to a *T*. He gave him the most amazing advice, brought up his spirits and made him believe, and then capped it off by being an ass. It was his way. "I think I can handle it."

"Ian, did he run?" Case rounded the corner. He caught sight of them and took a deep breath, as though relieved to see Theo was still there. "Good. Nick is changing and Robert just got here. We should be ready to go in thirty minutes or so."

Was his twin still worried he was going to up and disappear? How much had he cost Case?

He'd been living at Case's place, letting his brother handle the load while he disappeared into a world of video games and TV shows and tried to forget what had happened to him. Case had gotten married and Theo hadn't bothered to get to know Mia. He'd decided he didn't know anyone, so why should he know her?

He'd discounted them all because he was so fucking angry.

"I'm ready," he told his brother. "And I'm not going anywhere. I'm here to stay."

Case nodded, but didn't look like he believed it. "Go and get changed. You can take a shower if you need to. I'm going to get everything ready for Nick."

Theo followed Ian into the locker room to change.

Thirty minutes later, Theo stared up at the screen and felt sick to his stomach. There she was.

Hope McDonald was stepping out of a limo, her eyes covered by designer sunglasses. The sun glinted off her blonde hair and she looked like a pretty socialite, like some rich lady who was probably attending tea with her friends.

She was a sociopathic monster who believed she was owed the world.

After everything I've done for you, why can't you give me this? I'm not really your mother, you know. I'm only a few years older than you. Can't you see? I want you to be my prince, Theo. We

149

belong together.

He reached out and grabbed the water in front of him.

"Don't," his sister-in-law said. She passed him a can of lemon-lime soda. "Drink this. It'll settle your stomach better."

He gripped the can and flipped the top open, sending Mia a nod. "Thank you."

She smiled back at him, her hand slipping over Case's. "No problem."

Well, that was one thing he now knew about the woman Case had married. She was kind. He took a long drink, the cool soda easing him. It was enough to ground him and allow him to focus on the picture again.

"She looks good." Robert's voice was flat, his eyes unwavering.

"She looks psychotic," Charlotte shot back.

Robert turned to her, shaking his head. "Oh, but she doesn't. When she wants to, she can look as normal as anyone. She can smile and you believe her. It's only when you're alone with her that you realize she doesn't care about anyone or anything but herself. Ask her sister. Faith thought Hope cared about her. That's how she gets you. You think what she's doing is kind, but she does nothing at all that doesn't serve her agenda. Trust me, if that woman smiles your way, it's because she's thinking of how she can use you."

"I promise not a single person here is going to underestimate her," Ian assured Robert. "Nick, where and when was this taken and do we have eyes on her?"

"It was taken by Kayla Summers of the London office. She works under Damon Knight. She and Owen Shaw were tracking her around Asia when they got a tip from a reliable source that she was making her way to Europe. This was taken outside the Parisian offices of a pharmaceutical company with Collective ties. I also have tracked your man Hutch to the same city, but I lost him again."

"I knew he was going after her," Case said.

Alex shook his head. "We can't be sure of that. Paris is a big place."

"I think we can." Eve ran a hand over her husband's. "I told you what I thought he was doing. He's going after her, but he's ashamed. He doesn't feel like he can come home until he's made things right."

"Why would he be ashamed?" Case asked. "No one blames

him."

In this, he was an expert. "He blames himself. I assure you of that. I know because I blame myself. It's not rational or right, but it's true and it's not something he can stop. He was made to feel weak. He's gone to a place where he's in control again. She didn't take his memory, but she did give him to Tony for training. Tony used pain to ensure cooperation."

"Is he why you have four broken bones you didn't have before?" Case asked, his voice tight.

Theo shrugged. After he'd gotten back to Dallas he'd been subjected to numerous tests. MRIs and blood work and CT scans of every part of his body. It had told a story he hadn't fully remembered. He'd been brutalized. "I don't recall and now I think that might be a good thing. Maybe. I don't know. Do you want to remember Hell, or is it worse that it sits in the back of your brain and you can't quite catch it? You can't remember why you're so fucking afraid of a baseball bat sitting in the corner of your brother's apartment. Would it be better if I knew it had been used to break my bones? That's where Hutch is. He knows what happened to him. He can't forget."

Robert held a hand up. "I'm totally glad I can't remember. I think it would suck ass. So I salute whoever gave me the DNA that enabled that fucking drug to take over so easily."

He wasn't mentioning the fact that he woke up screaming in the middle of the night, fighting invisible demons. Theo had to hold him down sometimes until he was fully awake and back to being Robert. But Theo wasn't going to mention that. They all dealt with the same thing in different ways. Robert denied it. Theo pushed away everyone who cared about him.

And it looked like Hutch was out for vengeance. "I think this information could have come from Hutch and that means we might have a shot at finding him and getting some good intel from him. We can convince him to come home and he can tell us everything he knows. If he's been following her for a while, he likely knows what she's up to."

"Are you sure you can trust him?" Nick asked. "He could be angry. You left him there for a long time. The operation to retrieve Theo was a long game. Don't look at me like that. I understand it, but I'm not the one who was left in that woman's clutches for months."

"I know Hutch," Eve said with surety. "I believe Kai would back me up. It's not in his character to hurt the men and women he considers his family. His father wasn't around much and from what I can tell he and his stepmother never got along. From his psych reports he felt out of place while he was growing up. He was the only child his mother and father had. The dad remarried after she died and there was definite preference shown to the children he had with the new wife. I believe Hutch found his place in the world when he joined the CIA team. He might not be willing to face them right now, but he wouldn't ever hurt them."

"So we have to figure out why and how he needs our help." Ian sat back in his chair, his fingers coming up to steeple in front of his chest.

His brother's *I'm thinking* face.

God, was Ian right? Had he fought so fucking hard and it was all going to come back at some point and he would have lost everything? His mind was making connections faster and faster when he didn't try to force it.

Had he lost her tonight because he was so afraid he wouldn't even look at his son?

Nick began talking about the pharmaceutical corporation and who Kayla and Owen thought McDonald had been meeting with. Theo let it all sink in. The meeting went on with discussion of how and why she would be working with The Collective again.

He was useless here. What was he going to tell them? She had been very careful about hiding her "boys" when The Collective came around. At the time, their connection had been through a pharmaceutical company named Kronberg.

He didn't know anything, but maybe Robert did.

He turned to his friend, who had kept his mouth shut after his initial advice. That was kind of Robert's way. Maybe being quiet was a protective measure, or perhaps it had simply been a part of who he'd been before. Either way, Theo thought Robert might know more than he thought he did. "Do you remember when the money ran out?"

Robert frowned. "She didn't talk about that kind of stuff around us."

"But think back. Why did she say we were leaving Argentina?"

"The second base?" Robert asked. "That's kind of how I thought of it. The first base was her dad's place in the Caymans. At least that's the first one I remember. I woke up in the outer building."

They'd gone over all of this when they'd first gotten back. Eve and Kai had spent hours with both of them going over everything they could remember with a fine-tooth comb.

"Did she not say anything when we suddenly moved to Colombia? I get flashes of doing it at night sometimes. Like we were on the run."

Robert sat back. "I overheard Tony talking to Victor. I think Kronberg wanted one of us. I think they wanted some proof the drugs and the therapy were working. She wasn't willing to give anyone up."

"That doesn't make any sense," Ian said. "According to everything we've discovered, Kronberg cut off her funding over that. It's precisely why she had you robbing banks a month later. She also had another stash of experiments in Asia. Why not give them one and continue on? Nothing was more important to that woman than her research."

Robert's eyes came up. "That's not true. Tomas was. I mean Theo. He was her favorite. I think they didn't want just one of us. They wanted him."

"Why would Kronberg insist on Theo?" Case asked.

Ian had gone a little pale. "They knew it was you. They knew you were my brother. This is a smart group. They know all the major players. Kronberg wanted to know if she could turn a Taggart, a Navy SEAL, a former CIA team member. They wanted to see if she could turn the best."

Robert nodded. "I think that's what happened. She wouldn't give him up. She knew if she let them examine Theo, they would find out he wasn't as perfectly controlled as the rest of us. It would have fallen apart."

"And they probably would have terminated the experiment," Charlotte concluded. "So instead she decided to run. The question is, what has she got now that would tempt The Collective to take her back into the fold? They were looking for her pretty hard for a couple of months."

"Every agency in the world has been looking for her," Ian murmured. "I wonder what I could get out of Fain if I shared this information with the Agency."

Nick turned on Ian. "You'll get us in the back seat of this op, Tag. That's what you'll do. I know you have your brother back but I'll never get Des back. She's not coming home to me. Don't even think about passing this off to the Agency."

"I wouldn't be passing it off." Ian was using his most patient voice. It was the one that sounded only slightly annoyed. "I would be sharing intel to get intel. Do you trust me? Because if you don't, I'm not sure why you're here."

"I trust Knight and he trusts you," Nick allowed. "I can't get left out of this."

"You won't, but Ezra Fain is a different kind of agent. He proved that when he didn't storm the building and try to take Theo," Case said.

"There was a lot of pressure on him to do exactly that, according to Chelsea." Charlotte looked up at Nick. "I would go to her, but we try to keep a wall up. She works for the Agency. I can't put her in a position where she has to choose, but she thinks Ezra is trustworthy. He seems more interested in actually serving his country and the Constitution than he is in moving up in the Agency."

"Which is why he'll get his ass fired and show up on my doorstep with his hand out eventually," Ian complained. "Let me get some use out of him now before he turns into Adam 2.0."

Charlotte's hand moved out, slapping at her husband's chest. "What are you going to do when Adam leaves? Who are you going to kick then?"

The rumors were Adam and Jake were almost ready to start their own business. Not that they would get far. They intended to lease space in the same office building and work cases in tandem with the main company. Adam had developed a facial recognition software that was supposed to make him an incredible amount of money. He was already joking about how much he was going to charge Big Tag for use.

"I find everyone annoying, baby," Ian replied. "Finding another Adam will be a breeze." He pointed at the screen. "How did she give Kay and Owen the slip? Was the Scot in a pub drinking?"

From what Theo had read about the two London team members, Kayla was a former double agent, serving the CIA by spying on Chinese intelligence, and Owen had been SAS in the British military. Both were highly trained, and it would have been hard to lose them.

"They got her out by helo," Nick explained. "She was in the building for three hours. Kay managed to get in by stealing a key card. She talked to some of the workers and figured out that McDonald had been in the CEO's office for most of that time. They traced the helo to Reims. They think she actually crossed the border shortly after and went into Luxembourg. That's where they lost her."

Ian's eyes widened. "In Luxembourg? They lost her in fucking Luxembourg. Oh, they're so fired."

Charlotte rolled her eyes. "Please tell them to keep looking and we would love anything and everything on the company she met with. I want the entire corporate structure and everything you have on the products they make."

"Owen is targeting a female employee back in Paris. She's an upper-level executive who might have the information we need," Nick explained, completely unfazed by Ian's outburst. It made Theo wonder how Damon Knight ran his team. "He's already got a meeting with her. Our tech guys set him up as a potential client. The lady is divorcing and apparently has a thing for British men. We'll see what he can find out."

"See, Damon's got man meat," Ian said to his wife as though this was an argument they had often. "No whiney married guys who can't romance some info out of a woman. All I've got are whiney married dudes. Even Theo comes back, his memory wiped out, and I still can't use him as a man trap because the one thing he does remember is that his dick is attached to a female."

Charlotte's mouth dropped open. "Ian!"

But Theo threw back his head and laughed. It was true.

Robert looked at him after the laughter died down. "You know it's why she was so hard on you. You wouldn't forget Erin. You wouldn't play her games because of Erin."

Her games. It sent a chill through him. Her games had included running her hands over his body and trying to get a response. What had he given her? How much of himself had he given up? Had she taken?

Robert turned back to Ian. "I will happily be man meat, sir. You know, once you decide I'm not going to explode like a land mine of horror. I thought that was colorful language for a formal report."

Ian frowned. "A report you weren't supposed to get."

"If I can't get a report on myself, what good could I ever be to the team?" Robert asked. "I want to be here. I want to give back, even if it's in a small way. Let me read the reports on the new players. I can condense the information so it's something everyone can understand."

Robert was giving him time to recover. He took a deep breath. They needed to have a talk. Robert obviously remembered more than he was telling Theo. Perhaps he was trying to hide the truth, but Theo needed to know.

He had to find out what had happened to him in those tiny cells when the lights had gone out.

The door flew open and Theo turned, his heart starting at the sound. It clanged against the wall and for a second, he thought about reaching for the Colt he carried. Thank god he didn't because she was standing in the doorway, her curly hair floating around her face.

And she wasn't alone. Her arms were up, cradling a blanketed thing that could only be a baby. He guessed it could be something else. She could be holding a really big gun. She was the kind of woman who might bundle up her pet gun and hold it close to her heart.

God, that was his son in her arms. She cradled his head and bounced gently as she spoke.

"Ian, I need to talk to you."

It bugged him that she was looking at Ian and hadn't spared him a glance. She turned away from him as though protecting the child in her arms.

"What's wrong?" Ian asked, standing up. "Did something go bad with the police? Should I call Derek?"

She moved back and forth like the baby was heavy and she had to shift around to stay comfortable. "No. The police were fine. It's what I found on my baby monitor that has me freaked out."

The door opened again and Li strode in, followed by Avery. He held up a thumb drive. "I've got the relevant data, but Erin's right. It's disturbing. We have to find this woman, Ian."

What had happened? Avery put a hand on Erin's shoulder and held her arms out as if to take the baby.

Theo had a choice. He could let that happen and then she probably wouldn't look at him again all night long. She might not come back to the club. Yes, he'd signed a contract that stated he would take care of her inside the club, but that was bullshit. Life happened outside the club, and they, in particular, weren't a couple who could be confined to a damn contract. He'd died. She'd had his baby. They were twelve kinds of fucked up, and that didn't get fixed with a contract. It didn't get fixed with sex.

Maybe it could start to heal with a little compromise.

"I'll take him."

The room seemed to freeze, every eye on him.

"It's okay," Erin said. "Avery can handle him. He's had a rough night and he needs someone he knows."

She was giving him an out. The baby was asleep, his eyes closed and mouth sucking on a pacifier. He wouldn't know who was holding him. The blanket had slipped and he could see the baby's head. There was a cap of blond hair there. He could take the exit ramp she was offering him and sit back down and quietly listen.

And nothing would change. If there was one thing he wanted out of tonight, it was some damn change. Ian was right. He couldn't sit in that apartment anymore. He had to try. He'd spent all his time trying to remember what he'd had back then and none trying to figure out what was his in the now.

"I'll take him."

She sighed and started to hand the baby to Avery. "It's fine, Theo."

Sometimes she needed a firm hand or she would walk all over him. "Erin, I said I will take my son. Hand him over to me or we are going to have trouble."

Her skin went the sweetest shade of pink and he couldn't figure out if she was about to argue with him or if she'd gotten a little hot.

Either way, he needed to start finding his real place in their relationship, and that began with the baby in her arms.

No matter what had happened to him, he owed that kid a chance to know his father. A chance to have his father not be a total asshole who tried to live in the past.

Well, she was finally looking at him. Oh, she kind of looked like she wanted to kick him in the balls, so that answered his previous question. Though the fact that she was pissed at him didn't mean she wasn't also hot. She was kind of perverted. He liked that about her.

She moved toward him, the room completely silent. "If you drop him I will kill you."

He should have gone with her. He'd been scared, but now he could see how rough the night had been on her. He should have sucked it up and taken care of her, but he'd been a coward. "I'm not going to drop it."

She stopped and cradled the baby closer. "Him. Not it. He's a baby, not a thing, and he has a name."

"He has my name, Erin. I'm trying, okay. You wanted me to try. Well, this is me trying, and I will fuck it all up. But I won't drop my son."

Her shoulders came down from around her ears and she closed the space between them. "You have to make sure to hold his head."

He held out his arms and she shifted the baby over. He was eight months old. It wasn't like he was some tiny, fragile thing, and yet he felt that way as his body sank against Theo's arms. "I'm not going to hurt my own son."

He wasn't. It finally hit him. He wasn't going to hurt the kid. He might not be able to love him the way the other Theo would have, but he wasn't going to bring him to harm. He could do this. He could ease some of her burden and maybe she would let him back into her life. He'd been distant and that had to hurt her. Distance hadn't worked. Closeness felt so much better.

She stood there as though she wasn't sure she should leave him with the sleeping baby.

"Case, could you get Erin a seat?" He blinked through the pain, his hands perfectly steady. It was about half and half at this point when he said or thought her name. He would take it.

"I'll sit by Nick," she offered.

"Are we or are we not still in this club? It might be the conference room, but we're still at Sanctum. You will sit beside me."

The look she sent him told him they would so be talking about that later.

At least they would be talking.

Case grinned as he presented the chair. "Here you go. You know the old saying. Be careful what you wish for…"

She shot his brother her middle finger and sat down. "Li, will you please show them the footage?"

Liam started messing around with the laptop and Theo settled back.

He took a deep breath. He was holding his kid. Yep. Here he was holding his son like a regular old, hadn't-been-dead-and-had-his-memory-wiped-over-and-over-again father.

"He likes to be held higher," Erin said, her eyes staring away from him.

"He is higher. I'm taller than you."

"You have to bounce him when he gets fussy."

"He's not fussy. He's asleep." Theo looked down and that pacifier was working. Like he was dreaming about eating. Typical Taggart. Jeez, he was kind of cute. His tiny hands were fisted against his chest. Tiny hands that would reach up for him.

"He won't be for long if you don't fix his blanket. He doesn't like the cold."

She was going to micromanage everything he did and he was going to have to deal with it. If things had been normal, they would have learned all this together. They would have sat up nights trying to figure out if he needed his diaper changed or another feeding. They would have worried and fretted.

She'd done all of it alone.

He resettled the blanket over his son, who snuggled closer, his face rubbing against Theo's chest. "I should have gone with you tonight."

"It was no big deal."

Shit. He was in trouble. Big old trouble. He didn't have to remember. Any man with half a sense of self-preservation knew that tone. It was worse with Erin since she knew how to kill a man a hundred different ways and had named her gun. "It was a big deal and I screwed up."

She sat back as though simply relaxing. "I handled it. I'm used to handling things."

"I know and you've done it so well. I'm sorry. I should have done this the moment I got home. I should have taken over some of your work. You're not alone now."

"Not in the club, I suppose."

She wasn't going to give him an inch.

"I'm trying. I'm sorry. Sometimes it hurts, but I'm going to be better. I'm going to get to know him."

Her head turned and she was looking at him like he wasn't the worst human being on earth. "You hurt? Where? Kai told you. You have to stop trying to remember, Theo. Do you need something for a headache?"

Ian cleared his throat as if to say "told you." "I think Princess Theo can survive a few minutes. Li, you ready?"

She put a hand on his arm. "If you're in pain, I can stop all of this. It can wait."

His brother was a fucking genius. "I'm fine. It only hurts a little. Maybe if you kissed me I would forget."

Erin looked around as though she knew she was being had, but couldn't quite wriggle out of the trap. "Well, I suppose since we're in the club, I have to."

She leaned over, brushing her lips against his, their child between them.

It was over almost before it began, but it struck him that it was the first time she'd kissed him.

Maybe not the first, but the first he remembered.

She settled into her seat, but leaned toward him this time.

The baby wasn't trouble at all. He kind of liked having something to hold on to. The weight was good in his hands. It was chilly in the room though. He tucked the blanket around TJ's head. Didn't most of the body heat get lost through the head? Shouldn't the kid be wearing a hat?

"Okay, so this asshole broke into Erin's place around midnight tonight," Li was saying. "That's the best we can tell since he managed to take out the security system."

"And he did it without setting off the alarm that would normally go off if the electricity was cut," Erin added. "So I have to think he hacked into the system, and that means he's not some two-bit burglar looking to make some cash."

"Which this video proves." Li touched a key on the laptop and the screen in front of them filled with a grainy, black-and-white feed. "He didn't break in to steal anything…well not anything of financial value."

Theo watched the video. It was TJ sleeping. How did he sleep like that? His body was kind of bent in two and his butt was up in the air. He'd kicked off his blanket and looked small in the crib. There was a mobile above his head. It looked like airplanes.

"Are you trying to ruin him?"

Erin's eyes went wide. "What?"

"I told her you wouldn't like the airplanes." Case leaned in, his voice quiet.

Erin huffed. "For god's sake, it's a mobile, you two."

"It's going to send that kid straight to the Air Force." He would never have allowed that in his poor kid's room. "We're a Navy family. He's going into the Navy. You're switching that thing out for boats."

"I was in the Army, jerk. And we can talk about this later. There he is." She pointed to the screen.

Theo forgot about the highly inappropriate mobile and started thinking about the man who crept into his son's room.

"How tall is the crib?" Robert asked.

"What does that matter?" Why the hell was Robert interested in the crib?

"The side comes up to my waist. I know because I bend over that sucker every single day," Erin replied, standing up and putting her hand at her waist. "I'm five foot eight. Do you think you can figure out how tall he is?"

The man on the screen stood over the baby's bed, his masked face to the camera, though he didn't seem to know he was being taped.

"I need to look at it on a computer, but I would estimate he's roughly six foot and weighs about one ninety." Robert was studying the screen carefully. "Theo, do you recognize the balaclava?"

It was hard to tell because the screen was in night vision, but the man's face mask did seem familiar. "It looks like there's a change in material around the neck. Do you think it's leather?"

Mother always made them wear the masks when they worked. She insisted on protecting their throats. It wasn't a common balaclava.

"I think so. I think it's exactly like the ones we used to wear. He's from Mother."

Ian shuddered. "I thought we weren't going to call her that anymore. It's creepy. What the fuck is that in his hand?"

Erin went stiff beside him. "It's a medical grade swab. It's in a container to keep it sterile."

The man pulled out the swab and rolled TJ over. The baby yawned and his pacifier fell out. The man pressed the swab inside TJ's mouth and ran it inside his cheek.

Theo's arms tightened around his son. Erin's hand went to his shoulder, as if trying to soothe him.

"Did he take TJ's DNA?" Mia asked. "Why would he do that?"

The man eased the swab into the container as TJ started to flip over again. The man put the container inside his jacket and exited the room.

That bitch. He felt his heart rate jack up. She had his son's DNA. His fucking DNA.

What the hell was she going to do with his son's DNA?

Soothing hands moved over his shoulders. Erin was standing behind him. "Take a deep breath, babe. Your eyebrow is doing that weird thing where I'm pretty sure you're about to have a heart attack."

"I'm going to kill her." He watched in horror as the window shattered and TJ started to howl. He couldn't hear a damn thing, but his son's face screwed up and he started screaming. Kori rushed in, covering TJ's body with her own and pulling him away.

"I'm going to kill her."

"I know, babe," Erin replied. "I know."

He sat and held TJ and wondered if he hadn't brought hell down on his son.

* * * *

Erin kissed TJ and settled him into the crib with Aidan. The boys had bunked down before and Aidan didn't even move as TJ settled in. She wanted to keep him in bed with her, but Avery and Li's guest bed was one of those monstrous things that was high off the ground, and she worried because TJ sometimes woke up early and liked to roll around.

She could sleep in here. There was a rocking chair. It wasn't like she would actually be able to close her eyes and fall asleep. She was fairly certain that the moment she tried, all she would see was that man standing over Theo Jr. It would likely shift and change into that crazy fucking bitch looming over her Theo.

The door came open, light spilling in from the hall. Liam's big body blocked most of the illumination. "Come on out. The boy's will be fine. We need to talk."

It was so late. She didn't want to talk. She wanted to go back to the moment in the evening when Theo had been her Master and she hadn't thought about anything but the way he made her feel. Before all their problems landed back on her doorstep.

It had been a good plan, but the first crack had already shown up and it had fallen apart. She wasn't sure she could go back to the club now. She might never leave her child again.

Still, she followed Li out. He'd gotten down to a pair of PJ pants, his hair wet. It was obvious the man was ready to end the night, but here he was still dealing with her. This Irishman who shared no blood with her had been more her brother than the three she had. He'd been more of a father, too, though she would never say that to him since they were practically the same age. Still, when they'd become partners he'd been so much more mature than she'd been, settled and confident with his life.

He walked in front of her and she couldn't help but stare at the tattoo on his left shoulder blade. It was a glorious piece of ink. The *A* in the middle was for Avery, and the Celtic knots that wound around it, protecting the precious letter, were all about his heritage.

She'd thought so often about getting a *T* somewhere on her body, but she wasn't sure what she would want around it as protection and honor. Roses and guns didn't seem like a proper way

163

to pay respect to the love of her life.

Who'd died. It struck her finally today that the Theo she'd known had died and wasn't fully coming back. That Theo wouldn't have waited months to meet his son. He wouldn't have sat around and played video games while she struggled.

Could she trust the Theo who'd shown up tonight? He'd asked to hold their baby and he'd been quite tender with TJ. Of course, it was easy to be a good caretaker when the baby was asleep.

But when it had counted, he'd told her she was alone. He'd stood right there and chosen to let her walk away. That wasn't the Theo she'd known. The Theo she'd known would have been all over her, trying to take all the responsibility. He'd craved it.

Still, her heart had ached at the sight of this Theo cradling their baby boy. He'd done a good job. He'd cuddled TJ close and he'd been mad when he should have been.

He'd promised to kill the woman who'd threatened their boy.

She followed Li to the kitchen. There was no other way to interpret what had happened. She wasn't sure why McDonald had stolen her son's biological material, but it seemed like an all-out declaration of war to Erin. Not that she wouldn't have gone there. That bitch had declared war the moment she'd stolen Theo, and there would be no quarter. Woman to woman. She might appreciate that Theo was willing to kill her, but that bitch was Erin's. No question about it.

"You've got a visitor," Li said, stopping before they reached the kitchen. He turned to her. "I can send him away right now. You need to rest, not play nursemaid."

She stopped, staring at the door behind Li's back. It was freaking two in the morning. Who the hell would come and visit her? There was only one person she could think of. "Theo's here?"

"I'm pretty sure he drove your car. It's sitting out in the driveway, but I don't see his truck." Li crossed his arms over his chest. "Do you want to talk to him? I told him you're tired and he should make an appointment with you tomorrow, but he said he wouldn't leave until he saw you. I assure you, I can make him leave."

Such a big brother. "No, I'll talk to him."

She wasn't sure what he was going to say, but it meant

something that he was here. He'd retreated so often lately that she was surprised he would show up. No one would have questioned him if he'd gone back to Case's with Robert. It had been a long day.

He was here. He was waiting behind those swinging doors.

Li's lips curved up. "So the boy's coming around then?"

"I think he's trying." He'd held TJ and even been a bit reluctant to give him up at the end of the conference. It was all she could ask.

Li nodded. "All right then. Set the alarm again when he leaves. If he leaves. Goodnight, Erin. Avery and I will take care of the boys. You get some sleep."

He stepped away and she was confronted with that door. What was he going to say to her? Was he going to retreat? Would he tell her he couldn't do this with her? Or that he was too disturbed by the thought of McDonald to continue down the path they'd started?

She pushed through the door because she didn't believe in waiting. Waiting was for pussies and people who actually had a lick of patience. Rip the damn bandage off and start the bleed. It was going to happen anyway. She needed to know. It was time to stand in front of him and figure out what he truly wanted.

Theo was standing in the middle of the kitchen. He was staring at the door as though every cell in his body had been waiting for her to walk through.

"Hey."

Damn but that was a beautiful man. He might think that scar on his face was an issue, but she hadn't lied to him. It made him even sexier. It meant he'd survived. "Hey."

"I brought your car," he said, his voice breaking a little. It did that when he was nervous. "I thought you might need it tomorrow. Though no one would blame you if you stayed here."

All the things she needed to do in the morning rushed in on her. "I can't. I've got a full day. I have to go to the office in the morning and then spend the afternoon overseeing the new security system install. I hate changing passwords. I also have to get all up in Adam's business because I need to know how that asswipe hacked into my system."

"I'm sure she used Hutch's protocols," Theo explained. "One of the things I do remember was the fact that she forced Hutch to write a bunch of hacks for her. I suspect it's one of the things he feels guilty about. Don't judge him too harshly. The punishment was pretty bad for disobedience."

She could only imagine. "I won't ever blame Hutch. I just want him to come home. Speaking of home, it's late. You should probably get there. Did Robert follow in your truck?"

He stepped around the table. "I don't want to go back to Case's. I was hoping you would let me sleep here. With you."

Tears immediately sprang to her eyes and she fought them back. He had to understand what he was saying. Or rather, she needed to. "We're not in the club anymore, Theo."

"I know that. We were stupid to think we could keep it there. We left that behind a long time ago. We have a baby. We can't keep it to the club, but that doesn't mean we can't play."

Ah, so he wanted to finish what they'd started. He'd been left in a pretty shitty place and he probably felt like she owed him. She did. It might be nice to fuck him hard.

She shook her head. "Theo, I can't tonight. I'm sorry. I know it was a shitty cock block earlier, but I can't be in that place right now."

He frowned. "In what place? In the club? We can't leave here. We can't leave TJ. I wouldn't ask you to do that."

"Subspace, Theo. Sex space. I can't do that right now." Why did he always have to make her say it? In the beginning she'd thought it was because he was dense. Later, she'd realized it was a way to force her to be comfortable with him. Now she was dealing with a different man and she was unsure all over again.

She wanted to cry. It had been so long since she'd cried. It was like she'd shut down that part of herself after he'd died and it had only come back the moment she'd realized he was alive. Now she was numb again, anger so much easier than the anxiety she felt at the thought that the Theo she'd loved was gone forever.

He moved in, stepping close to her. "Is that what you think of me? I suppose the old Theo wouldn't want what you'd promised him. He wouldn't show up on your doorstep after an awful night and demand sex." His voice went low and he stared down at her. "I'm not sure how I feel about you thinking I'm capable of that, but we're starting over so I need to reintroduce myself. I do want to finish what I should have started earlier tonight. Come here, baby. Let me hold you. Let me rub your back and your feet and massage your head until you fall asleep. Let me get up in the middle of the night to take care of our son. Let me sleep with you so I can do what I should have. So I can take care of you. It's all I want to do."

His hands sank into her hair, gently pulling it out of the bun she'd fashioned. He ran his fingertips over her scalp with firm pressure.

Some people liked foot rubs. This did it for her. Having her head and shoulders rubbed properly always relaxed her.

"I've done this before, haven't I? When you got wound up, I would get you naked and lay you out and rub you down. Then you could sleep. When you walked in here looking so worried, I got a flash of doing this to you."

"So many times." She leaned against his strong body, her hands finding his waist for balance.

His fingers rolled over her shoulders and back up again. "Why did you love me?"

It was the first time he'd really asked about something important. She knew he and Case had talked about his past, but before the meeting with Kai earlier, he hadn't asked more than simple questions about them. She sometimes wondered if he thought she was tricking him into believing he'd loved her.

But answering why she loved him was easy. "Because no one in the whole world ever loved me the way you did. No one ever fought for me the way you did."

"Who did I have to fight? Were you with someone when we met?"

She shook her head and bit back a groan as he lightly pulled her hair. Yeah, she loved that, too. "No. I was divorced, but I hadn't been dating. You fought me, Theo. I was the one you had to fight. I didn't like myself much back then. I didn't believe in myself. You gave me that."

He tugged on her hair and she let her head fall back. He stared down at her and she could see how tired he was, too. "Then let me sleep with you. I'm not the same man. I don't know that I can ever be the man you fell in love with, but let me sleep with you. Let me try to be here for you. No sex. Just comfort. We've had a long day and I want to end it the way we should have spent it. Together."

167

She wrapped her arms around him and let her head rest against his shoulder. "Did you like holding TJ?"

His hands ran down her back and up again, soothing her. "I did, but Erin, I don't feel like his dad. I'm going to try. I'll spend time with him, but I don't feel like a dad."

Was that what he was worried about? She looked up at him. "Are you serious? Theo, it took time for me to feel like a mom. Don't get me wrong, I loved the kid from the moment I saw him, before really, but I had months to get used to it. You've only known he existed for a couple of weeks. I also knew why he was conceived, so I had a leg up on you in the parenting department."

"Case told me a condom broke."

So at least he'd asked. "That was part of it, but I think there was more. I think the universe gave him to me so I wouldn't give up. So I wouldn't do something stupid."

"Something stupid?"

She wasn't sure how much to tell him, but she didn't want this intimacy to go away. He deserved to know. "I went dark when you died."

His hands tightened around her as though he was afraid to let her go. "And after you knew you were pregnant?"

"I didn't think those thoughts again. I couldn't go and be with you because I had a piece of you inside me, and I had to protect him and love him and give him everything you couldn't. I'm not super religious, but I can't help but think some things happen because they need to. Some things are meant to be."

"Do you think we're one of those things?" He whispered the question.

"I know we are." She couldn't give up on him. No matter how mad she got or frustrated he made her. She had to remember what he didn't. She had to remember that he'd never given up on her.

She stepped back and saw his face fall. Did he think she was going to reject him? She held out her hand. "Come to bed, Theo."

His fingers tangled in hers and he let her lead him through the house and back to the bedroom.

"Is TJ asleep?" Theo asked as she shut the door behind him.

"He's with Aidan." How was it so awkward? She'd nearly fucked him earlier this evening. They'd slept together a hundred times and yet she was suddenly shy. "That's Li and Avery's son. They've got the monitor on and way better security than our place."

"But we're upgrading tomorrow. Do you need money?"

Ah, the things he didn't know. "I've got all your money, babe. Case made sure of it. We'll be fine. I guess I should give that back to you."

He shook his head. "No. I want you to have it, but maybe I could move back in. Test the waters. Maybe being home will help."

Fake it until you make it. She was willing to try. "I would love that."

"I can help around the house. Get used to it again. Maybe do some upgrades. I like fire pits."

She smiled. "We have one. You insisted and made everyone come over to help build it out. You were nice though. We provided the beer."

"I had a lot of friends," he said, as though the idea made him a little sad.

"You have a lot of friends, Theo. You might not remember them, but they will never forget you." She needed to get past the awkwardness. He was trying. That was all she could ask. "Give it time. I think you'll find you like these people."

He looked over at the big bed. "I already like them. They're nice people. I didn't bring anything with me."

She was wearing pajama bottoms and a T-shirt. The bottoms had to go. She shimmied out of them. "I think Li can help you out. Avery's kind of the greatest hostess ever. If you look in the bathroom, you'll find travel-size toothpaste and shampoos in there. There's even a new toothbrush. She's serious about guests."

"Good." He turned to the bathroom door. "I guess I didn't think this through."

"You don't have to stay." She wasn't going to make the night any harder on him. She'd been pissed as hell earlier, but she couldn't stay mad at him. "You can take my car and we'll talk in the morning."

He looked back, his hand on the bathroom door. There was a smile on his face that made her heart race. "No, I wasn't talking about sleeping with you. That's the best idea I've ever had. Don't be too impressed. I've had less than a year of ideas I remember, and most of them were bad. No. I was thinking about the fact that I can't shave in the morning and I want to be as attractive as I possibly can for you. I might roll out of bed early in the morning and shower and steal a razor so I can shave and brush my teeth and then slip back into bed so you think I wake up this pretty."

Oh, sometimes her Theo showed up and she wanted to cry in relief. "I remember what you were like before, babe. Not all that interested in grooming. And I happen to find your scruff incredibly sexy."

He ran a hand over the beard that was coming in. "I bet I used that to great advantage. I'll be back. Don't forget the alarm."

She could barely breathe as he closed the bathroom door. She ran down the hall, not caring if Li or Avery caught her in her undies. She set the alarm and checked the back door and hustled back to the bedroom.

He was already in bed. "Is it okay if I take this side? I like the right side."

"Unless the door is on the left," she said quietly. He'd said that to her the first night they'd shared a bed in Africa. The bungalow they'd stayed in barely had room for a double, and Theo had taken up all the space. But he'd ensured his body was closest to the door so he could protect her. She hadn't even realized that was what he'd been doing until they'd gotten to Munich and suddenly he preferred the left side of the bed.

"Then I would probably like that side," he agreed.

He'd shed his shirt and was probably down to his boxers. He usually slept naked and would never allow her to sleep with him with clothes on.

Maybe they needed them tonight. Maybe they needed something more than sex.

She climbed in on her side and turned off the light, plunging the room into darkness.

He was here. That had to be enough.

She felt him roll over, his hands moving out and reaching for her.

"Come here. You don't need a random warm body in bed. I think you need me, baby. I don't know everything that means, but I want to give it to you. Let me hold you." He cradled her to his chest.

And there in the dark, she held him and let go. It didn't matter than he couldn't tell her how they'd met or when he'd first told her he loved her. She cried because he was here and he'd always been her safe place. She cried because it had been a shitty day. She cried because he never could.

CHAPTER ELEVEN

"So how'd it go last night?" Robert asked.

Theo turned down Pearl Street and started toward Klyde Warren Park and thought about how to answer that question. How had it gone?

"I had the dream again." Naturally the moment he'd fallen asleep he'd found himself in a nightmare. "When I was awake, it was perfect. I like being with her and it's definitely getting easier to use her name, but I fell asleep and I was right back in the same place again."

Robert kept up with him. He'd come to the office this morning to help Adam with the security footage from the night before. Robert had been studying the footage over and over, trying to see if anything else about the man who had broken into Erin's place the night before might be meaningful. "Shit, I'm sorry to hear that. Is this the one where you kill her? Erin, I mean."

He nodded, stopping at the light. "Yeah. I can't seem to help myself. This time it was Mia who turned into Erin. Did I shoot my sister-in-law?"

It had felt so real. He'd been in some kind of industrial room with metal shelves around them. There had been a door at his front and another to his back. He'd been able to feel the chill of the air conditioner and the weight of the gun in his hand.

Mia had been there. She'd been in a pretty cocktail dress, but her mascara had been smudged, her hair mussed, and she was crying, begging him to let her go back to Case. He'd shoved her and she'd fallen behind a shelving unit. When she'd looked up, it had been Erin staring down the barrel of the gun he'd held. She'd stared up at him and he'd been so cold. He'd leveled the gun at her head as she'd begged for her life.

The light turned and they started toward the park and the numerous food trucks that surrounded the big green space in the middle of downtown. Normally he would eat in the deli at the bottom of the building, but today he needed to get outside, needed to breathe.

Robert strode beside him. "No. You didn't. You're talking about what happened in Colombia. You were ordered to kill her but you wouldn't. This is what I'm talking about, man. You have to ease up on the guilt. You got into so much trouble for not killing Mia, but you saved her anyway. And I think you pulled your shot when you took on your brother."

He'd shot his own brother. It was so hard to imagine. He stopped at the edge of the park, his head starting to ache. He was glad he'd nabbed Ian's sunglasses before he'd decided to take a break. The sun was bright in the sky, the grass of the park almost too green. "So the place I was at in the dream was real?"

Robert faced him. "Yes. It was real. I was there. Uhm, I might have tried to take your sister-in-law with us, but Moth...Dr. McDonald had other plans. Sorry. Big Tag's taken to hitting me upside the head every time I call her Mother. It's working. He hits hard."

His brother was a giver and it was creepy to think of why Robert would have tried to take Mia with them. "Did you try to keep my sister-in-law as your closet girlfriend?"

If there was one thing he could remember about that time, it was Robert's constant whining about the lack of female company.

Robert flushed a bright red. "I don't know if you've noticed but she's pretty. I guess I'm the kind of guy who needs a woman around. I was probably one of those serial monogamist dudes. I'm not proud of that, but at least I admit it. My fake name is Robert and I would like to be pussy whipped."

Sometimes Robert could be obnoxious. "You need to chill."

Robert's eyes rolled. "Says the man who got to sleep with a girl last night. Look, I might not remember sex, but I'm pretty sure I'm good at it. At least when I think about it, I'm good at it. One of these days I'm going to convince your brother I'm sane enough to play in the club."

Theo looked around. The park was popular with Dallasites, and many young people who worked downtown flocked to enjoy the sunshine and to eat al fresco from the multitude of gourmet food trucks that surrounded the park at lunchtime. More than one woman glanced Robert's way. He was a tall, muscular man with a thick mop of dark hair and a perfectly square jawline. He looked like he should be wearing a cape and saving the world, not whining about his lack of a sex life. "Why don't you ask someone out? The receptionist seems interested. What's her name?"

"Sadie," Robert replied.

She worked part time now that Grace had started working more and more as Sean's business manager. Sean was opening a second restaurant and was now appearing on some national shows. Sadie Jennings was Grace's niece and fresh out of college.

"Ask Sadie out." From what he understood, she didn't have a boyfriend.

He shook his head. "No. I talk about it, but I'm not doing anything outside a club where someone can watch me."

Theo was pretty sure that wasn't about Robert wanting to be an exhibitionist. He shook his head as he started into the park. His stomach was growling and he was supposed to be in a meeting in an hour. "It's funny because you tell me to hop in bed with Erin, but you're scared to do the same."

Robert's face lit up. "No, I'm not. I'll totally hop in bed with Erin. She can handle me. I do something weird and violent and she'll put me on my ass. Hey, we should think about it. You know it works for Jake and Adam."

Theo groaned, but he had to laugh because there was a lot of truth to what he'd said. "Dude, stop thinking about my girl. We are not going to do the threesome thing, but she could handle you. I don't think that anything fazes that woman. I woke up screaming my head off and she hit me with a pillow and told me to stop crying like a girl and go back to sleep. I tried to explain to her that I'd murdered her in my dreams and she snorted and said that was the only place I would ever be doing that. Then she cuddled against me and started snoring again. Is it weird that I think her snoring is kind of soothing?"

It had been heaven and hell. He'd loved holding her. God, when she'd finally cried in his arms, he'd felt like he was doing something for her. He'd felt necessary for once. Being there for her had made him feel worthy.

And then he'd fallen asleep and gone right back to the cold piece of shit the doctor had turned him into. He'd slipped back into that world and hadn't come out until he'd pulled the trigger on the woman he'd been sleeping beside.

She'd acted like it was no big deal and when he'd woken up, he'd found she'd left a note. She'd let him sleep because she'd known he'd been up late and then had what she called a whackadoodle dream, so she'd gone into the office with Li and left her car behind for him. After a super awkward breakfast with Avery, who made incredible pancakes but wasn't sure how to talk to a dude who couldn't remember anything, he'd gone to the office. Erin was still in a meeting and TJ was in daycare, and he was back to wondering why the hell he was here.

"I talked to her last night about moving back into my house," Theo admitted.

Robert slapped him on the back. "That's awesome. I mean it. You should do it today."

"I thought you would be worried."

"Because I've clung to you like a baby duck since we left the creepy medical-induced nest we were in?"

"Yes."

Robert was quiet for a moment, his arms going across his chest. "I have to be on my own sometime. I'm not as broody as you, but I still feel it, too. Hell, in some ways it's worse because I know damn well she broke me. I never fought the way you did."

"How many women did you kill?" It was a game for their "trainer." Tony would bring in a prostitute and then try to force

175

Robert to kill her after he'd spent time with her. Victor would do it in a heartbeat, but Robert would take the beating or whatever punishment.

"You know I didn't, but I thought about it. Especially since I knew Tony would kill her anyway. He snuck one in my bed one night. I woke up next to a dead girl. Sometimes I wish she'd wiped that memory."

He sat down at one of the green tables that dotted the park. Food could wait. He needed to have a talk with Robert. "When was the last time she wiped your memory?"

He sat down across from Theo, his hands knotted on the table in front of him. "It was before you came to us. I remember that day. We had to go to Havana and we were in a hospital. I paid off the administrator so we could use the surgical unit. Look, I hate her, but she was brilliant when it came to surgery. You should have died."

Sometimes he wished he had. "How did she explain my appearance? Was Victor already there?"

"Yes. I'm not honestly sure which of us was first. The drugs make it difficult to remember, but by the time you came along, we were both there and had been for a while."

"Do you ever have any flashes of your previous life?"

Robert's eyes stared through him. "Not anything that resembles memory. It's why I tell you you're stronger, Theo. Victor didn't have flashbacks either. He didn't care. He liked our life. He liked the violence. But you...she loved you."

A chill went down his spine. "It wasn't love."

Robert held out a hand. "I'm sorry. You're right. It was a sick obsession, but you have to understand when I was in therapy every day, it felt like something I should be jealous of."

And yet Robert had shown him nothing but kindness. Sometimes he wondered if he would have survived if Robert hadn't been there. He would sneak to Theo's bedside when he was in the infirmary after Tony's sessions and talk to him. He would tell him to be strong. Not once had he told Theo to forget. "Why didn't you turn me in when you knew I was getting some of my memory back?"

Robert shrugged. "I don't know. I hated the punishment, I guess."

"Or she never really broke you either. Have you considered that? She might have been able to take your memory, but she didn't change the core of who you are. You were my friend in there. When I was in hell, I had you to help me through."

"You were my brother," he said quietly, not looking Theo in the eyes. "I think she didn't know what that would mean to me. She told me I had a brother and I held on to that idea."

"But wasn't Victor your brother?"

His jaw tightened. "Victor was mean. I hated him. I hated you at first, and then you were you and you were my brother. I know now that you're not. Not in a biological sense. You have a bunch of brothers and they're amazing. But I don't remember a time when anyone gave a shit about me the way you did. I knew Mother didn't care. I could look at her and see I was nothing but a pawn."

"Did she ever try anything more with you?" The question made his stomach turn, but he needed to ask it. There was so damn much he didn't know. He needed to. He'd slept beside Erin the night before and the whole time he'd wondered where his body had been. God, he was thinking of his body like it was something that was separate from his soul and could do things he'd never done. It wasn't true. If it happened to his body, it happened to his soul, and that was why he should never have touched Erin.

Robert frowned. "What do you mean?"

He shouldn't have mentioned it. No. No. He fucking needed to know. "She never touched you sexually?"

"Oh," Robert began. "No. Not that I remember. She called me her son. But I always knew you were different for her. I knew she was obsessed with you and not in a good way. She talked about how you were going to be her greatest creation. You would be the one people remembered her for."

His stomach was in knots, but he proceeded anyway. "She would come into my room at night. After lights out."

Robert finally looked him straight on. "I knew that. She trusted me. She didn't lock my door. Sometimes I would sneak out and hear her talking to Tony. You frustrated her. She was so angry because you wouldn't give in to her."

"What does that mean?"

Robert shook his head. "It means you wouldn't do it with her.

She tried and tried and at the end of the day, you can't rape a man who won't get hard. I don't know. Maybe you still can but she didn't get any satisfaction from you. Why do you think she was so rough on you?"

"You don't think I…" He couldn't say it.

Robert shook his head. "No. I don't think you did. I wasn't there, but I don't think so. Why do you think she worked so hard to make sure you couldn't even think Erin's name without hurting? She thought if she could break you of your attachment to Erin, that you would look at her differently. But you never did."

"I didn't even remember Erin existed."

"Your brain might not have, but something inside you did because you wouldn't do her no matter what."

"You weren't there though. You don't know what happened." He could still feel those cold hands on his skin, still feel how his whole body rolled at the thought of what was going to happen next.

"I know you." He stood up. "Look, Theo, I get that you feel like you're out of control and you don't trust anything or anyone around you. I understand that you don't think you can trust me. No one does. They're all waiting for me to turn or go nutso or something. I know I won't. I like it here. I can be patient. I get a feeling and I follow it because I got nothing else, man. Reality might change on a dime because some crazy chick injected me with a drug, but I know some things are real and one of them was you. This place, these people, they're another thing that's real, and I won't let go because it's one fucking good thing and that's all I need. McKay-Taggart and that club are all I need. Maybe I don't have a claim on them, but I'll hold on until I'm forced out. You're already in. Why can't you see how good that is?"

"Because I don't know that I deserve it."

Robert put a hand on his shoulder. "That's not how it works, I think. We get what we get and we choose how we handle it. We let it go or we hold on. We rise or we choose to fall. I don't think you should fall, brother. I'm going to try hard not to, and I will hold on to you as long as I can. I think Erin loves you. I think you have a baby who will love you no matter what, as long as you're there for him. You have a family who fought so hard for you. How can you not try to hold on to them no matter what?"

He wanted to, but things were complex. "And if I hurt them?"

"Trust that you won't. Do everything you can not to." Robert stepped away. "I'm getting something for lunch because I'm not in a bunker, hidden by a crazy doctor. I'm a free man and it's a fucking gorgeous day. You can sit there and be sad or you can be happy that it's sunny and gorgeous and you've got a shot. And there are empanadas. I'm not sure what they are, but I know I'm going to like them."

Robert strode toward the food trucks and Theo watched him walk away.

Why couldn't he be more like Robert? From what he'd learned about the old Theo, he and Robert would have had a lot in common. Case had been the broody twin and Theo the optimistic, sunny one. It had been his role in the family. Now he was the one everyone worried about.

Had she not woken him up this morning because she'd wanted to avoid him? She'd seemed so nonchalant about it in the middle of the night. She hadn't seemed afraid of him, merely a bit annoyed that he'd woken her up. Even then she'd curled up against him, her body giving him warmth. If she'd noticed how stiff he'd been, she hadn't shown it. She'd simply held on to him and drifted back to sleep.

But she'd been gone in the morning. Was she rethinking him moving in? She'd taken TJ with her. Had she realized how dangerous he might be to their kid?

Theo put his head in his hand and groaned. He really was a whiney asshole. He should have walked into her office, ordered her to put that sweet ass over his lap, and given her a nice thirty smacks for leaving their bed without telling him.

They needed rules. She liked rules. God knew he liked it when she broke them and gave him the opportunity for some domestic discipline that would please them both.

He had to be confident with her.

Okay. What would Old Theo do? He likely wouldn't have spent his entire morning avoiding her. He would have walked in and talked to her and let her know he didn't like waking up alone, and from now on there would be punishment when she snuck out on him.

And then he would kiss her and touch her and maybe remind her that he was the one who could make her feel good. Yeah, show her what she got when she let him back into their house.

He stood up. It wouldn't hurt to bring her something. Ice cream was too messy. Maybe a turkey leg. Erin looked like a girl who liked some meat. She would either eat it for lunch or laugh at him and then he could see her smile. Either way he would feel good.

"Hello, brother."

He stopped, his whole body going cold because he didn't recognize that voice. He forced himself to turn and there stood a tall man with broad shoulders and hollow blue eyes. He was dressed all in black, from his T-shirt to his pants to a pair of boots that sparked something in Theo.

"Excuse me." There was some mistake. He didn't know this dude. The boots were familiar, but he didn't have anything for the man wearing them. He looked over and saw Robert standing in line. Two men dressed in black were moving toward him.

They were wearing the same boots.

The same boots Theo had worn when working a job. The same black uniform he'd worn when he'd robbed banks.

He started to back up but strong hands cupped his shoulders and he realized he was trapped.

"Come, brother. It's time to get you home."

* * * *

Erin looked up as Phoebe walked into her office, two familiar cups in her hands.

"One mocha for you and a decaf for me," Phoebe said with a smile as she set the cup down and settled into the seat across from Erin.

Erin closed the folder in front of her, the final report on a corporate case she and Liam had finished up last week. It included all the details of the small ring of spies in the multinational conglomerate and ended with a ridiculously large bill. "You beat me to it. How's your first week back?"

Phoebe Murdoch sat down with a glowing smile on her face. "So good. Don't get me wrong. I loved being home with my baby boy, but I missed this place so much. It's way better than any soap opera. I went down to close cover to ask Fisher about his weird way of reporting hourly payroll. He sent me handwritten notes. Not kidding. One of them was nothing more than *Mr. Harrison wanted late-night sushi*. Two hours. Really? That whole department is a massive mess. Anyway, as I was walking in, some blonde chick slapped the shit out of the new guy and yelled that he better hope she's not pregnant and stormed out. Remy laughed his ass off."

Close cover was McKay-Taggart code for the personal security section of the company. Private bodyguards. In the beginning, the founding members had handled those jobs themselves, but now Big Tag and the others preferred more cerebral jobs to throwing their bodies in front of bullets.

"Please tell me she wasn't a client." Unfortunately, most of the close cover guys were young and unattached. Erin liked to avoid the frat house if she could.

Phoebe sighed. "I didn't even think of that. Big Tag is going to have to get a whole legal team. Between those boys and the fact that Boomer can't text and walk, someone's going to sue us."

Erin shook her head. "Boomer swears he didn't fall into that elevator shaft. He jumped because he heard a kitten crying. Scared the crap out of the marketing unit on fifteen. He climbed back up the shaft with that dumbass cat and crawled over to the air vents. But the dude is so big, the ceiling wouldn't hold him and he dropped right in the middle of their conference table. Now he's got the world's most clueless cat because the damn thing won't leave him alone and they threatened to sue Big Tag. Charlotte fixed it though. We paid for the repairs and Top is catering their weekly lunches for a month."

Charlotte was excellent at cleaning up the messes the boys sometimes made.

"See, I missed that," Phoebe said with a frown. "I love my baby, but I missed the chaos." She sobered a bit. "How are you doing?"

Well, there was some chaos Erin knew about personally. "I think Theo's going to move back in."

Phoebe sat back. "Are you happy about that?"

"Why wouldn't I be?"

Phoebe held a hand out. "I'm not being mean, just cautious. As a woman who is married to a man who goes nuts from time to time and literally tears throats out, I have to worry that Theo's only been home for a few weeks."

Jesse Murdoch had been held and tortured for months. He'd watched his friends die. He'd been a mess when he'd come out. Still, not everyone reacted the same way. "I don't know that Theo ever felt truly alone. He had Robert."

"He's a weird one."

Phoebe had worked for the CIA for a very long time. She'd been so good at her job, she'd managed to fool Big Tag for years. Erin was interested in anything she had to say. "What do you think of Robert?"

"I think he's hiding something, but that doesn't mean he's a bad guy. I do think he knows more than he's been willing to tell us."

She worried about how much hold Robert seemed to have over Theo. "I don't know. I haven't talked to him much, but he seems to handle things better than Theo."

"That's why I think he's hiding something. And the fact that we can't figure out who he is makes me worry. Someone should have been looking for him somewhere. There's always a record. We figured out who Victor was."

The third and most vicious of the men McDonald had kidnapped had been a third-rate thug according to his police records. She'd taken him from a prison in Cambodia where he'd been caught for drug trafficking. As far as she could tell, McDonald had purchased him from corrupt guards. Erin had managed to track the man named Vince Costman back to Omaha and his shitty childhood in and out of juvie.

Robert would be someone Hope would have come in contact with, his name somewhat similar to his real name. She'd come up with nothing so far. No visual recognition software. Nothing on AFIS. Nothing anywhere that she could tell. Robert didn't exist.

And that made her nervous as hell.

"Is there any way he was Agency?" It was the only thing she could think of. He was some kind of spy who'd had his existence erased.

Phoebe's leg bounced, a sure sign she was thinking. "I've

worked every angle I could to try to figure that out. Ten tried as well. I have to believe that if Chelsea couldn't figure it out, he's not one of ours."

Chelsea Weston was Charlotte's sister, and she worked as one of the brains of the Agency. She would tell them if she could. Erin had to think it meant Robert was a serious mystery.

"Keep looking. He can't be no one."

Phoebe nodded. "I will, but you're naïve if you think he can't be no one. When I say he's not one of ours, I only mean he's not an operative the way we would understand. Kayla Summers wouldn't have shown up as one of ours."

Kay had been a double, recruited by Ten Smith to take her twin sister's place as a Chinese operative. She'd recently left the service and come to work for McKay-Taggart London. "But she would have shown up as a missing UCLA student."

Phoebe's left shoulder moved up and down in a negligent shrug. "If the Agency wanted her to. Otherwise, she wouldn't exist. I wonder if he wasn't a deep cover operative. That could explain why we can't find him. Or he worked for a criminal organization that could make him disappear. I know of some who could manage it."

She'd thought of that, too, but she'd never seen Robert in the field. She hadn't been there when the team had taken Theo back. She'd been told Robert allowed himself to be taken fairly easily, but that didn't mean he couldn't fight. It merely meant he was smart enough to know when not to.

"I'll keep looking, but as to your original question, I think it's the chance I have at getting him back. I think Theo needs to be surrounded by us if we're going to have any kind of a chance. I'm hoping sex might work."

Phoebe's lips curved up in a smile. "Well, he is a man."

He was a man who only seemed to be interested in her. It gave her great hope. She'd watched him carefully the night before, and he hadn't had eyes for anyone but her. Not once had he looked at another sub, and there had been so many beautiful ones.

"He seems to want me."

"Of course he does. He always did." Phoebe huffed as though irritated. It was one of the reasons they were friends. Phoebe rarely prevaricated. She let Erin know how she felt. "Are you seriously dipping back into your old insecurities about him? Because he loved you, Erin. He adored you. I watched it happen."

It was hard to think about it sometimes, how well he'd loved her, how much he'd loved her. It was everything she was fighting to get back. He'd worked so hard for her. Didn't she owe him the same?

"I'm trying to be patient. It's why I let him sleep in today. He showed up at Li's last night and asked to sleep with me."

"He wanted to sleep with you after everything you'd been through?"

"He wanted to make sure I was okay. He was a dick at first and then he came through. He held me and let me cry. He felt like Theo again. And then around four in the morning he woke up screaming something about murdering me." She sighed. "It was all super dramatic. He was obviously freaked out so I told him to get his panties out of the wad they were in and go back to sleep."

Phoebe laughed. "That is the most Erin thing I've heard in a long time. You have no idea how happy I am to hear that."

"Do you think that's why Theo's been so distant? Ian and Case do. They think he doesn't recognize me anymore."

"Well, he has the whole memory-wipe thing."

Phoebe could do some of her own damage on the sarcasm scale. Erin rolled her eyes. "Believe me, I know. Do you know the one thing I think he does remember? Taylor Swift. I caught him blasting freaking Taylor Swift two days ago, so his girl-power ballad love is alive and kicking. I thought about smacking him in the face and putting on some Five Finger Death Punch and begging him to act like a man."

She made a face but she'd taken to listening to the singer because Theo had a love for her music Erin didn't understand. Except the time he'd sung to her. Something about belonging with him. He'd taken her teasing and turned it around on her, and she'd found herself under him, holding on while he made love to her.

"Hey, I realized one of the preprogrammed channels in Jesse's truck is the love song station. He tried to convince me that it was the dealership that had programmed it in, but I know a man who listens to Celine Dion when I see him," Phoebe said with a shake of her head. "So you're going to let Theo back in?"

It was everything she wanted. Theo back in her life, back in her bed. "I'm going to take it slow and easy. We'll play at the club and figure out the home situation as we go. I'm not going to smother him the way I did when he first came home. That did not work."

"Jesse told me he seemed like he was trying to distance. I guess I can understand that in a way. It must be weird to walk around and everyone knows who you are but you have no idea. He can't know who he loved or hated, who was kind to him or played him for a fool."

That was her real fear. "I worry he thinks I'm lying to him."

"About your relationship?" Phoebe asked.

Erin shrugged. "He can't remember how we fell in love. He comes home and sees me. I'm older than him, harder. I'm not anyone's idea of the perfect girlfriend. He might think he made a mistake and knocked up someone he never intended to spend his life with."

Phoebe whistled at that statement. "I wouldn't tell Theo that. Not in the club at least. Damn. We need to work on your self-esteem. I know I haven't been here at the office, but I have been at a couple of parties and family gatherings and Theo can't take his eyes off you. When you're not looking, he watches you, and it's not in a 'what the hell was I thinking' way. It's in a 'how do I get my hands on that' way."

Erin felt her mood lift a bit. "Yeah, he got his hands on me last night and it was every bit as good as it ever was." She took a long breath and banished her insecurities. Theo didn't need them. He needed her strength. "So I'm going to give him his space and take what he offers. I'm going to let him get to know TJ and not flip out on him."

Her cell trilled. She glanced down. Unknown number. She thought about ignoring it, but Hutch was still out there. She also had a couple of contacts who might want to stay off the grid.

Phoebe stood up. "Don't let me keep you. Lunch tomorrow?"

Erin nodded. It was good to have Phoebe back. She liked Charlotte and the others, but somehow she'd clicked with Phoebe once the former CIA agent had gotten out of scared-of-her-own-shadow mode. It hadn't hurt that Phoebe had shown up when she'd come back from the Caymans and sat with her, told her how she'd felt when she'd lost her first husband. Phoebe had understood. "Absolutely." She flicked her finger over the screen and touched the speaker option. "This is Erin."

"Hello, Erin. It's been a long time," a smooth voice said.

Phoebe stopped in the doorway, turning around.

Erin frowned. "Who is this?"

"You know who this is. You have something of mine."

Phoebe's eyes went wide and she mouthed, "McDonald?"

Holy shit. Hope McDonald was on the line. That bitch had the nerve to call her? "Dr. McDonald, do you have any idea what I plan to do to you when I find you? And he was always mine."

Phoebe had disappeared down the hall. Likely running for Adam's office. It was a cell so she wasn't sure what Adam could do, but he would try.

"I'm sure you would love that," McDonald said over the line. "Tell me something. Is he all right? How is he handling withdrawing from his regimen?"

"His regimen of drugs and torture?" She was a crazy bitch. The woman sounded almost sincere. "How is he handling no longer being beaten and having his flesh carved like he was a fucking side of beef?"

"That wasn't me," McDonald replied quickly. "That was Tony and I made a huge mistake bringing him in. I met him through my father's connections and he seemed like a reasonable man. I didn't understand what he was doing to my boys until much later. I suppose I should thank you for taking care of Tony for me. I believe he intended to take over my organization once the work was complete. You can't trust anyone these days."

"First World problems, lady. Why are you calling me?"

Adam showed up in the doorway. He stepped inside quietly and looked down at the cell phone.

"Tell Mr. Miles that this is a burner phone and I'll chuck it the minute we hang up. He won't find anything at all."

Erin felt the hairs on her arms stand up. She looked up at Adam. He immediately shut her laptop.

"Well, what fun is that?" McDonald sounded like she was pouting. "I called because I wanted to know if Theo is all right. Is he eating properly? Is he being taken care of?"

"You have no right to ask me anything about him. You did this to him."

"I saved him. He's alive because of me and that's why he belongs to me and always will. All you could do was hold his hand and cry while he died. I brought him back. I did that."

"You're the reason he died in the first place. You and your father. If you're expecting some kind of a thank you note, well, I don't know where to send it. Why don't you give me an address and I'll send you a cookie bouquet." A poisoned, make her wretch and contort before it finally stopped her cold heart cookie bouquet. She was sure one of the Top guys could come up with something. The special ingredient would be arsenic.

"Oh, you and your sarcasm," McDonald shot back. "You know it really is the lowest form of humor, but then you never were the smartest brick in the box, were you? Didn't even go to college if I recall."

Erin couldn't care less about the insults. "Oddly, it didn't hold me back and it won't save you."

"Oh, I think it will. You see, I'm going to get my boy back and there won't be anything you can do about it. I'll prove that you're a slut, too. I doubt that kid is Theo's. He's too smart to end up with a child with you."

"Is that why you sent your man into my house last night?" Erin asked. "You want to run a paternity test?"

"If he is Theo's son, then I'll come back for him. I wouldn't want to separate father and child even if the mother is inadequate. If the boy has Theo's genes, he could be used as a control mechanism. I had thought that having brothers would settle him, but Theo obviously needs more. He needs to feel like he has a family around him. Perhaps his child will work where brothers did not. Especially if he looks like Theo. I think the Taggart genes run true. From what I can tell from the photographs, the boy seems to have avoided that brassy hair of yours. "

Something about the words made Erin pause. What had she said? She would come back for TJ? Not come for him and Theo. Come back for TJ. "What have you done?"

Ian showed up in the doorway, Charlotte right behind him.

There was a smug satisfaction in McDonald's voice as she

spoke. "I told you. I'm getting my boy back. Theo is mine. He belongs with his family and he's coming home today. By tomorrow he won't even remember you exist. If that brat of yours turns out to be his, I'll convince him the baby is ours. It's what I needed, Erin. I needed something to bond us together. Thank you."

"I'm going to rip your heart straight out of your chest and feed it to you." Rage pounded through her, but there was something even more urgent rising in her. Pure fear.

She was here. If not McDonald in actual presence, then her people were here, and there would be only one thing they would want to do.

She hung up. There was no more talking. "Where's Theo? We have to find Theo."

Ian had already turned and was running down the hall. Erin followed.

There was no way she was letting Theo go ever again.

CHAPTER TWELVE

Theo punched out at the first man, panic threatening to take over. His fist connected and pain flared but all he could think about was running. He was surrounded, but that didn't mean a thing if a man was trained.

He kicked back, knowing how they would come at him.

One at his six. His foot connected, sending the man back with an audible *woof.*

One at his nine. He shoved his elbow back, cracking at the asshole's jaw. That hurt, but there was zero time for pain. He'd made a gateway for himself, a path to get the fuck out of here.

He knew the drill. It was a public place. They wouldn't fire weapons here. Couldn't. Mother wouldn't allow it. Civilian deaths equaled scrutiny. All he had to do was get away and everything would be fine. He had to be faster and get back to base. He glanced over and Robert was being led away from the food trucks.

Shit. Robert struggled, but three men surrounded him. The crowd was staring as though sensing something wrong was happening around them.

He needed to run, but he couldn't leave Robert behind. Already Robert was craning his head, looking around, and then he heard it.

"Run, Theo! Run!"

The fact that he hadn't called him back, had ordered him to get the hell out of here, made him stop. He couldn't let them take Robert. Robert needed him.

"Hey, stop fighting, Tomas." The first asshole had recovered and seemed to be the team spokesperson. "There's nothing to fight about. We're here to take you home."

"I am home."

"Mother told us you might think that." He nodded as the rest moved back in behind him. They would try again.

They would fail.

He wasn't being taken back. He wasn't forgetting her again. Never again.

"I'm going to scream if you don't let Robert go." Privacy was tantamount in their world. Never scream. Never let anyone know something was wrong. Keep it in the family no matter what. Those rules had been drilled into him.

Beaten into him was more like it. It was time to break them.

He glanced around, hoping to see some DPD hanging out. They moved through the community, sharing in the afternoons and ready to jump in when they needed to. He didn't see a single familiar uniform.

That didn't mean the police couldn't be there. The men Mother had sent would have to get him to a car and they weren't close to a lot. They would have to get him back to the DMA or perhaps they had valeted at Savor. He wasn't going to go peacefully, so good luck to them. Someone would call the police.

Up ahead of him Robert threw a punch and lurched to get out of the tight circle they had him in.

Four and three. Seven other "brothers." Doctor McDonald had fucked up seven other men's lives. They weren't the enemy. She was. He couldn't kill any of these men. They had families, lives they could go back to. Some of them probably had children.

Like him.

The dark-haired man in front of him nodded toward his right hand. "I won't leave you out here, brother. We're all dedicated to bringing you and Robert home."

There was a hypodermic needle in his hand.

So that was their game.

He wasn't going down. "Come near me and I will end you. She's lying to you. She's a psychopath who's taken your memories and your lives."

"She told us you've been compromised," the one to his right said. "You need to come home so you can see the truth."

Robert was struggling. Were they dosing him up right now?

It was time to get this shit done. He kicked out again, catching the dude with the needle in the gut. They were hesitant and that could be his saving grace.

Had she told them not to hurt him?

He was her golden boy, after all. He was the one she wanted above all others, the one she touched at night, trying to find a connection with.

He ran for Robert. "Call the police!"

Chaos. He needed some chaos. Texans were damn good at putting their noses into violent situations they probably would be better off ignoring. And someone would be packing.

He heard cursing behind him.

"FBI! Take cover!"

So they had come in with a plan. Smart. He had to assume they would have something that looked like proper ID. Still, someone would call the police. They had little time to bring him and Robert in.

He watched as Robert was surrounded and he lost visual.

Fuck. He couldn't leave Robert behind, couldn't allow him to be taken again, but he had to think about her. Erin. He had to think about Erin and their boy.

Suddenly the group around Robert exploded out, like he was some real version of the Hulk. Robert was on his feet, his body moving with a grace Theo hadn't seen before. He took out the man closest to him before pivoting and striking the one at his back.

Robert ran toward him and Theo realized they had a shot.

"Everyone down! Federal Bureau of Investigation!" a masculine voice called out behind him.

All around him, people in business suits and dressed for jogging hit the ground, leaving Theo and Robert vulnerable and on the run.

"What the hell?" Robert caught up to him and they started to run toward the other side of the park. They had a shot if they could get through the park and across to the museum. The street was packed with fast-moving traffic.

All he needed was to get lost in the hectic downtown bustle. The Nasher Sculpture Center was across the road and then he could lose himself in the museum district and its never-ending rounds of tourists. He could circle back to the McKay-Taggart building and figure out what the hell was going on.

If he could just keep moving.

He glanced back and McDonald's men had efficiently taken care of the crowd. They were all down, hands covering their heads in a way they wouldn't have been without the authoritative presence.

He caught a glint of metal and then felt something zing by his shoulder. Shit. "They've got guns."

"Probably tranqs," Robert replied, not showing a single sign that sprinting was causing him strain.

They raced down the tree-lined walking path, Theo taking one side and Robert the other. Robert leapt over a green bistro chair that someone had abandoned in their determination to get out of the line of fire. The green tables dotted the park.

Theo turned one over on his way toward the outer edge of the park, hoping the other guys weren't as good a hurdler as Robert.

Up ahead he saw Robert fumble and hit his knees.

There was a dart sticking out of his shoulder. Shit. Theo rushed to him, pulling the dart from his shoulder and tossing it aside.

It didn't matter. It was already doing its work. Robert's eyes were going glassy. "Go. Leave me. You can find me later."

When his memory would be wiped again? When McDonald got her talons back in and tried to remake him into something he wasn't?

He hauled Robert up. They had to make it to the street. If they could make it across, they had a shot.

In the distance, he heard the sound of sirens.

Thank god.

That was when he felt it. His left side flared with pain and then an immediate numbness set in. Theo pulled the dart out.

Had to keep going. He wasn't letting them take him without a damn fight.

But then he'd fought so hard the first time and it hadn't mattered. He'd fought McDonald. He'd fought his own weakness. He'd fought to remember her. He'd sat in bed every night staring at the white walls, telling himself to remember Erin.

And he'd forgotten her. He'd forgotten them all.

He couldn't forget her again.

Adrenaline rushed through his system and he forced himself to move, dragging Robert beside him. Water. There was a fountain up ahead and misters where kids and dogs played during the long summer heat waves. The water could wake him up.

He felt another dart hit him, this time in the leg. He was getting nauseous and the world was starting to spin. His vision was clouding, but he kept moving.

"Brother, there's no reason for this. We're taking you home. You'll feel better once you're home. Mother is so worried about you." A hand on his shoulder pulled Theo back.

He went down on one knee, pain shocking through his system as he came in contact with the concrete. He heard a thud as he lost hold of Robert.

They were both down. Theo tried to turn, tried to punch out. He couldn't control his arms. The world was getting dark.

"Don't worry, brother. We're going to get your son," the man standing over him said with a beneficent smile. "You're the first of us to have a child. We wouldn't leave him behind. Sleep well. When you wake up…"

"If you lay a hand on him, I will pull this trigger right here and right now. Don't think I won't. I would love to blow your brains out, scoop them off this sidewalk, and mail them to that crazy bitch you call Mother," a heavenly voice said.

He looked up and Erin had a gun at the back of his would-be captor's head. Her hair had come loose, like a curly red halo around her head. She was the prettiest thing when she was threatening to kill someone.

His avenging, foul-mouthed angel.

"Try to remember he's not the real enemy, Erin," Ian said.

"The cops are coming." Adam ran up behind them. "Time to lay down weapons and get our hands in the air. I already asked Alex to call Brighton to back us up."

He watched as Erin cursed and laid down her weapon. The two "brothers" they'd caught took off running, the police in hot pursuit, while Erin knelt beside him, her hands up in the air.

He managed just enough movement to get his hand on her and then he let go.

She was here and he could rest.

* * * *

"What do you mean they're both dead?" Erin felt her heart squeeze as she looked up at Lieutenant Derek Brighton. Theo lay in a hospital bed, an IV in his arm and a monitor on his heart because they'd pumped him so full of drugs the doc was worried.

She'd received a pat down from an officer who likely would enjoy a couple of nights topping subs at Sanctum as a Domme and a trip downtown in a police car that could have used some scrubbing. Naturally she'd gotten shoved in with Adam the germaphobe, who complained mightly about everything from the smell to the stickiness of the seat he was in to how tight his handcuffs were. Sometimes she understood why Ian randomly slapped him upside the head.

It had been three hours before she'd gotten here and found out how Theo was doing. She wasn't in the mood for shitty news.

Brighton frowned as he looked from Theo back to her. "I'm sorry, Erin. There wasn't anything we could do. We chased them to the edge of the park. They ran out into the street and when they got to the railing, they jumped onto the freeway."

"Suicide?" Ian asked, his arms crossing.

"It was definitely a deliberate act. You can't fall off into the freeway," Brighton explained. "They ignored the officers orders and ran straight for the railing. They climbed and jumped without hesitation."

"As though they were programmed to do it," Ian said with a shake of his head. "Well, we know how she manages to not get her boys caught."

"They kill themselves if they're on the verge." It made Erin's stomach churn for the fiftieth time that day.

"It has to be something new because we didn't run up against it at all when we found Theo's group in Africa. Trust me Victor wasn't trying to take himself out." Case stood up from his seat by Theo's bed. He'd been the one to come to the hospital and watch over him while Erin and Ian had been explaining themselves. Luckily a quick call from Ezra Fain's boss had allowed Brighton to get them out of interrogation and released without further issue. DPD had given the whole case up to the feds who would deal with everything quietly.

Though there would definitely be some news made about what had happened in the park today. She prayed no one caught her face on cell phone footage.

What a clusterfuck.

And what a near miss. That man had his hands on Theo, ready to drag him back into hell.

If she'd been two minutes later… If Ian hadn't known where Theo had been going for lunch…

The horrors of those possibilities would haunt her.

"I would tell you that I'll get you the results of the autopsies, but oddly enough the government has already moved the bodies. Not oddly. I should have known the Agency would work quickly." Brighton looked over at Theo, his face softening. "I'm more surprised that they didn't take him when they could have."

Ian's jaw tightened. "We cooperated. Theo and Robert both gave blood samples and spoke to analysts. We'll give them updates."

They'd done all of those things, but something about the way Ian's voice had deepened made her wonder if he wasn't lying. Or at least hiding something. Had he given something up so his baby brother wouldn't get taken in by the Agency? How much did she owe Big Tag?

"How are they?" Brighton asked, looking between the two beds.

"Theo took two doses," Erin explained. "Robert took one. According to the docs it was a strong sedative. They're not worried about Robert. He's sleeping it off. He can leave when he wakes up. They want Theo to stay overnight."

"So she's coming after him again." Brighton stepped up. "Erin, you have to know the DPD will do anything you need us to. I gave the chief a briefing and he's spoken with the Agency. I know you've got bodyguards, but if you need us, we'll watch the house or put him in protective custody if we have to."

Theo would hate that. "I think we should handle this in-house, Derek, but I can't tell you how much I appreciate the offer."

Brighton nodded and took a step back. "It's an open offer. Let me know if you need anything else, and please text me to let me know Baby Tag's okay."

Erin couldn't help but smile at that. "He insists that Baby Tag is TJ. I think we should call him Forgetful Tag from now on. They're like the dwarves. I expect to find a set of triplets out there any day now."

"God, don't even joke about that," Ian said. "My father was a bastard, but he had sperm that worked overtime."

Brighton smiled and gave them a wave. "All right then. I'm off. You take care."

The minute the door closed Ian sighed. "A DPD tail is only going to work for so long, and you can't live the rest of your life with a bodyguard."

Case stood up, his hands on his hips. "Have we considered hiring a professional? I'm not kidding. I'm saying we find the bitch and we pay someone to take her out."

"Are you offering to hire an assassin?" Ian asked.

It wasn't necessarily a bad idea. "Charlotte's cousin knows people. I can be on a plane to Saint Petersburg tomorrow morning."

Ian held out a hand. "I'm not being a priss. If I thought it would work, I would call Dusan myself in a heartbeat. I've done wet work myself. I'm old now. I can hire that shit out, but I'm worried that even if we take out McDonald, it won't end."

"She's the one with the obsession with Theo," Erin argued. "Even if they bring someone in to complete her work, why would that person come after Theo? He's a hard target."

"He's also the only man so far who's actively fought the drug," Ian replied. "They will want him and not only his records. They'll want the anomaly so they can perfect the treatment."

Case groaned. "What the fuck are we going to do? We don't even know where she is right now. I doubt she's here in Dallas, but she'll send men in after him."

"And my son." It was horrifying. They would come after her

baby, and he couldn't fight the way Theo could. "She's interested in having a real hold over Theo, and his son is perfect leverage in her sick brain."

Case's hands fisted at his sides. "I can't believe she called you like that. Why would she do that? Why would she tip you off? Not that I'm complaining, but it's why we got to save him."

"She hates Erin," a weak voice said.

Erin turned and Robert was trying to keep his eyes open. "Hey, are you all right?"

"Only because Theo is a dumb fucker." Robert's face twisted with emotion. "He wouldn't leave me. Damn it. He should have left me."

She wanted to agree, but then he wouldn't be Theo. Theo gave a damn about this man and she needed to get on board. When she thought about it, Robert had no one. He didn't remember who he was, what he'd done, where he'd grown up. No one. She'd felt alone before.

Erin moved to Robert's bed. He had no family but Theo. Theo was hers, so that kind of made Robert hers, too. Was this how Tag felt whenever he took in another stray? She put a hand on Robert's. "He couldn't leave you. That's who Theo is."

Robert's eyes opened, red showing. "I would do anything for him. You have to know that. I would die for that man. And I'm going to tell you that she hates you. You can use that against her. It's her weakness. She needs to win at all costs. You think she loves Theo, but the truth is Theo is incidental. He's the prize. You're the competitor."

"Why? I barely knew the woman."

"But Faith loved you. Her sister thought you were the most amazing woman. You had everything she thought she wanted. You were strong and Faith looked up to you in a way she never did with McDonald. You understood Faith. Hope didn't approve of her sister's lifestyle. You brought her further into it. You had the man she thought she deserved. And she knows you killed her father. She hates you."

"The feeling is entirely mutual," Erin murmured. It was interesting information. She'd always thought she was an afterthought in this little war she found herself in. But if she had power, she would use it. It was a tool. She would think about how to make it work for them. "How are you feeling?"

"Like someone hit me over the head." He groaned, but his hand tightened around hers as if he desperately needed the contact. "I heard something before I went out. Theo dragged me along and when he finally went down, the man who followed us said he was coming after the baby. He said he wouldn't leave without your son."

Yep. There was that familiar nausea. "She said something similar, though she told me she was going to wait until she could prove the baby was actually Theo's."

Robert sat back, obviously exhausted. "She knows. That's all about insulting you." He sniffled, emotion clear on his face. "I can't believe how many of them there were. Did the police catch them? Can we talk to them? I might be able to talk them down."

"I'm sorry, Robert." She hated being the bearer of bad news.

Robert's eyes closed, but not before she saw the pain there. "Did they force the police to kill them or did they do it themselves?"

"They jumped onto the freeway. Cars did the rest." Ian joined her at Robert's side. "Did she train you to kill yourself rather than be taken in?"

"No, that wasn't our highest directive," Robert said, his voice hoarse. "We had a different motivation."

Erin could guess. "To save Theo."

Robert nodded. "We were never to leave Theo behind. He was the most important among us. We were never to allow anyone to take him. It's why Victor fought so hard."

"But you didn't." Case glanced over. "I was there. You tried hard not to hit anyone, and most of the time you kept your head down."

Robert's lips curled slightly. "I knew who you were. I figured out why you were there. I worked hard to seem completely obedient because I knew she would spend less time on me if she thought I was broken. It got easier after Hutch showed up because she was interested in seeing if she could turn him without the drugs. By that point I'd gone a whole month without a booster. I took the daily meds, but she seemed to need to give us boosted doses every couple of weeks or we started to slide. She could be forgetful when she started in on a project, and she didn't like bringing new people in.

She was paranoid. At that point her main assistant had run away and she was counting on Tony to remember the majority of the extra duties. He couldn't give a crap about routines, so I got through."

"How did that make you feel? Did you remember anything at all?" Robert seemed to process the drug differently than Theo did, but any information was good information.

Robert's head rolled back on the pillow as though he was too tired to hold it up any longer. "Sometimes I get flashes. I don't understand them though. I see a woman but it's like I'm small because she bends over to touch me. Sometimes I remember what it feels like to stand on a mountain road and breathe the air in and know I'm okay now. And sometimes I know I've done bad things. Dark things. And it could all be bullshit. What I do know is when the main drug cleared my system, I wasn't so ready to obey anymore. So when that shit went down in Africa, I knew I would do anything to get out. I hoped you wouldn't kill me, but getting away from her was worth the risk."

"I'm glad Tag here didn't kill you," Erin said with a smile she hoped was encouraging.

"It wasn't like I was looking to kill the other victims," Ian huffed with a roll of his icy eyes.

"Killing Tony was fun." Case sat back down near Theo.

"Yeah, I wish I'd been in on that one. Vic wasn't exactly an awesome dude either." Robert looked up at Erin. "I'm afraid she's going to come after you."

"Bring it on." She would love to get this over and done. "Somehow I think I can take her down if I can get in the same room with her."

"She won't play fair," Robert warned. "And I don't think she'll come after you physically. She knows how strong you are."

Erin knew she was dreaming if she thought that woman would come after her like an honorable opponent. "She's going to come after my son. She'll go after Theo. You remember what that man said to him?"

Robert nodded. "He said they wouldn't leave TJ behind."

She looked over at Theo's brothers. "Is there any shot he won't remember?"

"He did get two full doses," Case pointed out.

"And kept on moving." Ian put a hand on Theo's arm. "That was something. Still, he could have short-term memory loss from the drugs. We won't know until he wakes up."

"I'll have to tell him." Robert sounded apologetic, but sure. "I can't keep it from him."

Ian shrugged. "I could smother you with a pillow, but I want to know why Erin doesn't think Theo should know there's a threat to his son."

"Good. I would hate to have survived everything only to be taken down by a pillow," Robert replied. "And I think I know why. She knows Theo's going to flip his shit and want to distance himself from her, but he'll do that anyway. What happened out there today freaked me out, too. I thought she would stay away. The first time she took Theo, she knew no one would look for him. Everyone thought he was dead. It was easy. This time she would be courting war with McKay-Taggart."

"Oh, she's declared it." Ian's eyes had hardened. "We're definitely at war. She walked in to my town and tried to take my family. There's no turning back now. I wasn't planning on letting her go free, but she's upped my timetable."

"I'm with Robert," Case added. "I can't imagine how she thinks she can win this one. We won't ever let her take him and god, she thinks we'll allow her to kidnap my nephew? She's high."

Oh, but she wasn't. "She's drunk on power and feeling good about her position again. I find it interesting that she has a high-powered meeting with a Collective conglomerate and suddenly we're dealing with her boys."

Ian pointed her way. "Exactly. She's cut a deal and is feeling protected."

"Which means we have to cut her off from her resources and take her out," Case concluded.

"And make sure the company doesn't continue her work, right?" Robert had managed to sit up, his legs dangling off the bed. "That drug is dangerous. It's ruined so many lives. I know you want to get McDonald, but we have to save the others, too. We have to save an entire generation of people she could use that drug on."

Ian put a hand on his shoulder. "I promise you, I will not forget them. Whatever happens, we'll remember those men and we'll take care of them. And I vow I'll do everything I possibly can to end this, the entire thing."

Case stood by his brother. "I promise you, too. I won't let this go undone."

Robert seemed to release a deep breath. "Thank you. I know you don't trust me yet, but I want to help. Anything you need. I won't complain when you hand me the grunt work. I mean it. Anything."

She believed him, but she was fairly certain he wouldn't be hanging around here. "And when Theo asks you to run with him? Because there's zero chance he heard that threat against his son and doesn't take off to try to put some distance between us and her. Oh, he'll make a plan with Ian, Sean, and Case to put me and TJ in a box somewhere, but then he'll attempt to martyr himself and I can't let that happen."

"Erin, you know we're going to have to figure out a plan to protect you and TJ," Ian said, his hands coming to his hips.

"You can't stay at your house," Case agreed.

God save her from overprotective men.

She held up her hands, knowing when she couldn't win. "I get that, but I have a plan and it's a plan that won't separate us, but might put us in a position to protect our son and find that crazy bitch."

Ian's eyes narrowed. "I'm listening."

"Let's go and grab whatever they'll call dinner here," she began. "I want Robert to be able to honestly say he knows nothing."

Robert gave her a smile. "My lips are sealed, but it's probably best I don't know anything. I've been told I talk in my sleep."

She didn't even want to know. Erin looked down at her own sleeping beauty and vowed to do whatever she needed to keep them together.

No matter what.

CHAPTER THIRTEEN

Theo sat back in the black car that had come to pick them up and yawned. A solid week had passed since that horrible day he'd realized nothing was over. He was still having nightmares about the doctor getting her hands on his son.

A week since Erin and TJ had been sent into hiding without so much as a kiss good-bye. He could still see her standing there, asking him to come with her, to keep them together.

All of his memories had to do with disappointing her.

"I'll have you to The Garden in no time a'tall." Owen slid behind the wheel and relaxed back. "Well, as fast as London traffic will allow. You see, this is one of the many ways my native country of Scotland is better than this pale land. Not as much traffic. God knew that if he made too many Scots the world wouldn't be able to handle it."

Nick groaned from the seat beside Owen. "Stop. No one wants to hear about your Scottish pride. I understand there are more sheep than people in the upper lands."

"Highlands," Owen quickly corrected. "It's the Highlands, you Russian barbarian."

"Yes, well, I'm fairly certain all Scots descend from Russian explorers." Nick clicked his seatbelt on. "It is little known fact that all of Europe was first explored by Russians. We were exploring when your people were still worshipping trees."

"Little known because it's a complete bloody lie," Owen said under his breath.

Robert leaned over. "They're insane."

He couldn't argue with that. The London office of McKay-Taggart was run by a man named Damon Knight, and he'd put together a multinational team Ian liked to call the Mutts of Europe.

"They're good at their jobs," he whispered back. "And The Garden is extremely well protected. We should be safe there."

Robert frowned. "I'm not worried about safe for me. I'm worried about Erin. Do you even know where she is?"

Theo felt his whole body stiffen. After twenty-four hours on three different planes, the fact that he could get more uncomfortable was saying something. "It's better I don't know."

It was the plan he'd worked out with Ian shortly after he'd woken up in the hospital that terrible day when he'd learned the danger he was to Erin and their son.

She would never forgive him if he cost her their son. Never. He wouldn't forgive himself.

It was better this way, but still, not knowing where she was made him ache inside.

They'd been so close to starting over again and he had to wonder if she would give him another chance. Hell, he didn't even know how long it would be before he could see her again. She could settle down and figure out how much trouble he was. If he took too long, she could meet someone new. How would he handle it if he went through everything and then came back to get his family and there was another man in his place?

He should picture it, prepare himself for being magnanimous. After all, it wasn't like he remembered their past together. She could move forward and have a nice, normal life with a man who never attacked her because he had visions of killing her. She could be with someone she could trust. Someone who could open his whole heart to her and TJ.

Or he could quietly assassinate the fucker and slip back into his own bed.

Yeah, he was going to have trouble if that scenario played itself out.

"Your partner is very stupid man," Nick said, his Russian accent deepening. Theo had noticed when Nick wasn't trying to sound more American, he tended to drop articles. When Nick was angry, his accent went thick and deep.

Well, he'd known the man didn't like him. "Thanks a lot. Your opinion is noted."

Owen turned toward London from the small private airport that had been their final destination. They'd taken two commercial airliners, and then a private jet provided by a friend of Drew Lawless had taken them from Chicago to London. The paper trail would lead anyone looking to a car rental at O'Hare and a hotel off the Miracle Mile.

"Why is the baby Taggart stupid?" the big red-haired Scot asked. "That's not what I'd heard. Kay likes all the Tags. She says they're awesome."

Nick snorted a little. "Kay thinks everyone is awesome. She's far too positive to be in this business. And Kay's sister apparently slept with at least one of them." He sobered a bit. "I call him stupid because he leaves his woman behind. He leaves child behind. They are in danger and all alone because he's too stubborn to hold them close to his heart."

"My heart is the fucking target." He was guilty of many things, but not giving a shit wasn't one of them. The fact that she wasn't with him was a genuine ache in his gut. "I'm not going to use my wife and child as a shield."

Robert's right eyebrow rose over his eye.

Theo waved him off. "You know what I mean."

Robert shrugged. "Never heard you refer to her that way."

Theo stared out the window at the ridiculously green countryside. "She's not legally, but I know what the old me wanted. I bought her a ring. I was going to ask her."

"Or you bought ring and chickened out," Nick said.

"I know what I would have done." He wasn't going to discuss this with a man who hated him.

Nick sighed and sat back. "I'm sorry. I'm being an ass. You're right. You were going to ask her while we were on the island. You told me this. I felt bad because Desiree wasn't ready to marry. I was jealous of you. I knew Erin would agree. You planned to ask her after we were through with the mission. You had even picked out a place to do it."

"Are you fucking with me?" He wanted to believe it was true.

Nick didn't look back, but his voice had gone low. "I do not fuck with you. There was a restaurant at the resort Brody and I worked at and you were planning to ask her there. You had a reservation. Things did not go as you planned, but that does not mean they must be through."

"They're after me, Nick. They won't stop until we stop them."

Nick shrugged. "Yes, the operative word there is *we*. Your *we* should include her. She is much smarter than you. You need her."

Again, nothing he didn't know. "I'm not putting TJ in the line of fire and that means not putting Erin there either. She can't leave her son."

"Don't you mean *our* son? You act like you had nothing to do with the boy's conception. Wasn't that one night the only time you've held the child? I've held him more often than you," Nick said dismissively.

"Good for fucking you." He was just about done with the Russian. "I hope the two of you will be very happy together."

Nick shrugged as though he couldn't care less what Theo thought of him and went back to watching the road. They were in London proper now, leaving behind the vibrant green fields of the surrounding countryside.

Had he ever been here before? He'd forgotten to ask. Things had been so hectic that he'd done nothing but study Nick's case files on McDonald, work with Adam trying to trace the call to Erin and the hack to Erin's computer, and sit up at night worried sick that she wouldn't ever forgive him.

"I think what Nick here was trying to say got lost in translation." Owen's light brogue filled the car. "You see, Russians speak arsehole most of the time and it's hard for him to tread lightly."

"I say what I meant." Nick was unrelenting. "He is coward."

"Hey," Robert began, "you have any idea what it means to have your whole fucking life blinked out of existence, asshole? Any conception what it means to wake up and not know who the fuck you are? Because if you don't, maybe you should recuse yourself from commenting."

Nick looked back at Robert. "Interesting turn of phrase, counselor."

"Yes, it is," Owen agreed. "You were right. You can tell an awful lot by getting him wound up and talking."

"What?" Robert was looking between the two men.

They were assholes, but they had a point. "You used the word *recuse*. It's a specific term that not many people outside the legal profession or politics would use. You were likely highly educated, though I'd already figured that out."

"He's got a mathematical brain," Nick commented. "He could be self-trained, but I doubt it. And no, I don't know what it's like to have been through what you've been through. I do know what it's like to lose woman I love. I know what it means to be Erin and you've hurt her terribly by leaving her behind. You've shown her she's nothing but piece of property to be put in safe and guarded. She's not a partner. That is how I would be feeling."

"That's not how it is." He felt his fists clench at his sides. It wasn't what he meant at all. "I care about her and TJ. I can't have them in the line of fire. How am I the bad guy here?"

"You're not," Robert assured him. He put a hand to his head, a sure sign that he was hurting. The information Nick had given him was probably causing him to think about things he shouldn't. "You're trying to take care of her."

At least he had one friend in the world. Even Ian had tried to talk him out of what he knew was the only right path. Case and Sean had told him he was a dipshit. Awesome. "I am trying to ensure she's not a casualty of my problems."

Nick looked at Owen, nodding his head in a knowing fashion. "See what I mean?"

"Aye. I understand that he's got memory problems but it appears he's got some judgment trouble as well if he thinks that woman is soft," Owen replied.

"I didn't say she was soft." How far was it to The Garden? He hoped it wasn't some actual garden. Ian had said it was the most fortified place he could think of, but Theo wasn't sure how plants and butterflies and crap would protect him and allow him to work in peace.

But she was soft. She could be. She could be so fucking soft.

"She's a warrior." Nick turned to stare out the passenger window to his left. "If this were happening to O'Donnell or Miles and Dean, I would agree with the plan. Their women are strong, but they're not trained. Can you imagine what Charlotte would do if Ian suggested she hide away for months, possibly years?"

"She would need to protect her children." He wasn't wrong about this.

"Scottish women can protect their children, do their jobs, cook a meal, and still make a man feel like a man at the end of the day," Owen piped up. "Perhaps you should find a Scottish lass."

He ignored Owen completely. "Charlotte would understand that Ian needs to keep a clear head and know his children are safe."

"Have you watched Big Tag around Charlotte?" Nick scoffed. "That man talks good game, as you Americans would say, but he knows the score. Doctor wins if she breaks up family. It's what she wants."

"She wants me," Theo argued.

"And to hurt Erin. There's no doubt in my mind she's thrilled that you're not with her," Robert said.

Robert had explained his theories of McDonald's motivations. Theo wasn't sure he bought the idea that he was the prize two alpha females were fighting over, but it didn't matter. He wasn't putting the female he actually gave a damn about in danger.

"You think she's got eyes on you?" Owen stopped at a light, his gaze searching the streets before the light went to yellow and then green.

Nick fiddled with his phone, not looking back as he spoke. "You'll have to forgive him. He took a week off to gather new venereal diseases. He's not up on the recent intelligence. McDonald's been watching Argent for weeks. From what Adam can tell, it started a few days after young Taggart was rescued."

"She hacked Erin's system." How much had she seen?

"I didn't think McDonald was particularly adept with a computer system, and I can't help it that all the lovelies want a piece of me. It's that show." Owen winked in the mirror. "All I have to do

207

to get an American girl to hop on me is call her *sassenach*. There was a pretty redhead named Angel at a club in LA. Worked like a charm on her."

Nick sighed heavily but seemed ready to soldier on. "McDonald's not adept with computers. It's why she took Hutchins in the first place. She needed someone who could get her into systems. Which makes me wonder how she's doing it now."

"She's got backing again." Theo would love to know how she'd gotten in good with The Collective again. "They're the ones providing her with what she needs. Cash, research materials, and apparently hackers."

Nick shook his head. "This began before the meetings with the new firm. I have a theory but you won't like it. Big Tag tells me not to even talk about it, but he is wrong."

Theo hadn't heard anything about a theory.

Robert sat up. "I think you should listen to Ian."

Nick turned, his face fierce in the last light of day. "No. I don't listen to Putin when he tells me to shut up, either. Adam said it himself. No one but an insider could have busted through his firewalls."

What the hell was he trying to say? "You think someone we know is helping her?"

"I think Hutchins is helping her." The words dropped from the Russian's mouth like a bomb waiting to explode.

"He is not." Theo bit the reply through clenched teeth. Hutch was his friend. Hutch had been there. "He would never help that bitch."

"I'm sure he left protocols for her to follow when we got rescued. He wouldn't have thought to destroy them," Robert said quickly, as though he could find a way to defuse the situation if he talked fast enough. "It's why he was there. He was supposed to teach one of us how to do what he does, but Theo kept forgetting and Victor would rather punch the computer than use it. I spent the most time with him. He wouldn't help her."

"Yes, this is what Big Tag says, too." Nick crossed his arms over his chest as he slumped against the door to his left. "No man of his ever goes bad. No one he trained himself could ever have his brain washed. No one of his employee could be bought. But Hutch is the one who ran and two days later a woman who couldn't hack a system to save her life begins watching her greatest enemy through a system that should be safe from everyone."

Owen whistled. "Damn me, but the Russian has a point. Put like that it doesn't look good. And the boy hasn't called anyone?"

They were wrong. They had to be. "He's having trouble with the fact that he was taken by a crazy lady and tortured. He needs time and space. He wouldn't do this and no amount of money would make Greg Hutchins betray his team."

"Of course," Nick said dismissively. "You would know better than I."

Nick and Owen exchanged a look that told Theo they wouldn't let this go easily.

"He's out there and he's looking for her," Theo insisted. Nothing else would make sense.

The car made one last turn as silence fell. Up ahead, Theo could see a door opening.

It looked like they'd arrived.

Twenty minutes and three layers of security later, Theo held his hand out as Damon Knight entered the room. The big Brit was wearing a T-shirt over a pair of leather pants, his dark hair slicked back.

"Damon, thanks for having us." He'd been told he'd met the man in front of him many times. He went over everything he knew in his head. Knight had been a commando, winning the Victoria Cross at one point. He'd joined MI6 until a heart condition had sidelined him. His wife was named Penelope and they had a son who was slightly older than TJ.

Where was his son now? Was he cuddled against his mother being rocked to sleep? Was she thinking about how angry she was with his father?

Knight shook his hand and nodded toward the elevator doors. "Not a problem, Taggart. You're more than welcome. I would give you a full tour, but The Garden is open this evening and I have to get back. Nick can show you to your room. We have to go through the dungeon to get to the lifts that take you to the residential part of the building. The only access points are here in the garage and the street level door. Both have guards twenty-four seven. They will ask to see your identification even if they've seen you walk in the building every day for ten years. I still show ID when I enter so if I hear you complaining, there'll be a nice thrashing for you. I run a tight ship."

"That's why we're here." Theo followed him into the elevator. The garage was utilitarian, but the elevator was anything but. It was lush and elegant, with shiny gold fixtures like something out of an old Hollywood movie.

"Can I ask what's the point of the guards checking ID on people they know?" Robert stepped into the big elevator beside him.

It easily held all five large men. Unlike that tiny lift in the hotel in Frankfurt. He and Erin had barely fit, their bodies pressing against each other. Her breasts had brushed against his chest and he could feel her nipples tightening. He'd known in that moment that he would have her and damn soon.

Another memory. They'd started coming more often in the last few days. He'd recalled the day his father had walked out and had a vision of his mother crying while Case had stood stoically beside her. He'd had a flash of looking back at the trailer they'd grown up in and knowing he wasn't ever coming back.

Mostly though he had visions of her. Always her. Erin was going to be the ghost who haunted him the rest of his days.

"If you're being watched or forced to do something, you show your ID and ask the question 'how are your kids today,'" Knight explained. "It's another layer of protection. If you ask the question, an alert will go out to everyone and we'll quietly figure out what's happening."

"It's a normal question to ask," Owen continued. "One that won't raise eyebrows, and we deal with things quietly so we don't tip anyone off. One of the easiest ways to hurt an operative is to take a loved one and force the operative to do the kidnapper's bidding. We've got protocols for almost everything. Except the zombie apocalypse and I think that's an oversight."

Knight groaned as the elevator doors opened again. "The only protocol I'll need is for someone to shoot me. I don't want to live in such unsanitary conditions. Nick, if you'll show our guests to their room. Normally you wouldn't be allowed to walk across the dungeon floor in street clothes, but I have to make an exception tonight. You're going to share a room on the fifth floor. We have another refugee we're protecting, so I'm short on guest rooms. My whole team lives in the building. I had the fourth and fifth floors redone as flats. I'm on the sixth and the lower floors are our offices. Obviously the ground floor is The Garden. You have the same rights at The Garden as you've been given at Sanctum. Robert, stay with someone who has Master rights when you're in the dungeon. You can take classes while you're here. I left a schedule in your room."

Robert's eyes were wide as he stepped out into the dungeon.

Dungeon was an odd word. Its name was much better. Garden. The whole center of the building was hollowed out, the floors above overlooking the magnificent courtyard. Night blooming flowers scented the air and the walls were covered in deep green ivy and winding plants.

Industrial music thudded softly through the building, and when he looked up he could see the sky.

"This place is incredible," Robert said, obviously in awe.

"We like it." A petite woman strode forward wearing a lovely blue corset and a teeny-tiny skirt. No shoes. Submissive. Curly blonde hair brushed her shoulders, and she had the sweetest smile for Knight. "Hello, Master. I missed you."

He grinned down at her. "I was only gone for a moment, love, but I missed you, too. Is our wild thing down for the night?"

"He's sleeping peacefully and Clarissa is watching over the children tonight. Her Dom is out of town so she doesn't mind playing nanny this weekend." Penelope Knight barely reached her husband's shoulders, but it didn't matter. He leaned over to kiss her.

"Then let's play, love. It's been so long." His hands went to her face, cupping her cheeks before he kissed her again. He pulled his shirt over his head and looked back at Theo. "If you need anything...don't bloody need anything until tomorrow."

So the man was planning on getting some. Awesome. The party would be going on down here and he would be up in a tiny apartment with Robert. Exactly where he'd been before. Hiding. Away from her. Essentially alone.

He glanced out over the dungeon. There was a bar to his right.

That would be where all his free time was spent. Yeah for him.

"Come along, Taggart." Nick nodded toward another elevator across the dungeon floor. "Tomorrow morning we have a meeting scheduled. We're getting the Dallas office wired in so you'll want to get some sleep."

"I would rather take a look at the files you've got here." He wouldn't sleep at all. He'd sit up all night going back and forth between knowing he'd done the right thing and calling Ian to ask for her contact information. It would be better to drown himself in work.

Owen clapped his hands together with obvious relish. "You lads can work all you like. I'm going to change and have some fun this evening. I've heard the new girl needs some stress relief. I'll be happy to oblige her. What was her name again? She's stayed in her room most of the time."

Nick's lips curved up slightly. "I believe she told us to call her Red on the dungeon floor."

Theo stopped. "What did you say?"

"I said you were a stupid man. Your woman is not," Nick replied. "I am sorry. She's not yours, of course. Don't worry about it. You do your thing and we'll take care of Red. I believe I'll change into my leathers as well. Your room is the fourth on the left. The key is in the lock and someone will bring up your things. Good evening, gentlemen."

He stepped in front of Nick, stopping him in his tracks. "Are you telling me Erin's here? In this building? She's somewhere in this building with our son?"

Robert put a hand on his shoulder. "Uh, I think he meant she's here in the dungeon. Damn. She looks good."

He followed Robert's line of vision and realized his work for the night was far from over.

* * * *

"Are you nervous?" Faith asked as they walked through the dressing room and out into the dungeon.

Erin breathed it in. She loved Sanctum, but The Garden was a rich experience. She loved the smells. Jasmine and leather and the underlying hint of sex. Sanctum was so modern, with its colorful lighting and industrial feel, while The Garden was pure theater. Like she was walking into an ancient forest. There was something primal about the place. She would love to play out a scene with Theo here. She could be the warrior princess and he her enemy. Their battle would end in the sweetest way, but not before he tormented her with his hands and mouth and cock.

Somehow she didn't think that would be the way she ended her evening.

"I'm not nervous, but I'm also not looking forward to the coming confrontation. Nick promised he wouldn't say anything until it was obvious. There's a part of me that hopes like hell that will be tomorrow morning at the conference." It might be easier to face Theo there.

Faith wrinkled her nose. "Coward. You know you want him to walk in and immediately see you and fall to his knees."

"The problem is I'm pretty sure he won't be doing that. He's going to be angry with me."

Faith stepped out onto the path that led to the scene spaces. They were cleverly hidden all over the garden. In between the trees and vines there were benches and sawhorses and St. Andrew's Crosses. "There's angry and then there's angry. I think he's going to be the latter. I can't imagine he hasn't missed you."

"He hasn't called or asked where Ian sent me." That hurt most of all. "He hasn't asked about me or TJ."

Faith reached for her hand. It was something Erin had gotten used to. Faith was a huggy friend. At first it had been a real struggle, and now she was used to it, Faith's easy affection becoming something she'd come to rely on. "He needs time. I know it feels like it's been forever, but it's only been a few weeks. And you said he was ready to move in with you. That was a huge step for him. He was trying."

"Yes until…" She let it go. It wasn't Faith's fault that her sister was a ho-bag.

"Until Hope reared her ugly head." Faith lost a little color but squeezed her hand. "Have I apologized for how awful my family is lately?"

She'd been so happy when she'd gotten to London and

discovered Faith here. Faith was in between jobs and planning to move to Dallas in the next few months, but her husband was working somewhere in Europe. She was staying at The Garden where he could visit easily, and it was so good to have a friend here. Erin liked the women on the London team, but Faith was special to her. Faith was the first female she'd ever felt totally comfortable with, the first she'd allowed to get truly close to her.

"You don't have to." She wasn't about to make Faith feel bad for something she'd had no real part in. The minute Faith had realized what her father and sister were doing, she'd worked to try to help Erin and Theo fix things. She'd tried so hard to save Theo when he'd been shot. Faith had been the one to get her to break on that horrible night. Faith had been the one to hold her while she wailed out her pain. She loved Faith. "You are not your sister. But I do have some questions for you."

"Anything."

She meant that. Faith would tell her anything if she thought it would help. "Robert mentioned something to me. He thinks your sister hates me. He thinks that's why she truly wants Theo. Did you ever talk about me to her?"

Faith moved into the bar area and sat down on one of the settees. "I did. She called quite often when I was in Liberia. Now I know she was looking for information on what was happening since she'd switched my drugs with her own, but at the time I thought it meant we were closer."

"I thought you were fairly close." She settled on the settee beside Faith, deeply aware she wasn't wearing a collar. The Doms would be polite, but it was so much easier when she'd worn Theo's collar. It was upstairs with the rest of her precious possessions. She'd packed light, but hadn't been able to leave behind a few items, including the delicate silver collar Theo had offered her that first night in Africa when they'd been exhausted and anxious about the new op. It was all for show, he'd said, but the fire in his eyes and the satisfied way he'd looked at her after he'd clasped it around her neck had told her differently.

Faith shook her head. "No. We weren't close, even when we were young. We went to different schools after elementary. She was four years older than me so we didn't spend a lot of time together.

After she showed her true brilliance, father sent her to school in Europe, a specialized math and science program. She was the youngest one there."

She would have felt isolated and alone, the youngest, likely one of few Americans. Had that been the place her psychosis was born? Or had its impetus begun the moment she'd been conceived, something warping in the womb? "So Robert's grasping at straws."

"I don't know that I would say that exactly." Faith shifted, drawing her legs up so she looked as modest as a woman in a thong could look. "When she would come back, she would get a bit clingy. Father said it was because she missed her family. I think it's because somewhere along the line, she decided we belonged to her. Not in a nice way, but in an overly possessive, arrogant fashion. She was taught that she was better than anyone else, that her brain put her above the rest of us. She came to think she was above the law, above morality. If she was doing it, it must be right."

It made sense. Eve had labeled Hope McDonald a sociopath, incapable of true empathy. She was highly intelligent so she could fake it, but there was no feeling inside the woman for anyone but herself. She would view the world and other humans as nothing but useful objects. "Your father used that moral flexibility to insinuate himself into The Collective."

"Yes, that's what Ten's figured out," Faith agreed. "My father knew about The Collective, but he didn't have any real power in the organization until Hope started working for Kronberg. That was when he met the real power players. Hope wouldn't care as long as someone was funding her and leaving her alone."

"So why Theo? He's a beautiful man, but surely she's been around handsome men before. When I put aside my rage at her and look at her objectively, she's quite lovely, and she was very wealthy. If she wanted a boy toy, she should have been able to find one."

Faith sighed and sat back. "Robert's right. I didn't think about it at the time, but her curiosity started after I told her about you. I didn't exactly mention Theo as anything but your boyfriend. I talked about you a lot though. You were the first friend I'd made in a long time."

She felt the same. "Do you believe she targeted Theo to take him away from me? To punish me for taking you away from her?"

"I think she seized an opportunity," Faith allowed. "I think she found a way to hurt both of us and she took it. She knew how much you both meant to me and she didn't bother to tell me Theo was alive. She wanted me to hurt. She wanted you to hurt. And somewhere deep down, she thought if Theo was my friend and your lover, then he must be the best. So she took him for herself."

"I wish I knew everything she did to him." It haunted her at night. "So much of his tenderness is gone. All that seems to be left is the Dom, and that's not how Theo was. Sometimes I see a glimpse, but when I try to catch him, he slips through my fingers."

Faith reached out, touching her hand. "He's still there somewhere. I think his memory will come back in fits and starts. You said he was already getting flashes. The first version of her drug didn't work on everyone the way it did Robert. Brain chemistry is an odd thing. It's why we need different drugs for the same use. Ten thinks she's working on a second version of the drug, one specifically made to work on a brain like Theo's. If she ever gets her hands on him again, I believe she intends to wipe his memory completely and rebuild him as her mate."

"And why would she take my son's DNA?"

Faith went a little pale, even in the low light. "DNA is a useful thing to a doctor. It might be she wants to see how much of Theo is in TJ, what genes she can isolate as pure Taggart. Or she did it to split the two of you up. She could be ensuring that TJ is Theo's so she could use him as leverage. My sister is capable of anything."

Yes, that was something Erin knew well. She had to think on it. Being out of her home allowed her to focus solely on the problem at hand. Though her mind constantly went back to Theo, but then he was the problem. He should have sat down with her and worked through how to deal with McDonald, but he'd behaved exactly as she'd expected. He'd woken up and immediately asked for his brother. She'd found herself packed up and on her way with TJ a few hours later.

Of course, she would have fought if she'd thought it would make a difference.

"Are you going to play tonight?" Faith asked, her voice uncertain.

Erin leaned back. She should relax while she could. "I'm pretty tense. I could use a session. It's not like I'm cheating. He's the one who sent me away."

"I doubt he thought you would come here. I'm sure he believes you'll only be separated for a brief time."

"He was in full-on martyr mode." It wasn't his best look and she couldn't blame that on his torture. He'd been willing to throw himself on his sword for his loved ones long before he'd met the doctor. "He told me I shouldn't come out of hiding until McDonald was dead and that could take years. He didn't even seem all that sad about it."

In fact, he'd seemed more focused and level than in the weeks he'd been home. He wanted to go after Hope McDonald more than he wanted to stay with her. Vengeance was more important to Theo than their family. Yes, she'd thought about that for a solid week as well.

She had some decisions to make but so much would be determined in the morning. Tomorrow morning he would find her sitting in the conference room and she would know how he truly felt. He would be cold or hot. Anger wasn't in question. He would be angry that she'd ruined his plans. The question was which Taggart temper would show. If he was cold, she would have her answer.

But if he went white hot on her, then there was still some passion left.

"I don't think he's going to like it if you play with another Dom," Faith said.

"I'm not having sex with anyone. I'm not planning on doing anything at all but finding some stress relief," Erin explained. "I'm not sure who to ask though. Brody is good with a whip, but I prefer a flogger with a nice sting. It's faster. The trouble is Nick is best with the flogger, but Theo wouldn't like it. Penny offered to share a scene with me. Damon can flog us both and then they can go at it in the privacy room. Mind doing my aftercare?"

Faith grinned. "I can certainly put some ointment on your butt. I am a doctor after all."

"Just not an evil crazy one." She would feel so much better after a nice long flogging. There wasn't anything sexual about it. That was the crazy part. She'd discovered she was one of those people for whom pain brought relief.

Faith's hand squeezed hers. "I'm so sorry, Erin. I wish I could change things. Do you think I should try to talk to her?"

"No." The last thing she wanted was Faith in her sister's clutches. Faith was smart and strong, but she had no real idea of how to deal with a woman like Hope. Faith would never be able to think like her sister so it would be difficult to read her moves and outmaneuver her.

That was Erin's job and she needed time and information in order to do it.

The key would be in isolating her again, in taking away her resources and forcing her to run. If she panicked, she would make mistakes. If she made mistakes, Erin would capitalize on them.

"Not that I would know how to call her," Faith said with a sigh. "You have to know that if I did, I would share the information with you. She might be related to me biologically, but you're my real sister."

Stupid emotions. She never used to blink back tears. "I never doubt, sister. Never."

"Hello, subs," a deep voice said. "How are you this evening?"

Erin looked up and there was a gorgeous man standing over her. Clive Weston. Ah, Simon's brother was a lovely man and one of the few Damon trusted to be a member of his club. Each member outside the team was carefully vetted. She'd never met the man but knew him from pictures and the stories Simon told.

She'd also heard he'd recently lost both his long-time submissive and a close friend. Clive, like Adam and Jake, was heavily into ménage. It was a lifestyle for the man, but he'd had two partners instead of one. Now, according to gossip, he was playing solo and running through subs like they were candy and he needed a sugar fix.

She could understand the need for solace. "Good evening, Sir. My friend and I are doing well this evening, thank you."

"A Yank? You're new here. Can I buy you a drink? I see your friend is collared, but she's welcome to chaperone us, if you like."

Wasn't that polite? It surprised her since she'd been told Clive was the resident manwhore Dom and didn't spend time getting to know a woman. "Are you attempting to negotiate with me, Sir?"

Faith gasped at her side, sitting up as though she was going to put the Brit in his place. Erin held a hand out. She was intrigued. Not by the idea of playing with Weston. She wouldn't do that since he was obviously looking for a lover, but she was interested in his state of mind. His brother was worried about him. If she could tell Simon anything at all, she would.

He put his hands on his muscular hips. "I think I'm attempting to get to know you, sub. We don't have to play tonight. Unless you want to, but even then I think I would like to talk a bit first. I'm in a mood tonight, you see."

Very interesting. "I would love to sit and talk to you if you don't mind my friend joining us. I would appreciate a chaperone. Her Dom is a good friend of mine. I intended to play a bit tonight, but only with a married Dom, if you know what I mean."

He nodded her way. "You're cautious. I understand that. I find myself more cautious these days, too."

"That's not what I've heard."

He winced a little. "So my reputation precedes me. You'll have to forgive me, dear. You know me, but I don't think we've met. You must work for Knight. I suspect that since you're not wearing a collar and he allows so few people outside his business in."

He was a smart man, but then his brother was one of the smartest she knew. "I actually work for Ian Taggart."

That sensual smile on his face turned upside down. "Then you know my brother."

And he didn't like that. It told her he wanted to hide his real state from Simon. "We're acquainted, but I work more with Liam O'Donnell than anyone else. I take it that means you're going to change your mind. I can give you several other reasons to walk away. I have a baby upstairs. I'm involved with a man who might never remember how that baby was conceived, much less that he ever loved me. I'm in love with him and that won't ever change so if you're in the mood for sex, you should look somewhere else. I know your brother is worried about you. I know he loves you and so does Chelsea. So it's all right if you want to run away and find someone easier to talk to. Or to not talk at all. You have no idea how much I wish I could."

Clive's jaw tightened as he looked down at her. "Life was easier before I loved someone. Before I needed others." He looked away for a moment and she was sure he would walk. Instead, he turned back to her. "I think we might have a lot in common. You must be Erin."

So he was in the know. She held out a hand. "Erin Argent. It's nice to meet you, Clive."

He grasped it and there was a certain softness in his eyes. "I don't want to be alone tonight, but I also don't think I want to fuck senselessly. How about we pass the time together? As friends? As people who've lost? Drink with me."

There was something in his eyes, something dark and yet pleading that made her rethink her plans for the evening. "Of course. You know there's a two drink max."

"Only if we're playing," he replied. "We can drink as much as we like if we forgo the play. Tell me your sad story and I'll tell you mine."

That might not be such a bad idea. She'd thought to let her stress out by taking a Dom's discipline, but maybe there was another way, too. It was inconceivable, but she missed the sessions with Kai. Once she'd given in and let herself go with it, she'd blown off some steam there. Having a person who listened was a beautiful thing. "You've got a deal."

He gave her a sad smile, his hand coming out to reach for her. "I think you're what I need tonight. I need to talk more than anything else."

She placed her hand in his. He was big and warm and moved her not a bit because everything inside her called for Theo. It didn't matter that he'd been the one to split them up. He didn't seem to want her but that didn't matter to her stupid heart.

She bet Clive wanted someone else, too. It was right there in his eyes. He was weary and heartsick. Perhaps they would be good for each other. She allowed him to help her up. Drinking with another sad sack might work. She started to stumble, but Clive put a hand on her hip, helping to steady her. It made it easy to reach up and put her hand on his leather vest, right over his chest.

"Uhm, Erin, I think you should probably stop touching Master Clive." Faith's suggestion came out a bit breathless.

Erin followed her line of sight and felt her eyes widen. Theo was standing there looking like the most decadent man candy she'd ever seen before. Well, except for the righteous anger in his eyes.

His lip curled up and he started toward her, long legs eating the distance between them. "Take your fucking hands off my sub."

Clive took a step back, his hands coming up. Erin felt bad because the night wasn't going to go the way she thought it might. She wouldn't be helping Clive Weston find his calm. But she had her answer about Theo.

White-hot rage was right there in his expression. No doubt about it.

"She doesn't have a collar," Clive said, his shoulders squaring. "You have no rights to tell me what I can or cannot do with her. It's up to her."

Theo stood right in front of the big Brit. "You want to tell me what I can or cannot do with my sub? You want to tell me a collar makes a fucking difference? That woman lives in my house and gave birth to my child. You step back before I decide to take the anger I feel right now out on you."

She had to do something or the night would turn out very wrong. The last thing she wanted was Theo spending a night in a London jail.

Erin dropped to her knees in front of her love and hoped it was enough to calm her Master down.

CHAPTER FOURTEEN

Theo watched as Erin sank to her knees in front of him. She was stunning, so fucking stunning his heart nearly stopped. It made him take his eyes off the snake who'd been closing in on his woman.

His. Fucking his.

No matter where she went, what she did, she was his. He could forget his entire damn life, but he would know she belonged to him. Always. Forever.

That was the sweet sense inside him. She belonged to him. But there was another. The primal piece of him that wanted to savage the man who'd dared to fucking touch her. The dark-haired man stood back a bit as though giving the predator some room. Theo still wanted to wrap his hands around the other man's throat and squeeze until he was blue and cold.

"Master, I was hoping to play tonight." Her words came out so breathy and sweet.

Play. He wasn't going to play. He meant business tonight. "You're not supposed to be here, sub."

"Theo, you need to stay calm," the woman who'd been sitting with her said. "She meant no harm or disrespect. She was simply looking for solace."

Solace? From his wounds? He stepped in front of Erin. She was well trained as she never once looked up, merely stared at his boots. Her head remained submissively down. He still wouldn't let it pass. "Is that what you wanted? Solace from this fucker? You wanted him to take you to bed so you could forget me?"

He knew deep down that he wasn't being fair, but it didn't matter to him in that moment. All that mattered was the ache in his gut, the feeling that all was wrong in the world. She was his anchor and it didn't matter that he kept pushing her away. All that mattered was she was drifting and he couldn't stand it.

"I wasn't planning on sleeping with anyone, Sir." Her voice was calm, perfectly even. Her hands were on her thighs, flipped up in offering to her Dom. "I will admit I was looking for a scene in order to ease my stress level, but I'd already set up something with Master Damon. He was to flog both me and his wife. Faith was ready to handle my aftercare as Damon would be happily fucking Penelope. It's her you should be jealous of. Faith, I believe my Master would like to challenge you to a Dom off."

The brunette standing beside her grinned his way. "Swords or whips? I'm equally bad at both, Sir. Perhaps we should wait until my own Dom is here. He lives to defend my honor."

Such fucking brats and he wasn't putting up with any of it tonight. "I will have a word with your Dom. Who is he?"

Her chin came up. "Tennessee Smith, Master Theo."

Fuck a duck. "You're Ten's wife."

Her smile was brilliant, absolutely no fear of him in there at all. "It's so good to see you again, Theo. You look wonderful. Seriously, Erin wasn't planning on having sex. She was going to scene in a nonsexual fashion and then I was going to ensure that her butt didn't scab over. It's what subs do for each other."

He didn't care about what subs did for each other. He cared that his sub had blatantly disobeyed him. "I'll have a long talk with your Master when he returns. Tell me something, Faith. Did he know my submissive would be here? Was he involved in the conspiracy to make me look like a complete fool?"

Faith's smile faded. "You don't look like a fool."

A low chuckle came from behind him. Nick. Naturally. "Oh, I think he's definitely the fool."

"Hey, if you don't want that pretty sub, I'll take her," Owen said. "If she needs to scene, I'll relieve all her stress."

"I can kill you, too." It could be a nice night. He could bloody up everyone and then maybe he would feel slightly better.

She was here. She wasn't in some random place where McDonald couldn't find her. She was right here with him. There was zero chance that was a coincidence. She'd known exactly what she was doing, and that also meant Ian had known what she was doing.

So much betrayal.

And his dick didn't care because she was right here.

Her head came up and there was a bit of fire in her eyes. "I don't have a Dom so it doesn't matter who I play with."

She didn't have a Dom? "Do you forget that we signed a contract?"

Yep, there was fire in that glare. "Do you forget you told me to go away?"

Ah, the beauty of a well-written contract. He silently thanked his brother for being such a tight ass when it came to a contract. "There was nothing in the contract that stated you were allowed out of the contract unless we sat down and signed off. I sent you away for good reasons. It's my job to protect and shelter you and I held up my end. What was your job?"

"To serve you. To protect and shelter you. You didn't allow me to do my job."

Frustration threatened to boil over. "You have more than me to worry about."

"And I can protect TJ while working with you." She held a hand up, but not to him. She turned to Faith, who helped her stand. Her whole body went tense as she stared at him. "Not that you think I can. Look, it's fine. I get it. You're upset to see me. I'm sure you think I should be upstairs watching my son sleep because women with children shouldn't have needs. I'll play privately so I don't offend you, Sir."

"Is there a problem here?" Damon Knight stood looking over the scene with a dark expression on his face.

That was when Theo realized everything had shut down. The scene that had been playing out to the left of the bar area had stopped, the Dom glaring at them, his submissive clinging to his leg.

"Not at all." He could still save this. Maybe. "We'll keep it down."

Owen's face had lost its constant devil-may-care look and he suddenly seemed damn serious. "I'm sorry, Master Damon. Nick and I were going to take these two up to their rooms when young Taggart gave us the slip. We'll leave the dungeon floor until we're properly dressed."

"Apologies, Master Damon." Nick nodded to his boss and the woman at his side. "Penny. I'll speak to the Doms who had scenes this evening and ensure them Owen and I will attempt to make it up to them."

"It's not the two of you I'm concerned with," Knight said. "It seems to me Big Tag's sent me all his drama. I don't like drama. Perhaps I should reconsider your rights here since you obviously have no idea how to behave in a dungeon. Either that or your brother's standards have fallen far."

Shit. The last thing he needed was to start a war between Damon and Ian. He needed The Garden, needed Damon's team, but he wasn't about to hang his head. He did know his rights. "Your standards are in question, too. Since when did The Garden allow a contracted submissive to play without her Master's permission. You intended to play with my sub tonight, from what I understand. Were you going to bother to mention it to me or do you not honor contracts here?"

Knight's jaw tightened and he looked over at Erin. "She told me she didn't have a Dom."

"She's not wearing a collar," the dark-haired man insisted. "How was I supposed to know she's taken? And I wasn't intending to play with her. I asked her to sit and drink with me."

Knight's eyes rolled. "Certainly, my lord. You had perfect intentions. You wouldn't at all have fallen into bed with her if you had the chance."

"Not tonight I wouldn't," he shot back. "I'll take my drinking binge elsewhere, Knight."

The man turned and stalked out.

Penny glared up at her husband. "Damon, it's been a year tonight. Do you know what it took for me to get him here? I have to catch him before he gets to the locker room. I'm not allowing him to be alone on tonight of all nights."

Damon sighed as his wife ran after My Lord. My lord?

"Who the hell was that?"

Erin had lost her submissive posture and the bitch he loved was back. Her hands went to her hips and she shot him a stare that could have peeled paint off a wall. "That was Simon's brother, the Duke of Norsley's heir. He's sixth in line for the throne or something, but at the end of the day he's a man who lost one of his best friends and their shared sub in a car accident. He wanted someone to talk to." She turned that stare to Knight. "As for your accusations, he broke our contract when he sent me away. Besides, our contract was specific. Our interactions were kept to Club Sanctum. He has no hold over me here so don't look at me like I'm some kind of monster."

"That's not what the language of our contract meant, Erin." She couldn't be right about that.

Erin shook her head. "Nevertheless, I'm the problem here so I'll leave. I'll go back to my room and I won't come back to the club since it offends Theo's sensibilities. I assume I can still work in the offices?"

Knight ran a hand over his head, a weary gesture. "Of course, Erin. I'm sorry I got so angry."

She held a hand up. "It's your first night to play in a long time. I understand. You've had a kid recently and that shuts everything down. Believe me, I understand. I'll remove myself so you can get back to your wife and your evening. Thank you for attempting to accommodate me, Master Damon. Please apologize to Clive for me. I'll see you all at the morning conference."

She turned and started to walk away. He reached out for her, gripping her arm. "Where do you think you're going? We're going to have a long talk, you and I, and then you're going to pack your bags and you and TJ are going to do what we agreed on. You're going into hiding, though I now see I'll have to handle that as well since you're not capable of following a few simple orders."

He heard a groan from Robert right before Erin used her free hand to attempt to break his nose. Theo hissed and stepped back.

"Take your orders and shove them up your ass, Taggart." She

turned away but not before he saw a sheen of tears in her eyes.

Fuck.

Faith stepped in front of him, a frown on her face. "Who the hell are you? You sure look like Theo, but you don't act like him at all."

She turned on her heels and stalked off after Erin, not even offering to check Theo's nose to see if Erin had broken the cartilage. Theo wiped the blood off as he stared after her.

He'd ruined everyone's night.

Nick clapped a hand on his shoulder. "You see, I told you you were foolish man."

"Fuck you." He stepped back, breaking the contact as he thought seriously about walking into the ladies locker room after Erin and dragging her out. Of course, if he tried that she would likely pull his balls off and shove them down his throat. That's what Erin did when she was threatened.

"Of course." Nick bowed slightly. "I couldn't possibly help you. Good luck, Taggart. Owen, shall we get changed?"

He watched as Nick began to turn and walk off. Robert stood next to him. At least he always had Robert. Robert, who had no idea what he was doing either.

"Dude, you did not handle that well." Robert was shaking his head.

It was time to retreat. He would go up to his room and play some inane game on his tablet and have a beer or something. He would sit up again all night trying to figure out how to handle things.

Or he could man the fuck up.

"Markovic?" Theo rushed to catch up to the retreating Russian.

He turned around, one brow climbing over his right eye.

"Let me buy you a drink and maybe you can tell me what you think I should do." Everyone else treated him with kid gloves. Well, everyone except Erin, who punched him in the face when he was an asshole. His brothers would all tell him to be patient, that time would work everything out. His sister-in-laws would baby him.

Markovic might tell him some hard truths and he needed to hear them.

Markovic nodded at Owen and then toward the bar. "Come

then, I have good vodka in the back. There no one will care we're not in leathers."

"I'm heading to bed." Robert stepped back. "Good luck."

Theo followed the Russian to the back of the bar and through the door that led to the kitchens. It was quieter here, and there was something soothing about the distant thud of music. "Who was I? Was I this asshole I seem to turn into whenever I'm around her?"

Nick chuckled, a deeply amused sound. He strode to one of two professional-sized refrigerators and opened the freezer drawer. "You were always possessive, but you were a much smarter man then. Whatever drugs the doctor gave you took all your finesse away."

He could believe that. "You knew me well?"

Nick pulled out a frosty bottle of vodka and set it on the counter before seeking out two shot glasses. "I watched you and Erin closely on the last op. Before that we'd worked together once when Ian was testing me. It was a short job, but we were friendly enough."

"You liked me?" God, that sounded stupid, but he kind of wanted to know.

"Well enough. I did think you were very smart man." He poured out a healthy swig of vodka. "You were reckless, but you were also young and arrogant. I allowed you that. It was the way you handled your woman that made me think you were an intelligent man who would one day be as good an operative as she was."

The old Theo seemed to have been a bit behind his girl. "Did that bother me? That everyone thought she was so much better than I was in the field?"

"Does it bother you now?"

It wasn't something he'd spent much time thinking about. He had plenty of other things to worry about. If Erin was better in the field than he was, it was because she was smart and quick and she'd earned everyone's respect. "I don't care. She's got way more experience than I do and she's smarter. It doesn't make me mad. It makes me proud of her."

"There's the Theo I knew." He slid the shot glass Theo's way. "Many men would be intimidated by how competent Erin was, but you were not. You knew your worth, and your masculinity wasn't tied up in being stronger than all the women around you. You saw past her walls to the jewel she could be inside if she was simply loved and made to feel safe."

"You got all that from watching us?"

"I recognized a kindred spirit. I knew what you were doing because I went through it all with my Des." Nick held up the shot glass. "To fierce women and the men who are smart enough to love them."

That was something he could drink to. He shot back the cold liquid and came up coughing. "What the hell was that?"

Nick's lips curled up and he sighed in obvious appreciation. "That is pure Russian vodka. None of that fancy French shit."

He'd had some pretty strong liquor in his brief time, but this was something else entirely. Still, he was intrigued by the conversation. "So how would old me have handled that scene tonight?"

Nick poured two more shots. "The old you wouldn't have found yourself in that position. The old you would have sat with Erin and decided together on what you would do. The old you respected her and never treated her like a piece of property."

"I'm not treating her like property. I'm treating her like someone I should protect."

"As I say before, I would agree if this was another woman, but there is a core to Erin that will never accept being left behind when her man goes to war. She's a warrior herself."

"She's also a mom."

"And you are a father," Nick shot back. "Does this mean you will hide away? Or are you clinging to the idea that the woman should give up herself when she has a child? You can continue on, though we've agreed she's the better operative. Is this because you have the penis?"

He growled in frustration. "I didn't say that."

"No, but your actions speak louder than words."

"Are you trying to tell me if you could go back, you wouldn't try to protect Des? You wouldn't ensure that she stayed home where she would be safe?"

"If I attempt this, first she takes my balls, as you Americans would say. Second, if she allow me to do this, she wouldn't have been my Des. That is the true problem you're faced with. You try to make your woman into something she is not and now she has to wonder if you love her at all or if you simply are with her because your family told you to."

"That's not it. I knew there was something about her even when I didn't know who she was. When I was on the drugs, I could still…I don't know how to explain it. I could still feel her. When McDonald would try to get me to…"

Nick's face went grave. "When she would try to rape you. Is that what you're saying? There's no shame in it, brother. You were the victim. Again, let go of old ideas about what it means to be a man. A man survives. A man keeps going no matter what happens. A man can be hurt and wounded and torn up inside and still come out on the other side. The shame is not in that it happened. The shame is in allowing it to cost you what you truly love."

"I don't think she did." Theo took another shot. It warmed him at the very least, even though it tasted like fire rushing down his throat. "But I can't remember. I dream about it at night and then I wake up and try to attack anyone close to me."

"Good thing your woman is so competent then. She'll put you on your ass."

"And if I manage to hurt her?"

"She'll handle it, Taggart. She'll count it as little payment for having you alive. She hit you earlier. Does it make you want to run away and hide?"

Theo rolled his eyes at the silliness of that idea. "I grabbed her and was a complete dick to her. I deserved it. She doesn't deserve it."

"What does she deserve?"

He thought about that all the time. "A man who can take care of her. A man who's whole."

"You don't remember this but one night we had dinner with Brody and he asks you if you don't deserve better than Erin, and I will never forget what you say to him."

Theo frowned. "The Aussie? He thought I deserved better than Erin? Asshole. What the fuck did he think was wrong with her?"

Nick waved him off. "That doesn't matter. What you say back to him does. You told him it didn't matter what you deserved. It mattered what your heart needed. You say you need her more than all other women. What she deserves is meaningless. What her heart needs is you."

"I don't exist, Nick. Not the way I did."

Nick shrugged. "Then you should wish her well and leave her. The heart is a funny thing. It heals for some. Perhaps it will heal for her and she will find someone who she can be content with. Not to love. I don't think she'll truly love again, but she can find companionship, a measure of happiness. And you can move on to someone you can be happy with. If you have changed so much you can no longer love her for who she is, it is best to let her get on with her life, but either way, I suggest strongly that you don't give her more orders. She doesn't take them well."

He ignored the last bit. He'd already figured that out. "Do you think I haven't thought about walking away from her? I've tried to keep my distance. I don't think I'm good for her or the boy."

Nick's eyes narrowed. "If you can't even admit that he's your child, then walk away now. I'll buy you a fucking ticket out. If you've changed so damn much that there's no room in your heart for a child, get the fuck out of here because the doctor defeated you. You might as well have died. I think about it a lot. I wonder what would have happened if it had been Desiree and not you who came back. I wonder does the universe only give so many chances and you took hers. I wonder why God would bring you back when you so clearly wish to be dead. You ask me why I am angry with you. This is why. Because you get a chance she does not and you waste it. You waste it on anger and fear when you should open your arms and embrace the fact that you have a life, that you have a son."

"Even if I could hurt him?"

Nick pointed at him, his face flush with emotion. "You hurt him by rejecting him, by walking away, by not fighting for him. But do it. Walk away because one day he'll figure out his father is a walking corpse. It won't matter because that woman of yours won't ever stop fighting for her son. That's who she is. She'll take the love she would have given to you and pour it into him. She'll be fine. Walk away."

Something dark was in Nick's eyes. Theo had dismissed him because there seemed to be animosity between them, but how would he have felt in Nick's shoes?

He'd focused so much on his own struggles that he'd

completely forgotten what it meant to empathize with another human being. All their lives Case had been the strong one, the stalwart one, but Theo had been able to understand the people around him. It had been his strength and he'd been proud of how he'd treated others.

It was why he was a good partner to Erin, who so often viewed the world as a puzzle to be solved and needed someone to draw her out and pull her into her humanity, to remind her she was a woman as well as a warrior.

The ideas floated in his brain and any other time he would have pounced on them, attempting to grasp and hold them. Tonight he was content that he'd had them and allowed them to sit, not chasing some mystical connection to his past. Wasn't that what Kai had told him to do? Let it come and go as it wished. He had the answer to at least one of his questions.

"I loved her for everything she was. I loved every part of her. I sense that, but I can't quite tap into it," he said quietly. "I want to love our son, but I don't feel it. What if I never feel it?"

Nick leaned against the cabinet, another shot of vodka in hand. "Then you aren't the man I thought you were."

How would he know if he didn't really try? He'd taken the first shot he had at distancing himself. From her. From them.

He was fighting it so hard, not trusting that he would ever fully remember. Not trusting that he could be who he'd been.

How would he know if he didn't truly try?

What did he want to do tonight?

He wouldn't be able to sleep unless he'd done something, unless he'd handled the situation in some way. The only question was what should he do?

"What would the old me do? I don't think she'll accept a simple apology at this point and she's not a hearts and flowers girl." He didn't need memory to tell him that.

The door opened and Damon ushered the man who'd been hitting on Erin inside. "I'm pretty sure this is where Nick keeps the strong stuff."

He'd ruined Knight's evening. He'd ruined Erin's. Should he go to bed and start over in the morning?

Or prove he wasn't as soft and cuddly as the old Theo had

been?

"Has Erin gone up to her room yet?"

Knight didn't look happy to see him. "She's still in the locker room with Faith, but I swear I'll toss you out on your arse if you barge in there and start another fight. I won't care how much I owe your brother. I won't have a sub treated like that in my club. I'll have Ian send me a copy of your contract in the morning and I'll settle the dispute between you, but understand my word is law in this club and in that business."

Naturally Damon couldn't stand him. Theo had run the mission that led to one of his operatives being killed in the field. He was surprised Nick had even tried to help him.

"I'm going to take care of her. If I can't make things right with her tonight, you can kick me out in the morning. What room is she in?"

Knight's brow arched in a regal fashion. "I thought I told you I didn't want more drama."

Nick stepped up, bottle of vodka in hand. "Give him a break, Damon. And the girl. She loves him and they have a child. If he tries to get her back, who are we to stop him? Besides, she'll kill him if she's upset and then the problems are all solved. Now, my lord, why don't you come with me? I'm in a drinking mood tonight. Let us sit and drink and remember our departed."

"I could use a drink," Weston said. "But god, please call me Clive. I know this one means it as a dig, but I want to be me here, not some aristocrat."

Nick put a hand on his shoulder. "Well, drink with the peasants then. This is Russian vodka. It will make even the highest king into a man of the people. I'll make sure our friend gets to one of the guest rooms this evening. And Taggart, don't forget what I said."

Knight nodded to Nick, murmuring his thanks as he escorted Theo out. "You need to get to bed. You can sort out your problems with your woman in the morning. We've had enough drama for one night. There. That's Frank in the back moving toward the lifts. Catch up with him and he can show you to your room. He's got your baggage. He's also got keys to all the rooms. I'm going to find my wife and try to salvage something from this blasted evening."

"I'm sorry, Damon. I assure you we'll keep our drama to

ourselves." It was obvious the man wasn't going to help him. Or had he already helped him? He'd said Frank had keys to all the guest rooms. If Erin wasn't already up there, all he needed was a passkey and some slick talk to convince Frank to let him in her room and not Robert's. He turned to Knight. "And I'm sorry about Des. I can't tell you how sorry I am about what happened to her and what your team went through. It was my call and my responsibility."

Knight turned dark eyes on him, but there was a measure of sympathy there. "We've all made calls in the field that cost our people. You don't even bloody remember it."

That didn't matter. "It's still my mistake and I'll live with it. Unless the doc catches me again and then I'll totally forget again."

Knight's mouth dropped open. "That's nothing to joke about, brother."

"If I don't, I'll end up with Nick and his lordship, and I don't want to cry into my beer tonight…or whatever the hell that was Nick had. I'll see you in the morning and I intend to have that woman sitting beside me." He ran across the dungeon floor.

He was a man on a mission and he wasn't going to mess this one up.

* * * *

Erin slipped TJ into the crib in the room next to hers. The last few nights she'd slept cuddled up with him, but she was fairly certain she wouldn't sleep at all tonight. She would pace and try to decide how to deal with her asshole ex.

That was how she was going to think of him from now on. He was just another asshole who thought he owned her.

No. She forced herself to stop. That was the old Erin talking, the Erin she'd been before Theo, the one who always saw the worst in everything and everyone and who thought the world was always going to shit on her so she walked away first.

She looked down at her sleeping boy. She couldn't be that Erin anymore. She had to be this kiddo's mom and that meant sticking it out and working for the best. No more walking away.

Kai's words came back to her. Was she going to give up on Theo? He'd never given up on her. Of course she might have settled that issue tonight since she'd punched him. He was much more Dominant than he used to be so that had likely been a big mistake on her part.

She leaned over and kissed her baby one last time, a wistful feeling coming over her. They were safe here at The Garden. Damon Knight knew how to build a shelter. Bulletproof glass, well-guarded points of entry, a highly vetted staff, all of whom were deadly loyal to Knight and his guests. It was the perfect place to stay while they hunted McDonald down, but she would have to leave now. Despite what she'd said earlier, she wasn't going to fight Theo if he pushed her. That would be dangerous for both of them. She glanced out the window before closing the blinds. She'd thought she could show Theo they could stay together, but he didn't want to.

She couldn't force him to love her again. Maybe the part of Theo that had loved her was truly gone and he wasn't coming back.

It didn't matter. She had to try to reach him, not for her sake but for his and TJ's. If they couldn't be lovers, she would settle for being his friend.

She would love him until the day she died and that meant something to her. It meant she couldn't rage against him in an attempt to get her way. It meant she had to find a place to hide so he could do what he needed to do without the distraction of dealing with her.

Erin walked out of the small nursery, her heart heavier than before. Somehow she'd imagined she would walk into the conference room in the morning and he would realize how much he'd missed her and forget the dump-Erin-and-TJ-somewhere plan.

That only worked if he loved her.

She needed a beer. That would help. That and maybe she would pop open her tablet and take a look at Serena's latest book. The woman knew how to write a sex scene and didn't scrimp on the action. Blood and sex. Yeah, that could kill a few hours.

A cold sensation snaked up her spine as she realized she wasn't alone. There had been no creaking of floorboards or whispering of an unfamiliar voice. She simply knew. Someone was here with her, watching her.

And she'd left Bertha in her bedroom. The tiny skirt she'd worn into the dungeon didn't leave room for her precious Beretta M9, not that guns were allowed on the dungeon floor. She looked to her left, gauging how quickly she could get to the bedroom where the gun was locked in its case.

Or she could go for her phone. That was on the bar in the living room. One call and the cavalry would come running, but perhaps not before someone got to her son.

She couldn't help who she was and she wasn't a damn damsel in distress. She would call Knight after she'd killed the motherfucker who'd broken into her room. Or at least gotten the asshole to pee himself.

Two steps into the bedroom and she could see the gun case, but it didn't matter because a hard arm came around her waist and her attacker's other hand covered her mouth.

She immediately kicked back, but he'd moved his legs apart and angled his body so she found nothing but air. Adrenaline started to rush through her system. The fucker was good. He'd wrapped her arms up when he'd taken her waist, but he couldn't stop her from head butting him.

She hoped he had a nice hard head because she intended to make him hurt.

"Baby, everyone keeps telling me how much better you are than me," a deep voice whispered into her ear. "But I seem to have the upper hand right now. Have I ever told you how fucking good you smell to me? I could forget a lot, but I never lost your scent, and don't think I'm talking about your skin cream. I'm talking about you. I never lost that spicy sweet scent you get when you fight or you fuck. It's intoxicating."

Theo. He was here. She knew she should fight him, but damn it felt good. His body was hard against hers and she could feel that he was moved by the experience. His cock was pressed to the curve of the small of her back.

But she also couldn't be the girl who took shit from her man and then welcomed him between her legs. She'd thought sex might work to connect them, but he'd proven otherwise earlier this evening.

Sex might get them in more trouble. Sure, New Theo still wanted her body, but that wouldn't make a real relationship.

Old Theo had taught her that.

She went still in his arms.

"Are you going to scream if I let you go? Because I've got a gag prepped and ready. I know you used to be able to manhandle me, but I'm stronger than I was back then and a little meaner. I can have you tied up and gagged before you can fight me. Is that what you want, baby?"

What the hell was going on? Did he think he could tie her up and ship her out before morning? He wouldn't even give her a single night before he shoved her away?

Maybe they weren't done with the fight for the night. All her good intentions were flying right out the door.

Still. She had to be still and lull him into a false sense of confidence. He'd asked if she intended to scream. No. This was definitely between the two of them. When she was done with him, she'd drop him on Robert's doorstep and let his bestie take care of him. It was obvious he cared more about Robert than her or their son.

She would leave, but she wasn't about to let him tie her up and ship her off. He'd humiliated her enough for one night.

He eased his hand away from her mouth. "Be a good girl and I'll take care of you."

Yes, he'd ensure she was out of his life as quickly as possible. "I'll be good. Let me go and we can talk."

"I know we need to talk, but before that I'm going to show you how it's going to go from now on."

Oh, the arrogance of that man. It was an actual ache in her body that he would treat her like this. Her Theo might make mistakes from time to time, but he wouldn't have ever treated her like this. He would have apologized and talked to her. He would have made her feel precious and wanted.

Tears threatened because she fucking missed him. She missed him so damn much and he was gone. His body was here, but he wasn't hers.

Loneliness threatened to swamp her every sense. She'd never been lonely until she'd met him, until he'd taught her how to truly need another person.

And then he'd died on her.

It hit her so harshly. He was here, but he was so far away.

She couldn't show this man her softness. That had been for her love and this man simply wore her lover's skin.

The minute he released her, she brought her elbow up and back. Shock raced through her when he sidestepped her and swiped her feet out from under her.

"You need to fight, I'll fight, baby," he said as he loomed over her. His hand came out, catching her hair and twisting it lightly. "How hard do you want to go? Tell me now because the last thing I want to do is hurt you more than I already have."

He tugged at her hair, lighting up her scalp. Her whole body responded. It was a trigger sure to send her straight into the warmth of sub space. What was he saying? "I don't understand."

He got on one knee, his hand forcing her head back. "I mean I was a complete jealous ass and I want to make it up to you. You need some play? I'll give it to you. You need to relax, I'll see that you do and I won't take a damn thing in exchange. This is about you, baby. All about you. I hated seeing that fucker's hands on you, but I should have trusted that you would handle it."

The sweetness of his words pierced through her and she could feel the tears welling. "You're not sending me away?"

He frowned and then his hands were out of her hair, arms coming around her, lifting her. He stood up, not showing that her weight bothered him at all. "I was wrong. If you want to stay here, I won't force you to leave. But if you stay here, I'm staying with you. I know you think it's annoying, but I was trying to protect you. And what the hell is it with you and royal assholes? While I was waiting for you, I remembered something about you and a manwhore and we were in Dubai and he hit on you. He was the king of something, right?"

She felt like she was floating. He was here and he was saying all the right things. "Are you talking about Kash? The king of Loa Mali?"

He frowned down at her as he stalked toward the bed. "I had a vision of you walking out of his bedroom. I didn't like it, Erin. I wanted to murder someone. I felt it deep inside. I wanted to wrap my hands around that asshole's throat the same way I did tonight, so I was better at hiding it then. I wasn't different. I was smarter, but I was exactly as much of a possessive dick as I am now."

She clung to him like shelter from the storm she'd thought was coming. "I missed you so much this week."

He laid her on the bed, his eyes softening. "I missed you. I missed you before I remembered who you were. You were a hole inside me. I shoved you away because I'm afraid you won't ever be able to accept the man I am now. I don't know that I'll be able to love you the way he did."

She lay back, happy to just look up at him. He was the single most beautiful thing on the planet with one exception. His son matched him. His son was proof that there was good and light in the world. "I'll take that chance. Do you know what I was doing in Kamdar's suite that night?"

They'd been on a mission in Dubai. It had been early on. She'd only known him for a few weeks at the time, but she hadn't been able to stop thinking about him. Kash Kamdar was the king of a small but wealthy island nation and he'd made it plain he was more than willing to have some fun with her while they were working. He'd told her she was beautiful, but she hadn't believed him. She'd rolled her eyes, though she'd found him incredibly sexy.

She hadn't been able to take her mind off Theo Taggart.

"I don't know that I want to," he said, his voice dark. "We weren't together then. It doesn't matter."

"You remember that?"

"No, but I know you. You wouldn't cheat on me, which is precisely why I shouldn't have acted like a massive ass tonight. You were going to do what you said, play for comfort, not for sex, and I took that away from you. I made it dirty when it's not. I'm sorry, Erin."

She'd already forgiven him. The minute she'd realized he'd come to her seeking connection and not to send her away, she'd thrown out all her anger. Could he even understand how much of a change that was for her? Could he know that he'd been her impetus for change? That he'd shaken her whole world and turned it into a kinder place?

"I didn't sleep with the king. I'm going to be honest. I thought about it because it would have hurt you and at the time, you scared the hell out of me, Taggart. I was pretty self-destructive back then. I didn't think it was possible that you could ever truly care about me

239

so I thought long and hard about making you hate me so I wouldn't
be tempted."

"I think you should probably tell me this story naked and with
your ass in the air." His face had flushed a soft shade of red, a sure
sign he was getting angry again.

Not that it frightened her. Theo's anger—even this Theo—had
never been a thing to be afraid of. He could be righteously angry
with her and never hurt her. It seemed like her Master needed the
play tonight every bit as much as she did.

This was what she'd been hoping for. Erin had those pants off
quickly and was back on the bed, her backside on display for her
Dom. She didn't worry that he would reject her or that her butt
wasn't pretty enough. He'd told her so many times she believed him.

Maybe she should take a page from his playbook.

"We belong together," she said with a sigh as she settled into
her position. There was something about being half naked that was
almost more erotic than being fully undressed. He'd given her an
order and she'd followed it to the letter. He wanted to concentrate on
her backside and she wanted so much to please him. And to find that
glorious place where she worried about nothing but connecting to
him.

His big palm nearly covered her whole backside. "I feel it, but I
don't trust it, baby. I don't trust that I'm good for you or the boy.
There's a place inside me that's hollow now and I'm not sure
anything can ever fill it up again."

"We belong together." He needed to hear it over and over again.
"Stay close to me and you'll see. I'll take care of TJ. You take care
of me. In bed, in the dungeon."

His hand moved over her skin, warming her and making her
shiver in anticipation for what he would do next. "You take care of
the things that matter and I'll handle our sexual encounters, huh?"

"Don't make light of sex, Theo. I've gone without for a long
time."

"I want to talk about safety protocols in the morning, but if
you're staying here, I'm not about to sleep with Robert. I want back
in our bed." The words sounded stubborn coming out of his mouth,
as though he fully expected her to reject him.

"Of course."

His hand stilled. "Because that's what you planned all along, isn't it, brat? It's why you didn't fight me when I told you I was sending you away. You knew exactly where you would go and what you would do."

This could end up hurting more than she'd planned. "I knew The Garden was the best place for me and TJ, Master."

He slapped her ass. Hard. A rush of heat coursed through her body when she realized the first time hadn't been a fluke. Theo was playing hard. He wasn't holding back on her and that made her ache for more.

"And you knew I would end up here." His fingers brushed her backside as though he was tracing the mark his hand had left.

Yep, she would feel this in the morning. It would sit on her skin, a delicious ache that would remind her she wasn't alone. "I knew. It's the best place for you, too. It's the safest place for all of us. Though Knight might kick us out now since he has to deal with Clive Weston when he was going to play with his wife."

A nasty smack cracked through the air and Erin could barely breathe. "The Russian took care of it. I think Master Damon is happily balls deep in his sub by now, so we owe Nick. Tell me what you were doing with the king of Loa Mali that night. I'm remembering more. Something about spanking your pretty ass shakes the memories out."

Because he wasn't concentrating on them. Kai had told her it would be like this when Theo focused on other things.

"We were in a hotel room," Theo continued as he gave her two more smacks. They were languid as he took his time, caressing her after each one. "Something bad happened after I found you with him."

"Jesse was taken." Maybe if the damn doc would stop interrupting their scenes, Theo would remember more. Again, a good reason to be here in The Garden. "You caught me coming out of his bedroom because there was a diversion meant to throw us all off."

He smacked her right in the center of her ass, a hard tap that made her spine shake. "That's right. You were in his bedroom."

She'd seen the look on his face when she'd raced out of Kamdar's room. They'd had words about it, but she doubted he'd believed her when she said nothing happened. "We were talking, Master. That was all. Believe it or not, he told me I was a fool if I didn't give you a chance. He's the one who made me think I should try. Not that I did for a long time. I was slow back then."

Four hard smacks and she could feel the heat starting to coat her skin. It began in the flesh of her backside and swept outward.

"Why did you go into his room in the first place?" He settled in, the smacks becoming a rhythm she could breathe to, her heart could beat to.

"I was his bodyguard, Theo. And I liked him. He was a nice guy. I understood him. He was a man who enjoyed sex and wanted nothing more from a woman than a fun time. He didn't want my soul. He didn't ask for my love. He didn't need anything more than a good time in bed. And I still couldn't bring myself to touch him even though I convinced myself that was what I needed at the time."

"How long did I chase after you?" He smacked her thighs suddenly, causing her to groan.

This Dom knew how to keep her off balance. It was so stimulating. She had no idea what he was going to do next. She'd always gotten the feeling that Theo had studied D/s because she needed it. He'd been good, but he'd never brought this sexy sense of anticipation. "For a very long time, Master."

"And you held me off because you thought I was too young and pretty."

There was danger in his tone, but she couldn't lie to him. Not here. Not in this headspace. "Yes. You were younger than me and shiny. You could light up a room by walking into it and I was never that girl."

"I'm not shiny anymore, Erin. And I don't fucking feel young or pretty."

"You are the single most beautiful thing I've ever seen in my life, Theo Taggart. No amount of scars can change that. I told you, I think you're even sexier than before."

"Get up." The order came out on a harsh bark, but Erin complied, getting to her knees before he continued. "Take off the shirt. I want you naked."

He was in a mood, but then she'd turned all his plans upside down. Theo needed control and she'd wrested it from him this evening so she would do anything she could to give him some measure back.

Besides, she liked being naked with him. She definitely loved the contrast between the fire in her backside and the cool air that made her nipples tighten. Between the dry heat of her skin and how wet her pussy was getting. It made her feel alive in a way she hadn't in forever.

"Get in front of me."

His low growl went straight to her pussy, but she couldn't help but notice how different he was. His voice was deeper, harder and more real than ever before when they were playing.

Because they were no longer playing. It came to her as she dropped to her knees in front of him. She'd gotten hints of it before, but now she truly got it. Hope McDonald had stripped him down, peeled layers of him off, exposing that space every man needed to remain secret. He'd been laid bare and he would never be the same.

And it didn't fucking matter. Not at all. He'd been broken and shattered and left on the floor and he was still precious.

She gave him her submission, kneeling between his legs, but keeping her head down because he hadn't told her what he wanted yet. It didn't matter. She would give it to him.

"You have to understand that I'm not that shiny idiot who worshipped at your feet."

Patience. "He wasn't an idiot."

His hand found her hair, tugging hard so she was looking up into his eyes. A dark storm brewed there. "This is time for you to listen to me. Can you do that for me? I don't want to fight more tonight, but there are things I have to say to you."

She settled back down. No more pushing him this evening. Sometimes she had to remind herself that not every encounter was a battle to be won. Sometimes she had to bend. Like he'd done for her. "Yes, Master. I can do that."

He released her, but stayed close. "I'm not shiny anymore. I get flashes of how I was. I see it in my brothers' eyes. They're disappointed I'm not the same man. I think my function in our family was to be the one who pulled everyone else out of their darkness, but Erin, I'm a black hole now. I pull them into mine and it hurts them. It will hurt you and the boy. I dream at night of killing you."

She held her tongue even when she wanted so badly to speak, to argue with him. He wasn't dreaming of killing her. He was playing out a scenario in his head he was trained to. It wasn't his fantasy. It was his nightmare. If he thought he could scare her away, he would soon find out she was made of way sterner stuff.

His hand found her head again, but this time he stroked her softly, almost absently. "I want you, but I don't know that I'll love you like he did. I don't know that I'm capable of looking at the world the way he did. What happens if I have that dream tonight and I wrap my hands around your throat?"

A direct question. She could answer that. "I put my knee in your balls and hope I don't take away our chance for more kids, Master. But you've slept beside me and it was only annoying. You went back to sleep when I yelled at you so I think we'll be okay. It's a risk I'm willing to take."

"And if I can't give you more than a good time in bed? It's what you were looking for before you met me. What if that's it for us? Are you willing to risk that?"

She would risk anything for him. "Yes, Master."

"I don't know how we had sex before, but I know what I need now."

She felt herself tense because they might finally be getting to the heart of the matter. "I'm ready to give you whatever you need."

His face was slightly cruel as he looked down at her. "And if I need you to take care of me? Even after how I treated you tonight?"

She could tell him so many stories about what a bitch she'd been to him. "I think I can handle it."

"I'm not quite that much of a bastard yet, but it's a close thing. The only thing that's going to save you tonight is how tired I am."

Because he'd been on planes for two days and he'd likely gotten little sleep. He needed rest and he'd gotten emotional turmoil. She wished she could spare him that. "Then you should sleep, Theo."

"You haven't gotten what you need yet."

She went up on her knees, touching his face suddenly. "I only need you here with me."

He stared at her. "Anyone else touches me like that and I flinch." His eyes trailed away from hers. "Erin, what if I can't stand to have sex with you any way but with you tied up and submissive?"

"Then I'll get used to being bound. I need you to understand one thing, Theo. I love and adore you and that means we're going to make it through this because we'll find our way together. It means we have to hold on tight and not let her break us."

"And if I'm already broken?"

"Then I put you back together. You might not be exactly the same as before, but you'll still be beautiful to me. You'll still be the center of my world."

"You make it sound so easy."

It was the easiest thing in the world now. "It wasn't in the beginning. I made it hard. I think now it's your turn to pay me back."

He stood up, holding a hand out. All the sexual tension in him had fled and what was left looked like utter exhaustion. Despair. But he helped her stand and his hands went to her waist, hauling her close. "I don't deserve it, but let me sleep with you. Kick my ass if I do anything wrong in the middle of the night and know deep inside you're the last person I would ever mean to hurt. Let me stay with you."

If she said a word, she would burst into tears, so she let her hands drift up and began to unbutton his shirt. Without talk between them, she worked the clothes off him. After she'd folded his shirt, she ran her hands over his chest, slowly so she wouldn't startle him.

He caught her hand and brought it to his heart. "Don't be tentative. I know I have problems with people touching me now. It's because she would come in and touch me and it made me sick. It made me sick because only one person owns this body and I don't think it's me. It's you and it's always been you, hasn't it?"

She leaned forward and kissed his chest. "We belong together, Theo. I'll take you any way I can get you because you were made for me. I won't ever turn you away or make you feel like you're less than the best thing that ever happened to me."

"I thought that was TJ."

Then he misunderstood. "TJ only exists because you loved me. I'm the woman I am because you loved me. Let me love you, Theo. Let me help you be the man I know you can be."

His jaw tightened. "I don't want to disappoint you. I don't think

I can ever be that man again. Even if I remembered."

She couldn't lose him now. "Come to bed with me. It's late. Can't you brood tomorrow, babe?"

His lips curled up. "I can try."

She got him undressed and slid into bed next to him, his skin warming hers as his arms wound around her.

For the first time since he died she felt safe. Her men were here, close to her heart where she could fight for them.

"Tell me a story." Theo soothed a hand over her head. "Not a story. Not really. Tell me how I caught you. Tell me how I finally took down the mighty Erin Argent, and don't leave out details. I want to know how I used to make love to you."

"It doesn't matter," she said. "All that matters is now."

"Not to me. Tell me. I want to know our story. It's mine, too. Give it to me, please."

It was a request she couldn't refuse.

CHAPTER FIFTEEN

Liberia, Africa
Two years earlier

T he heat was going to kill her. She was absolutely sure of it and she was a woman who'd spent time in the desert while she was in the Army. Of course, her version of the Army hadn't included Theo Taggart with his shirt off.

Please don't actually be drooling. Please. Maintain some semblance of dignity.

She watched as he kicked the soccer ball to a kid who couldn't be more than nine. He'd lost his father to the Ebola outbreak ravaging the country, but Theo had managed to make him smile again. His mother was one of the few recovering at Faith McDonald's small clinic.

The clinic was tiny, but damn the doc was a force of nature.

Erin leaned back, fighting the emotions that threatened to take over. She'd started this trip as a mission, but Africa had changed her. Faith had changed her.

Theo was threatening to turn her into an entirely differently human being.

A little girl named Teta leaned against her, hooking her arms through Erin's and cuddling close.

Weird. So fucking weird, but her arm came out to cradle the five-year-old girl.

Africa was making her soft. She'd gotten close to the children, especially this one. The tiny orphan girl had clung to her since the day she'd made it to the compound, her sick mother hauling her miles to come for treatment only to succumb to Ebola twenty-four hours later.

"Mister Theo is so nice and he plays well." Teta was smiling as she looked out at the field.

Mister Theo was a son of a bitch who played a long, manipulative game that she wasn't going to win. The athletic shorts he was wearing rode low on his hips, showing off the ridiculously sculpted notches there.

"Mister Theo is very nice and Ms. Erin is a lucky woman," a familiar voice said as she sank to the ground next to Erin.

Faith McDonald was the target. She and Theo had been tasked with getting close to the doctor in order to gain an invitation to her father's island getaway home where Big Tag was certain all the secrets were kept. They'd been in Liberia playing a happy D/s couple for six weeks and they would be here for the rest of the summer, making the target comfortable enough with them to allow them to set her up with a Dom. Tennessee Smith. The former CIA agent would find all the intel they needed once he was in Faith McDonald's bed.

If she didn't watch it, Erin was going to end up in Theo's bed.

In a biblical sense.

She was already there in a literal way. For forty-three days she'd slept in the same way-too-small for both of them bed they'd been offered. Every single freaking night she went to bed clinging to the side and every morning she woke up with her face pressed to his chest, a leg slung over that hot bod of his. Sometimes she hiked it up high enough that she woke to the feel of that massive Taggart cock of his saying good morning, and it took everything she had not to hop on top of him and ride that monster to paradise.

She looked over at Faith and gave her a smile. It wasn't like she could explain how sexual frustration was causing her to be even more violent than normal. Some asshole had tried to bully his way into the clinic today. Very likely he was looking for pain meds. Erin had ensured the fucker needed them. Of course he wasn't likely to get them in the local jail. If he came back, Erin had plans to break both his legs.

It still wouldn't make her any less hungry for that man. Theo Taggart was going to be the death of her.

Or the utter and complete rebirth of Erin Argent.

She'd started to think that it would be one or the other.

"I would like to marry Mister Theo," another girl said.

There were ten of them sitting on the edge of the field wearing the shorts and shirts Faith's clinic provided to them. There were also knee-length skirts that allowed the girls to attend the privately funded school not two blocks away. Faith made sure every child who stayed at her clinic was able to keep up his or her studies.

"I think you'll have to talk to Ms. Erin about that," Faith said with a bright smile.

The sun was beginning to set and Theo pulled the children playing around him, getting to one knee and likely promising more fun tomorrow. They all put their hands in, Theo included, and made a happy roar as they disbanded. There were no losers in Mister Theo's games. These children had seen far too much loss to count points or call out winners.

So much loss it sometimes weighed down her soul and only one thing could spark her back to life.

Theo had become necessary in a way no other person had done, and that scared the hell out of Erin.

Still, she remembered she had a role to play. She gave the girl a grin. "I'm afraid you'll have to find your own Taggart. That one is mine. The good news is he has a twin brother."

The girls all started giggling as Theo made his way over. They dispersed quickly, whispering about him behind their hands like schoolgirls. They *were* schoolgirls thanks to Faith McDonald.

The job had started as just another op but had become so much more. Faith had turned her back on her privileged existence in order to fight the good fight. She was a naïve, overly sentimental do-gooder, the type that made Erin roll her eyes and threaten to vomit because they didn't understand the way the world worked.

Here in Africa, Faith was changing the way it worked.

"Why do they run away like that? Is it the fact that most of the time I've got a P90 strapped to my chest?" Theo frowned as the gaggle of girls made their way back to the dorms Faith had set up for them. Some were orphans, others clinic patients waiting on their families, but all seemed happy to have a place to stay, food in their bellies, and doctors around during the worst outbreak of Ebola the world had ever seen.

Yet even among the death and horror, Theo was able to smile, able to bring his unique optimism into her world.

"I don't think that's fear, Theo," Faith replied. "They want to marry you."

He actually blushed. Damn but he was cute when he was embarrassed. He tossed his shirt back over his head, but it didn't mean anything. She still knew how muscular that chest was. Every single morning she was treated to the sight of Theo Taggart in his surprisingly tight boxer shorts slamming down a set of a hundred push-ups followed by that gorgeous body hefting himself up and down the pull-up bar. She was fairly certain he didn't work out mostly naked at home. No. That was totally for her benefit because the bastard was smart enough to know that she craved his hot bod.

He was also disciplined enough to not give it to her.

"Well, I hope you informed them I'm taken," he said as primly as a six-foot-three-inch hunk of a sex god could be.

And that was pretty prim since Erin still hadn't managed to get into his frilly boxers. He'd kissed her senseless, slept by her every night, offered all manner of play, but wouldn't even let her touch the monster in his pants. He'd been serious about needing some kind of declaration of love or some shit.

He wasn't getting it. She didn't do love. No way. No how.

But she was getting desperate. They had at least another four months here in Africa. No way she was going to make it that long without breaking down and begging him to fuck her. Especially since he had zero problems playing the Dom.

"If I catch you touching yourself, you won't like what happens, baby," he'd said to her the first night here. *"This is a deep cover operation and that means living the part. She could walk in at any time and she will find you in bed with me at night. If Faith shows up at our quarters, she'll find you at my feet or cuddled up on my lap.*

You will sleep with me, shower with me, take your every meal with me because for the course of this op you belong to me."

He'd been utterly true to his words. She slept wrapped around him. At night when she read or they watched movies, he cradled her on his lap, his hands moving over her like she was a kitten he was soothing. Every night before they went to bed, he was the one who washed her body, fingertips worshipping her and forcing her to know herself in a way she hadn't before.

She didn't even want to disobey him when it came to masturbation. It wouldn't be as good as the real thing. It would be a soulless imitation.

"I offered them Case," she replied, allowing Theo to haul her up. She knew what came next because he did it constantly, but she was still breathless with anticipation.

His hands went to her waist, drawing her close as his lips descended on hers. "I'll be sure to let him know you've arranged a good woman for him."

Her whole body was awake and alive at the touch of his hands. "She's twelve."

His lips curled up in the most sensual smile. "Then she's at Case's mental level. Next year, she'll pass him right by. We should jump on it now."

His lips brushed hers and she forgot about Case and the op and everything else but the feel of Theo. All too soon he was straightening up and bringing her to his side.

"If you don't need anything else tonight, Doc, I'll take my pretty here and get some R&R in," Theo said, smiling Faith's way. "Murray and Clancy are on duty and I'm certain they've got our protocols down now."

The first thing they'd done when they'd gotten here was whip the small six-man security team into some semblance of shape. Faith was too nice to try to force some kind of routine on the men she paid to guard her clinic and the compound around it, but Erin didn't mind playing the ball-busting bitch for her friend. She'd immediately convinced Faith to let her fire two of the lazy guards and bring in some actual specialists.

"No problem, you two." Faith started toward the clinic again, her break clearly over. She glanced back, a wistful look on her face.

"Have fun."

It was so obvious Faith was lonely. According to the good doc, she hadn't taken a Dom in months, not since her last one proved so douchey. Of course, they were counting on her loneliness. It was what they would play on to get her to come back to Dallas with them and put her firmly in the clutches of Ten Smith.

"See you in the morning." She looked forward to having breakfast with Faith every morning before her and Theo's shift began. Maybe it was because Faith's version of girl talk included blood and disease and surgical discussions, and she never flinched when Erin described a firefight. Or maybe she'd clicked with the chick. It was a first for her and like the deep connection to Theo, she wasn't sure she could trust it.

Especially not when the friend in question was actually the target of her op and would one day hate Erin for lying to her. The one real friend she'd made and it would all go to hell over her job.

"Absolutely," Faith said with a wide smile. "I'll expect all the details."

Theo frowned but before he could say anything, there was a shout from the girls.

"Doctor, please!"

Faith took off running. Erin did the same once she saw the small child who was on the ground.

Teta.

Another nightmare had begun.

Forty-nine hours later, she found herself being led back to their small quarters by Theo. He'd tried to pick her up and haul her out of the hospital several times, but Erin wouldn't leave. She'd sat next to Teta's bedside, her whole body encased in a Hazmat suit as she'd watch the girl lose her battle.

She'd napped briefly in the hospital's on-call room, but every time she closed her eyes she saw Theo lying on a bed, blood seeping from his clear blue eyes. She'd seen him dying and hadn't been able to touch him. She'd never been able to touch him the way she'd wanted to because she'd been so scared.

And then she'd seen herself on that bed, but she'd been alone because she'd pushed everyone away. No one had come to sit with her and as she'd died, she'd known no one would remember her at all because she'd never allowed them in.

Not even him.

Teta had died a few hours before and Erin hadn't cried. Faith was too exhausted. The whole staff was numb. The nurses had carefully prepared the girl's body for what was to come. There was no burial for Ebola patients.

"Hey, let's get you in a shower and get you to bed. I've already made arrangements for the others to take our place for at least the next two days. You need to rest."

If she closed her eyes she would see all the death again. She would be alone again. She pushed away from him. "They've taken my place for days. I can manage a shift, Taggart. Faith has checked me over every single day. I don't have a fever. I've followed all the safety protocols. I'm not sick so I don't need you to babysit me."

It was his fault. It wasn't Africa that had made her soft. It was Theo Taggart, with his whispers and caresses, always lying to her about how pretty she was. She wasn't fucking pretty. She had a damn mirror and she could use it.

She wasn't buying his bullshit. Didn't need it. Didn't want it. He was playing some kind of game with her and it stopped now.

"Hey," he called out, catching up in a few strides of his long legs. He had a hand on her elbow, trying to pull her back.

It was the perfect excuse to get a little violent with him. She kicked back, catching him right in his perfect six-pack. There was a muffled groan and he went down on his ass.

"I said I don't need a fucking babysitter, Taggart. That's all you are, you know. A babysitter. You feed me and put me to bed and make sure my hair's done right but other than that, you obviously aren't man enough to handle me." Something nasty had taken root in her gut and she spat bile his way because he was the only one around who could give her the fight she was desperate for, the only one who couldn't ruin their mission.

It would utterly ruin their relationship, but she hadn't believed in that anyway. It was better to break it than to be broken by it.

"What is that supposed to mean?" He hopped back to his feet and his shoulders squared as he stalked toward her.

This was what she needed. She needed a good fight, needed to destroy something, and if that ended up being something important, then so be it. The need to tear and rip was threatening to overwhelm her.

"It means I'm done playing your games," she shot back, her voice low. They were well away from the clinic and the dorms, but she wasn't giving up the op. They would still have to pretend, but she wasn't doing it anymore when they were in private. That had been a terrible mistake.

"Game? What the hell game am I playing?"

"The limp dick game," she shot back. "The one where you pretend to want me in order to control my behavior, but the truth of the matter is you can't get it up and don't want anyone to know."

A harsh laugh came from the back of his throat. "Oh, my love, you are excellent at rewriting history, aren't you? I've showered with you. You've seen how hard I can get around you. You're angry that I haven't treated you like a piece of meat. You're pissed as hell that I won't prove myself to be as bad as every other man you've known, but I'm not going to start now. This isn't a game. This is our life and I won't allow you to goad me into ruining it. I understand that you're tired and emotional, but I won't let you self-destruct on me."

Of course he wouldn't because he was Theo the fucking Great. He couldn't be goaded. He was far too good and smart and upstanding to be goaded into acting like the rest of them.

"Fuck you, Theo. I'm done with you. Do you understand me?"

He stared at her, but there was a nauseating sympathy in his blue eyes. "Far more than you think I do. Baby, don't do this. Tell me what you need and let me give it to you. Let me ease you tonight. I know how bad you feel."

He couldn't possibly. He'd always had that face and that sunny air. He'd had a brother who loved him. Hell, when he'd found two brothers he hadn't known before, they'd welcomed him with open arms and made him part of the family. Maybe he hadn't had all the money in the world, but he'd had respect and love. She'd had none of the three. She'd had a father who'd actively hated her. Theo wasn't capable of understanding her. No one fucking was. "You don't know a damn thing and you'll step back if you know what's best for you."

He stood his ground. "I know something better, Erin. I know what's best for you. Me. Give over and let me take care of you."

Why the hell couldn't he take a hint? "I don't want you, Taggart. I don't trust you and I have zero interest in you. I want a real man. I want a man who doesn't whine and cry and need my undying love in order to fuck me."

"I need your undying love because you have mine," he said slowly. "But I'm beginning to think I'm going about this the wrong way. Maybe you need more."

"More than you."

He moved swiftly, his big body capturing her and pulling her close. He stared down at her. "Do you need me, Erin? I'll take that. I'll give you what we both need if you'll admit that we belong together. No words of love. Simply tell me this works for you and I'm not like the other men and we'll move this forward."

This. Them. Nothing special because she wasn't truly special, but then she knew that. She didn't know what his real game was. Did he have a bet with his brother? With the other boys from Ten's unit? Was he the kind of man who needed to know that he could have absolutely any woman in the world?

"You don't work for me, asshole. None of this works for me. I'm playing along because I don't want to lose my job. I'll have to leave this job because the boss's brother is an asshole who can't take no for an answer."

He paled a bit. "That's not what's happening and you know it. Your job isn't in jeopardy. Am I wrong? Have I scared you? It wasn't my intention."

His face was so earnest. He had scared her, but not physically. He wasn't the type of man who would impose his will on a woman. He would never force himself on her. He sure as hell wouldn't fight her and that pissed her off.

But his existence made her antsy, anxious. Angry. He was a prize she could never be worthy of. "Fuck your intention."

He sighed. "Let's go to bed, Erin. One day you'll understand that you are everything to me. You're the reason I was born. You're the reason I'll hold on long after I should have died. But today, let me comfort you. Let me do what I was born to do."

The words pierced her, so sweet and so untrue. She didn't deserve any of it. Not a single syllable. He was wrong. Or he was cruel. She wasn't sure which but either way she hurt. She ached with love for him and she couldn't stand it.

She punched him. Hard. In the nose. It was what she did. She felt bad, she did some violence.

Theo shrank back, cursing. "Damn it, Erin."

"Fuck you, Theo." It was all she could say. What the hell was she supposed to do? Beg for forgiveness and comfort and solace because he might—god, please—love her? She couldn't do that. Couldn't get super soft and subby for him.

His eyes went hard. "Don't do this. I want to be tender. I want to hold you and let you feel precious. But if you push me, I'll do what I need to do. What you need me to do."

Her hands fisted at her waist. Maybe she would still get her fight. "Bring it, Taggart. I'll fuck you up. That's what I need."

"It doesn't have to be this way."

But it did. "Screw you."

"All right, baby. Whatever you need." He was still for a moment and then turned away. He was leaving. He was walking away from her. There went the violence she needed. He turned back, his face falling like a fucking sad-sack baby. "Can I grab my bag? I'll work the shift. You do need some sleep."

In their bed. Alone. "I'm not sleeping, Taggart, but you can definitely get your bag and get out."

Her mind started whirling with bitter possibilities. She could use this breakup to get closer to Faith. Yes, maybe that would work. Maybe she could even stay with Faith and get the shifts moved around so she wouldn't have to see much of Theo. If Big Tag fired her, so be it.

She started walking toward the small building that had been their home for weeks. Domesticity had drugged her into becoming something she wasn't. She'd begun craving the time they spent together in their tiny house. They would eat at the commissary with the rest of the staff, but every morning he would wake up early and prep her coffee. He would climb back into bed and they would sit in the early morning light and drink coffee and talk.

And at night, after a long shower, she would pour them each a glass of Scotch and sit on his lap and watch a movie.

How long would it be before she felt like that again?

"What is it?" Theo had stopped, his hand on the doorknob.

Tell him. Tell him you were a bitch and that he's right and you're so tired you can't think straight. Ask him to take you to bed and hold you and maybe you'll find a way to cry and get the toxic shit out of your system because it's killing you.

Instead she rolled her eyes. "You're being slow, Taggart. Grab your bag and get out."

"Not going to give on anything, are you?"

She didn't have anything to give him. That was the real problem. He brought sunshine and she was used to rain. "Could you hurry it up?"

He opened the door and stepped away to let her in first. She stepped through the door and he was on her in a heartbeat. He caught her completely off guard, tossing her over his shoulder in a fireman's hold.

"What the fuck?" She started pounding on his back with her fists.

There was a loud smack as the flat of his hand rained fire down on her ass. He managed to grip her legs so she couldn't kick at him and still had the strength to smack her ass hard. "You want to do it your way, then I can be the hardass Dom. What's your safe word?"

Safe word? He was asking about her safe word? It was something they'd agreed on a long time ago as part of their cover.

"It's Winnebago." The worst vacation she'd ever had had featured a Winnebago. She'd been seven and her father had left her in a bathroom in Wyoming. It had been eight hours before he realized she wasn't there and he'd punished her for forcing him to drive back to get her.

"Use it if you need to."

"I don't need to use my fucking safe word, Taggart."

Another hard smack. "I think I'd like some courtesy from you. I'm bending. I'm doing what you need so you can either stop cursing me or I'll punish you for real."

She knew she should stop this here and now. Spit out her safe word and then chuck him straight out of their house. It would be easy enough to do. Theo would follow the rules.

He was also a sneaky bastard who would make her admit what she wanted one way or another. Not saying her safe word was basically the same thing as admitting she needed him.

So her best option was to get out of the game altogether. In this case, retreating would win her the war.

And leave her alone.

"Fuck you, Baby Tag." She knew how that annoyed him, knew how it rankled to have everyone compare Case to Ian but label Theo as the baby, the one who needed the others to watch out for him. Yeah, she always knew where to stick the knife in.

He moved into the bedroom. His kit was in the closet, but he hesitated. She could practically hear his mind whirling. If he put her down, would she run? He didn't trust her.

He shouldn't because she would run. She would make it as hard on him as possible without saying her safe word. She would make him hurt her because she did need it. She so deserved the pain and none of the real pleasure.

If she could draw out the nasty Dom, the man deep inside who needed to hurt someone a little to feel big, maybe they had a shot at a D/s only relationship. She could curb her need for him by bottoming. She would never be his girl, but she might be his submissive with clearly drawn boundaries and limits placed on them both.

He proved more creative than she'd given him credit for. Theo grabbed the long cord that charged her laptop and tossed her on the bed, face first. He immediately covered her body with his, his hands drawing her wrists together and binding them quickly.

Fuck, he'd been fast and that did something for her. The horrors of the day were slowly receding as she concentrated on giving her Dom as much hell as she possibly could. He hadn't gotten her feet yet so she tried to bounce him off her.

Theo put a hand on her back. "You stay down or I'll clamp those pretty tits of yours before we get down to business."

He eased off her cautiously, like a cowboy unsure as to whether the calf he'd so recently tied would hurt him or itself.

She was in the mood to do both. Erin flipped over and started to kick out, but the room was too small and he caught her before she could truly connect. His mouth twisted in a vaguely cruel grin as he held both her ankles in a single hand.

"All right, sub. Clamps it is. You want to go for a plug? Yeah, I checked my whole kit. I'm sure whatever passes for TSA in the various countries we've visited loved looking through that. Do you know what I do every day while you're having breakfast with Faith?"

"Jerk yourself off while listening to teen pop?"

He reached over to the tiny closet they shared and came back with the single tie he'd brought. One suit. One tie. Just in case, he'd told her. It looked like the tie would get some use in. He wrapped it around her ankles as he spoke. "I take out every toy and I carefully wash it and make sure it's ready for use because I wake up every morning hoping you'll decide today's the day you'll finally love yourself enough to let me love you, too."

"Don't spout that psychological shit to me."

He shrugged and continued on. "I look over all of it and I remember that I bought every single toy with you in mind. Not a one of them has been used on anyone else. They're for you. They're to torture and pleasure only you. You're the only sub I'll ever take and if you can't find the bravery to say yes, I'll pack it away and never use it again."

She could feel emotion strumming through her and it made her sick inside. She couldn't handle it. If he kept it up, she would be a sobbing mess and she didn't fucking cry. Never. Crying made her weak. "I don't want this, Taggart. I want the play, but I don't want this sentimental shit you're pushing."

His jaw tightened. "I thought I told you to stop cursing me. I don't curse you. I expect a modicum of respect when I'm topping you."

He flipped her over and she heard him rustling through the closet, likely reaching for his kit.

What was she doing? He didn't truly want this. He'd even told her. He was playing at being the top. He didn't need it the way she needed to bottom. It wouldn't work because he was pretending something he didn't feel.

Then she groaned because something hard and nasty came down on her butt and she couldn't breathe for a moment.

"It's a cane. You like a bite of pain, well I can give it to you.

You want to howl, baby. I'll make you scream." He brought it down on her again, this time hitting the backs of her thighs.

The pain bloomed through her, crisp and right. It flared and then sent shivers through her body. Her skin was suddenly alive when she'd felt flat for so long.

He caned her with a steady hand, the strikes moving from the flesh of her ass down her thighs. The ache began, but it was physical and so much easier than the one in her soul. This ache was a gateway to something else, something freeing.

He stopped and she heard more movement and then she felt him tugging at the waistband of the scrub pants she'd taken from the clinic. The sound of fabric tearing made her tense.

"Don't move. I don't want the knife to cut you."

She went still. "Those aren't mine. And don't even think about cutting my underwear off."

She felt it go.

"If you wanted to save it, you wouldn't have forced me to tie you up," he growled her way. "Damn, but you're pretty."

"I told you no sentimental crap, Taggart."

"And I told you to show me some respect."

She couldn't see what he was doing. After a few seconds, she felt him tug the pants and underwear off her, leaving her naked and exposed from the waist down.

"I don't give a shit what you think about your own ass. I think it's beautiful and fuckable and my dick hurts looking at it so you can keep your opinions to yourself or I will gag you. I think this whole evening might go better if I shove a ball gag in your mouth and take away your right to degrade yourself and the experience. Do you treat all your Doms like this? Or is it special because you don't have an ounce of respect for me?"

That question made her feel nasty. She'd always respected the lifestyle. Since the day she'd found it and knew she had a place in D/s, she'd given every man who'd topped her the respect they deserved. They'd all been carefully selected. None had ever hurt her and Theo Taggart wouldn't physically harm her on any level.

"I'm sorry, Sir. I do know the rules." No Dom wanted to listen to his sub moan and complain about her body. Self-denigration was frowned upon. Doms in her world took pride in building their submissives' confidence.

He gripped her hips and she found herself with her backside in the air. "It's pretty when it's all nice and pink."

He slapped her ass, this time with his hand. His hand was on her, cupping her and holding in the heat from the smack. After a moment, he ran his hand over her, fingertips tracing across her skin.

Yes, that did make her feel pretty. The trouble was she wasn't treating Theo like any other Dom. If they were going to try a pure D/s relationship, she had to start and that meant trusting him to bring her peace and pleasure. It meant giving over to him and letting herself find subspace. She could fight him again tomorrow. In the morning she could lay out all the new rules and they could sit down and bang out a contract that was for more than the operation.

But less than her soul.

She would be satisfied with that. Until he found the woman who could match him. Some day he would find a woman with his same shiny sunniness and she would be left out in the cold, but at least with that contract in place, she would never forget it. She would always know she was a placeholder for Theo Taggart's real woman.

"I think you're beautiful, Erin." He smacked her again, every stroke feeling like admiration to her. He said the right words to go with the very same actions that the vanilla world would deem cruel. They were perfect for her. Kind words. Hard hands. Agreed upon actions.

She groaned as he tore her tee shirt apart and then unhooked her bra. At least that would be salvageable. She had so few of them. He ran a hand along her spine.

"I think I promised you something about those pretty tits of yours."

She clenched her teeth because he had. He'd promised to clamp them, and her nipples tightened in anticipation. He flipped her over suddenly, her body twisting and the world shifting positions. He frowned as he looked down at her and she realized that the bra was about to bite the dust. "If I promise I won't move, you could untie my hands and ease the bra off."

His knife was already doing its work. "I told you."

Damn it. She was down to four now as he cut the bra off her body. He flicked the straps and she was naked to his eyes.

He stared down at her, her breasts outthrust because her hands were tied behind her back. Her knees bent to her left and she was absolutely sure she looked about as submissive and vulnerable as a woman could look to a man.

"I'm not saying my safe word, Theo." She couldn't take her eyes off him. He was still wearing his normal T-shirt and khakis as he loomed over her, but she knew what was under all that fabric. He'd been right earlier. She'd taken in every inch of his gorgeous, athletic body when they showered together. She'd memorized the whole of him from his broad shoulders to his muscular legs. There wasn't a piece of him she couldn't recall because she took him in every chance she got.

"Then you'll get more of me than you've ever had before, brat." Theo stared down at her breasts, his eyes hot as embers. "I'm not stopping tonight. I need you, too. Maybe I need you more than you need me. Maybe I've fooled myself all along, but I'll have you at least once if you let me."

She would let him. Already, she could feel herself sinking into that place where she didn't have to think about anything but her body and the sensations coursing through her. It was easier, faster because it was him, because he held the cane and the key to her pleasure.

One night. She could wake up in the morning and be wide-eyed and reasonable. That was when she would talk to him about a contract, but tonight she would sink into him, pretend briefly that they could work. He rolled her over, putting her on her belly.

"I think I promised you something and then I proved to be a terrible Dom by allowing myself to be sidetracked by this gorgeous ass." His hand came down and then the cane, the one two crack making her skin sing and the air leave her lungs. He laid the cane down and spread her cheeks.

Erin fought the urge to try to wriggle away. She'd agreed to this, still agreed to his topping her this evening, and that meant her body belonged to him until she stated otherwise. He was inspecting her, every inch and private part. She should have known the bastard would get nasty once she gave over. It was always the uptight ones who turned pervert when they had the chance.

The good news was she was a total perv herself. The fact that he was staring at her asshole made her heart start to race.

"Tell me something, brat. Has anyone taken this pretty hole before?"

She had to disappoint him. "Yes, Sir. I've had anal sex before. Not a lot here that's virgin."

His hands dropped, allowing her cheeks to come back together. "Oh, I can think of a few things, but you mistake me. I don't give a damn about your experience. I want you all the same. I don't care how many men you've had before. I only care that I'll be the best of them, the one who takes the finest care of you, the one you remember to your dying day."

He would be perfect if only he would stop with the sentimental shit. She would have to ignore it, to view it as one of his peccadillos that had little to do with her and everything to do with himself. She could ignore it all and focus on the feel of his hands, his ability to give her the sensation she required to get through this day.

He picked her up and flipped her over like she weighed nothing at all. It made her feel delicate and feminine when she usually felt neither. Not even close. She was tough and rough, but here when finding her submission, she could pretend she was a BDSM princess.

And damn but he was a Dom prince. At some point while she'd been face down, he'd dragged off his T-shirt and for some reason his khakis always rode low on his hips, showing off the gorgeous notches she wanted to lick and worship. He stood over her, his blue eyes roaming her body. His face had a nice amount of scruff on it since he'd barely left her side at the hospital. He'd forced her to eat, begged her to sleep, watched over Teta when Erin couldn't.

He'd been perfect.

She let that float away because she couldn't go there. The minute she started to think about how good it had felt to have him watching her, how she'd trusted him enough to fall asleep with her hand in his, she would lose it and she couldn't lose it.

Above all she had to stay tough. Weakness wasn't acceptable. Not even for a moment.

"I believe you promised me clamps, Sir." She needed to get his mind back on the play. They were fine while he was topping her.

Though hadn't he been doing that for days? Since the moment

they'd gotten on the plane to Frankfurt. He'd been bossy and wouldn't take no for an answer when he thought she wasn't comfortable. Sometimes he was sneaky about it, but now that she was staring up at him, she could see he'd been quietly topping her the whole time.

He loomed over her. With her hands bound behind her back, her breasts were thrust out. Her nipples were already hard points. He reached down and gripped the right one, twisting it with a wicked turn.

Erin whimpered. Maybe he was normally a quiet top, but he seemed fairly fierce today. That was what she needed, his hardness, his unrelenting will to dominate her.

"I promised I would make these sweet buds hurt. That's what you want, right?" He twisted her left nipple and she couldn't help the short shout that came from her throat. "You like this. It gets you hot."

Everything about him got her hot, but it was far better for him to believe she was only interested in the D/s. "Yes. This is what I want. This is why we probably can't work. You're not this guy."

He frowned, reaching down into the kit he'd snagged from the closet. "You let me worry about what kind of guy I am. I don't think you would be able to tell a good man from a bad one if he had it tattooed on his forehead."

She opened her mouth to reply in the snarkiest fashion possible but he stopped her by leaning over and dragging his tongue over her nipple. He laved it for a moment, spreading a wildfire through her system. That sensual mouth she'd longed for sucked at her breast, drawing the nipple between his teeth and then nipping her hard.

Erin gasped and squirmed as he tortured her breasts, going from one to the other and lashing her with his lips and tongue. While one breast was enjoying his affections, the other was tormented by his hands. He pinched at her, twisting the nipple in the most sensual of fashions.

She moved with him, offering him more and more.

That was when he slipped the clamp on.

Erin gasped, the alligator teeth of the clamp biting into her flesh. It was hard and rough and perfect. Even with her feet bound securely, she could feel her toes curl, and he went to work on the other breast.

He clamped her other breast and then stepped back, looking down on his work.

She was completely at his mercy, trussed up and open for him. Nowhere to go. No way to fight back. He had her totally and utterly.

It wouldn't work if she didn't trust him. She would fight and win, but she didn't need to now because he would stop any time she asked him to. All she had to do was say one word and everything ended, but she wasn't going to say it.

God, she might never be able to tell him no again.

"I'm going to get you up now," he said, his voice dark and deep. "I'm going to get you on your knees and you're going to apologize for the hell you've put me through. I don't want words. Words mean nothing from you. Your words come from a place I can't understand so I want action. I want the solace of your lips and tongue. Can you do that for me?"

Get that gorgeous cock in her mouth? Hell yes, she could do that.

"Please, Sir. I want it." She was far gone now. She wanted nothing more than to serve him and then he would reward her. He was that kind of guy. That kind of Dom. There would be no punishment after this if she behaved. Only pleasure.

When he picked her up, she was sure she would find heaven.

* * * *

Theo settled her on the ground, his dick throbbing in his khakis. What the hell was he doing? This was exactly what he'd promised he wouldn't do. He wasn't going to allow her to see him the way she saw all the other men in her life. As someone who used her and discarded her because she wasn't worthy. Some dickwad—or several—had convinced this amazing woman she wasn't worthy when she was.

He'd watched her for days as she attempted to save that child in any way she could. She didn't have the medical knowledge so she'd offered her will, her energy. She'd opened herself when he knew how fucking hard that was for her. She'd done it because the child had needed her.

And now this was all she would allow him to do to ease her grief.

He was a bastard because he didn't care in that moment. All that fucking mattered was the fact that he was going to have her. He was going to sink himself inside her and he knew he wouldn't ever want to come back out again.

She didn't have any trouble finding her balance despite the fact that her hands and feet were bound, a testament to both her long knowledge of the lifestyle and the fact that she was a magnificent physical specimen. She'd nearly taken him out and he'd been prepared for her. Had she caught him unaware, she would have easily taken him down.

It was stupid, but that did something for him. She was a serious alpha female and the fact that she was kneeling in front of him, ready to suck his cock made him feel about ten feet tall. She wouldn't bow for just any man. Hell, she wouldn't bow for him in an everyday setting. If he got his way and made her his, he would understand that the woman needed her place of power in their relationship. He would happily let every other man in the world call him pussy whipped. He wouldn't care because he loved her. He'd fucking loved her from almost the moment he'd met her.

"Sir, I can't actually open your slacks. Should I try with my mouth?"

"Hush." He wanted to remember this moment. Their first real sex. He'd taken care of her a few times, but had nothing for himself. Then he'd been a dumbass and withheld his cock, though he'd given her plenty of affection. He would never withhold affection from her. Not ever. Even when she didn't deserve it, he would give affection to her because she'd so obviously been deprived. He was her man. It was up to him to lavish her with everything she'd had too little of.

Too little love. Too little praise. Too little attention.

That's where he'd miscalculated. She viewed play sessions as positive attention. She needed permission to receive affection because she'd had so little of it before. She needed this and she might need the sex.

He would put aside his desire for some words in the face of her needs. He would sleep beside her every night after he'd brought her to a screaming orgasm and he'd wake her up in the morning with his cock deep inside her. He would be all over her and she wouldn't be able to deny him. If he had his way, she would forget that there had ever been a time he hadn't been on top of her, surrounding her, protecting her.

"Do you have any idea how beautiful I think you are?" He knew she didn't want the sentimental crap, as she would put it, but he couldn't let the moment go without telling her how gorgeous she was. She deserved to know he thought she was the most beautiful thing on the face of the earth.

"Thank you, Sir." But her eyes trailed away.

He caught her chin, forcing her to look at him. "If you don't believe another damn word I say, believe that. I've chased you from the minute I saw you. Give me the benefit of not being a complete idiot to chase something I don't want so desperately. I know you don't believe me, but I've never lied to you. Not once."

She remained perfectly submissive, but she wouldn't look up at him. He let his hand find her hair. Perhaps if he told her enough, showed her how much he wanted her, she would believe. He had to make her believe because he was fairly certain if he couldn't, he would lose her to her own insecurities.

He wasn't about to lose her. Not when he'd worked so fucking hard to get this close. Now that he was here, he could feel the warmth she kept hidden from the world. She was scared and he was going to show her there was no need to be afraid with him.

He was her safe place. He simply had to prove it to her.

He'd gone about it all wrong though. She needed to serve, needed to submit in this one place, and he hadn't given her the chance. She might accept his worship of her if he gave her a place to give back. She wasn't the kind of woman who wanted everything to be one-sided. Erin had to belong. Erin wanted so desperately to have a place for herself and he hadn't given it to her. He'd let his own fears keep them apart.

No more.

He leaned over and kissed her forehead and then stepped back. If this was what she needed, he could give it to her. No one else in the world would balance her the way he would.

And no one would move him the way she could.

Perhaps he'd started this BDSM journey because she needed it, but there was zero chance that he wasn't moved by the way she looked tonight. Her body was tied and trussed for his pleasure. She was open to him in the way she could only be when she was in this space.

Her breasts were small but perfect, the nipples a deep red from the tight clamps he'd placed on her. He couldn't leave them for long, but he would enjoy this moment of perfect submission before finding their connection.

That was the key. Finding the balance between the D/s she needed to feel safe and the affection in their everyday lives she was so thirsty for. He had to find a way to make her believe that she deserved both. He'd learned it was different for all couples. Some needed nothing more than the space to play and explore limits. Some needed a twenty-four seven hard contract to feel like they had sanctuary. Nothing was wrong as long as it was right for the couple.

Figuring out what Erin needed was the question of his life because the answer would set them both free. Free to love and be together as they'd been made to be.

It was pretty nice that it would start with a blowjob.

He unclasped the button on his khakis and shoved his boxers and slacks down. His cock bounced free. The damn thing knew exactly what it wanted. Hard and pulsing, it was ready for the feel of her mouth. He kicked off his boots and managed to get as naked as she was. He didn't want anything between them. She watched him silently as he undressed, her eyes on his body. Next time he would demand she undress him. There was an eagerness in her eyes that told him though she enjoyed the bondage, she wanted to play more of a part.

He gripped his cock, already hard and wanting. "I want you to get me ready to fuck you, brat. There's nothing I want more than to get deep inside you."

"Anything you want, Sir. And I apologize for what I said before. There's no limp dick here. I was mistaken."

She was a brat who wanted to make him insane, but he would play with her. He stroked his cock, making sure he was hard before he stepped up. She licked her lips, her tongue dragging across the bottom of her mouth and making his spine straighten.

"Damn right you were and if you spit bile my way again, I'll have to show you exactly how hard I can get for you. Kiss my cock. Drag your tongue over me and get me even harder for you."

Her eyes were up, a light in those emerald orbs. This was what she needed to hold back the horrors of the last few days. She needed respite, but had to be pushed to take it. Topping Erin would require careful thought and all his attention. Her self-destructive tendencies could be curbed if he gave her the right amount of dominance and affection.

She didn't play with him. No. His girl went right for the kill. She rolled her tongue over him, starting at the tip and dragging all the way to the base before starting back down again. Heat flashed through him, burning him in the best way possible.

He let his fingers find her hair, pulling it out of the sensible ponytail she usually wore and setting all that soft stuff free. Her hair brushed the tops of her breasts and he decided from now on she would leave it flowing and free for him. Only for play. It wouldn't work while they were patrolling, but it would be one more thing that was special for when they were alone. One more way to let her know she didn't have to be practical with him.

Besides, he couldn't control her with her hair in a bun. He couldn't tug her this way and that. There was so much about her needs that called to him. She needed permission to enjoy herself on a sexual level, needed her partner to take charge. He could do that.

"Suck me, brat." He tugged on her hair, watching as her skin flushed. He tugged again and she whimpered. "You like that?"

She nodded. "I love it. It feels so good."

She leaned forward again, her lips opening. He watched as his cock started to sink inside. Her tongue laved the underside of his cock, licking pleasure along his flesh. His whole body was tight with anticipation as she sucked the head between her lips. He tugged her hair again, forcing her to take more of him. She hummed around him, her head bobbing easily, going with the pressure of his hands in her hair.

Erin found the rhythm he set and worked over his cock with determination. Her tongue whirled as she sucked hard. She wasn't dainty about it. She enjoyed what she was doing and it showed in her enthusiasm.

He'd never had a woman have so much power over him. Her

smile made his day. If he saw her frowning, he couldn't stop until he'd turned it around for her. He'd never wanted anything in his life the way he wanted this woman. She was it for him and he knew he wouldn't find anyone else like her. Strong and smart and precious.

"Take it all." He wanted to feel her everywhere. He wasn't going to come down her throat. Hell, no, he was getting all the way inside her tonight. He was going to stroke into her and finally bring them together, but he wasn't about to skip on how good her mouth felt.

He could feel his balls drawing up, readying to shoot off, and he tugged on her hair to draw her away.

"There's time for that later. For now, give me permission to take you. Just once and then I'll play all the nasty games you like, but I need to know you want this. That you want me. Not some random-ass Dom. Me."

She sat back on her heels. "You should untie me."

His whole soul sank. He shouldn't have pushed her. Now she wouldn't get what she needed and they would be worse off than they'd been before. "Erin, forget I said anything."

Her eyes flashed at him. "I asked you to untie me."

He had to honor the request. With a clenched jaw and aching cock, he got to his knees and undid the bindings on her feet and hands, unwrapping her more slowly than he'd tied her because his eagerness was gone. He'd fucked everything up because he was selfish. Tonight was supposed to be about her. She was the one in need, but did he care? Fuck, no. He had to have his words. His ego wouldn't allow him to be used. Fuck his ego.

"Erin, I'm sorry. I knew what you wanted." He winced as he undid the clamps, but he seriously doubted she would allow him to soothe the ache the way he should, with his mouth and tongue.

She hissed as he unclamped the second breast and then allowed him to help her stand. When he thought she would turn away, she stepped close to him, her hands going to his shoulders, body brushing his in a way that had his cock right back to eager-puppy mode. "First, you have to replace the bite of the clamp with the suction of your mouth, Sir. Am I the first sub you've clamped?"

He wasn't sure what the hell was going on, but he wasn't about to question it. She was here and not stalking away. Those same nipples he'd tortured were grazing his chest. She moved like a sensuous cat who'd found her favorite scratching post. What did it matter that he was about to blast her hopes of a dream Dom? She was here with him and he was the dumbass he was. The one who wanted only her. "I practiced, but I let other Doms perform the aftercare."

Her jaw tightened as she looked up at him. "Why would you do that, Theo?"

How to explain that to her? "It was too intimate. I was only learning so I could top you. I didn't want that intimacy with another woman. Only you. I won't ever take another sub, Erin. I know you don't believe me, but I worry if you walk away from me, I won't have another woman at all."

"Fuck you, Taggart." But she'd gone up on her toes and her lips hovered close to his. "I swear to god if you're fooling me, I'll make your life hell. Do you understand me?"

She wouldn't take kindly to him being a liar or a cheater. Yes, he'd figured that out about her. The good news was he'd never been either of those things. "I do, brat."

"Next time you clamp me, you better take care of my poor breasts," she said. She was silent for a moment, looking up at him as though memorizing his face. "I want you, Theo. I know deep down I probably shouldn't, but I've started to wonder if that's the part of me I should listen to. She's kind of a downer bitch and I think she listened far too much to people who didn't matter. You'll kill me if you change your mind. You should know that."

His heart practically thumped out of his chest. They weren't through the woods, but he could see some light. It was all he could ask for. "You won't regret it. I'll take care of you. I'll need you to take care of me, too."

"I think I can handle it. You're a delicate flower," she said with a hint of a smile.

He let his right hand smack her ass hard, loving the way her eyes lit up. "Watch it. I'm still in control here. I'm going to kiss you now and you need to understand that I mean it. I mean every kiss, every caress. I'm going to eat you up because you're what I need to survive."

He lowered his mouth to hers and she flowered open, allowing him entry. Their tongues danced against each other and he could feel the difference. Always, she held a part of herself away from him. This time her hands moved up his neck and over his head, exploring and holding him close. This time she'd decided and she was in.

He wasn't ever going to let her get away again. He would take such good care of her that in a few months she wouldn't recall why she'd ever fought him.

Her skin was silky and smooth under his hands, though at times he could feel the slight raising of the scars she carried. He adored them. Each and every one. They meant she was tough, that she'd survived in a world that hadn't been built for her. He intended to create one where she would thrive. A private world for the two of them where she was the queen and she learned her worth.

He backed her toward the bed as he let his hands explore. She sighed and offered more and more of herself to him. This was what he'd been doing in the shower and late at night with her, making her comfortable with long, slow caresses. She didn't realize it, but she'd changed over the weeks. At first she'd been hesitant, a bit chilly. Now her back arched, a veritable demand that he pay attention to her breasts.

He lowered his head and did what he should have done when he'd taken the clamps off. He gently sucked one bud into his mouth. Her body shuddered, her arms dropping away as she let him take complete control.

He lowered her to the bed, knowing he had to please her first. He'd waited so long there was zero chance he was lasting once he got inside her. Later he would fuck her for hours, but tonight he feared was going to be more perfection than he could handle.

Theo followed her down, covering her body with his. Her legs moved restlessly against him as her hands eased over the muscles of his back and ass. She squeezed him there.

"Have I ever told you how pretty you are, Master?"

The first time she'd said the word Master and he believed she was talking about him. He would give her the pretty. If she wanted him to be pretty, he could handle it. He could handle her. "I try for you, brat."

Erin's eyes closed as he played with her other nipple. She was stunning when she let go, a creature of pure sensuality. He'd sensed it in her but rather thought this was a first. She wouldn't let go for anyone. She would find her pleasure, but this utter submission was only for him.

He sucked her left nipple into his mouth, his teeth grazing the sensitive flesh. Her legs moved against his, allowing him to find a place at her core.

His cock throbbed, but his cock wasn't in charge. Learning what brought her the most pleasure was the quest of the day. And comfort. Even while his body was engaged, he couldn't forget how hollow she'd looked as she realized her friend had passed away. He needed to give her something soft and safe, something to let her know the world wasn't as awful as it seemed.

He needed to know it, too.

"You're as beautiful as I thought you would be." He kissed between her breasts, starting to inch his way down her body.

"I never feel that way except with you," she admitted.

"You should feel that way every single day, every hour. You should walk around knowing how fucking gorgeous you are."

"Somehow I don't think the rest of the world thinks freckles are gorgeous," she murmured. "It's the price I pay for being a natural redhead. You wouldn't believe all the bullying I got."

He found one of the tiny dots she was talking about. "I love your freckles. One day I'm going to kiss each one, moving from one to the other like a connect the dots that makes my perfect woman."

"I wish I'd known you when I was in high school." She groaned as he dipped his tongue into her belly button.

He wasn't about to point out that he'd been in elementary school. She was sensitive about that but he kind of thought he needed the advantage of youth with her. She was too fierce, too strong. He needed all his damn energy to keep up with her.

"I would have carried your books and been the nerd who worshipped you." So close. He brushed his lips over her pelvis and breathed in the scent of her arousal. It was better than any perfume.

"You've never been a nerd once in your life."

Thought she knew everything, did she? "You didn't know me during my Dungeons and Dragons years, brat. Hush. I want to enjoy this. Hold on to the sheets. Don't move. This is my time."

She whimpered as his mouth hovered over her pussy. "God,

Theo, you're going to kill me. Please kiss me. Kiss me there. It's been so long and it was never any good. It's going to be good with you, isn't it?"

She was beginning to understand. It would all be good because he loved her. "Oh, baby, we belong together. This is going to be the best. I know. This is going to be the best, sweetest pussy I've ever eaten. It's going to be the last pussy I ever eat and I won't ever get my fill."

He lowered his mouth and kissed her briefly before getting down to what he'd wanted to do pretty much five seconds after she'd put him on his ass that first time. He'd wanted to get a taste of the most interesting woman he'd ever met.

He'd been right. Her arousal coated his tongue, and he couldn't help but want more. He knew he should tease her, draw out the play more, but he wanted her too much. He was a starving man.

He parted her labia and let his tongue explore.

"Do I have to be quiet, Master?" Erin's voice was reedy and thin. "I'm being still, but it's hard to stay quiet when your mouth feels so damn good."

"Make all the noise you like." Her clit was a pearly, creamy jewel poking out of its hood and tempting him.

She gasped as he ran the flat of his tongue over her clitoris.

When he sucked her into his mouth, she screamed out his name.

He eased two fingers into her pussy, but she was already coming. Her body tensed under him, though she held herself beautifully still. So disciplined. He sucked at her and curled his fingers deep, drawing the orgasm out while she moaned and her hands fisted in the bedsheets.

He let his eyes gaze up her body, seeing the way her head thrashed, but she kept her body still. She was biting her lip as she rode out the rest of the orgasm. Her chest was heaving as she dragged air in.

He got to his knees and reached for the condom he'd put on top of his bag. He tore it open and rolled it over his dick with shaking hands. He was so hard he could easily cover it. Theo stared down at her flushed body. She was a damn goddess. He didn't deserve her, but he was going to take her. Someone had convinced her she wasn't the stunning warrior princess she was and that she didn't need a prince. Well, that opened the way for the lowly soldier to take his queen and make her the center of his world.

He spread her legs further, lining his cock up with her pussy. "This is serious for me, Erin. Tell me to stop if you don't want this. If you don't want to try with me, let me know now."

He would fucking die if she turned him away now, but he had to give her the chance.

"Shut up, Taggart. We're together. I get it. Take me hard."

That was his girl. He gripped her hips and thrust inside.

His vision focused down to her, to her face, her body. He pressed inside, lowering himself down so their bodies were pressed together. "I don't want to be apart from you again."

Her hands came up to his back, nails lightly sinking in. "You talk too much."

She shoved her pelvis up and her legs wound around his waist.

He couldn't hold back a second more. She was everything he'd ever wanted and now she was his. He wouldn't let up. There was nothing she could do now. Erin was in his trap and he wouldn't open it again. He'd played fair and given her every opportunity, and now he was going to be the bastard who kept her close at every single turn. She wouldn't be able to get away from him now.

He thrust in and dragged his cock back out, the sensation spiraling through his system. She was tight and perfect. The heat of her body sent him reeling but he held on to her. He fucked inside her, working his way in inch by inch. The deeper he got, the more she gripped him.

She sighed under him, her body soft and submissive, and he couldn't wait another second. He fucked her hard, his hips pumping in and out. He rode her because she was his in that moment. Her hips pumped up, matching his rhythm like she'd been born to make this particular music with him.

He ground down on her, hitting her clit with his pelvis. Every breath brought him closer to paradise, but he was determined to keep going until she'd found her pleasure again. He twisted and shifted. He leaned over to kiss her, letting his tongue penetrate her as surely as his cock was.

She was his home. It struck him firmly as she took every inch of his dick that he'd searched all his life and this woman was his home.

Where he belonged wasn't a place. It was a person. Erin Argent. His soul mate.

"God, I'm crazy about you." He couldn't not say it. It wasn't what he wanted to say, but she might not be ready for that yet. *I love you.* He loved her so much. He'd always known it.

She smiled up at him, but her eyes were hot, her nails biting into his back as she worked with him.

He felt her clench around him and watched as her eyes dilated. She opened her mouth and moaned out his name as she came again.

He went wild. He didn't have to hold back. He could fuck her as hard as he liked and she wouldn't care. She'd been built to take him the same way he'd been born to please her. Made for each other. He thrust in and pulled out, his spine starting to bow. His balls drew up and he couldn't hold it back a second longer.

His body went tense as the orgasm rushed through him, shooting out of his body. Every muscle seemed infused with pleasure, with energy.

And then he collapsed, the moment passing and a sweet languor seeping through him. He didn't hold himself off her. He didn't have to. His girl was stronger than anyone he'd ever met. She could handle him.

The moment lengthened as he breathed her in, loving how their bodies meshed together.

A sudden shudder went through her.

He lifted his head and was shocked at what he saw. His warrior queen had tears running down her face.

"Baby, baby, it's all right." This wasn't about him. It was about what had happened. She'd finally found a place where she would cry. He'd given her that. He kissed her cheek and her forehead. "It's all right to mourn her. She needs someone to mourn her. Baby, I'll cry with you."

She was silent for a moment, but her arms were still around him. He shifted off her, still holding her close. After a long minute where he thought she might ignore him, he heard the sweetest words ever.

"She was so young, Theo."

She trusted him with her grief, trusted him to share it and take some of it from her. If she could do that, perhaps she would let him double her joy. That was how the world worked when you were loved well. The pain was lessened. The happiness was multiplied.

He held her tight, trying to give her the comfort she needed. Erin required intimacy to admit her vulnerability. "She was, love. You were close to her. Tell me everything."

He would listen all night if it helped her shed an ounce of pain. He kissed her over and over, taking her tears.

She sniffled and settled her head on his chest and slowly began to talk. Her arm wound over his chest and she tangled their legs as though she couldn't stand to not have an inch of their skins touching.

And Theo knew it was the beginning of their lives.

CHAPTER SIXTEEN

London, England
Present day

Theo sat in the conference room, unable to forget what had happened the night before.

He'd remembered. Not a foggy, distant, maybe that vision was real thing. He'd remembered how it felt to have her mouth on his dick, her tongue rolling over his flesh. He'd recalled how her eyes had lit up and he'd realized she needed to serve as much as to be served. That had been the moment he'd known they could work.

The conference door opened and Erin strode in looking cool and collected and totally calm. If he'd expected drama from her because he'd left the bed before she'd gotten up, he wasn't getting it. In fact, she barely looked his way. She walked right to Penelope Knight and smiled and started talking as Penny handed her a cup of coffee. There was another woman standing with them, a pretty woman with raven black hair. He was almost certain she was the London team's psychologist, Ariel Adisa. She smiled, greeting Erin with a hug and then pouring her own cup.

No crappy paper cups for McKay-Taggart and Knight. Nope. While Big Tag might be happy with that, the Knights obviously needed something a bit more formal. One side of the conference room was a beautifully laid out buffet complete with coffee and tea service and lovely china cups and plates. There was fruit and Danishes, but Theo hadn't been able to eat.

Because he was an idiot and when he realized that his "dream" was actually a memory, he'd tried to force it. He'd tried to shove through the cobwebs and ended up throwing up from the migraine he'd brought on. He'd stumbled down the hall to Robert's place so he wouldn't wake her up and spent the rest of the night shaking.

He hated Hope McDonald.

What should have been a peaceful night with his sub had been turned into gut churning hours away from her, and now she was acting like none of it had mattered. She was talking to Penny and joking with another chick when she should have come and greeted her Master, offered him her morning kiss, allowed him to be the one to get her coffee and see to her comforts.

McDonald sucked ass.

"Dude, I don't think that's a good sign." Robert leaned over.

"She's fine. Look, she just smiled at me." It was a bad fucking smile. It was Erin's fuck-you smile, but he had to play it cool. He hadn't told Robert exactly what had happened the night before. He hadn't mentioned that Erin had fallen asleep telling him the story of how they'd first made love and that his own memory had taken over and finished it. She'd almost been to the really good part when her eyes had closed and she'd drifted off. His own mind had taken over and he'd lived it. He hadn't told Robert how he'd rolled out of bed, desperately seeking the rest as though a few moments couldn't possibly be enough. He'd needed more. He'd needed everything so he could be the man she'd loved, the man everyone had loved.

He wanted so badly to be Theo Taggart again and not the pale, sad imitation.

He wanted to scrub the scar off his face and be beautiful again. She'd thought he was beautiful. She'd thought he was good.

He wasn't good now.

Robert sat back. "I don't know, man. I might have forgotten everything I know about women, but that looks like a fuck-you smile to me."

Robert hadn't forgotten everything at all. He had good instincts.

"I left her room because I got sick. I wasn't trying to hurt her. If she can't get that, then she isn't the woman I thought she was."

"Did you tell her you were leaving? Because I got the idea that you kind of snuck out."

"I didn't want to wake her." He wasn't the bad guy here. He'd had the best of intentions. He sure as hell hadn't wanted to wake up the baby. Then he would have had to deal with the baby.

He would have to deal with the fact that Erin would have chosen the baby over him.

Yep, there it was. He was certain Old Theo would never be jealous of a baby. Old Theo wouldn't have sat up all night holding his head and puking and hating the whole damn world. He even hated his old self. For a few moments he'd been able to feel it, to feel how good it had been that first night. He'd been alive and happy and he'd known he was good for her. His life had settled into place and he'd known what he wanted to do for the rest of his life. He'd wanted to be Erin's husband, to be her best friend, her Dom, her happy partner. He'd known he could be the man who made her happy.

He was no longer the man who made her happy. He was the man who disappointed her, who constantly made her life difficult.

He had to wonder if it wouldn't be better if hadn't come back at all. She would likely be happier. She would be at home with her son, finding her way back to the world. Not stuck in his own personal hell.

Erin said something to Penny and then began to move his way, coffee cup in hand. Dr. Adisa slid into the seat across from Robert, gracefully settling herself in.

Erin sank into the seat beside him, giving Robert a polite smile. "Good morning, you two. If you haven't met her, this is Dr. Ariel Adisa. She's the profiler for Knight's team. She's an Oxford trained psychologist who previously worked for Scotland Yard. She also swims through the sea and sings."

Ariel laughed. "Yes, I'll never forgive my parents. They were immigrants and they desperately wanted their first daughter to fit in. For some reason they decided naming me after a Disney princess would do the trick. I suppose I'm lucky they didn't choose Cinderella. It's nice to meet you both. I hope you found the accommodations comfortable."

"This place is amazing," Robert said. He didn't have Theo's issues. There was a plate with every kind of Danish available sitting in front of him. "I like the catered-in breakfast idea. Not that the last place I worked at didn't feed us, but it was all nutritionally balanced so our boss could easily keep us in tip-top shape to do her evil bidding. All in all, I'll take pastries any time."

Erin grinned at Robert. "That's the spirit, my man. You know how to handle the dark shit. You shove it down deep and make quirky jokes about it. I like you."

Ariel was still smiling as she tipped her head Robert's way. "Yes, that's terribly unhealthy. Don't listen to Erin. She's done quite well in therapy. I hope you'll continue yours while you're here."

Robert was staring at the gorgeous Brit. "Sure. I can do that."

Theo hoped Dr. Adisa was ready to have a two hundred pound lovesick puppy following her around. She started to ask Robert a question, but Theo had his own worries.

Erin turned back to settle into her seat. "I'm sorry for falling asleep on you last night. I certainly would have tried harder to finish the story if I'd known you were going to leave if I didn't. Should I have your bags moved to Robert's room? I assume that's where you went. From what I understand the guest rooms are all full."

"Yeah, I went to Robert's." He hated the fact that she wouldn't look at him, but he'd brought it upon himself. He'd promised to stay with her and hadn't lasted more than an hour without breaking it. That was the story of his life now. He was as unstable an influence as the man in his memory had been a rock. "I couldn't get to sleep and didn't want to wake you."

Ariel looked over at him, her intelligent eyes focused. "You're having trouble sleeping? Kai did mention you had nightmares in the beginning."

"It's nothing." He didn't need a second shrink up his ass. Getting away from Kai was one of the good things that had happened. He didn't want another doctor asking him to talk about his issues.

"He was vomiting like a crazy person because of his migraine. It was awful." Robert gave him up with what seemed to Theo like an unholy amount of glee. "He really would have kept you up. He kept me up. You should probably take tonight's shift."

Erin turned to him, her eyes going wide. "What? You got sick and didn't wake me up? What's wrong? Do we need to bring a doctor in?"

This was what he'd been trying to avoid. "No. It was a bad migraine. That's all."

She paled visibly. "It's because I fell asleep. I was right in the middle of a story and I drifted off and you tried to remember. It's my fault."

"It wasn't your fault." He reached out for her hands, grasping them in between his and holding them. "It was mine. I didn't try to remember. When you fell asleep, I think I did sort of stumble into the memory. Unless my mind was playing tricks on me."

"Which story was it?" Robert asked, watching them like they were the best TV show ever. "How you two met? He didn't tell me, just said that after he remembered he pushed it and tried to remember more. Always a bad idea. It leads to the headache, which for most people is enough of a deterrent, but if you push it hard, it'll lead to an insane migraine where you can't move or you throw up. Theo's awesome at getting to that point. He used to do it all the time back at Forgetful Base Camp. Dude liked to vomit."

"It's an extreme conditioned response," Ariel explained. "She placed triggers in his brain that cause his body to react. It's quite fascinating. Evil, but fascinating."

Erin's hands started to shake in his. He was going to beat the shit out of Robert. No doubt about it. He hadn't wanted Erin to see him like that and now she was going to worry he was some insane mental bomb waiting to go off.

Which he kind of was.

It didn't matter at that moment. All that mattered was calming her down. She had enough stress. He couldn't do it like this. Erin had always required touch over words. He tugged her up and had her sitting in his lap before she could protest. He wrapped his arms around her and held her tight, trying to give her that bound sensation that would make her feel safe and secure.

"I'm fine, brat. It was a rough night, but I got through it. Calm down. I'm okay." He kept his voice low. She would hate their problems being aired in front of everyone, but he couldn't let her sit and stew.

It took a moment, but she finally relaxed against him. She curled on his lap, her face turning up. "You're sure we shouldn't call in Faith? She could take a look at you. She's coming to the meeting so it wouldn't be out of her way or anything." She looked over at Ariel. "You have some medical training, right?"

"Some," Ariel agreed. "But this is more a mental problem than a physical one. As long as he stops thinking about the incident that triggered his response, he should be all right."

"I'm fine this morning." He was way better now. Holding her was calming him down, too. He breathed in the scent of her shampoo. Milk and honey. The damn smell always seemed to send a wave of peace through him.

"Did you really remember?" Erin whispered the question.

"I think so. You ended up crying in my arms. You cried for a long time, but holding you made me feel right. It was almost as good as making love to you."

"Dude, it was a sex story?" Robert said. "She's telling you sex stories?"

Erin turned Robert's way. "I'm beginning to not like you."

Theo couldn't see the look she'd sent him, but it had Robert on his feet, plate in hand. "I'm going to go and get a second helping before the Aussie shows up. I heard he can eat anything."

Ariel stood as well. "He's right. Brody is like a lion. He comes in and picks the buffet clean. I'll keep Robert company for a moment."

"That's my brat. She scares all the boys away." He felt grateful to the shrink as she walked away. Somehow he couldn't bring himself to set Erin back in her own chair. He knew he should, but she felt so fucking right sitting there in his lap, and it wasn't like anyone would think them unprofessional. Damon Knight had walked in and swept his wife up in a passionate kiss.

"I thought you changed your mind," she said quietly.

He had to be honest with her. "I change my mind on an hourly basis, but it's not because my feelings for you change. It's because I worry I'm not what's best for you."

She groaned, but her head nestled in the crook of his neck. "You're not smart enough to know what's best for me."

He had the almost overwhelming impulse to turn her over his knee then and there. "Watch it, brat. You know what I'm talking about. I've brought you a hell of a lot of trouble these past few weeks and it won't stop. It might never get back to normal."

"Then we find a new normal, Theo." She huffed, a frustrated sound, and moved off his lap, straightening her slacks and the prim white button-down she was wearing. "The fact that you had a full-on memory should tell you that you're not so far gone. Even if you were, even if you never truly remembered our past together, has it occurred to you that you could make new memories with me? Or does life have to be over because one fucking bad thing happened to you?"

He sat up straighter. "It was a big bad thing, Erin. Don't treat it like I got a hangnail and decided I couldn't continue with life. I was tortured. I had my memory erased. It was awful and it changed me."

"So change back."

Like it was that easy. Like he could make the decision to be someone he no longer was.

"You know what your trouble is, Taggart?" Erin's voice was so low he could barely hear her. "Your trouble is you didn't know what real heartbreak was until now and you have zero idea how to handle it."

He felt his face flush. It was a damn good thing she was doing this in front of an audience and not in the club because he didn't like the way she was talking to him. Not one fucking bit. He might have been a soft-hearted Dom in the past, might have played around with it, but he was harder now. She was pushing him, and he already knew so well that he could break. "Are you serious? Because growing up with an absentee father who left us when we were kids was awesome. And you know I was a freaking Navy SEAL. It's not like I haven't known a day's hardship or sacrifice."

"And yet you used to be so beautifully optimistic despite what happened to you. Forgetting all your pain really fucked you up, baby."

He was pretty sure his jaw dropped. "Are you kidding me?"

She was saved from having to answer by the door opening and the rest of the crew striding in for the meeting. Including a newcomer. He was lean and tall, looking more like a cowboy walking off the range than a former CIA agent. He knew it was Tennessee Smith because Faith was clinging to his hand and looking up at him like he was the sun in the sky. Or the dude who needed a shave. Ten Smith was a grim-looking man who lit up when he stared down at his wife.

This man had been his CO, a close friend. It had been trying to save this man that had cost him his life.

Why the hell couldn't he feel something?

Another man walked in behind Ten, and this one Theo remembered.

Ezra Fain. CIA agent. Ten still worked for the Agency as a contractor, splitting his time between McKay-Taggart and government work, but Fain was a company man. If he was here then Ian needed something from the Agency.

"Theo, man, I can't tell you how good it is to see you." Ten crossed the distance between them, his hand out.

Theo shook it. "It's nice to meet…see you again."

Ten stared for a moment. "Damn, brother, I'm sorry about what she did to you. I was only in that woman's tender care for a day or so. I can't imagine what months with her could do."

He didn't want to think about it. He was tired of all the sympathetic glances. This was exactly why he thought about walking away. No one would ever look at him without feeling sorry for what he'd gone through. No one would look at him like Erin had that first night, like he was everything. Everyone here knew he was damaged beyond repair.

"I'm fine," he replied, knowing no one in the world would buy it. He looked past Ten and Faith to the only man in the room he was certain didn't know him before. "Fain, good to see you. What's the Agency up to these days?"

Ezra Fain was a dark-haired man who looked like he had way too many secrets. Despite the fact that Theo was sure many women would call him handsome, there was a darkness to the man that made him wary. Fain's lips curled up in a smile that didn't quite reach his eyes. "A little of this and a dash of that. You know how we are. We like to keep our hands in all the pies."

"Yeah, well he came up with some intel that we need so I offered to bring him along. He's heading back to the States in a couple of days so we don't have to put up with him for long." Ten rolled his eyes and ran his hand across the beard that totally needed a shave. All that scruff made his former CO look a little like a dangerous hobo.

A genuine smile crossed Fain's face as he walked over to Erin. "Ms. Argent, it's a pleasure to see you again. How is your son doing?"

She gave him a grin that threatened to light up the room. "He's good, thank you. Growing like a weed."

Fain held her hand in between his. "I'm so glad to hear that. The last time I spoke with Case and Mia he'd been sick."

She shook her head. "An ear infection, nothing more, but I'm sure for Mia it seemed like the end of time. My boy can cry. He lets the world know he's in pain, if you know what I mean."

"You can let go of her hand now." What the fuck was that asshole doing standing there holding her hand like they were old friends or something?

Fain let go, holding his hands up as though to show he meant no harm. "I apologize if I was too familiar. I'm afraid I spend most of my time out in the field, so when I meet a woman like your sister-in-law or Erin, who is completely forthright and honest, I tend to enjoy their company very much."

According to Case, Fain had been more than half in love with Mia. Was he thinking of coming after another Taggart woman? "You should find your own then."

Ten was staring at Theo like he'd grown horns. "What's wrong with you?"

Erin merely rolled her eyes. "Don't bother, Ten. He's a dog with two bones. Let him be. Ezra, it is good to see you. Don't mind Mr. Grumpy."

"You probably should mind Mr. Grumpy," Knight said, sitting down at the head of the table. "From what I understand, he's also turned into Mr. Beats on People."

"Or Mr. Stabs Assholes who can't keep their hands to themselves in dark alleys." Robert had his back.

"We'll have to work on that." Ariel sank back into her seat, obviously ready to get the meeting started. "If he attempts to murder everyone who flirts with his sub, it could get nasty around here. Our men are all manwhores."

Nick chuckled as he grabbed a cup of coffee. "This I can promise is true. He tries to kill me, but we all know Russian fighters are the best in the world."

"Why don't we stop worrying about Taggart's understandable jealousy and get down to the task at hand?" Knight nodded to his wife, who sat down beside him.

Ten and Faith took seats across from Theo. Just as Fain was about to sit beside Erin, Brody Carter claimed the seat. The massive Aussie smiled his way. "Sorry, mate. This is my seat. Custom done because as we all know, Aussies are bigger than other men. More respectful, too."

Yeah, he liked the Aussie.

"Tell me I didn't miss anything." A sprite of a woman slipped into the room, her dark hair sleek and falling to her waist. She was Asian-American with a Cali accent he couldn't mistake. "I heard there was drama last night, but I was busy downloading a member of parliament's hard drive."

"Kayla." Knight's voice was a sharp bark. "New friends."

She looked over at Fain and shook her head. "Dude, the Agency knows all about corrupt politicians." When Knight wouldn't smile she sighed. "Fine. I was out in the West End with girlfriends having fun and not slipping anyone a roofie so I could avoid sleeping with them. Thanks for that, Ari. It was so helpful. He went down fast. And Damon, next time find someone hot for me to not sleep with. That dude was the poster child for the need for better body odor elimination technology. Not that he existed or anything."

It was Knight's turn to sigh. "Theo, this is Kayla Summers. She's our resident close cover expert. Owen and Walter are out on assignment this morning so this is the crew for now. Mr. Smith and Mr. Fain have come to us with some new intel."

Finally he could stop worrying about his personal life and get down to business. One of the reasons he was happy to be out of Dallas was the fact that perhaps Damon Knight would let him work in a way his brothers wouldn't. They gave him desk jobs and research work. He needed to be out there in the field hunting her down.

Or being the bait for the trap that brought her in. He didn't care which as long as he was involved. Work would take his mind off things, give him focus.

Work would make him forget that fucking Ezra Fain had made her smile because he'd asked about TJ when Theo wouldn't even check on the kid. He'd held him, but the boy had been asleep. Anyone could hold a sleeping baby. It was an awake one that made him worry. An awake one would need his father and Theo wasn't it. No matter what biology said.

Ten sat back. "I've been following up on some leads we got back in Africa when Erin here managed to lure McDonald to Stephanie's clinic."

"I thought that was my brother." This was the first he'd heard of Erin being involved.

Fain snorted slightly. "As if. Case didn't come up with that plan and neither did Ian. That was pure Argent. One of the smartest, meanest women I've ever met. I totally mean that as a compliment."

"No offense taken. I am quite mean," Erin replied. "And it was my plan, but it was Avery O'Donnell who made it happen. She took something awful that happened to her and turned it into me getting my…into bringing Theo home. So she gets all the credit and there's not a damn thing mean about that woman."

What was that about? There was a tremor to her voice that told Theo she was emotional about something. Li's wife, apparently. They were close, but he wasn't sure what she meant about her being the woman who saved him. Then again, he'd thought his brothers had been behind the plan to rescue him.

What had he thought? That Erin would be sitting at home like a good little woman? Not a chance. She was fierce. She would have been right there, making plans, taking chances.

Erin cleared her throat and turned to Ten. "So you've been following her? Physically?"

"When I could track her, yes. I even managed to take a shot at her while we were in Malaysia. Had her right in my sights, but she dodged a dog that was coming at her and I missed," Ten grumbled.

"It's a good thing since we now know she has a whole other unit." Fain had his tablet out. "I'm sure by now she's got some support, but I worry what would have happened to those men if you had managed to take her out. She didn't exactly leave their cell doors open."

"They could have starved," Robert agreed. "One time she left Victor and I alone for three days and had to rehydrate us. That was when she started leaving us with Tony. He'd been around some, but he came on full time then." Robert stared at Ezra. "He was with the Agency, too."

"I'm still not so certain you weren't, too, lost boy." Ten Smith's Southern accent was deep as he stared Robert's way.

Fain gave him a nod. "I was wondering about that, too. If he was deep cover, the higher-ups wouldn't admit they lost him. You see the footage?"

"The footage from the CCTV cameras at the park?" Theo knew exactly what they were talking about. Robert had fought brilliantly. He had to be well trained. "My first thought was Special Forces."

"The military would look for him," Ten pointed out. "There would be records."

Robert leaned over. "Can you figure out who I am?"

Fain considered the situation for a moment. "I can try, but if you are what I think you are there's likely not a trail to be followed. You would have signed away your life."

"And I would have to have been the stupidest asshole operative if I got myself caught by Hope McDonald." Robert shook his head. "I'm not with the CIA. I'm not smart enough. I'm just an asshole no one cares about. What have you found out about McDonald? Where is she now?"

Theo wanted to push the subject, but it wouldn't matter until Robert was willing to deal with it. When they found the threat, he could quietly start trying to figure out the secrets of Robert's past. "And do we know where her base is? She'll have to have a suitable place to hold the men."

"She had to move fast when we caught up with her last time," Fain explained. "So I managed to find a few things she left behind. She wiped all the computers, but we went in with a team and took everything from the sheets on the bed in the cells to the drinking fountain."

"Did you get a sample of the drug?" Erin asked quietly.

Everyone in the room went tense.

This was the question. Who would get control of that drug?

There was zero question every government in the world wanted control of it, wanted to test it, to see how it could aid their cause. It was what governments did.

Fain grimaced. "Yeah, she was careful about that. You know how doctors can be."

Faith leaned forward. "Luckily, I did manage to come into a small dose."

Ariel leaned forward. "I would love to help you break that down, though you understand the drugs are only a part of the problem."

"How did you do that?" Nick asked. "I thought you had no contact with your sister."

"How small a dose?" Knight talked over Nick.

"Has it been analyzed?" Penelope pulled out a notebook.

"I want to know how she got hold of it, myself," Brody was saying.

Ten sent the Aussie a nasty glare. "Back off."

It was so obvious. He was the one who'd forgotten everything. Why was he the only one who could see what Fain had done? Case had told him Fain was solid for an Agency man. Fain had been the reason he and Robert hadn't been hauled into some government hospital and put through twelve million tests. "Guys, Faith isn't dealing with her sister. Fain slipped her the sample so if anyone asks he simply doesn't know. Give the dude a break."

Maybe it wasn't the worst thing in the world that the asshole had made Erin smile. It wasn't like she was flirting with him. He was being a jerk again, making Erin feel bad about something she had zero control over.

What had she said? Change back. He couldn't change back, but he could acknowledge when he wasn't treating her right and try to fix it.

Fain's hands came up in the universal sign of "that's not my problem." "Whoa. I have no idea what you're talking about. I didn't find anything like that, but if I did, I would probably need a doctor to figure out what all was in it so we could use the components of the drug to try to find her new place of business."

"Ah, you're going to look for shipments." Erin turned to her friend. "Have you managed to break down the components of the drug?"

"Not entirely," Faith replied. "It's more complex than merely breaking it down. I need to know exactly how she formulates it and that's about more than a recipe. She could be mixing certain drugs to form the base. She could be changing materials with heat or cold or separating them and putting them back together but changed. The point is, I think she's manipulating the materials to create something completely new. I need to know exactly how many doses she's making in order to look for what she would order. I'm still working on it, but I have a lab set up here in Chelsea and Walt is going to help me figure this thing out. Dr. Adisa, you're more than welcome to help."

Ariel nodded. "I would love to be there, but Walter is your best bet. His CDC experience was extensive and we all know he's good at breaking down chemicals."

"He'll be on it tomorrow. I'll recall him. We know there were seven cells at the center in Malaysia," Knight pointed out.

"And there were seven men who attacked me and Robert." He'd counted them carefully, tried to memorize their blank faces, seeing his own there. He'd known that mere months before he would have been one of them. He would have been the man trying to bring the lost "brother" home.

"Two are dead." Robert's face had gone blank, likely thinking what Theo had been. He would have been one of those men, too. Perhaps one of the ones who threw themselves into traffic because failure was not acceptable and the "family" secrets were more important than individual lives. "So unless she's found some more subjects, she's dosing five men roughly three or four times a week depending on how long they've been with her. Or how stubborn their systems are."

Ten's hand ran over his wife's as though seeking comfort or perhaps giving it. "The trouble is we now believe she's refined the drug."

"I haven't done all the work I need to do, but I do believe there are some differences between the drug she gave to Robert and Theo and the one she's using now," Faith explained. "We believe she's managed to amplify the drug that targets the long-term memory center of the brain. Ezra found some handwritten notes she tried to

291

burn."

"She didn't get them far enough into the fire," Fain continued. "It was the only break we caught. According to her notes, she can wipe a memory with one dose now. We believe she was using the secondary site to experiment. She had her primary team, Theo, Robert and the man they called Victor. She used the first iteration of the drug on the primaries. The secondaries were more, shall we say, expendable."

Nick's lips turned down in a fierce frown. "And how do you know this? You say you didn't find other notes."

"Bodies," Ten said, his voice flat. "They found fourteen bodies."

Theo's stomach threatened to go south again.

Robert stood up, his skin pale. "I need a minute."

He strode out the door. Theo stayed in his seat. He knew what Robert was about to go through and he would want some time alone. It wasn't easy to figure out how expendable you were, how close you'd come. If Robert hadn't been in the right place at the right time, he could have been on that secondary team.

"All right, so we're waiting on the components of the drugs to be fully identified," Theo said, trying to keep his voice even. "After that we're going to do what? Look through every pharmaceutical vendor to figure out where they're sending these drugs?"

Erin shook her head. "She's got a new partner. She'll use them. All we have to do is figure out where that company is sending the right mix of drugs and we'll know where she is. I suspect we could also hack into their systems and track new real estate acquisitions or older properties that have been recently renewed. What kind of equipment would she need to formulate the drug?"

Damn but she was smart. "They'll send it to her. If we can find the big-ticket items, we can find her. The invoices won't be so obvious, but they also can't simply ship expensive equipment without leaving a paper trail. The majority of employees in Collective companies have no idea they work for one. It's only the men at the top who are committing the crimes."

Knight's fingers tapped along the conference table. "Yes, it would be easier to track the equipment than the drugs. That kind of equipment requires careful handling. I'm sure they'll use some kind of a cover corporation, but we can guess from the time and type of equipment. I believe she's somewhere in Europe. I think we should start looking for shipments to Eastern Europe."

"We should call Adam in," Erin offered. "He can hack into the system and get us the data we need."

Something was wrong. Ten and Fain should be jumping all over this discussion. They should either be agreeing or explaining why everyone else was off base. They were used to running meetings, not sitting by quietly with grim eyes as though they knew something no one else did.

He looked down and saw that Ten's hand clutched Faith's. His face was perfectly passive but that hand told the tale. He needed comfort.

"What's happened?" The question came out in a croak. His throat still hurt from the night before and now it felt parched and ragged.

All eyes were suddenly on Ten and Fain.

"We're worried she's got a reliable man working for her. Someone who could potentially get around Adam," Ten explained.

"You think The Collective is supplying her with a hacker?" Knight asked. "So they would go through the proper channels and then the hacker would go back and erase it?"

"Or send us on a wild-goose chase." Fain stood, his tablet in hand. He moved toward the back of the conference room where he connected the tablet to the media system.

Ten began to talk as Fain set up the projector. "I started to suspect something was wrong a few days ago when Big Tag gave me the heads up about what was happening with Erin."

"Are you talking about the fact that someone managed to tag her laptop?" Brody asked. "I found that surprising since we use one of the best firewalls on the planet."

"It's a specialized system that Adam, Chelsea, and Hutch came up with," Erin explained. "And it's fairly new. We've been using it for about eighteen months. They test it constantly. I couldn't believe she managed to get in. Adam is still trying to figure it out, but Serena's been traveling so his focus is a little off. It's hard with Chelsea working for the Agency and Hutch gone. We need a second communications person."

He was definitely getting nauseous again because something bad was coming. He could still see the tension in Ten's face. They hadn't gotten the bad news yet.

"I think I've figured out who got McDonald onto Erin's system." Fain killed the lights and a single photograph appeared on the wall in front of them.

Hope McDonald was smiling, walking down a street with a tall, thin man. There were two men walking in front of them and two behind them, obviously protecting the two between them. McDonald appeared to be talking, a designer handbag tossed over her shoulder.

"This was the shot I could get of him." Fain's voice floated through the tense air as everyone seemed to have stopped breathing. "Apparently Ten trained him well. Or maybe it was Big Tag. It definitely explains how he's kept an eye on the team. He used his own backdoor into the system. From what we can tell he's downloaded a ton of documents on McKay-Taggart operations."

The man in the middle was glancing up but there was no way to mistake him.

Hutch.

CHAPTER SEVENTEEN

Erin stared at the screen, trying to make it turn into something else. They'd gotten it wrong. That couldn't be Greg Hutchins on the screen with Hope McDonald. It was some kind of a joke.

Except Ten and Ezra looked pretty damn serious.

"I don't understand." It was all she could think to say. She thought about reaching for Theo's hand, but he'd withdrawn, turning his chair away from hers.

One step forward, a whole mile back. Every time they made the tiniest breakthrough something shitty happened.

"Where was this taken?" Theo ignored her, staring at the screen. His voice was flat and she could see his hand was fisted in his lap. "And when?"

"Three days ago," Ezra replied. "And it's a street in Tallinn, Estonia. We believe that's where she's got her new lab set up. The pharmaceutical company has a small base there. And it's close to Russia. We're fairly certain she's found ties to the Russian mafia."

Then they could have an in. "With the Denisovitch syndicate?"

Ten shook his head. "Already tried to work that angle. Charlotte's relatives claim they know nothing about it. I don't think they're involved, but her cousin also won't work with us unless there's a direct threat to his family. He's got a reputation to protect. We're on our own here."

"So we think we know where we're looking." Theo turned toward Damon. "I'll be on a plane to Estonia in the morning."

Erin felt the room go cold. "No. No, you won't."

Theo turned hard eyes on her. "I will. She's got Hutch. I can't leave him with her. You have no idea what she could be doing to him."

Ten frowned Theo's way. "I don't think you understand."

"Theo, he walked away from us," Erin said gently. "He left us. No one took him. We even tracked him getting back into Europe. He was alone."

Now that she thought of it, Hutch had used press identification to cross the border. He'd claimed he was a Western journalist covering the immigrant crisis caused by the Syrian civil war. Posing as journalists had been one of the ways McDonald had gotten Theo and the others around the globe.

"So she found him later and took him," Theo argued. "Like she tried with me. She's trying to get the team back together. Can't you see that?"

"His body language is relaxed." Ariel was studying the screen. "There's nothing about the way he's standing that tells me he's tense or doing anything he doesn't want to do."

Theo turned on the profiler. "It's one picture. One second of the day. You can't possibly figure out what's happening from one picture."

If his harsh tone bothered her, Ariel didn't show it. She was serene, her voice soothing and calm. "That is true, but I've been given more than a simple picture. I've read Mr. Hutchins's files. I find it interesting that during his first incarceration by Dr. McDonald he managed to work with you, and yet this time he's obviously the one who gave her access to Erin's computer. There's no evidence he did anything like that the first time."

"He fought her. He fought for us," Theo insisted.

"But according to all accounts of the operation to rescue you, Mr. Hutchins didn't fight. The only person he hit was you," Ariel pointed out.

Ezra turned the lights back on. "It's true. I was there. He had multiple opportunities to help us out. He chose to retreat to the plane where from what I can tell he was preparing to move out when Case managed to get inside. We have to accept the probability that she turned him."

"No." Theo wasn't listening at all. "He was upset. He went after her. She somehow found him and forced him to work for her again. He's the one who sent us the intel that she had a new backer."

"He needed a way in," Nick explained. He was going through the files he'd brought in. "Yes, here it is. I got the notes from Miles. Hutch sent the e-mail and that granted him access to the systems. That was when he pulled all the files down and found his way into Erin's system."

"You're wrong. I'm calling my brother. You're all fucking wrong about this." Theo stalked out.

Erin stood, but Ariel shook her head.

"He won't listen to you right now," Ariel said. "He needs time to process."

She was probably right. Theo—this Theo—wasn't always rational and if she pushed him, it might start a fight she couldn't win. "I need to process. You guys don't know Hutch. He's a good kid. Ten recruited him."

"Out of prison," Brody pointed out. "Am I right? He was in prison for hacking?"

"It was juvie and he fell in with a bad crowd. I actually talked to him while he was in. He got released right before his eighteenth birthday. I told him I would consider him for the Agency if he could survive a year in the Army." Ten looked like he could use a couple of days' worth of sleep. "I wanted to make sure he learned some discipline and that he was serious about changing his life. Hutch was smart and he was kind, but there was a lot of anger in him at the time."

"And that's not why you recruited him." Ezra sat across from Ten, his eyes on the former agent. "Don't bullshit me. We both know why you went after Hutch in particular, and why he left when the Agency tried to keep him. It's relevant information."

Ten sighed heavily before speaking. "Damn it. I recruited him because it was so obvious to me the kid wanted a family. His dad died when he was a teen. He came back to the States with his stepmother, but it wasn't long before he ran away. He lived on the streets for a while. He finally found a place with a group called The People's Revolution."

Erin had never heard any of this, but she knew that name. "Damn it. The anarchist group? The ones that hack political figures to prove the government is corrupt?"

"That same one," Ten agreed. "He got caught when he hacked a university system to prove they were glossing over a series of rapes perpetrated by the football team. His evidence forced the prosecution that landed three footballers one-year suspended sentences because, boys will be boys you know, and Hutch was sentenced to three years in juvie for hacking. No suspension for him."

"Our justice system in action," Erin said under her breath. "How long was he in before you made a deal with him?"

"Six months. I got him out, put him in the military and before long he was ready to work for me. I was right. He viewed me as a father figure and that kid was more loyal than any man I ever had." Ten's head fell back on a groan. "And then I dumped him on Tag."

"He had the opportunity like everyone on your old crew to stay at the Agency," Fain pointed out. "He turned us down."

"Because his loyalty wasn't to the CIA, Mr. Fain." Ariel sat back, obviously considering the situation. "His loyalty was to Mr. Smith and to his team. His team left so he did as well."

"He was loyal to us." She hated the fact that they were talking about Hutch like he was some kind of unsub. He was their friend. This all had to be a mistake. "You don't understand how sweet he can be. And I'm not talking about his blood sugar level. When Theo was gone, he stayed with me when Case couldn't. He never complained."

"He wouldn't. I doubt Mr. Hutchins would complain seriously about anything. He would view service as a way to make a place for himself inside the family unit," Ariel explained. "He likely volunteered often."

Hutch was always the first to offer to stay late or to go grab pizzas for everyone. He would hang out with the guys, and his apartment was always open if anyone wanted to play games. "Yes, he did, and the guys adored him. He had a place in a family. Our family."

"And then you left him with Hope McDonald." Knight's face was grim as he looked at her.

"We didn't leave him."

"You could have saved him sooner, but you wanted to be careful. You wanted to leave him in so he could lead you to Theo Taggart." Nick said the words casually, as though they weren't devastating. "That was your plan. If Hutch had told you exactly where he was, would you have gone in guns blazing?"

After what had happened with Theo the first time they'd tried that, no. "Theo was too far gone. He nearly killed Case the first time they met up. We needed a carefully laid trap in order to save him."

"Yes, Theo," Knight agreed. "Not Hutch. Hutch was smart. He could figure out the plan. He was the inside man. It was his job to take whatever she gave him while you waited for the perfect opportunity to save the man who really counted. Theo."

"It wasn't like that." Erin hated the way it sounded. That hadn't been their intention at all.

"Wasn't it?" Nick waved a hand. "I'm not saying Taggart was wrong. If I am placed in this position and it is say, Brody, we were trying to save, I would do this for him. He is only an Aussie. He would need someone strong to take care of him."

Brody snorted. "Yeah, you'd save me. That's a fine story, mate. But you're right. Any one of us would do what it takes to save a teammate, so I'm with the girl here. I don't quite buy it. And I never did understand why he walked away. All he could talk about that night was getting back to his place and taking up some game he'd been playing."

"He could have been planning his escape the entire time," Ariel explained. "I've never met the man so I can't know anything for sure, but if he does have problems with abandonment, he could have been angry with the whole group. I know McDonald didn't give him the same drugs she gave to her soldiers, but you have to consider some amount of brainwashing was done."

"He would hate her." She couldn't accept this.

"Hate is a weird thing," Ezra said. "Sometimes it can transfer to someone who doesn't deserve it. I can think of a scenario. Hutch had been dragged in to find Theo. He knew how much everyone loved Theo, but when it was his life on the line, you all were willing to wait."

"It wasn't like we could barge in and save him," Erin argued. "The plan of action we agreed on was best for both of them."

"I didn't say it wasn't, but we have to look at this from Hutch's point of view," Ezra shot back. "There's no guilt here. But if you stand in his shoes, everything in his world was all about Theo. He gets kidnapped and his new 'mother' is all about Theo. The plans to rescue him have to wait for Theo. When he was finally saved, was anyone concerned with him? Or did you all gather around Theo?"

"We thought he was dead." Ezra might have said there was no guilt, but Erin felt it deep in her gut. She'd greeted Hutch, given him a hug, but all her energy had been on Theo. She had to admit, they had a point. He could have felt abandoned and Theo was right, too. No one knew exactly what had happened to Hutch while he was with McDonald. The doctors had looked him over and then moved on to Theo and Robert.

"Then we have to acknowledge the fact that Hutch might have left on his own and sought her out on his own," Ezra explained. "We have to consider that he's banking on his place with McDonald as more settled and secure than the one with McKay-Taggart. Or he could be angry enough that he wants power and this is how he's getting it."

"It's all conjecture," Ariel interjected. "But I'll contact Kai and Eve and get their takes on the new information. And Damon and Ten will have to get together with Ian to decide how to handle the situation."

"If he's been brainwashed, I'll clean it out for him again. Ian won't leave him behind and he sure as hell won't issue an order than might hurt him." It didn't matter what was going on. Hutch was one of them and that meant he didn't get left behind.

They'd made a mistake by not being careful enough with him.

How alone had he felt? Alone enough to learn to hate Theo?

Erin took a deep breath and banished the ache in her heart. She would take it out later and examine it, poke and prod it so she could find some peace with her actions, but for now she had to soldier on. "What's our next move?"

"I'm sending Brody and Penelope to track the lead in Estonia." Knight closed the notebook in front of him. "Darling, I hate to ask you..."

Her blue eyes had taken on a gleam. "Don't finish that sentence. I'm the only one who speaks the language. Well, I speak Finnish and that's close enough. Brody and I will be fine. And you'll take care of our boy."

Knight's hand reached out and held his wife's. "I will."

"I can totally babysit," Kayla offered. "You have fun, Pen."

Damon tugged her out of her seat and into his lap. "It's not fun. None of this is fun. Why don't you all give me a moment with my wife? We'll meet back here for tea and I'll hand out assignments then. You're dismissed."

Erin knew an order when she heard one. She stood up and Faith was suddenly beside her.

"I'm so sorry you found out like that," she said quickly. "Ten just walked in. He and Ezra didn't get here until right before the meeting."

"He had to know," Ten insisted as they walked out and into the hallway that led to the offices. Everyone was breaking up. The doors behind Nick, who was the last one out, closed and Damon shut the blinds.

"Where's Theo?" A spark of fear went through her system. He could be crazy enough to go after McDonald. He could do something stupid on an emotional whim.

"I instructed the guards not to let him out until Knight countermands my orders," Ten said. "I knew he was going to get upset. He seems different."

"He is different," Kayla said. She hadn't spoken the entire meeting, but she stepped up now. "Look, I know everyone's been through bad shit, but we all handle it differently. I don't know that therapy is going to work for him. I say that because it didn't work for me. I spent six months in a prison unlike anything you've seen. I did not do well. When I got back it was home to a place that wasn't home at all."

Kayla had been a double agent for the CIA. She'd worked in China's MSS for years before she'd finally come back. She'd taken a job with the London office. Erin had always wondered why she'd chosen London.

"But when you had the chance, you didn't go back to the States." She studied the younger woman. Kayla showed some scars of battle, but she had a bright smile and a sunny attitude. "I know Ian offered you a job in Dallas. You requested the London office."

"Because I wasn't the same," Kayla replied. "Because I needed something new."

"Theo doesn't need something new," Ten said with a frown. "He has a family."

A brow arched over Kayla's left eye. "And I don't? I assure you there are two men in Santa Barbara who would disagree with you. But I get that you're saying he's got a kid. I love my dads, but I spent very little time with them those first few months. It wasn't until they showed up on my doorstep that things changed."

"Why wouldn't you spend time with them?" Erin asked.

"Because I didn't think they could love me. Not the way I am now. I went into the service and I was so young. They knew a happy college student and I came back a thirty-year-old who'd killed more than once, who'd seen more horrors than they'll ever know. I didn't want to face the me I'd been."

Like Theo. "So you think being around me is hurting him?"

She shook her head. "Not at all. My dads showed up a month after I moved here. They knew I was doing something for the government that kept me away from home and out of touch most of the time, but they didn't know everything. So they showed up and demanded entry. That was when they found out about the kink. Yeah, that was a conversation. And they stayed with me. They were obnoxious and normal and the stupid thing was they brought a dumbass poodle with them. I grew up with dogs. I always had them around. It was the dog that finally did it."

"The dog?"

She sniffled a little, her eyes watering. "That dog didn't care. She only wanted someone to cuddle with. She didn't care that I've had blood on my hands, that I've been brutalized and done my own share of damage. I ended up holding that dog and crying my eyes out and telling my parents everything."

"Uhm, a lot of that was classified," Ten pointed out.

Faith slapped a hand on her husband's chest. "You hush. You're the one who sent her in there."

"My point is, you might want to give him space and time, but what he needs is that one thing to hold on to, that one thing that makes him feel new and clean." Kayla put a hand on Erin's arm. "He'll find it. I know he will. But you have to have faith. In him. In you. He loved you for a reason."

"He thinks he's a completely different man now." He kept telling her that. She couldn't believe it. Theo was still in there somewhere.

"He's pissed off and angry with the world," Ezra said. "Look, Kay's got a point, but Theo's a man and we process these things differently."

Ten leaned against the railing, looking out over the club. From this height, it looked like a dark, decadent jungle right there in the middle of the building. "He's right. We're not as willing to talk about it. We need other forms of expression. Has he been more violent? Did she train that into him?"

"He isn't violent." She wasn't going to have anyone thinking that Theo was hurting her. He had enough guilt and not once had he followed through on the impulses McDonald had planted inside him. "He's strong. He still resists everything she forced him to do, but I do think he's felt out of control for too long. Finding out about Hutch isn't going to help."

"He'll either believe that Hutch is working with McDonald and that a friend has betrayed him or he won't accept it and he'll be at odds with the rest of us." Ten cursed under his breath. "Or he'll think if Hutch was under her control, it's only a matter of time until he falls prey to her again, too. If there had been any way to have kept this confidential, I would have, but he had to know."

She understood, though she too wished he could have been kept in the dark. It wasn't smart because Theo had to know there was something going on or he could trust the wrong people. Still, the idea that Hutch would turn didn't sit well with her. "Are you sure about that photo?"

"There's no question the photo is real," Ezra confirmed. "Hutch is with McDonald. Why? That's another question entirely. The profilers will give us any range of whys, but until we stand in front of him, we won't know. I only spent a couple of days with the man, but this isn't the person I got to know. I worry he's gone rogue and he's got plans of his own."

"That makes him dangerous," Ten said. "The Agency won't care what he's doing there. Neither will any of the other groups out there looking for her."

"I can promise you MSS is going to want to get their hands on that drug," Kayla assured them. "And they will use it. They would love to be able to build their perfect operatives."

If they lost Hutch, she wasn't sure what Theo would do. "Is there anything you can do to protect Hutch?"

"Only if the Agency gets to him first." Ezra tucked his tablet into his bag. "I'll do everything I can, but there's only so much I can get away with. I've put Ten on the payroll for this one. We're going to head out tomorrow. I'm not sure at all that they're still in Estonia. We're going to try to work it from the pharmaceutical company angle. I've got Chelsea on it, too."

Ten turned around, reaching for Faith's hand. "You concentrate on Theo and making sure he doesn't get more whiny than he seems now. I always knew Taggarts were whiny. Has he been listening to vagina rock? Because I would love to put that in my report to Big Tag."

She rolled her eyes, but it was nice to laugh. "He's always listened to vagina rock. It's so annoying. I think he was a poet in another life. At least if things were going to change with him, it could have been his musical taste."

Ten looked down at her, Faith by his side. "He's in there, Erin. His sad-sack musical tastes haven't changed and neither has he. He's a bit harder, that's all. The good news is, you're a fighter, one of the best I've ever met. So don't give up. He needs you now more than ever."

He needed her in a way he hadn't before. Their positions had changed and it was up to her to break down his newly built walls. She couldn't fail.

It was the most important mission of her life. The only question was how did he need her this morning?

She intended to find out.

* * * *

Theo pulled his body up and down, sweat beading on his forehead. He wasn't sure how many pull-ups he'd managed, but his muscles were screaming.

It had been a couple of hours since he'd gotten the news that Hutch was back in the fold and he couldn't wrap his mind around it.

Robert was currently visiting with the shrink, but Theo had decided on another path. He'd found the small gym on the fifth floor. It had everything he needed. Treadmill. Weights. Quiet.

After a few miles on the treadmill, he'd lifted more weights than he should. Erin would kick his ass for not having a spotter, but he didn't care at that moment.

He pulled his body up one last time and dropped to the floor.

What the hell was happening? How could Hutch stand walking next to her?

Unless she'd used the drug on him. That was the only thing he could think of. He'd read Ten's report about what they'd discovered at McDonald's base. She'd made her grand breakthrough.

Had Hutch been her first victim?

"Dumbass." Hutch had gone after her on his own, likely seeking revenge, and now he was caught in her web.

His cell trilled and Theo groaned. Ian. Or Case. It could be Sean. It was most certainly one of his brothers calling to make sure he hadn't gone insane and fled the safety of The Garden. They'd been calling all week to "check in." Theo knew the truth. They were worried he would do something stupid.

He thought about not answering. It would serve them right to worry. Fuck 'em.

The phone trilled again and he forced his body up. They would call and call and send someone looking for him. It was better to answer the phone and get rid of them.

Asshole.

He stared at the phone and decided it was past time to be honest with himself. He was going to answer because he didn't want them to worry. Or rather up until now, he'd seen a bit of worry from them as his due. They were the ones who'd left him behind. They could worry.

Was that what he thought deep down inside? When he wasn't

rational, was he angry with all of them for not knowing he was alive and in pain?

Maybe he should be the one sitting on the shrink's couch.

He grabbed the phone and looked down at the number, expecting one of his brothers. It was an unknown caller.

A chill went through him. No one had this number. The cell was new. He hadn't given it out and it was strictly personal, so he shouldn't be getting robo calls or marketers.

Who would be calling him? Who would want to cover their number?

Only one way to find out. He dragged his thumb across the screen to accept the call.

"This is Taggart."

"God, I've missed your voice."

Nausea rolled through him at the sound of her voice. Hope McDonald sometimes affected a little girl tone and it made him want to wretch. His mind was thrown back by the sound of her voice and he could feel the chill of the examination room on his skin, feel the needle going in as she stared down at him, her hand running across his bare chest.

All you have to do is forget and we can be together. We're supposed to be together. Forget her. She's not good for you. I'm the one you were made for. You're my reward for all my hard work.

"Tomas, sweetheart, are you there?"

He forced his brain to function. He wasn't getting lost in nightmares. Not now. "My name is Theo."

She sighed over the line. "I'm sure that's what they've told you, but identity is a relative thing. When you were with me, you were Tomas."

"When I was with you, I was a drugged-out victim, you fucking freak. Tell me what you're doing with Hutch." Hutch was all that mattered. "You do understand I won't leave him to your tender mercies."

"You think very little of me," she said sadly. "I called because I know you met with Smith and that other Agency asshole today."

She knew where he was? "How do you know that?"

A clucking sound came over the line. "I'm smarter than you give me credit for. I've had someone watching you for weeks. You might have lost him back in Dallas but there's always a footprint. I knew you wouldn't leave your whore alone for long. All I had to do was figure out where she and the brat were to know you wouldn't be far behind."

Fuck. He'd known this was a mistake, known he would bring Erin and TJ nothing but trouble. He would have to leave and not see her again until he'd handled the situation.

"Look, I know you won't believe me, but it wasn't my fucking idea. I was trying to get away from her." It was a calculated risk, but one he was willing to take. If she thought he had no interest in her, perhaps she would leave Erin alone. "I don't remember her and I'm not sure why I ever wanted her in the first place. She's obviously not my type. I think it was all about the operation."

He heard a gasp and turned, his heart clenching because naturally there was Erin. She stood in the doorway, her face pale.

"McDonald?" She mouthed the word.

He nodded. Fuck. He'd ripped her heart out of her body and kicked it to the curb and he couldn't take it back. He couldn't let McDonald know a damn thing.

"Somehow I don't believe you," McDonald said.

"I don't care what you believe but I was surprised to find her and the kid here. She's desperate to get me back, but I don't want her. I don't remember her or the kid."

"I can tell you he is yours," she said quietly over the line. "I had a DNA test run."

He looked back and Erin was gone, likely running to get someone, anyone who might be able to trace a call that was probably untraceable.

"It doesn't matter. I don't want a kid." At least she wouldn't hear him say that. It wasn't that he didn't want TJ. Not precisely. He couldn't feel anything. He was numb and that was no way for a kid to live.

"I wish I could believe that. I felt I had to call because I'm sure they're spreading lies about me. If only you'd allowed your family to bring you back none of this would be necessary."

"Did you feel a damn thing when you found out those two men died? You did that. You trained them to kill themselves."

"I trained them to be excellent," she corrected. "I trained them to be the best and to accept no failure. Can't you see that's what a mother does? When she loves her children, she won't allow them to live with failure."

"I'm your failure." He let his voice drop. "You failed with me, Hope. You tried and tried, but you couldn't quite get me to forget. Guess what? I'm having real memories now. It won't be long before I get it all back so you've failed utterly with me. Shouldn't you walk out right fucking now and throw your body off a bridge?"

He would pay to see it. Hell, he would pay to push her off.

"It's different with me. I'm too important. My failures are merely stepping-stones to changing the world. It's a burden I have to bear. And you must, too. You're the perfect soldier and that's why you resist the drugs. I had to go back to the sounding board because you're the reason I'm doing what I'm doing. It's all for you."

She was beyond insane, but he might be able to use it. "Is it? Then maybe we should talk. You have Hutch, but I'm the one you want. You don't need him. You need me. Meet me somewhere and I'll exchange myself for him."

He heard a hiss and realized Erin was back again. She'd brought Knight with her. Both were looking at him like he was the biggest idiot in the world, except Erin wanted to cut his balls off and Knight wouldn't waste the time.

A long sigh came over the line. "I should have known you would be willing to sacrifice yourself, but unfortunately I think that would lead to a trap. You've spent too much time with those people and they've convinced you I'm bad. Besides, I need Greg. He's proven to be an invaluable resource, and before you blame me for all manner of evil, I've never had to give him a drop of drugs. He came to me of his own free will. He sees what we could all be."

That simply wasn't true. "He wouldn't betray us like that. You did something to him. He doesn't remember who he is. That's the only reason he would be working with you."

"He believes in what I'm doing. He knows the value of the family I'm creating," she insisted. "But I can see you're going to need convincing."

He touched the screen to hit the speaker. Not holding the phone to his ear made it feel less personal.

And then he wished he hadn't done it because another voice

came over the line. One he hadn't thought he'd hear.

"Hello, brother." Hutch's voice was deeper than usual. He was always so light, ready to make a joke, but now he sounded deadly serious. "I need you to understand that I'm here of my own free will. I'm not on any kind of drug because I need to maintain my skills in order to make the team stronger. You need to take some serious time and think about what you're doing right here and now. We need you for the good work we're going to do."

It was wrong. He was having another nightmare. "She's fucking with you."

A low chuckle came over the line. "You want to hear something different, Theo? You want to live in make-believe land where everyone worships you because you happen to have the last name Taggart? It doesn't work that way here. She's not interested in you because you're a Taggart. She's going to take that away and then we'll figure out exactly who you are."

Erin's face had gone red.

"Hutch, this isn't you." He couldn't believe what he was hearing. The man on the other end of the line couldn't be Hutch.

"Brother, I'm more me than I've ever been," Hutch replied. "I've finally figured out where I belong. Mother won't leave me behind."

Had he gone fuck-all insane? "Mother had two of your 'brothers' kill themselves because they didn't bring me in."

"They failed. They fell on their swords exactly as they should have. She teaches her children honor."

"Is that what's going to happen to you? If you screw up, are you going to put a damn gun to your head?"

"I wouldn't do that because that's not my place," Hutch explained. "I'm not a foot soldier. I understand that there's a hierarchical order that must be respected. It only makes sense. Some of us are more important than others. That's what you need to understand. You have to accept your place in the order."

"You already have a place. You have a place at McKay-Taggart. Damn it, Hutch. You don't have to do this."

A laugh came over the line, but it was dark and humorless. "Yes, I figured out my place at McKay-Taggart. I thought I was someone there. I was so wrong. That night when we were in

Colombia, when we came to find you, that's when I figured out how important I was to the Taggarts. Your brother let them take me. All he cared about was you. He didn't even try to find me."

Hutch didn't know the whole story. "We took you out a secret passage. He didn't know what had happened until later. Case was devastated at losing you. He's felt guilty about it ever since. He would have done anything to find you."

"Anything except actually come and get me. I gave them all the clues twice as to where we would be, but I assume they decided to not risk saving me if it jeopardized you. You're the golden boy. Everyone loves Theo."

Theo shivered at the chill in Hutch's tone. "It wasn't like that."

"It wasn't? Because that's not what I heard after they rescued us. What I heard was how brilliant Erin's plan was to save her boy. She left me there, but then I should have guessed that. I could have helped her out, been her friend, but she's going to choose her boy toy every time. I was nothing but the idiot who did all the shit work. Guess what, brother? I got a promotion. While everyone was ignoring me and salivating all over you, Mother called."

"She called you while we were in Africa?"

"She called that same night," Hutch explained. "I don't even know how she managed to contact me, but she cared enough to figure it out. She asked me to come home. All the rest of the team was too busy worrying about poor Theo to notice me. I left in the early hours of the morning and she made arrangements for me to join her. I've been working to rebuild what your clumsy brothers destroyed. And I don't think that Mother is to blame for my brothers dying. I blame you, Theo. You killed them when you wouldn't come home. We will try again and again, and every single man who fails in his mission will die. How much death can you have on your conscience? Remember that and I'll see you soon, brother."

The line clicked and the screen showed the call was dead.

Knight cursed under his breath. "Let's go see if they could get anything. I bloody doubt it."

Erin's face was pale as she started to follow Knight out of the gym. "I'm sure they were using a burner phone. They'll toss it out and use another one the next time they call."

"Still, I got Nick on it as quickly as I could," Knight was

saying. "He might have found something."

He couldn't let her walk out, not after everything he'd said. He followed her out to the hall. "Erin."

"Hutch is good." Erin continued to follow Knight, turning toward the elevators. "He'll either be comfortable enough to let us know where the call came from because he wants us to think he's there or he'll ping it around the globe so many times we won't be able to figure out where he's at."

"Erin, we need to talk." He'd said what he'd said at the time and he'd even thought he was doing the right thing, but he couldn't let her believe it. Deep down he knew that maybe it was all for the best, but he couldn't do it.

He might have found something worse than forgetting. The idea of hurting Erin that way…it ripped him to his core. It was wrong when he'd spent all his time before building her up. He was supposed to be the one man in the world who would never tear her down.

"Theo, we can talk later." Her jaw was tight, her shoulders up around her ears. "This is too important. We need to figure out if we can trace the call. Nick got on it as soon as I told him. Hutch talked for a long time. We might have a shot."

"I'm sorry," Nick called out across the atrium. He stood one floor down and on the other side of the building. "He pinged the call all over. I was still following it back when he hung up."

Erin's shoulders slumped. "Damn it."

Knight waved a hand to Nick. "Understood. I'll be down in a moment and we'll analyze the data. If she calls again, let us know."

"He's getting rid of the phone." Erin held out her hand. "Give it to me. He can track you through that thing."

"He knows where I am. He doesn't have to track me." But he handed her the phone anyway. "Someone has to call Ian and tell him what's going on."

"Ian is out of touch," Knight said. "I talked to Charlotte an hour ago. She says Ian and Case are on some kind of assignment. They've gone to ground and she doesn't even know how to contact them."

"Bastard." Erin handed the phone to Knight. "I'm sure we could call Top and find the executive chef has taken a mysterious and sudden sabbatical. I should have known he was playing some kind of angle. He obviously doesn't want Ten or Ezra in on it."

"Or he wants us all to have plausible deniability," Knight said. "All right then. You're my responsibility. I'm going to find another safe house. I'll have you out of here in a few hours. I'll find a place for the three of you to go."

"The three of us? Erin isn't coming with me and Robert." He knew she would be angry, but he wasn't shoving her into danger.

"I'm not sending Robert with you at all." Knight pressed the button for the elevator. "He'll stay here. I know you trust him but that's twice she's found you and Robert was with you. It's my call and I'm splitting you up."

"Then how are there three of us?" Theo didn't understand that math.

Erin's eyes went wide and he realized he'd made a horrible mistake. "Are you serious? You cannot fucking be serious. I get it. You don't want a kid, but at least you can admit he freaking exists. You know what? Fuck you, Theo. You might not want us to go along, but we're coming. Wherever we stay you can have your own room and when Big Tag's done doing whatever he's doing, you can go your own way."

Shit. "I wasn't thinking about the baby. He's not a one. He's more like a half."

She flipped him the bird and strode off, her hair swinging behind her.

The elevator door opened, but Knight stayed back.

"That was not well done of you, mate." Knight put a hand on his shoulder as they watched Erin stomp off. "You've got some work to do. They don't like it when you forget the children. I've found begging can work. Pathetic, really, but a man does what a man must do. Unless you meant what you said to the psychopathic bitch on the other end of the line. Are you trying to get away from Erin?"

"No. Of course I didn't mean that. I can't exactly tell McDonald how much I want another woman. She'll come after Erin, which is precisely why she can't hide out with me. She needs to stay right here. I'll leave. I'll go completely on my own or I'll go with Ezra and Ten. The Agency will protect me."

Or he could handle all of this on his own because Hutch had been right about one thing. He couldn't handle more people dying because of him. He knew it wasn't truly his fault. McDonald was making the choice, but Theo would remember those men for the rest of his life. They'd done nothing wrong. They were victims like him.

How many would die so he could remain free?

Knight shook his head. "We can't count on the Agency."

"Fine, then I'll go with Ten and leave Ezra out of it. You know I'm an adult who can make my own damn choices. If I want to leave, there's nothing you can do about it."

A chilly smile lit Knight's face. "Oh, watch me, mate. You have no idea the things I'm capable of. You try to leave and find out what will happen to you. I have a lovely cell on the fifth floor. Very neat and tidy. Soundproof as well. You won't be as comfortable as you are now, but that won't be my problem. You'll be alive and well when Ian comes back for you. That is my mission and I don't intend to fail. Am I understood?"

"Do you know what happened the last time a member of The Collective decided they wanted one of our team?" It had been the incident that led to his brother losing a truck and breaking a leg. "They blew up Sanctum. Are you willing to risk your club? Your son?"

"My son can go to our country house along with his nanny, who happens to be a six-foot-seven-inch former SAS commando. I assure you, I can perform my duties and protect my family if I have to. Are you going to make that necessary for me?"

"Damon, you have to see that there's more at stake than me. How many of those men won't go home to their families because they failed to bring me in?"

"Not my responsibility. I feel for them, but I'm not allowing a member of my family to sacrifice himself. We've lost too much already." Knight hit the button again. The doors opened immediately and he stepped in. "Don't attempt to leave until I've settled on where to send you and your family. Erin and your son are targets as well. If you choose to split up, then let me know and I'll assign someone to Erin. Robert is going to stay here under my supervision. If it helps at all, I believe Ian's up to something. That means we shouldn't have long to wait. If this is his last move, it should be over

313

fairly quickly and you can get on with your life. But if you want that woman to be in it, I suggest you follow her and beg."

The doors closed.

And Theo knew he had a decision to make. No matter what, he couldn't leave things with Erin. Not like this. He turned and prayed he could find the words to fix things between them.

CHAPTER EIGHTEEN

Erin slammed the door to her room and briefly thought about putting her fist through a wall.

He was the stupidest man alive. She'd figured that out long ago, but she'd let hormones take over and now she'd done it. She'd had a kid with the stupidest man alive.

He didn't even think of their son. TJ wasn't even there in the back of his mind.

She had to consider that he honestly didn't want a kid. All this time she'd been thinking that he simply needed time. Her Theo would never reject his baby. Never. He'd joked about it after the condom had broken the night they conceived TJ, but she'd seen it right there in his eyes. He hadn't been upset by the possibility at all. He hadn't exactly said it, but she'd known in that moment that he would welcome her accidental pregnancy.

Now he wouldn't even acknowledge their son existed.

She could deal with everything but that. She could handle the memory loss, the mood swings, the fact that he wasn't the same. All of that could be handled, but she couldn't be with a man who didn't love his kid. Hell, when she'd found out Theo was alive, one of her first thoughts had been that TJ wouldn't have to be an only child.

She'd thought about the fact that they might be able to have more beautiful babies, and this time he would be with her.

What if he could never love their first child?

Tears blurred her vision. How could he? How could he not see how amazing that kid was?

Maybe he didn't want to. She had to face that fact. He couldn't possibly be interested in being a husband and a father if he was so willing to sacrifice himself without even a word to her. He was willing to walk back into hell but he wouldn't talk to her about it or allow her to stand by his side. He wouldn't let her fight for him.

A pounding sound broke the silence of the room and made her start.

There was zero question who was standing outside. It would be Theo. He would be here ready to tell her all the reasons he was going to leave her and their son behind. He would explain why he needed to sacrifice himself. He would tell her why he would put himself in a position where he would take the needle again and forget everything he'd remembered.

She strode to the door and flung it open, ready to get this conversation done.

He was standing there, still dressed in his gym clothes, sweatpants and sneakers, a tank top that showed off his Greek-god body. Why did he have to be so freaking gorgeous? The very sight of him made her mouth water and her heart soften, but she couldn't allow what had happened.

"Go away, Theo. It's almost time for me to pick up TJ and we both know you don't want to have anything to do with our child."

He paled visibly, but forced his way in the room. "It's not like that, damn it. Erin, you can't think I meant anything I said to that woman. Please believe me. I didn't mean a word of it."

Well, she wasn't stupid. She knew he was lying about getting away from her, but now she worried he wasn't lying about getting away from his responsibilities. She'd tried her hardest to keep things easy for him, but it still hadn't worked. He'd held TJ once and then run away as quickly as he could afterward. He'd proven he could want her for sex and submission, but that wasn't enough. Not even close. At one point, she would have been happy to take it, but he'd taught her what it meant to be truly loved and now she couldn't settle for less. "It doesn't matter. You should go. I have to pack."

She had no idea where she would go now. She would be alone. It would be the first time she'd truly been a single mom. There was no question that up until now she'd had it better than most in her position. Even though Theo hadn't been there, she'd had his family and Li and Avery.

"Erin, I didn't mean to hurt you."

"And yet you managed to so beautifully." She sighed. It wasn't his fault. He hadn't chosen to forget. They'd had a second chance and it hadn't worked out. She held a hand up. "I know you didn't mean anything by it. You're forgiven. Now go back to Robert and let me figure out what to do for my family."

Her heart clenched because this might be the end. How could he be here and still be so fucking far away? He was standing right there and she couldn't touch him because he didn't want all of her. TJ was the most important part of her now and she couldn't be with someone who couldn't accept him.

It was an actual ache in her gut that she was giving up, but she wasn't sure what else to do.

"Erin, tell me why you're crying if you believe me. I had to say those things to McDonald." His voice had gone low, misery in his tone.

Well, she was pretty miserable, too. "You had to tell her you would sacrifice yourself? She needed to know that?"

His brows came together. "I was trying to save Hutch."

"Hutch sounds pretty comfortable to me." She had no idea what was going through Hutch's head and it was something she would think on later. She still wasn't sure she bought it, but right now all she could think about was Theo. Big Tag had been right to leave her out of whatever plan he was cooking up. She couldn't be rational. She was in far too deep.

He started to reach out, but right before he touched her, he pulled his hand back. It fisted at his side. "I don't know what he's thinking, but something's wrong. He wasn't Hutch. You don't know what she can do to you. Even without the drugs, she finds her ways. Right now she doesn't matter."

"She matters a lot, Theo, since you're letting her come between us again."

"I'm not letting anything happen," Theo shot back. "I'm dealing with the situation the best way I can."

This was the best way? "By splitting us up for god knows how long? By missing more of your son's life? Is that what it comes down to? You seemed so damn eager to give yourself up. Are you that desperate to run away from us? Guess what? You don't have to. I get it. It's finally through my thick skull. We'll leave you alone. I'll take my son and you won't hear from me again. When this is over and TJ and I are safe, I'll leave the company."

"What? Why would you do that? I told you I didn't mean anything by what I said. Not a word of it. Not about you. Baby, she's obsessed and she'll hurt you. I can't let that happen. I can't allow her to lay a hand on you."

She snorted. It wasn't the most ladylike sound, but it summed up her feelings. "Because I'm the poor woman who can't defend herself."

His jaw tightened. "I didn't say that."

"You can't allow her to lay a hand on me? You don't allow or disallow anything when it comes to me, Taggart. I'm my own woman and you would be lucky to have me as your bodyguard. Hell, if you had listened to me in the first place, you wouldn't have fucking died."

His face went a lovely shade of red. "Oh, how long have you been waiting to shove that in my face? You think I haven't read the files? You think I don't know where I fucked up?"

She wasn't sure he did. "Tell me. I would love to know if you've learned anything at all."

It was there on the outer edges of her consciousness that she should slow down. She should think about what she was saying, but she'd been so careful around him. Every word around Theo had been measured and applied with the strictest discipline, and now it felt good to unleash a little. Kai had told her to view Theo's situation from an intellectual standpoint when she could since emotion could cause her to lash out where she shouldn't.

But why shouldn't she? He had made mistakes. Why was Theo so above everyone else that he never should hear he'd screwed up? He'd cost them almost two years, cost their son his father. Why shouldn't she point that out? If they were going down, she would set fire to the rubble.

Theo stepped in front of her and planted his feet shoulder width apart, his shoulders squaring as if he were staring down a commanding officer. "I should have called back to base. I should have allowed Ian to make the decision as to whether or not we proceeded."

At least he understood what the problem had been. "You had no right to make that call. Not when we could have easily had input from base. But you were arrogant."

"I'm not arrogant anymore. If you think I have a damn ounce of self-confidence, you're high. I've been taken as low as a man can be so don't worry I'm making decisions based on my belief in my abilities. I get it. I'm a screwup. I'm only on the damn team because of Case."

She rolled her eyes. Sometimes he was a total drama queen. "Yes, the Navy SEALs accepted you because they couldn't survive without Case. Ian Taggart is known for risking his team on hard-luck cases."

"Everyone knows you should have been the lead." There was no way to miss the resentment in his voice.

"And that makes you upset. Don't want to answer to a woman, do you?"

A low groan of frustration burst from him and he turned away, stalking back toward the door. "Don't make me into something I'm not. Shit. I don't know what the hell I am. Do I resent it that everyone looks at you like the fucking Madonna and I'm some low-ball shit who got a teammate killed and can't make a decent decision to save his own ass? Yeah. I resent it. I'm sure the amazing god of a man I used to be would never feel anything so human as resentment. Wait, except this whole fight is about how stupid I used to be. Which one is it? God or man? You can't have it both ways."

"You were an arrogant, amazing, wonderful, flawed god of a man, Theo." Tears pulsed behind her eyes, but she was going to try not to shed them. "You were human, like the rest of us, but you were so good. You made me believe in myself when no one else could."

He stopped pacing, looking right at her. "I'm not that man anymore. I can't believe in myself much less help anyone else."

A spark of hope lit through her. He'd been her lifeline. If only he would allow her to return the favor, they might find their way out. "Then let me be the lead now, Theo. Stop pretending like I'm a delicate flower who needs protection. Stay with me. Let's wait this thing out together and maybe we'll find a solution. Have you thought about that?"

He shook his head. "It won't work. She'll keep coming. She won't stop."

"Unless we stop her." Frustration ratcheted through her. "Your real mistake was that you wouldn't listen to me. You wouldn't even think about what I said to you. Don't make the same mistake again. Don't split us up. Choose me this time. Choose us."

"Do you understand that she doesn't give a damn who I choose? She'll kill you."

"I won't let her kill me, Theo. And you won't let her break you. God, you talk about how you aren't arrogant anymore. I can't imagine why not. Bring my arrogant Taggart back, please, because he is a badass who never broke no matter what that bitch did to him."

A shudder went through him. "I broke. I am so fucking broken nothing can put me back together again. Do you understand that?" He pointed to the scar on his face. "You see this? It's not going away. It will never fucking go away. Neither will the stain on my soul. Saint Erin thinks she can cure me? I'm incurable. I'm toxic and no amount of fucking me is going to make it better. Do you really think that pussy of yours is so sweet it can fix what's wrong with me? You're the arrogant one."

She stared at him, her heart aching with every word he'd said. She knew what the old Erin would have done. The old Erin would have popped him hard and not held back. This Erin could do nothing more than stand and manage somehow to keep herself upright because no one in the world could hurt her the way this man could.

He went still, as though he realized what he'd said. He took a deep breath. "Erin, I shouldn't have said that. God, baby, I'm so sorry. I didn't mean that."

But somewhere deep in his soul he had. And he was right. There was a piece of him that had changed irrevocably. The time he'd spent with McDonald had altered him, darkening what had been an essentially light soul. She had no doubt given time, he would find some of his light again, but it would take a different woman to bring it back.

She had to accept the fact that she was no longer the woman for him. Life and tragedy had changed him, turning his needs into something she couldn't fix. Pain lanced her, making it hard to breathe, but she couldn't break down in front of him. They'd lost that right with each other. She forced herself to blink back tears and face him. "No, I'm sorry. I shouldn't have pushed you."

He shook his head as he took a step toward her, that volcanic anger she'd seen in him seeming to deflate. "I'm sorry I said what I said. Baby, I didn't mean it. It was awful and I shouldn't have said it."

She held out a hand to stop him from coming closer. "You're right. I can't fix anything and I'm only hurting the both of us by pushing as hard as I have. You've told me in so many ways that you need space and I won't give it to you. I'm going to honor your wishes."

She would leave and pray he did find the person who could pull him out of the dark place he found himself in, the person who could make him want to be better. She could talk all she liked about fixing him. No one could fix another person. Theo hadn't fixed her. Theo had loved her so perfectly that she'd begun to see the world through a different lens. Theo had given her a place where she could learn to care about herself in a way she never had before.

She'd tried to give that to him, but people and needs changed. Even if he hadn't died and come back, he would have changed. Life was change and any relationship was a delicate balance of staying close to one's partner while finding one's self. It didn't work for many people.

Who knew what could have happened if that terrible day had a different ending? But she had to deal with the man in front of her, and she was doing nothing but hurting him and not allowing him the space to heal.

Her soul felt heavy, weighing her down as she stepped forward and looked at the only man she was ever going to love. She might not see him again after today. TJ would be her priority. She would close herself off to all but him and try to make a life for them out in the world. God, his father was still the most beautiful man she'd ever seen and she knew how different she was because she wouldn't take a second of it back. Not the joy and not the pain. She would live through all of it again because knowing him had been the most important experience of her life. "Be safe out there."

She turned and walked to her bedroom, closing the door between them. When she was alone, she finally allowed herself to cry.

* * * *

Theo felt like the world had shifted and he found himself in some place he didn't understand, the landscape and the language utterly foreign to him. He didn't understand the look on her face.

Erin was his rock. She had been since that moment in the bar when he'd found her again.

No. It had been long before that. Long before he'd met her again. Long before he'd seen her face and tried so hard to memorize it in a way that he could never, ever forget again.

Even when he hadn't remembered, she'd been there. She'd been a whisper in his conscience to fight what was happening to him. She'd been the bedrock that wouldn't break, the reason he'd been able to hold out.

She was the strongest woman he'd ever known and he'd brought her low with a few careless words.

His anger wasn't under control. His anger was a never-ending pit waiting to boil over and burn everyone he loved because he wouldn't admit the truth.

He still couldn't because no matter what, he did have to protect her. He wasn't the man she needed any longer. She deserved someone light and happy, someone who could pull her out of her dark places. All he could do was drag her into his.

He walked to the door she'd closed between them and put his hand on it as though he could feel her one last time. "Don't leave the company, Erin. Don't leave Dallas. I need a new start. There are too many ghosts there. I want you to have everything you need. You…and the boy. I'll find a job and we can maybe work out something."

He would send her everything he had, but she didn't need to

know that. He would keep only what he needed to continue working and she would have everything else. He couldn't love her like he had, but he could provide for them. For her and TJ. He forced himself to think his son's name. It was hard. He wished like hell she'd named him something different because the kid shouldn't be named after the father who disappointed them all.

She was silent and he thought about walking away.

That was when he heard it. A small gasp and then a low sob. Such a faint sound, but then she would attempt to hide all her weaknesses from him now. He wasn't her man anymore so she wouldn't give him her pain. She would hold it close and shove it down. It would fester and eat at her, and he didn't want that.

He turned the knob, praying she hadn't locked it. The door opened and he saw her. She was on the bed, her fist pressed to her mouth as though she could keep all that pain in. He'd caused that. He'd hurt her, but that didn't matter in the moment. All that mattered was that she needed arms around her, needed to understand that she wasn't alone in this.

Her body curled in on itself. He easily picked her up and cradled her against his chest.

Her eyes flared open and for a moment he thought he was going to take one right across the jaw. He prepped himself mentally but what happened was so much worse. She wrapped her arms around his neck and sobbed into his shoulder.

"I miss you. I miss you so much." She clung to him.

He held her tight, sitting down on the bed. He started to tell her he was right here, but with a sinking heart realized she wasn't talking to him. Not really. She was missing the man who'd loved her so long and so well. The man he'd been.

"I'm sorry. I would do anything to go back to that moment and change things." Anything to have not died on her. He was a walking corpse, a shell of his former self.

She cried harder and he knew somewhere deep inside that she never did this. Almost never. She cried with him because he'd been her safe place. Now she would go back to crying alone or worse, she would hold it all in and be strong, never allowing herself a moment's weakness because she wouldn't trust anyone to take care of her. She would raise their child alone, live out her life alone.

She would mourn him alone.

It was far worse than thinking of her in another man's arms. At least she would get what she needed.

Fuck, he loved her. He loved her, but he couldn't be the man he'd been. And he couldn't bring her and a child into his fucked-up world.

He had made the mistake. It was on him, but he could give her some comfort. One last day. He could give her the barest minimum that he should. He could hold her. He could make the rest of the day easy on her.

It might be the last time he ever held her.

"It's all right, baby. You cry. Let it all out."

She held on to him for the longest time, her body shuddering in his arms. He rocked her, his heart aching. It felt good to hold her. Like this was his right. It was nothing but an echo from long before, the memory of the life he'd had.

Erin tilted her head up, her face blotchy and red and still the most beautiful one he'd ever seen. Her emotion wasn't given away easily. He'd earned it the first time around, earned being the one to stroke back her hair and tell her everything would be all right because they were together.

"I'm okay, Theo. I'm sorry I lost it like that."

If he didn't do something, she would get off his lap and they would be done. She would pull back into her shell, and he couldn't stand the thought of it being over. He did the only thing he could think to do. He lowered his lips to hers and kissed her.

It was a good way to get hit, but he was willing to risk it for another few moments with her. In the morning they would be apart, perhaps for a very long time. She would never look at him the same again. All his chances would be gone, but if they could have another hour together, something he could hold on to for the rest of his miserable life, he would take it.

He would even take a punch to the face if it meant one more kiss. Somewhere in the back of his stupid brain he was practically begging for it. Let it scar so he could see her there when he forced himself to look in the mirror.

Instead, her hands came up, cupping the sides of his face as the kiss turned incendiary.

Her mouth opened, tongue coming out to run along his bottom lip like she couldn't wait to taste him.

Pure need crowded out all the softer emotions he'd felt. The need to brand this one last encounter onto his psyche in a way no one could take from him. No drug could ever make him forget how good it felt to have her soften and open for him. She was the flower that had refused to bloom, preferring to protect herself with thorn after thorn. He'd been the man to ease them away so she could open and feel the sunlight, so she could be the warm woman he'd known her to be from the moment they'd met.

That had been his true talent. Ian was the strongest, Sean the smartest, Case the true soldier, but Theo had been able to see past all the bullshit of the people around, to find the core of beauty everyone missed.

She'd been his prize. She was still the prize. He simply didn't deserve her anymore.

He began to ease her over, but her hands came up, tugging on his hair.

He growled her way. She wasn't playing the way they'd agreed to. "Stop it, brat. Lay on the bed. Let me take care of you."

She twisted her body with the ease of an athlete, shifting in one swift move so she was straddling him. "I'm not your brat anymore. Doms don't leave their subs. Whatever contract we've had, it's broken, so this is my way or you can leave."

The alpha male inside him flared and threatened to take over. He could show her his way. Oh, he could pin her down and take her, and there wouldn't be a damn thing she could do except use her safe word on him.

Something about the stubborn set of her jaw made him stop.

He was leaving her, but sometimes Doms were just men who couldn't stop the tide of shitty fate. And sometimes Doms bent to their subs needs, shoving their own aside. Erin needed to take back the power she'd lovingly given him. She'd needed to break with him in a way that was clear and unforgettable. She would be alone and would need control.

It was time to give it back to her.

He eased himself back, giving her the dominant position.

She looked down at him, tears glistening in her eyes, but he knew his girl. There was no way she backed out now. This was her path and she would walk it. Taking him one last time would be her first step to moving on from him.

She reached down and took his tank in both hands, ripping it in a show of feminine strength.

She stared at him for a moment, her lower lip disappearing behind her teeth as though she couldn't figure out whether to lick him or not.

His dick throbbed in his sweatpants, so close to her pussy but not quite about to touch. There were layers of protection between them and he wanted to rip them all away until he was deep inside her. He could forget about the rest of the world, let it all narrow down to nothing but the feel of her silky body surrounding him, cradling him.

But this wasn't his show. He'd given that up when he'd given up her.

Her hands came out, palms flat on his chest as she ran them from his collarbone down to his pecs and abs. Warmth flowed between them as she explored him with her fingers. She brushed them over his nipples, making them tighten with need.

"Don't think this means anything, Taggart. After you walk away, don't come back looking for sex."

He hadn't dreamed of it. She wouldn't allow it. Coming in and out of her life would hurt her, but it would harm the boy worse. TJ would become the center of her world and she would fiercely protect him against everyone.

The harshness of her words didn't match the way her hands stroked over him, brushing over every muscle as though memorizing its feel. "I won't, baby, but you can't leave your job. You need it and you need to have family around you. I'm the one who needs to leave. My decision. My sacrifice."

Her hips moved, rolling her pelvis over his cock. "I don't think that's going to work forever. You'll want your family back."

His hands came up, touching her waist and flowing down to her hips. "I'll stay away as long as you need me to. I promise. You're more important."

"Shut up, Taggart." She hauled her shirt over her head and tossed it to the side.

He moved his hands to the cups of the lacy bra she was wearing, a whisper of a memory floating through his brain. "You never used to wear pretty things. I told you something. I bought you lingerie and then I said something to you."

"You said I was beautiful and I should only ever be allowed to wear beautiful things." She unhooked the back of the bra and tossed it to the side. Her nipples were already sweetly taut and his fingers itched to roll them and watch her eyes dilate. "Save the bullshit for the next woman. I want some stress relief. It's been a day."

He saw right through her. The tough chick was back, but it was armor she needed. He'd wounded her and it would take a long time for the scars to heal. She'd only ever let one man in and he'd turned out to be so flawed. "Take what you need from me, baby. Take whatever you need."

She rolled off him, getting to her feet. "Take off your pants and lie back on the bed."

They should talk. Her tone was harsh and he didn't want their final time together to be so rough. "Erin, please. Come here and let's get into bed and we can talk. I still don't think you understand everything that happened here today."

"If you aren't out of your pants and lying back on the bed by the time I finish undressing, I will walk out and I won't see you again. You're not in control of this. I am."

He groaned inwardly because either way he went he would hurt her.

In the end, he couldn't reject her physically. He'd already rejected her enough for one lifetime. She would shut down her heart because of him. He didn't want her shutting down her sexuality, too. It would be the only way to get to her. If she kept practicing BDSM, she might find a Dom she trusted enough.

Lucky man.

Lucky man he suddenly wanted to murder.

Theo kicked off his shoes and socks and shoved his boxers and sweats down. "I should take a shower. I'm sweaty."

"You smell like man." Her eyes were on his cock as he pushed his body up the bed to a comfortable position. He had the feeling he was in for a hard ride if that look in her eyes was any indication. "Stroke yourself, Theo. Do you have any idea how much I love that cock of yours?"

It loved her. It only fucking wanted her. Even when he'd been half out of his mind on drugs, the fucker had a brain. His brother always told him not to think with his dick because his dick was an idiot. Fuck Ian. His dick was the smartest part of his body since it knew damn well when to come to life and when to play dead.

No need for that now. His cock was straining. He took himself in hand, gripping his dick hard as he pumped up and down. She wanted a show? He could give her one.

She ditched the last of her clothes and his cock proved it could take even more blood from his brain. She was a fucking goddess. Slender with long limbs and graceful breasts. They were bigger than they'd been but still fit his hands perfectly. Her ass was a thing of beauty. A drop of pre-come pulsed from the slit of his cock, letting him know he wouldn't last terrifically long.

There had been a time when he could fuck her long and hard. Hours he would spend torturing his sweet sub and bringing her to orgasm over and over before he would give in and let go. Best days of his life. They'd been in one of the worst situations the world had ever seen, utterly surround by death, and yet most of what he could remember about Africa was the joy of being inside her.

"Don't ruin this, Theo. I can tell when you're trying to remember. Please don't. This is what it is. One last moment with you. Not the Theo from before. I had my time with him. I'm saying good-bye to you."

He let the memory float away and concentrated on the moment. This he could hold on to. This he could call up later when the nights were lonely as hell because no matter what she did in the future, he wasn't sure he would ever take another lover. She was it for him. She was everything, and the idea of anyone else made him ache inside.

"It's gone. No future. No past. Here and now with you, baby." He stroked himself from bulb to base, thinking of nothing but how gorgeous she was, how much he needed her on top of him. "Take me. I'll play your game because I think you need it, but take me soon or we're going to lose that chance. Just looking at you makes me want to come. That's all it takes. You walk in a room and this is what happens."

He kept his eyes steady on her, but he was certain his dick had gone a nice shade of purple. He would be ripe and ready to fuck, but then that was the state his body seemed to prefer when close to her.

"Don't you dare come without me." She climbed on the bed, kneeling next to him. "Stop. I want to touch you."

"I want to touch you, too. I want to get my mouth on you. You can be in charge all you like, but don't deny me this. Come up here and put that pussy right on my face. Let me taste you again." If she said no, he would regret it for the rest of his life, but he would give her what she wanted and not say another word.

She twisted and leaned over, her mouth nearly on his cock.

Fuck, he wasn't going to survive this. He wanted to give back to her, not be another asshole who took and took from her. His hands fisted at his sides as he swore he would be still. How many times had she taken what he gave her? He was determined to do the same for her.

Her leg hooked over his chest and he was gifted with the sight of the sexiest pussy in the history of the world not an inch from his face. Her scent invaded his every sense, heightening his awareness of how aroused she was. Her pussy was wet, the labia beautifully swollen as though it reacted to him the same way he reacted to her. Desperate. Needy. Hotter than hell.

"Do your worst, Taggart. I know I intend to."

He figured out what she meant in the next moment when her mouth covered his cockhead and sucked up the drop there. His eyes nearly rolled to the back of his head.

She wanted to make this a competition? Oh, he could give that to her. He shoved his nose in her pussy, breathing her in. So fucking good. He didn't play around this time. No teasing. Just a full-on feast for a man who would starve forever after. He would eat his fill of her.

He dragged his tongue through her labia, loving the spicy taste of her arousal. Slightly sweet, like the woman herself. He sucked at her, drawing her tender flesh into his mouth. He let his hands come up, gripping her hips and holding her down when she squirmed against him.

He knew he'd hit her sweet spot when she groaned around his cock. The sound made him shudder like a wave of cool water rushing along his skin, making him feel alive. It was washed away with the warmth that hit him as she worked her tongue over the slit of his dick. He could feel himself pulsing, giving her more.

He needed to make her come on his tongue. He had to make sure she found her pleasure because he was rapidly rushing toward his.

He shifted his right hand up, finding her clit and pressing down as he speared his tongue deep inside her body. He pressed his body up, fucking her hard with his tongue and circling her clit in a way sure to make her crazy. Circle, circle, press. He had the rhythm down. He'd preformed this service so damn many times. It was his favorite thing in the whole world. It was his home.

Circle, circle, press, fuck. Every long penetration of his tongue sent his senses reeling. His body was taut, every muscle tight and desperate for release, but he was soldiering on. He wouldn't give in to the need. All that mattered was Erin and showing her how he felt. He needed her to understand. If not in her mind, at least her body would know how much he cared about her, how much he wanted and needed her. It had to be enough to see her through the dark times to come, enough to show her how beautiful she was so she could accept the love of a worthy man.

Over and over he worked her clit until finally he felt the beginnings of her orgasm. Her body went tight and then he was shocked at the complete desertion as she rolled off him.

"No. It's not going to be that easy, Taggart." She turned and straddled him. She reached back, gripping his cock with an expert hand. She was a goddess looming over him with upthrust breasts and a haughty stare. "We come together or not at all. I know you're up to the task. That monster cock of yours always gets the job done."

"Let me get a condom." He wasn't going to leave her pregnant and alone again. He hadn't meant to in the first place.

She moved his cock into place. He could feel the heat of her pussy nearly scorching him. "I'm on the pill. I started after I weaned TJ. I knew you were alive by then and I felt optimistic. We're good, unless there's a reason you want me to grab one."

"I'm clean." He'd had all the tests after he'd come home. Still, it hurt to think about why she would ask. "I don't think I cheated on you."

She stared down at him and one hand came out, caressing his face as her eyes softened. "Baby, that wouldn't be cheating. That would be rape."

He traced her curves, feeling the warmth of her skin, the way she gave to him even when she didn't have to. "I don't remember."

Her lips curled up in the softest way. "It doesn't matter because I don't care, Theo Taggart. What could have happened makes no difference to me. Right here and now you're mine. Then, you were mine. The only thing that is separating us is you. Not her. She has no hold on you that you don't allow her to have. I'll beg you one more time. Choose me. Let go of what she did. Let go of the pain and pick me. You won't regret it. I'll work every single day of my life to make you happy."

He wanted it. So badly, but he couldn't believe it was real. "She'll hurt you."

The saddest look crossed her face and she nodded. "All right, Theo. Your choice. One last time, my love."

She moved his cock into place and began to lower herself down.

He couldn't contain the low groan that accompanied the pure pleasure of her pussy clamping down around him. Perfection. How he'd missed this. Would miss this. He'd made a horrible mistake because the truth was better than any fleeting memory. Wet heat engulfed him but more than that was the feeling of peace that swept through his body, sinking into his soul. This woman was his, made for him by God or the universe or whatever a man believed in. She was divinely created to take him and make him into a better human being with the pure will of her love.

He let all other thoughts go but the joy of thrusting inside her. His hips pulsed up, trying to move as deep as he could. She was controlling the motion and it threatened his sanity. So slow. She moved carefully, as though every moment was something to savor and store in her memory. Inch by inch she lowered herself. She didn't pay attention at all to his attempts to speed up the process, merely continued her slow exploration.

Her back bowed, thrusting her breasts out as she took his final inch and made them one.

So good. She felt perfect and good and all the right things of the world. He could feel her in his spine—a deep heat that suffused him.

She moved back up, sliding along his cock. Her pussy was so wet, she slid up and down with ease.

He caught her rhythm, their bodies moving fluidly as though born to make this particular music together. His whole being focused on hers as her back bowed and clenched around him. Her skin flushed and her mouth opened on a keening cry that seemed part pleasure and part loss.

He wanted to draw out the moment, to grasp it tight and stay right here with her forever. So the loss never had to occur. This was as elusive as his memories. His balls drew up as she clamped down on him and he couldn't help but let go. He came deep inside her, gripping her hips and fighting to hold on.

She fell forward, her body sagging into his.

He let his arms enfold her, pulling her close.

One last time.

He breathed her in and suddenly was shoved back in time. The memory crystallized as clear and pure as if he were experiencing it for the very first time.

* * * *

Dallas, TX
Eighteen months before

Theo pumped into her one last time, finally giving over to the driving need to come. How this woman managed to do this to him, he might never know. Only with Erin could he literally fuck for hours and still want more.

Peace wrapped him as he let his body fall to cover hers. He finally had her exactly where he wanted her. She was in the home he'd bought for them and while she might pretend this was all about the mission, he planned on her never leaving. She would wake up in a couple of months and find a ring on her finger and a collar around her neck.

"God, what are you thinking, Theo," she said, her breath still heavy from all the exercise. "Do I even want to know? You've got the most arrogant look on your face."

He kissed the tip of her nose. What was there to be humble about? He had the coolest job in the world. He had a whole group of ride-or-die friends. He had a family around him that was rapidly getting filled with nieces and nephews.

He had his girl.

Yeah, he was pretty much the shit. He kissed her again and rolled off her, feeling the cool of the air conditioning around him. Being back in Dallas with her was the perfect way to transition from the op to real life. "I was thinking that by morning Ten will likely be in a better mood."

She went still beside him. "I thought he was staying on the couch."

It was almost the end of their op. Months they'd spent in Africa, then three weeks outside Munich, and now they were back home in Dallas. Earlier that day, they'd introduced Faith to her promised Master, who happened to be Tennessee Smith. He'd shown up tonight wanting to talk to Faith, but Theo wasn't so sure he was going to end up sleeping on the couch. Ten had a job to do and he was moving quickly.

Once they had the intel they needed, his time with Erin could be over. So he'd been the arrogant bastard who'd had his brother buy them a house, move her lock, stock, and barrel in, and all for their "cover."

He wasn't letting the love of his life get away. No way. No how.

"He'll be in bed with her before morning," Theo said with confidence. "No doubt about it. I'm going to go get this thing off me. Can we think about getting you on the pill now that we're back here? Think of all the money we'll save."

"How about I cut your balls off and we won't have a problem?" She rolled over, putting a hand on his chest. "I'm joking. Yes, I'll look into it, but I'm serious about Faith not getting hurt. I like her. She's not involved in any of this."

There it was. There was the soft heart that beat under all those layers of stone. He pulled her hand up to his lips. "I think Ten's in deeper than he imagined. Sparks kind of flew when those two met. Don't worry about it, baby. It's all going to be okay. There's a chance she never has to know what we were doing there. It's not like Ten's going to the press himself. He doesn't want his face plastered everywhere."

It was a long shot, but they might be able to keep their friendship with Faith.

Erin yawned. "If you say so. I have a bad feeling about it."

"You worry too much."

"You don't worry enough," she replied as she brought her hand back and stretched.

Fuck, but she was gorgeous all sleek and sleepy and satisfied. "That's why we're prefect for each other."

She sat up, rolling those pretty eyes of hers. "So you say, Taggart." Those eyes went wide as she looked down at him. "Theo…tell me that happened afterward."

What the hell was she talking about? He glanced down and saw his swimmers were on the wrong side of the condom. "Shit."

He bounced off the bed and ran to the bathroom. On closer inspection, there was a decent-sized hole in the latex. He would bet it hadn't happened after. Nope. The thing probably hadn't been meant for hours of fucking.

He walked back, having cleaned up, and Erin was sitting up in bed. "Hey, you okay?"

She sighed. "I suppose if an accident's going to happen, it's a fairly good time for it to happen. It should be fine."

She was saying all the right things, but he could see that she'd retreated. She got up and disappeared behind the bathroom door.

He stared after her. She could be so tough, but he thought they'd gotten through this crap. Did she think if she stayed in there long enough, he would go to sleep? The minutes rolled by and he waited. Finally the door opened and she crept out.

He was waiting for her. He hauled her close and pulled her up against him, her feet dangling off the floor.

"Theo! What are you doing?"

He kissed her hard. "Would it be so bad? I think you would look cute all round and pregnant."

Even in the low light he could see the way she flushed. "It would be horrible. But I told you, it's not likely to happen."

He hauled her back to the bed. Something else was going on here. "Because of the timing?"

334

She shrugged and tried to turn over. He knew all her moves. He simply plastered himself to her back, spooning her and cuddling her close. After a moment, she sighed and relaxed back against him. "I've got fertility issues, that's all. I don't always ovulate and that makes it hard to get pregnant. The crazy thing is I'm supposed to be on the pill to regulate all that crap, but I stopped about a year ago because it didn't matter."

He hugged her close, knowing how hard it was for her to talk about her past, but he had to ask the question. "Is that why you didn't have kids with Frank?"

Her first husband. Frank, the limp-dick moron, as he liked to call him in his head.

"I didn't have kids with Frank because he was a cheating, lying sack of shit." She was silent for a moment. "It was one of the things that went wrong. We tried for a year and that's when the doctors found out the problems with my ovaries. It's not that I can't have kids. It's harder for me than most women. It might take patience. Might take fertility drugs. He didn't want to wait. Last I heard he'd married some chick he picked up at a party and they have two kids. Of course I also heard he's cheating on her, so there's that."

Between her father and her ex-husband, he'd been left with a hearty mess to clean up. He kissed her hair, pulling it back so he could run his lips along her neck. This was pure affection, with no intent to end in sex. This was nothing more than a man wildly in love with a woman, worshipping her body and soul. "I don't care. I want you to marry me when this is done."

She elbowed him, turning in a flash. "Theo. What is wrong with you? I tell you I might not be able to have kids and you ask me to marry you. Do you have a martyr complex or are you really that stupid?"

He reached for her hair, sinking his fingers in and tugging it back so she had to look at him. "Next time we're at Sanctum, that's a non-erotic spanking. Don't you tell me that I have a martyr complex because I love you."

She stilled, her body tense. Tears glimmered in her eyes. "You love me."

"Yes, I've been saying that for a while now." He softened his hand, bringing it around to caress her cheek. "I love you, Erin. If

335

you did happen to get pregnant from that condom breaking, I wouldn't be upset. I would use that sweet baby as leverage to make you marry me because that's what I want. I want you and me and any kids we get to have. None if we can't, but baby, there's always a kid out there who needs a mom like you."

Her arms went around him, clutching him like she would never let go. "You love me. You've said it before, but I didn't believe you. You love me."

"I love you."

"I love you, too, Theo." She laid her head on his shoulder.

The sweetest words he'd ever heard. He held her until she fell asleep and prayed that one in a million chance had happened that night.

A baby with his girl. Nothing would be better.

The world was kind of perfect and he intended to keep it that way.

* * * *

London, England
Present day

"Are you okay?" Erin's voice broke him out of the daydream.

That's what it felt like. He knew he was awake, but he also knew he was stuck in memory. Sweet, amazing, beautiful memory.

He'd been there, in their bed back in Dallas, wrapped around her. Now he was here in her bed and she was getting dressed again. Instead of being in his arms, cuddled close, she stared down at him with worried eyes. All in all he wished they were back home.

He let go of the memory. It was still in his head, but he didn't try to push it further. He didn't have to. He could ask. "Did Ten sleep with Faith that night?"

She shook her head as though trying to clear it. "What? I'm pretty sure he sleeps with her whenever he can. They're married."

Yes, it had worked out for them. He'd called that one. "The first night in our house. Faith came with us and Ten showed up. He was going to sleep on the couch, but I told you I thought he would end up in bed with her. I was right, wasn't I?"

"You remembered something." Her eyes glanced away and she suddenly seemed interested in making sure her shirt was smooth. "Yes, if it's the same night I'm thinking of, then yes, they were in bed together the next day, but Big Tag cock blocked Ten and it wasn't until later they actually had sex. Is your head all right? Your eyes closed so I thought you were going to sleep. I didn't realize you were trying to remember."

He moved to sit at the end of the bed. "It wasn't like that. I wasn't forcing it. Sometimes a scent or a sound will trigger a memory and I kind of ride it like a wave. As long as I let it go when it's time, I'm fine. I feel fantastic. And it was the night we conceived TJ. Unless there was some other night the condom broke. Or did we decide to go ahead and try?"

Her skin went pink. "No, we weren't trying. It was that one time. I didn't get a chance to go see the doctor about the pill so we were still using condoms. I think that probably was the night. Can you put on some clothes if we're going to talk?"

He didn't see why. She'd seen everything. "Why don't you take off your clothes and we'll talk? I haven't asked some important questions. How did you feel when you realized you were pregnant? Were you pissed at me? Think about it, baby. That had to be a one in a million shot. One mistake and you were knocked up. These boys don't mess around. Taggart sperm."

She stepped into her shoes. "I was terrified out of my mind since my mom cut out when I was a kid and my dad hated me. I spent the first few weeks thinking about who to farm the kid out to. Tell the next woman you sleep with to make sure she's up to date on her contraception or you'll leave her with a present, too."

He reached out as she turned, catching her wrist. "Erin, I didn't mean anything by it. I remembered and I was excited. I remembered how I felt when I thought you could be pregnant. I wasn't afraid."

"Well, you've made up for it now." She took a deep breath and her eyes were weary when she looked at him. "I have to go. I have things I need to do and not much time to do them. The babysitter can only watch TJ for another two hours. I've got to cram everything I need to do into those hours since we're leaving in the morning."

He didn't want to leave her. Still, he had to admit she was right. He had made up for his youthful arrogance. Now he couldn't see anything but how fragile they all were. But he could help her. "I'll take TJ."

TJ, not the boy. He had to stop distancing that way. The man he'd once been had longed for that kid because it had been a piece of him and a piece of Erin. He was gone now, but the least Theo could do was honor his old self by spending an afternoon with the kid. It would make Erin's life easier.

Erin huffed. "I don't think that's a good idea."

"You need to work. It might be the only time I get to see him. Look, everyone has said I should spend time with him. I can change a diaper, Erin. I'm not a complete moron. He's not tiny anymore."

She was silent for a moment. "All right, but you have to call me if things go sideways. I do need to get some work done. And I have to find a place for us to go."

"So let me handle TJ. How bad can it get?"

She frowned again. "Well, he is a Taggart."

The good news was, he was used to being around Taggarts.

"I'll let the babysitter know it's okay for you to take him." She still looked like she thought this was all a bad idea, but she grabbed her bag anyway.

It might be, but it was the last thing he could do for her. And maybe, if he did a good job, she would let him stay with her one more night.

Hell, if he wasn't a complete idiot and he managed somehow to kick Hope McDonald's ass into the great beyond, maybe she would want to date or something.

He followed her down the hall, a little optimism squeezing through his darkness.

CHAPTER NINETEEN

T heo walked back to the room, trying not to wake the kid. TJ. He was trying not to wake TJ. The kid was asleep, wrapped for now in a blanket. When he'd picked him up from the lady on the sixth floor, he'd tried unconvincingly to argue that maybe TJ should stay there for a bit longer. Just until he was awake and stuff.

The sub named Janet had swiftly explained to him that her hairdresser waited on no baby and if he wouldn't take his son, she could always call Erin.

She'd been touchy and quick with that threat. It was one every man knew well. It began early on in life. Don't screw up, kid, or we'll call your mom. That morphed somewhere along the way into a man not wanting to have his wife called in.

"Don't tell Mom on me, kid," he whispered as he approached the door. "I'm probably going to be bad at this. She doesn't need to know that though. We should keep some things between ourselves. The ladies don't need to know everything."

The baby on his shoulder kept right on sleeping, but his arms shifted out, as though trying to wrap around Theo's neck, but not quite making it. Baby? He was practically a toddler. He was a solid kid. What had he been like when he was brand new? All wrinkly and red and probably still cute.

He stopped at the door. He needed to get the key card out of his back pocket. There was only one problem with that. Apparently the sleeping prince currently being secured by his left hand required a lot of crap to get through a day. That was being held by his right hand. There was a diaper bag slung over his right shoulder and he was carrying a large stuffed dog named Spot that was needed to entertain the kid.

A real dog would be less trouble probably. He could train the dog to carry around all of TJ's stuff. Yeah, he kind of liked that idea. A big dog that would make people think twice about messing with his kid. He'd always wanted a dog, but the trailer had been too small.

Wow, they were coming faster and faster. Random memories that made up his life. Kai had been right. When he calmed down and let the world flow over him, the whispers of his old life came back.

What would Erin do if he showed up at the house with a puppy? TJ and the puppy could grow up together.

She would murder him because she would have to be the one to clean up after the puppy. And the baby. In the house he'd forced her to live in.

He tried to shift the stuffed dog under his arm, but the diaper bag was pretty damn heavy and when he leaned forward, it tried to come off his arm and go crashing to the floor.

Was this what Erin went through every day? Juggling everything with no help. That's what he was sentencing her to. He was sending her into hiding with no help. It was necessary. It wasn't being done to hurt her. It was all to make sure she was safe from the psycho who was after him.

Yes, because Erin Argent couldn't take care of you, a baby, and assassinate a psycho without breaking a nail. And then she would clean Bertha, cook dinner, and the house would be in perfect order. You're the one she doesn't need, dude. You're the one making things harder on her.

When had that voice started talking to him? It wasn't the normal, dark voice that told him everything was going to be shitty.

If you had half a brain, you would take this time to clean up her place, buy her some really good takeout, make sure the baby's asleep when she gets home, and be waiting to serve her dinner wearing nothing but an apron. Oh, and have a beer ready for her. Yeah, then she might take you back.

That voice was way too optimistic. And maybe a little sexist, though in a reverse way. It didn't matter. He needed to get inside and get TJ down for the rest of his nap, and he could prove to Erin that he was at the very least capable of not killing their sleeping son.

Why was that suddenly so important to him? A few hours ago he would have said it didn't matter because he would likely never see them again, but something had happened when he'd made love to her. He'd seen how good it had been once. Maybe they couldn't have that again, but if they could find even a quarter of the happiness he'd felt in his memory, wasn't that worth fighting for?

Was it fair to ask her to wait for him? Probably not and he likely wouldn't do it. He would be noble and let her find someone who wasn't so burdened with the past.

And who the fuck is that, dude? She's found her himbo with nothing between his ears and a six-pack to drool over. That was you. The next guy is going to have substance, and anyone with substance is going to have a past. Why not freaking you? She still has a total thing for your abs.

He sighed and tried to shut up his inner voice. He hadn't been a damn himbo. He'd been a decorated Navy SEAL/CIA operative who happened to have a nice six-pack. It wasn't like he showed it off to get stuff.

Mostly.

The freaking door. He'd been standing in front of the door for how long? Was this how she would find them both? Completely stumped at how to both hold his child and open a door. Some dad he was.

He dropped the dog. He could get it after he laid TJ down. He let the bag drop to the floor and reached for the keycard.

"Mama." TJ's head had come off his shoulder and he was staring at Theo, blue eyes sleepy as he obviously tried to figure out what the hell was going on. He was wearing overalls and a T-shirt with dinosaurs on it. His blonde hair was a mop around his head that needed to be cut into a high and tight to make the kid a little more masculine. Erin had let his hair grow out in a halo of ringlets that would get the kid beat the shit up when he went to school. Theo would know. His mother thought his curls had been cute, too.

It was always cute until someone punched him in the face.

"Hey, buddy. Mama's working. We're going to go take another nap. How about that?" He tried to give TJ his most confident smile. Weren't kids a bit like wolves? They could smell fear.

"Mama," he said insistently.

"Dada," Theo shot back. "All you got is Dada, kid."

TJ looked so utterly forlorn for a moment, his bottom lip quivering as though he realized he'd just been sentenced to life without parole for a crime he hadn't committed. "Mama."

"Dada. You need more words." He was arguing with a toddler. He should get inside and see what the kid needed.

That was when TJ's eyes widened in horror and he proved he knew more words. "Spot! Spot! Mama!"

His face went a bright red and his mouth opened but no sound came out. Theo watched, his whole body alert to the fact that something horrible was happening and he was completely helpless to stop it. Was he breathing? Theo wasn't sure TJ was breathing. That was bad, right?

And then an ear-piercing scream seemed to make the walls shake.

"What? What is it?" Panic ran through his veins. The kid was dying. He had to be. Something was attacking him because there was no other reason to make that sound except horrific pain and near death. What should he do? Was it some weird seizure? Should he call a doctor?

"Hey, what's going on here? Did someone lose a puppy?" Robert was suddenly beside him, holding up Spot. He made the dog move, coming in to touch TJ's nose. "I missed you, TJ. Ruff, ruff."

TJ clutched the dog as fat tears rolled down his cheeks. "Mama."

Robert cupped his head, easing a hand down his back. "It's okay. Mama will be back. But Dada can be fun."

TJ tucked his head into Spot's body.

"What the hell was that?" Theo felt battered, like he'd been left on the sea in a storm without a boat.

"That was a fit," Robert replied. "I was coming back from a

session with Ari when I noticed your trouble. You know it's bad when the mouth comes open but there's no sound. It's like the reverse of lightning and thunder. You count the seconds and every one that goes by magnifies the sound that eventually comes out of the kid's mouth. The longer it goes, the worse it's going to be. You got a set of lungs on you, buddy."

TJ was sniffling, holding on to that dog like it was a lifeline.

Robert bent over and grabbed the diaper bag. "Having a hard time juggling things? Kids need a lot of stuff. It's why so many parents get those things. The baby handler things."

He'd seen Ian in them. Ian and Charlotte were big proponents of what they liked to call "baby wearing." Now that the girls were two they had moved on to strollers, but Theo had seen pictures. "Like a sling? Ian says it's the only way he could handle Kala when she was tiny. She was squirmy. Apparently her sister was more chill, but he's got a ton of pictures of him with a baby strapped to his chest. He says when Charlotte has this baby, he's getting a manly sling."

"Sling. Yeah, that's it. You got the keycard?"

He handed it to Robert, quickly bringing his hand back because TJ was kind of squirmy too, and he didn't want to see what his son did when he was actually in physical pain. It may register on the Richter scale. "How do you know so much about kids?"

Robert used the card and the door opened. "I don't know. It kind of came to me." He stopped and smiled. "I think I used to like kids. Maybe I was the oldest of a whole bunch."

"Maybe you had one."

Robert shook his head. "No. If I had one, then wouldn't someone be looking for me?"

Sometimes Robert wasn't the sharpest tool in the shed. "If you had a bunch of younger brothers and sisters, wouldn't they be looking for you, too?"

"Yeah, probably, so there you go. I saw it on TV or something. Come on, I'll help you get him settled in. Where's Erin?" Robert held the door open for them.

TJ's head came up. "Mama."

"Sorry. Only Dada here," he said, patting TJ's back as he walked through. "Can you say Dada?"

His mouth pouted, a sullen look on his features. "Mama."

"Mama has to work. Believe me, right now I wish Mama was here, too." She would have known not to put the dog on the floor. At least now he could stretch his left arm. Erin had left a playpen fully stocked and ready to go in the middle of the living room. There were a few toys, what looked like a jack-in-the-box, some blocks. Theo eased TJ down. He sat in the middle of the playpen, his dog in one hand while he stared up. "There you go. Play with your toys while Dad talks to Uncle Robert."

"When did you become Dad?" Robert asked.

He shouldn't have called himself that. Luckily it wasn't like the kid would remember. "Well, I thought Theo was a lot for a kid who only seems to be able to say the words Mama and Spot. Though the Spot really sounded more like Pot. You want something to drink?"

He could use a beer, but then Erin would kick his balls up into his body cavity. He strode into the kitchen and grabbed a bottle of water.

"I'm good." Robert followed him. "Are you sure you want to do this?"

He didn't want to have this conversation for the fiftieth time. "I don't have a choice."

"You do."

"Yes, my choice is either to protect my family or put a big-ass sign on their backs saying 'hey, come and hurt me.'"

Robert shook his head. "They've got that on their backs already. If you think for a second that McDonald is going to leave Erin alone because you stay away from her, you're high. It's not going to happen. She's going to come after Erin and TJ because she knows they're the key to getting you under control."

"She can't use them if she can't find them."

"And if she does find them, Erin will be alone to protect herself and your child." Robert stood taller, his shoulders going back. "I want to go with them. That's my plan. I spent the afternoon looking into it and I'm going to take responsibility for Erin and TJ. One of the club members has a country house that's well protected. I'm taking them there."

Anger swelled in him, a white-hot rage. "She's not your fucking teddy bear. You think I don't know how you view women? Erin's a pretty good catch for you, isn't she? You want a woman to take care of you. She's not fucking yours."

Robert looked a little angry himself, his face flushing. "She's not yours either. Otherwise you wouldn't leave her alone. Someone might think you want something to happen to her. Is she an inconvenient reminder of your former life? Now that you've started to remember, it seems you've changed your mind. Are you going to play the jealous asshole, Theo? You don't want her but no one else can have her?"

"Not you. You have the same problems I do. Can't you see I'm trying to spare her?"

"Spare her from what?"

"From being saddled with damaged goods. You think idiots like us deserve her? Deserve that kid in there? We're dirty. We're fucked up beyond all repair."

Robert reached out, grabbing him by the shirt. "You might think so, but I'm not fucking beyond repair." He let go, his face a florid red. He hit his own chest. "I fucking survived. I'm alive, and that's more than I can say for you. You died in there. All this, this isn't about saving Erin. This is about walking in front of a bullet that can put you out of your misery, brother. Save us all the pain and do what you promised. Walk away so we don't have to watch you die."

Theo stood in the kitchen, his body numb. Robert had been his only friend, the only person who hadn't known the old Theo, the one who accepted him as he was.

"I think you should go."

Robert nodded. "Yeah, I should. Good luck. And Theo, when you're gone, ain't nothing going to keep me from showing up on her doorstep, because that woman needs someone who gives a shit about her. You care so much you're willing to toss her out into the woods alone rather than standing by her side and fighting like hell for your family. That's fine by me, brother. You don't want them, I'll take 'em. Have a good trip and tell Mother hello for me when you see her. Preferably with a bullet to the brain."

"I swear to god if I find out you've touched Erin, I'll kill you myself."

"You know what the funny thing is? You don't even flinch when you say her name anymore. You beat it. You beat McDonald and you're still going to let her win." He turned and walked out, slamming the door behind him.

What the hell had happened? When had he become the bad guy?

TJ had managed to get himself to standing, pulling himself up by the railing on the edge of the pen. His eyes were turned up, solemnly staring at Theo. One hand came up and he opened and closed his fist. "Up. Up."

Another word.

He didn't want to pick up the kid. He wanted to punch a wall. Theo paced like a lion stuck in a cage. "You know I'm doing this for you and your mom."

"Up." As though to explain to the silly man who wasn't listening, TJ bounced a little.

He was doing it for them. He wasn't some fuckup who was looking for a bullet with his name on it. He didn't belong in this world anymore. He'd been changed and he wasn't good for anyone.

"Up."

Damn it. He shoved back the frustration. The kid was going to fucking start crying soon. He picked TJ up, bringing him against his chest. "There. You're up."

He glanced at the clock. How long before Erin got back? Then he could...go where?

He could disappear. He could do exactly what Robert accused him of doing. One last mission. If he was gone, McDonald wouldn't have a reason to come after Erin and the baby. He'd died a long time ago, his heart's blood staining the dirt of that Caribbean island in a way that he couldn't come back from.

It would be for the best.

TJ twisted his body and his hands came out. One chubby hand landed on either side of his face, and he was forced to look into the eyes of his kid.

TJ's face was solemn as he rubbed Theo's cheek. His scar. The boy was running his hand over the place where they'd nearly taken off his face, but he didn't seem scared. He ran his hand over it again and that was when he leaned over and put his mouth on Theo's cheek. The scarred one.

His son was trying to kiss his boo-boo. Theo's heart caught, his vision blurring. TJ didn't know him, didn't know who he'd been or who he'd become. He simply knew he'd been hurt and that a kiss made it better.

TJ didn't know him. It struck him quite forcefully. His son wasn't going to look at him and wonder why he couldn't be the man he'd been. TJ didn't care. TJ only saw who he was now.

TJ pulled back and stared at him, a smile coming over his face, and in that moment Theo finally saw himself in the kid.

The best part of him hadn't died that night. The best part of him had already been alive inside Erin, already growing. While Theo had been lying there dying, his son had been beginning.

He stared, father and son locked in what almost felt like a trance of discovery.

Would this kid have his smile? Would he be the leader of his group? Or would he be like his dad had been? Would he be the one who tempered those around him? Who tried to force them to remember to be kind while they were being strong, to look past what was on the surface?

Did he have to lose the piece of himself that saw the good simply because he'd been confronted with evil?

A man who saw evil and then turned from good...he didn't deserve any good, did he? This was the fight. This was what Erin had talked about. What Robert talked about.

This was his fight, not surviving McDonald. That had been instinct and luck. Survival meant nothing if he wasn't really alive.

How would Old Theo have looked at the situation?

Old Theo would have been a dumbass who would have taken all the pain because it meant he was still alive, because it meant he could love. Old Theo would have let his wife coddle him. She would be his wife because Old Theo would have used the whole experience as an excuse to ease her into marriage, because damn, he'd been through some bad shit and the only thing that could ease his pain was knowing the woman he loved was wearing his ring. Old Theo would have accepted his new needs and known that he'd picked properly the first time. Erin could handle everything New Theo needed.

He couldn't take his eyes off TJ. Old Theo would have worshipped the ground she walked on for bringing this light into his world.

TJ touched his face again, this time his hand becoming wet with the tears Theo shed. He leaned forward again, trying so hard to hold his father in his tiny arms.

What would he hope for this boy? That he never experience the kind of pain his father had been through, that he live his life free of tragedy—but if it happened, oh, if it happened, he would pray that his son would try to find his way back. He would pray that his son fought to let his heart be open to the love he deserved.

His talent had been to see beyond the scars, but he'd never looked past his own. What was on the other side of all that ugliness? A woman who loved him. A son who accepted him unconditionally. A world of love, if he only reached out and grabbed it. He made the choice. Not Hope McDonald. She'd taken so much from him, but here and now he could choose to take a measure of himself back. The very best part. The part that loved and accepted love.

Theo held his son and finally, truly let himself feel again.

* * * *

"So that's the plan, then?" Damon looked around the conference table. "I don't know that I'm in love with this plan. I'm a bit worried about anything that we can code-name Harry Potter."

Damn Phoebe forcing her to watch those brilliant films. "It's the only thing I can think of. Unless you want to stop everything for a week or two so I can have a proper amount of time to come up with a plan. And you know what? It did work in that movie."

Penny's lips curled into a grin. "Well, they did have flying vehicles in that scenario. We're going to have to take another course. Five, to be exact. I can't pass for Erin, but I think if we put Kayla's hair in a ball cap and give her a pair of heels, she'll pass."

There were still a few things to work out. They didn't have a ton of time.

Kay smiled her way. "As much as any Asian chick can look like she's straight out of Dublin. For this to have the best shot at working, we need someone who looks and moves like Erin. I'm calling Daphne."

Knight thought for a moment. "All right. I have to admit she's perfect." He turned to Erin. "Like Big Tag, I allow certain helpful members of the city to apply for memberships. Daphne Carpenter is a police officer and quite good. She's also a five-foot-eight-inch redhead with an athletic frame. She's quite good humored and won't mind the adventure of it all. I'll call her CO. We'll send her to St. Tropez for the weekend. She'll enjoy the oddness of carrying around a doll in a baby seat. I'll see if he's got anyone else who can serve as our other Erins."

Nick sat back. "So we're set on this course of action? Five cars. Three decoys. Why not send Erin, Theo, and the child out together?"

She hated how her cheeks heated. Yes, that would be the smart way to do it. Five cars, all nondescript black, like all the cabs in London. They would all leave at the same time, going different ways. It would have been best to cut down on their chances of being caught by having only one car that held the three of them, but Theo wasn't going where they were. "Theo and I are splitting up. He'll go to a location I don't know and TJ and I'll head to Clive Weston's country home. His lordship promises me it's well protected. In a week or two, we'll reevaluate. I would like to go back to Dallas at some point."

Owen shook his head. "I don't like it. Not the whole plan, but putting the baby out there worries me. All she has to do is find the car the real kid's in and she's got everything she needs to bring us all to our knees."

"The plan is to not allow her to find the car," Nick replied. "If the driver thinks he or she is being tailed, turn around and come back to base."

"And if she's sent the brothers after the car?" Owen seemed intent on playing the voice of doom. "Erin can't fight if she's trying to protect her child. We know she's got at least five of the fuckers. Are any of you ready to swear you can take all five down if they get you in a corner? Not to mention the fact that you won't be able to use a gun since you would be worried about hitting the boy."

Her stomach dropped. She was going to lose both her men in one day. Sure she would get TJ back, but being without him would hurt. "Owen's right."

Kayla nodded. "I hadn't thought about it that way. Look, I'll stay behind with TJ. I'll play nanny and bodyguard and when we're sure Erin's spot is safe, we'll smuggle him out and take him to her."

Penny sent a sympathetic look her way. "We'll take the best care of him."

"If she believes you're all gone, she shouldn't have any reason to target the club," Damon mused. "I can't imagine how hard this could be for you. You could stay here. The decoys could work."

"No." She had to be strong. They couldn't stay here forever and there was no telling how long it would take. This might not be the last time they had to move around. "We should protect TJ. I'll go and make sure we're safe and we can decide from there."

Owen sat back. "All right then, so we've got five cars. We each take one along with our decoys and watch for signs that we're being followed. Anyone being followed turns tail and comes right back here to The Garden. I think it's a perfectly good plan. No way she's got five people with resources watching the place. We get Theo and Erin out and then figure out where the blighter is hiding. She'll show herself soon enough."

That was what scared the hell out of her. Hope McDonald had made it clear she was coming back. It wouldn't be long now and Theo would be out there all alone. Robert had shown up an hour before and explained that he would serve as one of the fake Theos because he was staying behind to help out with the search for McDonald.

Theo would be alone and he would find a way to get himself into serious trouble. He was reckless. Theo had been a bit reckless before, but nothing like what he was now. Before his recklessness had been about arrogance. Now it was because he didn't care about his own life.

Damon started talking about the ins and outs of the plan, how they would stay in contact without a computer footprint and so forth. She listened, but she couldn't help but wonder how she would handle it this time. When she got the word that Theo was dead, how would she accept it? Would she always be waiting for him to walk back through her door?

Why couldn't that giant ass of a man accept that she loved him as he was today?

"All right, you have your assignments." Damon stood up. "We move out at eight in the morning. I want to get lost in London traffic. I'm going to speak with a friend of mine to make sure the traffic lights are as friendly as they can possibly be for the route our Harrys will take."

Phoebe would be so proud.

Erin sat as everyone around her got to their feet and started talking about how and what they needed to do to get prepared.

"Don't worry," Kay said, putting a hand on her shoulder. "That was a stupid thing to say. Of course you're going to worry. I promise I will take care of your baby."

She nodded up at the younger woman, secure in the knowledge that she meant what she said. Kay had done a lot for her country, suffered for her work, and still a deep cloak of humanity and kindness clung to her. Somehow, this woman had come out whole. She wished like hell that Theo had.

"Thank you. I'll make sure he has everything he needs. The most important thing is his stuffed dog. You can't ever let him think Spot might get left behind. He can throw a fit about that."

"Take special care of fake dog." Kay gave her a sassy salute. "Will do. See you in the dungeon tonight?"

Not a chance. "No, I'm going to spend my night with TJ."

Because it could be a while before she saw him again. Even the few days it would take to ensure she was secure would feel like forever. It was hard to conceive of a time when she'd been alone. It wasn't that she didn't like those quiet times when he was sleeping, but she knew he was there.

Theo might have started the job of teaching her how to love, but TJ had driven it home in a way she would never forget.

God, she'd wanted a chance to catch lightning in a bottle again and give that kid a brother or sister. She would make sure they loved each other, accepted each other. They wouldn't be put in the situation she had been, her childhood a constant competition where the siblings were ranked and viewed as successful or failing.

"He could come around, you know."

She looked up and Nick was the only person left in the room. He sat back, his massive body making what should be a large chair look somewhat tiny. Nick. She should have known he would stay until she left. They'd formed a sad friendship, she and Nick. They'd both lost so much that day. "I don't think so. I think he's made his choice."

"He can always choose again."

"Taggarts are stubborn."

He stared at her for a moment. "Do you wish he hadn't come back? Do you think it would be easier than to lose him again?"

Before Theo she likely would have bristled at that question, but now she saw it for what it was. Nick was asking because he wondered what would have happened if Des had miraculously survived. He probably thought about it every day. "No. I wouldn't take back this either. Every second I had with him was precious. Even the ones where I was miserable."

"And if he shows up five years from now? If he goes out into the world and finally figures himself out? What will you do then?"

She wanted to say she would have moved on. She would be happy and dating and looking for love. That wasn't the truth and she knew it deep inside. She would move on, but not from him. She would build a life for her son. Hell, she might find one or two of those kids who needed a mom like her. She would give herself to her family. "I would open my arms and welcome him home. I can say anything I like, but that's the truth. I'll die waiting for him to come back to me. I can't do anything else."

Nick stood, pacing over to the windows that overlooked the quiet neighborhood below. "I think I owe Desiree this kind of devotion, but I don't feel it. Does that make me a bad person? I've been sleeping with subs. Many of them."

She knew a bit about their relationship. "I didn't realize you and Des had been exclusive."

One shoulder shrugged up and down. "We understood what it meant to work. In our line of business, sometimes seduction is the only way to get the job done."

"It never bothered you?"

He sighed heavily. "It would have stopped when we married. Des was caught up with the adventure. She would have settled down. I miss her, but I worry that I'm not as faithful to her memory as you were to Theo's. Does this make me a bad man?"

Her heart softened. "No. It doesn't. It makes you human. By the time I began to process that Theo was gone, I knew I was pregnant. I had TJ to concentrate on. Who knows what I would have done if I hadn't. I might have torn through Sanctum looking for solace. I don't think that makes me bad. But you might think about spending more than one night with one of them. Maybe learn a last name every now and then."

He turned, his brow furrowing as though the thought was disturbing. "This does not help me to pleasure them more."

Men. At least he'd made her smile. "The next time you're at Sanctum, I'll be sure to hook you up. I know a couple of subs who like to tear through some dicks, if you know what I mean. They won't mind helping you through a rough time."

He smiled, looking younger than before. "You are too good to me, Argent." He sobered suddenly. "But you understand that you cannot fix him, right? Where he is right now, it is not your fault. No one can fix another person. He has to want to find himself again."

And that was what hurt the most. He didn't want to find himself. He didn't want to be with her and TJ. She knew what today had been. Staying with TJ for a few hours had been a gesture of guilt. He was leaving and this might assuage his conscience a bit.

"He needs to find some peace and he doesn't think he can do that with us right now." She'd given him her ultimatum, but she knew the truth. She would take him back the minute he asked. Maybe she should be tough and put up her walls again, but he wasn't rejecting her because he didn't care. He'd been through something terrible and it had changed him.

Maybe forever.

She wished Nick well and started toward her room. How would she say good-bye to Theo? Her feet felt heavy, as though they knew it would be the last time and sought to hold back, to make the moment last so she didn't have to say good-bye.

Inevitably, she ended up at her door, and there was nothing to do but walk through and face what would happen.

Her mind went back to that first time they'd met. She wished she'd taken him down then and there, hadn't fought what turned out to be the best time of her life.

There was a masculine shout from inside the room and her heart nearly stopped. She fumbled for her card and rushed into the room.

"Dude, what is it with you and the peeing?" Theo stood over TJ's small changing table, his shirt a wet and stinky mess.

TJ was giggling, his little legs kicking as his father covered his

353

offending boy parts with a diaper.

She waited for Theo to explode, but he simply shook his head and grinned down at TJ. "I need you to do that to your Uncle Ian. He's only got girls. I don't think Kala and Kenzie have your aim. You're the only boy in the family right now. It's your duty to protect your female cousins and pee on your uncle as often as possible. And don't tell your mom how many outfits we've managed to ruin. Dada will get faster with the change."

She stood there watching them. They were so freaking alike. TJ was the spitting image of his father. Even with the scarred side of his face toward her, she could see the way he was smiling. Just like TJ. He had a smile that could light up any room when he wanted to. Her heart ached watching them.

"You have to put the teepee thing on him or he'll get you every time." She could watch them for hours, but it was time to wake up and face the music.

Theo's head turned at the exact time TJ's did, their expressions so alike it made her heart hurt. While TJ started doing his grabby hands thing, Theo changed the diaper quickly.

"I'm afraid I thought that was some weird kind of hat," he admitted with a grin. He pulled the offensive shirt over his head and dropped it on the changing table. He picked up TJ and walked him over. "Yeah, we might have played around with those. Our son is a menace."

She took her baby, cuddling him close. "He is not. He's a sweet boy."

Theo frowned in a shockingly paternal manner. "He peed on his dad on three separate occasions and giggled while he did it. He attempted to climb up the bookcase. He managed to pull on Daddy's laptop bag and dump the whole thing on the floor."

She gaped his way. "What was he doing on the floor? Theo, he has a playpen. If you didn't want to hold him, you should have put him in there."

Theo shook his head. "Boys need to be free. You can't cage him forever. He's a Taggart. He needs to be out in the wild, catching fish and learning to be a man. Climbing some trees and making his place in the world."

Had he lost his ever-loving mind? "He can't walk yet. Not sure how he's going to climb a tree. And you live in Dallas. You're not exactly a mountain man. What did you do to him?"

Theo reached over and put a hand on TJ's head. "I started his training. He needs to learn how to be a man. He's got the belch part down."

TJ flashed her a toothless grin. "Dada."

Erin backed off, tears starting up again. He couldn't possibly be this cruel. "That wasn't fair, Theo."

His face fell but he stood his ground. "Not a lot I've done to you lately has been fair, baby."

"I don't care what you do to me, but you can't make him love you and then walk away from him."

"No, I can't."

She continued on, her anger taking hold. "How can you walk in here and teach him to call you Dad when you have no intention of actually being his father?"

"I can't."

"He's a kid. He needs stability. He needs to know that the people in his life aren't going to come in and out. I would think of all people you would know that. Your father walked out."

He winced. "I don't actually remember most of that, but I know I can't do it to him. Or you."

She started to open her mouth to let loose a torrent of anger his way when she finally heard what he was saying. "You're not leaving TJ?"

He stepped up and this time his hand found the side of her face, his eyes shimmering as he looked down at her. "I'm not leaving you. Either of you. Please don't leave me, Erin. I know I might not deserve another chance, but I'm going to beg you for one. I've been scared and it might be the first time in my life I've ever been truly close to breaking, but I know what brought me through. It was you, baby. It was always you."

She held herself back even as TJ was trying to reach for his dad. "You said that before."

"But I didn't believe it." His jaw went tight. "You love me."

Her heart felt constricted with the sweetness of his words. They were even better than hearing he loved her. She'd said those words to him once. She'd said them the moment she'd opened her heart and truly let him in. She'd said it because she'd finally believed him, believed in what they could be. "I love you."

"You love me the way I am. It doesn't matter that I might never remember all of our life together." His hand stroked back her hair, his eyes on her like she was some miracle he was witnessing.

No one in the universe, no one for the rest of time, would ever make her feel as beautiful as Theo Taggart did. "We'll make new memories."

"I didn't want to be weak, but I can be with you. That's what I figured out. I can be anything I need to be with you. Let me hold on to you so I can get through this."

So they could get through this. She couldn't speak, could only manage to nod her head.

Theo's arms came around her, encircling her and TJ, completing them for the very first time.

"I'm staying here with you tonight and in the morning, we'll face this together," he promised. "As a family. But you should know something, Erin Argent."

Even if he said he needed some time, she could handle it. "What's that, Taggart?"

He leaned over, his mouth hovering above hers. "You're changing your name when we get married. And you will marry me."

There was nothing she wanted more. "Yes."

He started to kiss her, but TJ leaned forward, going in for a sloppy kiss.

Theo laughed, the sound freer than she'd heard in over a year. "He's going to make things difficult. We're going to have a talk, son. You can't interrupt Daddy when he's making out with your mom."

Somehow, she thought they would get by.

CHAPTER TWENTY

Theo kissed TJ's head and felt an actual pain in his heart. How could he leave his son behind? He'd just found him and now he was saying good-bye.

He'd sat up most of the night watching TJ sleep. They'd brought him into bed, cuddling their child between them and bonding as a family for the first time. It would be him and Erin for a few days, and though he craved the time with her, he already missed the little guy.

Erin leaned against him, her body a comforting weight. "It's going to be okay. It's a few days and then we'll decide if we stay or find another safe house."

Kayla put TJ on her hip, holding him with the confidence of a woman who liked and spent a lot of time around kids. "I promise, I'll protect him with my life."

Knight stepped in behind her. "We all will. He's going to be safe here until we're ready to get him out. He's going to be much easier to smuggle out. Besides, I have a feeling something is about to happen. Ian wouldn't leave his girls for more than a week or two. He's got something up his sleeve."

There was no doubt in Theo's mind that his brother was

definitely up to something. He wouldn't be out of touch if there wasn't something going on. He'd talked to Sean yesterday, needing to hear one of his brothers' voices, but Sean had no idea where Case and Ian had gone.

They were out there. They were doing whatever they could to deal with the situation, and he had to honor that by taking care of his own.

He found Erin's hand, threading their fingers together as they watched Kayla take TJ back toward the playroom. TJ looked over her shoulder, his eyes wide as the distance grew, but he didn't cry.

Oh, but his momma did.

"It's going to be okay." He drew her close, knowing damn well if he hadn't been here with her, she wouldn't have shed a tear. She would have bottled it all up and been the tough chick. He kissed her hair and murmured into her ear that they would all be back together soon.

Nothing in the world ever felt as good and right as soothing his woman's heartache. He was the only person who could. That was better than any memory, better than being the strongest person on the team. He was the only man for her and that was all he needed to be.

"It's time," Damon said quietly. "The cars are ready and we've found an extra Theo decoy. You're all wearing roughly the same clothes. I sent one car out early. It will have a police escort and travel toward Heathrow. I'm hoping if anyone's watching, that will throw them off."

They started to walk toward the elevator that would take them to the garage level.

"Have you seen any signs that the building is being watched?" Erin had dried her eyes, but her hand was still firmly in his.

"We can't detect that anyone's cut into the CCTV feeds, but then Hutch would be careful about that," Knight explained. "I have arranged with some powerful friends to have CCTV cut out for five minutes when we go. They'll be dark for three blocks around us. That doesn't mean they won't have people on the ground."

She would find a way to watch. He would spend the next few weeks praying she wasn't watching his family. He hoped that whatever Ian was planning, it happened quickly.

And with the maximum amount of pain.

"Who's driving us?" Erin asked. "Are we going all the way to Norsely tonight?"

The country house that was owned by Clive Weston's family was somewhere in the north of England, deep in a county called Yorkshire. He'd been told it was a hunting cabin, but that English royalty tended to "hunt" things like luxury and that they were all "posh bastards who wouldn't know how to rough it." At least that's what the Aussie had claimed at dinner the night before. The hunting cabin was apparently very comfy and secure.

It was good to know he wouldn't be roughing it with a baby.

"I thought I would send Nick with you, but he's not feeling well this morning," Knight said with a frown. "Damn Russian and his vodka. It appears he overdid it last night, so Owen is going to take his place. Clive has assured me he's got everything ready for you. It's a long drive, but you'll get there tonight."

He would have to send his deepest apologies to Simon's brother. Now that he was comfortable with his place in the family, he knew he'd been a possessive moron. Clive hadn't done anything a man with eyes wouldn't have done. His sub was gorgeous and every Dom in the world would want her. And she would politely turn them all down.

The elevator doors opened and he realized Clive Weston wasn't the only person he should apologize to.

Tennessee Smith stood in the middle of the garage talking to Owen, Brody, and the other men dressed as drivers. Faith was standing with him, but when she saw Erin, she broke away.

"I can't believe you're already leaving." She opened her arms to hug Erin.

He gave the women a moment to say their good-byes. Ten turned as he approached, finishing up his lecture and dismissing the men. He held a hand out to Theo.

"Brother, I'm sorry to see you go, but I'm glad you've got some company."

Theo took his hand and shook it. "I'm stubborn, but I'm not completely foolish. She's right. We belong together. We're weaker apart."

A grin crossed Ten's face, lighting up his blue eyes. "Damn

straight, and don't you forget it. We're nothing without those women."

"Ten, I've never said I'm sorry."

Ten put his free hand over Theo's, encasing him as he stared at him seriously. "There is nothing to be sorry for. That night went sideways, but your intentions were pure. There isn't a soldier alive today who hasn't made mistakes he wishes he could take back. I've got a million of them."

"How do you live with it?" That was the hardest part.

"You honor the people who died by having a life, brother. By being better than you were before, by remembering them and never taking things for granted." Ten let him go. "But you need to understand that some things happen for a reason. Now I'm not a particularly religious man, but I've seen enough to know that sometimes bad shit happens because we've got something to learn. I've thought about this a lot, especially when we thought you were gone. I think about what would have happened if you hadn't made the mistake of coming for me that night."

Theo thought about it constantly. "You would have been taken by MSS and Ian would have rescued you. Des would be alive. I wouldn't have gotten caught by McDonald."

"Yes, I would have been taken by MSS. Des would be alive, maybe. But I would be dead and I think Faith would be, too. So would Kay."

Theo shook his head. "MSS wouldn't have killed you right away. They would have tortured you, but they wouldn't have killed you. And Faith was with us. I don't see what Kay had to do with it."

"Because all you've done is worry about your own guilt. You didn't look at the bigger picture. Did you know the plane MSS took off the island had a mechanical failure over the Pacific? It's classified, but the CIA has confirmed that the plane went down and there were very likely no survivors. I would have been on that plane and so would Kayla. That was her last op. If I'd been taken in when I should have, she wouldn't have had an opportunity to save me. She would have sat back and waited and we both would have died. Faith wouldn't have stayed with you. She would have confronted her father, and he was damn good at getting rid of inconvenient women. She would have had an "accident" or been given to her sister to erase her memory. So your mistake saved us. Who knows what other repercussions your actions might have had? Des was reckless. Damon had been ready to let her go. Nick would have gone with her. No telling how that turns out."

He hadn't followed the direct order to kill McDonald and he'd regretted it. Until this moment. She'd been alive to save him. She'd been alive to return to Robert's cell and ensure he and the others lived. He couldn't be responsible for what she did. He could only serve his own sense of honor, and that meant not killing an unarmed woman he knew nothing about.

He'd made the call and in that second he realized he would make it again. He would walk past her knowing everything that would happen next because the pain was worth it. The pain meant he was alive and able to hold his wife and son.

He would stop her this time because now he knew what was at stake, but he forgave himself for that moment he seemed stuck in, that moment that had seemed to cement everyone's misery.

It had saved Robert and the others from being dispensed with as The Collective's dirty secret. It had saved Ten and Faith.

It had saved him.

Ten gave him a hint of a smile as he gave him a manly hug. "So trust your instincts. I know you don't remember everything, but remember that even when you fuck up, something good can come of it. See you on the flip side, brother."

"Stay safe."

Ten winked and stepped back. "You know it. I plan on letting Ezra take all the bullets on this one. We're heading out after you go, and then later today Knight's sending a team to Estonia. We'll keep you up to date."

Erin joined him while Faith took her husband's hand.

"Are you two ready?" Owen stepped up, looking dapper in his dark suit, a cap covering his red hair. "There's nothing like a long drive through the country. I'll have you there in no time a'tall, and then I'll head north for a few days to visit my mum and sis. So I'll be fairly close in case you need anything."

He stepped over to the door of the car, opening it for Erin. Their bags had been taken earlier. Erin slid on a pair of sunglasses, covered her hair with the hood of her jacket, and slipped inside.

"Hey, be safe!" Robert ran up. He was dressed exactly like Theo and had matching sunglasses.

It was damn good to see him. Being friends with Robert was one of the many things he would have missed out on if he hadn't survived. He held a hand out. "Not mad at me anymore?"

Robert smiled. "Nope. I got what I wanted so I can be magnanimous."

"What you wanted?"

"Yeah, my friend is happy again. And he's not acting like a dipshit, so there's hope for us all." He shook Theo's hand and then nodded back toward the car he would be traveling in. "My Erin is pretty hot. I think I have a shot with her."

That was Robert. Always the optimist. "I think you do, too, buddy. She'd be lucky to have you."

He waved at his friend and slid into the seat beside his girl.

"Are we doing the right thing?" Erin stared out the window as the car began to move.

He reached for her hand. "I think we are. We have to be sure we're safe before we bring him in. We have to put him first."

She squeezed his hand, but he could see easily she hated to be apart from their son.

"You're doing what every good mum does for her child," Owen said from the front seat. He turned and took his place in line. "You make sacrifices. You do everything you can. My own mum, well, I can't even begin to tell you all the things she's done for me and my sister. Your boy will love you for what you do for him. No closer bond than a son and his mother."

The car moved forward. It looked like they were third in line.

Theo took a deep breath and attempted to banish his fear. Erin needed him to be strong. She needed him to lean on, and he intended to be there. She'd shouldered so much on her own that he needed to bear more of the burden now that he was back.

The car started up the long drive and finally out on the London street. Theo looked out the tinted glass windows.

She was out there somewhere. "I don't think she's in Estonia. I think it was all a trick. She's somewhere here in England."

Erin turned to look at him. "I think so, too. I think the minute she discovered we were here, she started making plans. That's why we have to leave. I don't trust her to not bomb The Garden."

"I think that's a smart play," Owen said. "That woman is pure evil. She'll do anything to get what she wants. You're both smart to see that and kind to give a damn about the rest of us. The team will look after your boy. They won't let anything harm him."

He turned down a side street and Theo watched as the car carrying Robert went the opposite direction. They were breaking up, each going a different route.

They were silent for a long while, the tension seeming to fill the car so it was hard to breathe. Theo watched out the mirrors, looking for anything that would tell him they were being followed. Erin seemed to be doing the same thing, her eyes sharp and seeking out any predator coming their way.

Nothing. Owen turned and looped around the city, giving them every chance to find a vehicle that was following them. After thirty minutes, he took a deep breath and turned toward the M25. "I'm satisfied we don't have a tail. Could you text Damon and let him know we're beginning our route to the north?"

It was the "all clear" and the last communication they would have with base until they made it north. Theo pulled out the phone he'd been given, texted the word *test*, and sent it. It was the code they'd agreed on. If they'd been followed the word *home* would have been sent.

Theo pulled the chip out of the phone and destroyed it.

They were going fully off the grid for a few days.

How long would it be? How long would they hide before she showed her face?

The city gave way to green countryside as they left London.

The waiting was going to kill him. He slid closer to Erin. He would have to find a way to make the waiting worthwhile. Like maybe talking about trying to hit that one in a million shot a second time.

He leaned over, whispering in her ear. "Maybe by the time we get TJ back, we'll have a little brother or sister on the way."

She turned slightly, her eyes wide. "Are you serious?" A smile crossed her lips. "Only you could think of that at a time like this. We're literally on the run for our lives and you're thinking about sex."

It was all worth it to see her smile. "I think about sex all the time, baby. It's a man thing. Am I right, Owen?"

"Absolutely," he concurred. "Nothing we think about more. I was in a firefight once and I was thinking about the girl I was going to see that night. I can be rip-roaring drunk and unable to perform, but I'm still thinking about it."

Erin smiled but shook her head. "Men. You know, speaking of drunk, I'm worried about Nick."

"Why? He just had a little too much. I'm sure he was partying."

"Nick doesn't party," Erin insisted. "Nick is very controlled. He reminds me of Ian when he drinks. You can't tell he's had too much. If he was so bad he couldn't work, something went wrong last night."

"I was with him," Owen said. "He's still in mourning. That'll make a man drink like he's never drunk before. I need to get some petrol before we take off. I want to make sure we have a full tank. Won't take but a minute."

Owen took the exit that brought them to a massive travel complex. There was gas and food and a parking lot that seemed to go on for days.

"I've never seen him drunk at all," Erin mused. "The man can slam vodka and not show a single sign. Besides, when I talked to him last night he told me he was going to bed. He said he was going to try to give clean living a shot."

"I suppose he changed his mind." Owen moved the car into a slot.

"I thought we were getting gas," Erin said.

Theo got a sinking feeling. "Nick wasn't drinking last night, was he? You wanted to be the one to drive us."

Bertha made an appearance. Erin had her Beretta out of the holster and aimed at Owen's head. "Get out of the car. Theo, slip up front and get ready to drive like a bat out of hell. I swear, I'll blow your brains all over the dashboard, Owen, and that still won't stop us from getting away."

Owen put his hands up. "It don't matter. They're already here. I'm sorry. I did everything I could to save the baby. Please don't tell her that was my idea. She wanted all of you, but I couldn't give her the child. Not even to save my mother."

The sun was suddenly blocked, shadows covering the car, and Theo realized they were surrounded.

The door came open and Hutch smiled down at him. "Hello, brother. It's time to take you home."

His fist came out and the world went black.

* * * *

Erin shivered from the cold as she started to come to. Her head throbbed and she could feel her stomach threatening to go. What the hell had happened?

It came back to her in horrifying flashes.

She'd been with Theo, holding his hand and nervous about leaving the baby behind. But so fucking happy because he'd been beside her. They'd been in the car. Her plan.

Her plan that didn't work because the person who'd been watching them hadn't been outside. He'd been sitting in the front seat.

Erin groaned and started to open her eyes. It was so bright.

She'd pulled her gun when she'd realized the danger. She could hear herself threatening that Scottish motherfucker, who better be dead right now or she'd kill him herself.

They'd been in a parking lot but away from the rest of the cars. She could hear the traffic from the M25.

They'd almost made it. They'd been so close to being out and then all those men had surrounded the car and she'd watched as Hutch hit Theo and he'd gone down.

Erin managed to roll to her side. She fought back the urge to vomit as the memory of Theo bleeding assaulted her. She could still hear her scream. She'd been frozen. Her every instinct had told her to hold him, but she'd known that she had to fight.

And then the fight had been over because one of those lost boys McDonald collected had used her terror to his advantage. She'd felt the needle go into her arm and then the world had started to go dark before she could get a shot off.

Not that it would have mattered. It had been six against two and they had been stuck in a small space with no maneuvering room. They'd been lambs led to the slaughter.

Where was Theo? How far away from London had they been taken?

She forced a deep breath into her aching lungs. She felt bruised and battered, like she'd been beat the hell out of, but from the inside out.

"That particular sedative isn't easy on a body," a feminine voice said. "It's something I played around with. It's like an anti anti-inflammatory. Well, I suppose that would simply be an inflammatory. So all your nerves and muscles feel like you've gone ten rounds with a heavyweight, but I didn't have to actually expend the energy or resources to beat you up. Cool, huh?"

"I would call it evil." Erin bit back a groan. She wasn't giving that bitch a moment's pleasure. She turned and there was the demon who'd invaded her life.

Hope McDonald stood on the other side of the high-tech cell. There was a wall of glass between them so Erin could see her clearly. She was dressed in a chic sheath, her feet in a set of heels that would impress any woman. Her hair was coiffed in an elegant bob and colored to perfect colorlessness. Icy and blonde, she looked like she belonged on a fashion magazine, but she also had a lab coat on, as though she didn't want anyone to forget that she had those letters after her name. Hope McDonald, MD. Also EAF. Evil as fuck.

"Somehow, I don't think this particular drug is going to make it to market."

McDonald shrugged. "Some of the best never do. This drug will be useful on the black market. All the best intelligence agencies will be hopping on the Dark Web to buy it. It's one of the drugs I'm forced to use when the boys are bad."

"Ah, yes, you're their loving mother," she returned, sarcasm dripping.

McDonald stood so close, her eyes staring in. "Yes. A parent must discipline her children from time to time. You should know that. Like that one. He was bad. He was supposed to bring you all in."

Her eyes trailed to her left. Erin followed them and gasped. Owen was lying face first on the cot in his cell. He was naked, his skin a mottled mass of sores. Despite the fact that he was the reason she was here, she couldn't believe her eyes. "What the hell did you do to him?"

She sighed, a long-suffering sound. "Another drug. I used two on him. The effect was unexpected. He's either allergic or I shouldn't use them in combination. Not sure. I'll have to experiment a bit more. Nevertheless, I've already got my story for when he wakes. It's good to lay the foundation down at the outset. My boys are confused when they wake up. All those pesky memories are gone, but they fight it at first."

"You wiped his memory?" Erin's head was still fuzzy but she tried to work through it. If that bitch was here then she wasn't somewhere fucking with Theo. She had to keep her here as long as possible. Wherever here was. "But he was working for you."

"Yes, and he failed. He was supposed to bring me all three of you, but you seem to have forgotten your child, Erin. A mother doesn't forget her son."

What had she done to him? Erin had thought of killing Owen in the moment when she'd realized he'd betrayed them, but she wouldn't have done this. He was ruined. "You wiped his memory? You're going to make him into one of your soldiers? I assure you, Damon Knight won't forget him."

"Well, I figure in for a penny, in for a pound, as they say here," she said with the breezy nonchalance of a person who had never once in her life possessed a conscience. "Ian Taggart will come after me for taking Theo, but I'm ready for him this time. As for our Scottish friend here, well, it wasn't like he wanted to help me. He had to be persuaded."

"You took his mother." Erin remembered him saying something about his mother before everything had gone down. He loved his mother.

"And his sister," McDonald agreed. "I've found having leverage is important. He's the only one in the group who had someone I could get to. Penelope Knight's siblings are surprisingly well guarded. Knight himself has no one but his wife's family. The Australian's mother is isolated and good with firearms. The Russian's only family died off years before and honestly, the Asian girl scares me. So it had to be the Scot. His mother was easy to get to. Once we had her, the sister walked into my trap, and then it was simple from there. He agreed quickly once he heard her scream. You know, it's actually a mercy that I wiped his memory since I had them killed about twenty minutes after I was sure he'd done the job."

"No honor among thieves, is there?" She was so going to murder this woman. Slowly and painfully and with little mercy.

"I'm not a thief." McDonald stepped right in front of her. So close that she could almost get her hands around her throat. If there hadn't been that thick glass between them. "I'm a god, Erin. That's what you don't understand. There are people and there are gods. We're the ones who were touched. Nothing I do is wrong because I make the world."

Ah, the ramblings of the sociopath. "Open this door and I'll show you how god-like you are."

She rolled her eyes. "Violence is the refuge of the pitiful. It's all you know, isn't it? I have no idea what my Theo saw in you."

Her blood chilled. "Saw? Have you already used the drug on him again?" She couldn't cry. Not in front of this bitch, couldn't let her see how afraid she was. "It won't work. It didn't work the first time."

"I've perfected the drug since then." Her heels clacked against the floor as she paced in front of the cell. "I wouldn't use the experimentals on Theo. He's too precious. I had to perfect it on the others before I used it on my prize. Theo is the ultimate warrior."

"Seriously? I love the man but I know several better soldiers than Theo. He's too emotional, too optimistic to be a truly great warrior. He's the best man I know, but you could find a better mercenary. I suspect that's what you're building, isn't it? An army of mercenaries to back you up while you make as much money as you can selling a drug that will ruin an entire generation of men."

"I free them. I make life simple for them," she shot back. "Do you even understand how much happier Theo was before you ripped him from me?"

"You mean before you kidnapped and tortured him?"

"I saved him," McDonald insisted. "I did that. If it weren't for me, he would be dead, and that makes him mine."

"No, you insanely psychotic bitch." Erin's fingers itched to wrap around the doctor's throat. "Look, I thank you for saving him.

I truly do. Faith would have even looked up to you for saving him if you'd truly given him back his life. That's what a doctor does. She repairs the body so the brain can heal, so the soul can be with its mate. You perverted that. He doesn't belong to you."

McDonald's eyes went icy and narrowed. "Don't mention my traitorous sister to me. Believe me, I'll handle her at some point. I once thought I could bring her closer to me, but now I understand how bourgeoisie her thinking is."

Which only showed how little McDonald understood her sister. "Faith is a real doctor. She's a real human being and you didn't answer my question. Have you used the drug on him?"

Her lips curved into a devilish smile. "Wouldn't you love to know that? As it happens, I'll tell you. No. Not yet. He's not awake. I want to make sure the sedative he was given clears his system. I won't have him end up like our new friend here." She nodded to Owen, whose body twitched and then went still. "In about twenty minutes, he should be ready. I'll administer the drug then and give him his first orders. Can you guess what they'll be?"

"I'm sure I'm about to become your first female soldier." She wouldn't go into the darkness quietly. Not a chance.

McDonald's laughter filled the room. "No, silly. Women are useless, with certain exceptions. You show no signs of true intelligence, so you're nothing but a walking womb. I personally think we have too many wretched creatures in the world, so I'm going to have Theo kill you as his first act. Then we'll go and find his son. I made sure you hadn't lied and cheated on him like the whore you are. I'm satisfied that Theodore Jr. is his, so I'll raise him. I'm interested in seeing how my techniques work on a child."

Erin couldn't help it. She ran at the wall, beating at it with her hands. "If you lay a hand on my son, I'll rip your fucking throat out."

McDonald didn't move an inch. "I'm certain you would try. It's what an animal does. You have those instincts. But you'll be gone. Your dead body will be the final proof that Theo is mine. I intend to install him as my husband this time. When you die, know he'll be in my bed thirty minutes later. I won't even make him clean up."

"No matter what you do, Ian is going to come after you. He'll take you all down."

"I've handled Mr. Taggart," McDonald claimed breezily. "I have powerful friends, and Mr. Hutchins has ensured that we know when and where Taggart will strike. He's looking for us in Munich. I left a false trail that will lead him there. By this time tomorrow, he'll meet with an ugly death. I have a group waiting for Knight's people in Tallinn as well. They won't make it out of the airport. Hutch has been a miracle from heaven."

It was so painful to think that sweet Hutch was working with the devil, but she'd seen it with her own two eyes. "Yeah, I think Big Tag will take care of him, too."

McDonald chuckled, a cold sound. "Believe what you will. I wanted to come here and stand in front of you and let you know who the better woman is. Theo is the prize and he's going to be mine. My victory is over you. Know that when you're gone, I'll have your man and your child, and neither one of them will remember that you existed. I'll wipe you from the face of the earth, bitch. Think about that in your last few minutes. Good-bye, Erin."

She turned and walked out and Erin was left with rage and fear.

CHAPTER TWENTY-ONE

"Wake up," a voice insisted.

Theo didn't want to wake up. He'd been having a perfectly pleasant dream where Erin had been on her knees, ready to serve her Master. She'd been licking her lips and the world had been a perfect place. TJ was sleeping and they had hours and hours to play.

A hard slap across his face shocked him to consciousness. Pain flared through him and he blinked his eyes open. The world was blurry.

What the hell had happened?

"It's time for you to wake up, you fucker. Mother is waiting for you."

"Hutch?" Was that Hutch? He could sort of see the outline of a man and he kind of recognized the voice.

His head was spinning though.

"Yes, it's Hutch. Come on. Do I need to hit you again?"

Hutch had hit him. Fuck. It came roaring back. Hutch had been there along with all the other new friends McDonald had decided to bring into his life. They'd surround him and Erin, and now he was fucked hard and not in a good way.

He forced his eyes open, made himself focus. "You bastard."

"Yeah, I get that a lot lately." He smirked, a look that he hadn't seen on Hutch before. "Nonetheless, you need to man up and come out of dreamland."

There was the sound of something sliding. A high-tech sound and Hutch suddenly stood up straight. He loomed over Theo and it was obvious the kid had made some serious changes to his physique. His shoulders seemed broader and he'd definitely added a ton of muscle to his previously lanky frame.

"You finally going to wake up, Taggart? Welcome home. I have a lot to get off my chest before you go under again. It's about time for you to take your medicine."

Medicine. That got him awake really fucking fast. Medicine here meant forgetting. Forgetting Erin. Forgetting TJ.

He couldn't forget. Not ever again.

He started to bring his arms up, but they stopped moving. Theo looked down. He was strapped to the bed. He tried to kick his legs and found the same.

His heart rate ticked up. Here he was again, in a too-white room without the ability to move. He looked up at his friend. "Come on, Hutch. Tell me this is all a fucking bad dream. Come on, man."

Hutch merely rolled his eyes. "I thought I explained this to you on the phone. This is my home now and I'm the big dog here. You're the mutt who ran away, so don't expect to get a happy homecoming."

"Hutch, we talked about this," a new voice said.

He fought with everything he had not to throw up. Hope McDonald was here. He heard her heels hitting the floor as she walked toward him.

"Theo is your brother and I expect you to honor him," she was saying. "You know how I feel about him."

Hutch took a quick step back, his head going down. "Yes, Mother. I do and I will. I'm sorry. We weren't close in our previous lives. I never liked him. I tried to stay away from him. I hope we can be closer once you purify him."

Never been close? They'd spent most of their free time together until he'd convinced Erin to love him. He and Hutch, Case and Mike, Boomer and Bear and Deke, they'd all been close. They spent time at each other's places playing video games and drinking beer. How could he have thought Hutch liked him? Hutch had flown right under his radar.

McDonald stepped into his line of sight, her face staring down at him. Her hand came out, smoothing back his hair. "I want all my boys to be close. But you, Theo, you are going to be the head of our family."

He couldn't stand having her hands on him. He tried to shrink away. "Where is my wife, you crazy bitch? Where's Erin? Erin, the woman I love. Do you see how I can say her name and it doesn't even bother me now? You failed. I didn't forget her. I remember more and more every single day. I just remembered all the times I spent with Hutch. We were friends, man. How can you do this?"

Hutch shook his head. "We were never friends. I did what I had to do to stay out of jail. Ten gave me that lovely choice. Work for the fuckers in the Agency and then McKay-Taggart or spend my time in a lovely prison being someone's bitch. Is it such a surprise that I forced myself to hang out with you morons?"

So much for friendship. "Fuck you, Hutch."

Hutch puffed up, his shoulders swinging back. There was a cruel twist to his mouth as he looked down at Theo. "Back at you, Taggart. You know I'm going after Case next. I want to send Big Tag his brothers in teeny-tiny pieces, and when I've run through all of you, I'll start in on the kids. I won't stop until I've ruined your entire family."

McDonald stepped in between them, a stern look on her face. "I told you, Hutch. I won't stand for you hurting your brother. You can play your games with the other Taggarts, but not until we're safe in our new home and Theo has accepted his place."

"It's hard to deal with him." Hutch's eyes found the floor. "I'm sorry. I know how much his stubbornness has hurt you and it bothers me. I'm sure once he's had his medication, he'll be more acceptable."

She put a hand on Hutch's chest and patted him with an almost maternal familiarity. "I know. I can't question your loyalty after everything you've been through."

"I'll question the fucker's loyalty. He's a turncoat bastard. He'll betray you in the end. It's what he does." He watched Hutch closely, looking for any weaknesses. He needed to figure a way to get out of the bindings that held down his wrists and ankles. If he could get free, he could find Erin and run.

McDonald shook her head. "It's because you don't understand how our family works. Not yet. You were happy when you were with your brothers. I'm going to give you an even bigger family this time. And I'll get your son for you. We'll raise him together."

"Don't you touch my son."

"I would already have him if Owen hadn't failed me," she said with a tsking sound.

Hutch pulled out his cell phone. "Should I call off the boys and have his mother and sister returned?"

She waved a hand. "I had them killed an hour ago. It's better this way. You know I like things clean and simple."

There was no way to mistake how Hutch paled. So he wasn't so far gone.

"Did she make a deal with Owen? That's what she does, Hutch. The minute she doesn't need you, she'll cut you, too. Is he dead?"

Despite the fact that Owen had betrayed them, he couldn't help but feel for the guy. Would he have done the same thing if McDonald had Erin and TJ? Right now he felt desperate enough to promise anything to make sure she was all right.

"Owen will become one of your brothers," she explained. "He's already had the new drug. When he wakes up, he'll remember nothing. We'll give him a home and purpose and he'll serve us. He'll be a good soldier. And he didn't do as promised. He was supposed to bring me all three of you."

His whole little family. Ruined by this woman. "I will not accept this. I didn't last time and I won't do it again. I'll fight you every inch of the way and when I get the chance, I'm going to kill you. Do you understand me?"

"I understand that you're in pain now and I can fix that for you." She reached for him, stroking back his hair.

He struggled against his bonds. Her touch made him sick. "Let Erin go and I won't fight you. You remember what it was like? How hard I fought?"

"That's precisely why I reformulated the drug, love. There won't be a fight this time. The new drug requires no therapy. It will wipe your memory and there will be no coming back. Think about it. You won't get those pesky whispers that make your head ache. All my boys are happy now. You're going to be happy, Theo."

"I want to see Erin." Was she even alive? Or had McDonald already ended her? It was worse than dying himself. She couldn't be gone. She had to be alive. He could handle any of this if she was alive.

How had he thought for a second that he would rather die than live through this again? He would live through anything if it meant even the slightest chance of being with her again. Of being a father to his son. He would survive any pain for that shot.

Please let her be alive. Please.

"You'll see her very soon. Calm down." She kept touching him, her hand on his arm now. "I haven't hurt her. I want you to do that."

So that was her perverted game. "I won't hurt Erin."

"I think you will," she said quietly. "Hutch, will you bring me the dose I left on the medical tray? I would get it myself, but I don't want to leave him. Not even for a second."

"Of course, Mother." Hutch's footsteps echoed through the room as he walked away.

Theo heard the sound of a door sliding open and shutting again.

Where was Erin? How much longer did they have before McDonald would take his mind? He had to remember. He couldn't give in, couldn't allow himself to forget. Panic threatened. He wasn't going to get his shot. He wasn't going to have a way to get free and save Erin.

"Hope, do you want to start our life like this? With me tied down?"

She laughed. "Well, if you weren't tied down, I'm sure I would be dead right now. Don't even try it, love. I won't take chances with you. You're too important. Ah, there he is."

Hutch walked in, a syringe in his hand. He had no expression on his face as he passed it to McDonald.

"All right, I know you won't remember anything I say to you right now, but I feel like I need to prepare you," she said as she looked at his arm, searching for a vein. She reached to a tray on the side of his bed and carefully prepped his skin. "You'll sleep for a while. There's a slight sedative in with the drug so you won't feel any pain or anxiety while the drug does its work. When you wake up, I'll be there and I'll give you your first assignment. You'll be confused at first, but the drug will make you susceptible to suggestion in the beginning. You'll want to please me and so you'll do your duty."

He had a guess. "Kill the woman I love."

It was the only thing that made sense. McDonald would get a thrill out of watching him murder her rival. Erin would fight him. God. He prayed Erin would fight.

"That's the beautiful thing, Theo," she said as she pierced his skin. "After this, you won't even remember her name. Good night. When you wake up, we can be together."

She pushed the plunger and the world went black.

* * * *

How long had she been left in this cold room? Erin shivered, but her mind was still racing. It had definitely been hours. How many, she couldn't tell. There was no clock in this room. Everything was white, from the small cot she was sitting on to the floors to the sink and toilet in her cell.

She'd already tried to take those fuckers apart. She'd attempted to scavenge anything in her cell for a weapon. Nothing. She couldn't even get the handles off the sink. It was motion activated, and without tools, she couldn't get inside.

She would have to use her body initially. Even if the guard came in with a gun, she could kick out and at least stun the guy. She wasn't sure what these men had been told about her. She had to hope not much.

One had come by, as though making the rounds every so often. Likely every hour or two. There had been a different man the last time. A shift change? Were they on an eight- or six-hour rotation?

Both men she'd seen had been dressed in all black, what looked like semiautomatics tucked into a shoulder holster. They'd stared at her blankly, not saying a word before moving on to check on Owen.

They never said a word, even when she tried to taunt them.

One of these times, the guard would open the door and haul her out. That would be when she would strike.

Go for the throat. Disable the guard. Take the weapon and then she would go find her man.

And complain to management. This was the single shittiest jail she'd ever been in, though she would admit it was clean. No one had thought to bring her dinner or even water. Not that she would have eaten.

Damn, she wished she'd had a better breakfast. Her hands were shaky.

It wouldn't matter. She would find the strength. Everything depended on her finding the strength to get them the hell out of here.

Would Theo even go with her? Or would he be like Owen?

Owen had awakened a while before, a few minutes before the guard had shown up. He'd howled in pain and looked so confused as he'd stood. She'd tried to talk to him, but the guard had whisked him out of the room. It was the only time she'd heard him say anything.

I'll take care of you, brother.

Owen had entered a nightmare. Was Theo waiting for him somewhere in this building? Had his mind been erased? Was he somewhere wondering who he was? Not knowing there were people who loved him.

The sound she'd been waiting for reached her ears. The outer door slid open with a quiet hiss.

So the guard was back. She looked up and there he was, all tall and broad. He was a good half a foot taller than she was and likely outweighed her by seventy pounds of muscle.

She was going to take him if she got the chance.

"You have a visitor," he said in a thick accent. It sounded Eastern European.

Was McDonald back? Because she hadn't said everything she wanted to say to that bitch.

The door slid open again and her heart nearly stopped.

Theo was here.

She pressed her hands against the glass barrier between them. "Baby, I don't care what she's done to you. We can bring you back."

He stared at her, nothing at all in his eyes.

"Mother, do you have a good view or should I reposition the camera?" Hutch strode in behind Theo. He touched his left ear, obviously hearing something there. "Excellent." He turned to Erin. "Hello, Argent. Did I ever thank you for all the jokes about how soft I was? How useless I was?"

What the hell was he talking about? Had he made up some weird world in his head? "Hutch, I've never been anything but your friend. Please, don't do whatever you're about to do."

He pointed to a place behind him. Hutch was dressed exactly like his soldier "brothers" and had the same gun at his side. He looked far more dangerous than she could ever remember him looking. "Smile for the camera. Mother is watching. She abhors violence, of course, but she does feel like she needs to watch her experiment in action. Brother, do you remember what your orders are?"

"Why do I have to kill the girl?" Theo asked, his brow furrowing as if he was fighting some voice in his head.

"You don't, baby," she replied. How was she going to fight Theo? She couldn't hurt him. She needed him ready to run. "You don't have to hurt me. You don't have to do anything she tells you."

Hutch leaned in, practically whispering in Theo's ear. "You do, brother. We can't let Mother down. You don't want to fail your family, do you? We're all you have in this world."

Theo frowned. "I don't understand why the girl has to die."

He was still in there, still fighting it. They had a chance. She simply had to get through to him. "Theo, please listen to me. I'm your wife. I love you. We have a child together."

"Remember what Mother told you. She'll lie because that's what she does," Hutch said. "She has to die because of what she did to Owen. Owen, our brother. Did you see the sores he had? The way he bled? That was all because of this woman here. She's a doctor who preys on people. She's killed many children."

"Are you fucking kidding me?" The nerve was too much. "I'm a doctor who kills kids?"

Theo stared at her for a long moment before making his decision. "She told me you would try to trick me. Open the door. I'm ready."

Hutch nodded to the soldier. "I'm going to open the door. You keep your gun trained on her. Don't let her out of your sights."

He stepped forward and placed his thumb over the reader and the cell door slid open. Hutch pulled his gun out and looked perfectly competent as he aimed it at her head.

She held her hands up, waiting for the moment when he would be vulnerable. Erin looked between Hutch and the other gun trained on her. Hutch moved in, flanking her.

Theo wasn't going to use a gun, it appeared. A nasty knife was suddenly in his hand. It was big and wicked sharp. That knife had never been meant to cook with or to help a man survive in the woods. It had one purpose. To kill.

And the love of her life was going to use it on her.

Erin winced as she felt Hutch's gun on the back of her neck. While she'd been watching Theo, he'd eased behind her. He'd made it impossible for her to move.

There was only one shot she had and that was to convince Theo.

He stalked in the room, his eyes on her. He was focused now.

"Baby, I'm not what she says I am. She's lying to you," Erin pleaded. She couldn't die this way. This couldn't be the end of them. If he ever got his memory back, he would hate himself for what he'd done. "You love me. This is not what you want to do."

"Shut up," he snarled back. "I know what you are. I know exactly what you are."

Hutch grabbed her hands, pulling them behind her back in his free one. "Do it, Theo. Tell her who she is. Let Mother see it. It's time."

Her body was pressed out and completely vulnerable. She would kick back, but that would likely cause him to pull the trigger. And then there was the fact that he wasn't the only man holding a gun on her. Theo was so close. He could get hit and then she would have to watch him die all over again.

God, she was going to miss her baby. She was going to miss Theo and the life they could have had. They'd come so close.

"I love you." She looked at him with tears in her eyes. She wasn't going down without a fight, even if it meant fighting him.

He moved in closer and she got ready. She would lean back, using Hutch's body to help her kick up and get that knife out of

Theo's hand. It played out in her head. Kick up, catch the knife while twisting her hands out of Hutch's hold and ducking her head. With any luck Hutch and the other soldier would catch each other in the cross fire and then all she would have to worry about was Theo. Well, and every other crazed memory-erased soldier they would encounter.

It didn't matter. She had to take the shot.

"I love you, Theo." She was ready.

He moved in and the sweetest smile came over his face. "I know who you are. You're the love of my life. You're my wife and my sweet sub and the mother of my son. I'll never forget you, Erin Argent-Taggart."

She felt Hutch let go of her hands and then a roar damn near made her deaf as he shot out.

She watched as the soldier who'd been training the gun on her fell to the floor.

"What?" She was so confused, but Hutch was moving.

He stepped up to the camera and flipped it off. "Yeah, this is my letter of resignation, you crazy fucking bitch."

He pointed his gun at the camera and popped a round in, killing it.

Theo got into her space, his arms going around her. "Hi, baby. You have no idea how good it is to see you."

She stood there in shock as he kissed her. "I don't understand."

Hutch took the gun off his fallen comrade. "He'll live, but I don't know how we're going to keep the rest of them alive. I know you're all about saving the innocent, but the innocent are going to be trying to murder us."

Theo stood there, grinning at her like a loon. "If Ian said he's going to be here, he'll be here and he'll have a plan. Don't worry about it. It's going to be fine. You look gorgeous, by the way. Damn, baby, are you cold or happy to see me?"

She glanced down and sure enough her nipples were hard as rocks. "How can you be thinking about that? You walked in here with a knife ready to kill me."

He put his hands on her hips, having sheathed the knife at his side. "Never, baby. I might have violated you, but only in a good way."

Hutch frowned, glancing down at his watch. "He's not here. I thought for sure he would be here. We're so fucked."

Theo didn't take his eyes off her. "Chill, buddy. Big brother always comes through."

Erin held out a hand because if she didn't, Theo was going to shove his tongue down her throat, and while she was thrilled to not be gutted, she had some questions. "Hutch isn't bad?"

Hutch turned, his jaw dropping. "Seriously? You bought that? I must be a way better actor than I thought I was."

Theo was still smiling at her. "Apparently this was Ian's plan all along. He sent Hutch in. Hutch is totally the reason I'm not a drooling idiot right now. He switched the syringes. Instead of the drug, I got a mild sedative and a nice dose of B12. I'm feeling very energetic."

The lights blinked off and Hutch breathed an audible sigh of relief. "Thank god. That's Ian. Give it a minute because he's taking over the system. I built in a back door that will allow him to lock down the cells and open the doors to let us get out."

They weren't going to die? She threw her arms around Theo, the darkness enclosing them. They weren't going to die. "I was so scared."

His arms encircled her. "I know, baby. It's going to be okay. We're getting out of here."

The lights came back on and the intercom system flared to life.

"Hello, shoppers, this store is undergoing a change in management," a thoroughly sarcastic voice said. "All crazy-as-fuck doctors are currently on sale because their lives have recently lost all value. Please shoot on sight. And Theo, get your girl and ass out of here. Now."

Ian Taggart. Son of a bitch. The cavalry was here.

The lights blinked back on and Theo leaned over to kiss her. "Told you, baby. It's time to get out of here and get home. Our boy needs us."

Hutch walked toward her, holding out the downed soldier's gun. "Try not to kill them. They're not responsible for what they're doing. You have no idea what these men have gone through."

She turned to Hutch, whose whole body was tense. She reached out her free hand and touched his cheek. "I never should have doubted you."

"It was my job to make you." He smiled faintly. "Please tell Big Tag I did my job. We agreed to this that first night we got home. I left that night to put this plan into place. I've been maneuvering her so we can take down the entire Collective. What I didn't count on was her bringing you in tonight. I tried to stop it but I couldn't."

She hugged him. "I'm so proud of you. Please come home with us. I'm going to make you the biggest batch of cookies you've ever seen."

Hutch froze and then his eyes went watery, face going red. "I want to go home, Erin. I want it so fucking bad. Please take me home. How big is TJ now? I missed all the kids, but especially him."

How much had it cost Hutch to do this job? He'd been loyal to his family and his family was going to welcome him home with open arms. And a regular therapy appointment with Kai. She looked up at him, willing him to feel her love. How far had she come that once she'd been so alone and now she opened her heart to all her family? Family wasn't blood. It was made up of the people who loved her, who she loved. The family she chose was better than anything she'd ever found. The family she'd chosen was her true home and she got to bring all her boys back.

"He misses his Uncle Hutch." She went on her toes and kissed his cheek. "He loves you, Hutch. Like Theo and I love you. Let's go home."

Theo reached for her hand. "You stay close to me and we'll follow Hutch. He knows the place."

Hutch nodded, starting for the door. "We've only been here for a couple of weeks, but I know how to get out. Ian should have shut down cell access so we won't have to worry about anyone stuck in the soldier wing, but McDonald always has a guard with her. She also recently hired a bunch of security. They're being paid by The Collective to keep this place safe so they're totally evil and fair game. We have to be careful of them."

"And Case and Ian are somewhere out there," Theo said.

So she would be super careful. She checked the clip and made sure the safety was off. If she had a shot, she would take out McDonald.

The door opened and Hutch took the lead, storming out into the hallway.

Theo took her hand, leaving his firing hand free for the gun he'd produced after he'd tossed away the knife. Erin followed him, letting him take the lead because he needed it. He always would with her and she got that now. They would never be able to work together. Not ever, but then it might be time for one of them to retire from the field since they had a baby to take care of.

They could flip for it.

"What's Ian's plan?" She kept her voice low as they moved through what looked like an industrial compound.

"He put me in so I could infiltrate The Collective," Hutch explained. "We decided to keep it quiet in case they had anyone on the inside. I've been manipulating McDonald toward making a deal with the company I thought had the worst security. When I finally broke into their private network, Ian and Case came over. They got into the building of one of the main companies here in France, and that's where they found the mother lode."

The significance of what Ian had been doing hit her. "He's not after McDonald. He's after the whole Collective."

"Oh, he wants McDonald, too," Theo assured her. "But he knows after everything we've been through the only way to ensure our safety and to keep that drug out of the hands of people who would misuse it is to take the whole damn group down."

"Is that why Ten and Ezra had no idea what he was doing?" Erin asked.

"Plausible deniability." Hutch moved down the hallway cautiously, his voice low. "Ten might not be working full time anymore, but his ties to the Agency are deep. If they suspected either Ten or Ezra had something to do with destroying the drug and all the research around it, there could be consequences. Ezra's already put his neck on the line for this group more than once. Big Tag didn't want to put him in that position again."

"So it's the three of us, and Case is somewhere in the building?" Erin needed to get their resources in order. "Do we know how many men she kept here?"

They were coming up on a set of double doors.

"Well, Erin, she kept five men here," a new voice said. It seemed to come from all around her. "Yes, in addition to my other amazing skills, I can also read lips. Hello, Hutch, it's good to see your new evil persona was nothing but an act. You're looking good there, buddy. Your enforced no-sugar diet helped you to drop that baby fat."

Adam Miles was in the house.

Hutch flipped off the nearest security camera. "Yeah, Ian brought Adam in at the last minute. And he can't read lips. The whole place is wired for sound. She loves watching everything we do. And fuck the no-carb diet. Big Tag promised me he would install a cotton candy machine if I took this assignment. Why the hell else would I be here? Where's Ian?"

"He's coming up on your six and he's not alone, kiddos," Adam explained.

The sound of gunfire rolled in, the narrow halls making it sound like thunder.

Shit. She'd known it wouldn't be this easy.

Hutch was moving toward the double doors.

"I wouldn't do that if I were you," Adam said. "She's got a security team coming from that direction. You're about to get caught."

Erin looked around the hall. There were two doors, but one looked far sturdier than the other. It was labeled as *staff only*, but hey, she was a girl who believed in breaking a few rules. And she totally was counting on Big Tag being the well-prepared soldier he was. "Adam, can you get me in this door?"

Theo had already opened the door on the other side of the hall.

There was a hard bang against the glass double doors. The security team was here. Luckily they had a gatekeeper. The doors remained closed, though she could see the guard attempting to access it with a card.

"Give me a second, Erin," Adam was saying. "I'm going to keep the double doors on lockdown, but that door's tricky. Ian's about thirty seconds out and then you're going to be trapped. I don't know what his plan is."

"Come on, baby." Theo stood by the open door. It looked like it led into a supply closet. The door was flimsy as hell and wouldn't do for what she needed.

"They'll come through that thing in about two seconds," she

insisted. "Adam, get this fucking door open and tell Ian I'm holding it for him. Tell him it should provide enough cover for him to pull the pin on his favorite toy."

Theo's eyes went wide.

Hutch looked back as the soldiers trying to get to them began firing at the glass, attempting to break through. "Whatever we're doing, make it fast."

"Bingo." Adam's voice could barely be heard over the intercom.

The door lit green and opened. Theo rushed across the hall as Ian came into sight. His massive body turned as he fired behind him, but Erin could already see that he had his free hand reaching for the grenade he kept in his utility belt.

"Fuck," Theo cursed. "This door better hold. Get in."

"I don't have cameras in that room," Adam was saying as chaos was unleashed in the hall.

The glass finally cracked. They were almost through. The men following Ian were firing, the sound blasting her ears.

She felt a bullet whiz by and then Theo was forcing her into the room. Hutch held the door open as Theo covered her body with his. She could barely see what happened. Ian's body twisted as he pulled the pin on the grenade and tossed it out. He leapt into the room and Hutch slammed the door, putting his back to it.

There was a terrible blast, the room around them shaking, and for a moment she worried she'd chosen poorly. Hutch cursed but held his ground.

They were all silent for a moment and then Ian sat up, smiling. "Fuck, yeah, it's a good day to be alive. Hutch, I not only ordered that cotton candy machine, but we're going to bring in a stripper to serve it to you. Fun Fridays is what I'm going to call it."

"I think I need some damn aloe vera." Hutch stood up. "That door got hot. I don't think I blistered, but I felt that blast. What the hell is this place?"

Theo sat up. "It's where she does the therapy."

Erin got up, reaching for his hand. What Theo called therapy was actually torture. This room—one like it—had been where McDonald had fed him drugs and utilized techniques that had made it difficult for him to even think about his past. The room went dark suddenly.

"Damn it. Well, that was probably the result of tossing a grenade into the hall," Ian said, only a little guilt in his voice. "And the comms seem to be out, too. Is that door open?"

A lone light blinked into stark existence. Ian moved the flashlight to the handle of the door. Hutch tried to turn it but it held fast.

"We're stuck until Adam gets that door open again. Unless there's another way out." Hutch looked back at Theo.

"It's hard to remember." Theo moved around the room, sliding his hands over the walls. "I know what she used to say about always having a way out. She never took us anywhere there weren't tunnels or a secondary route out. She liked secret passages."

Ian didn't sound concerned. "I think it's safe to say we took out the security dudes. I feel no regret. They're Collective stooges and likely knew exactly what was going on here. We managed to trap the lost boys in a room, so hopefully they stay put. By now, Adam's talked to Case and he and Mike are on their way."

"How did you keep this from everyone?" As long as they were stuck here, she had a few questions. "Or was it just the two of us?"

"Nah," Big Tag replied, following Theo with his flashlight. He kept it level with his chest so Theo could see but it wouldn't blind him. Theo kept up his slow examination of the walls. "I couldn't let the whole team know in case the Agency came a calling. Mike and Adam didn't know a damn thing when I asked them to get on a plane and meet me. They didn't even know where they were going until they were in the air."

"How are you taking down The Collective if you're not handing over the information to the Agency? Are you going with the feds instead?" Erin had her worries about that. "You know if they think releasing it will hurt the economy, they might choose to bury it. Some of the companies involved have powerful lobbies."

"I'm not giving it to the feds," Ian replied. "I'm doing something way worse."

There was only one thing she could thing of that was worse. "Shit, you're going right to the media."

"We're giving it to Mia," Hutch continued. "And I'm releasing it to some of my hacker friends to make sure it gets as much coverage as possible. There won't be anywhere to hide and the government won't be able to cover it up."

Theo stopped, running his hand over the seemingly smooth wood again. "I think it's here. Hold on."

He pushed against the wall and it gave way. He disappeared into the tunnel.

"Hey, don't go without us," Erin called out.

"He's not going anywhere with you at all," a wholly unwelcome voice said.

The lights blinked back on just as Theo walked out of the tunnel, Hope McDonald behind him. She had a gun pressed to the back of his head.

Erin leveled the semiautomatic Hutch had given her, but she couldn't get a decent shot. Theo's bigger body was covering her, only the top of her head visible. "You've got nowhere to go, McDonald."

Hutch and Big Tag had her in their imperfect sights, too. They were in an even worse position than she was, and now they didn't have the added benefit of that flashlight to blind her with. Damn Adam's quick skills.

"You're wrong," McDonald replied. "I've always got an escape route and I'm taking Theo with me."

Erin felt her heart flutter. She knew how awful it had been for Theo. He'd been more than willing to do anything so he wouldn't come under her power again. If he moved the wrong way, that gun could go off. It could blow off half his skull. He could be so reckless, so careless with his own life. "Theo, I'm going to ask you to stay calm."

He looked over to her, his eyes finding her. "Not a problem, baby. I know you're going to handle this. You're going to wait and be patient and you'll come for me. I'm not doing anything but waiting on you. Do you understand me?"

Despite the horror of the situation, a peace descended on her. He wasn't struggling, wasn't panicking. He was quietly waiting for her to get him out of the situation. Earlier, he'd covered her body with his own, not knowing how the explosion would play out. Now he was ready to do whatever it took to come back to her.

He loved her. She had to remind herself sometimes, but every time she did it hit her like a bolt of lightning. He loved her. She had no idea why the universe had sent her this glorious, amazing man, but there was no fucking way that bitch got away with her prize.

McDonald had claimed this was between them. Well, she was about to find out who the winner was going to be.

"I'm going to back up and close off this tunnel. I've got men waiting at the end so don't think Theo's getting away. If I hear you open the door behind me, I'll shoot him and leave you the body," McDonald explained.

"Yeah, you're totally in love with him." Calm had settled over Erin. She was in the best position. McDonald seemed far more worried about Ian than her or Hutch. She edged a foot to her left, quietly trying to improve her line of sight.

McDonald sniffled. "I do love him. I love him so much I won't let him go back to you. He's miserable and confused around you. I won't sentence him to that kind of life."

"I'm fine, doc. I've got a real nice view." He smiled Erin's way. "Are you cold again, baby? You know I love it when you don't wear a bra."

She didn't really have to but it was nice to know he had something to focus on. "You know what danger does to me. You're probably going to have a good time tonight."

"You know it," he replied. "After we put the baby to bed. I don't care where we are, we're going back to London tonight. We're getting our boy."

McDonald moved back, but Theo stayed still.

That tiny distance opened a pinhole between them. If she was off, she would kill her soul mate. If he moved in the slightest, he would take the bullet instead of McDonald.

Erin didn't hesitate. Her whole life had been one long prep for this moment. If her father hadn't been such a bastard, she might not have spent long hours trying to please him. She might have found another interest besides the gun range. She might never have gone into the Army, might never have found her way to McKay-Taggart and to Theo. If one thing had slipped, she wouldn't be here for this moment. She'd worried she wasn't the right woman for him, but she took her shot and proved she was the *only* woman for him.

Faith. She had to have a little faith in herself. In him.

A neat hole split Hope McDonald's forehead and her eyes went blank.

Theo took a deep breath as she fell behind him.

"Holy shit," Hutch said. "What the fuck was that?"

Theo crossed the space between them and had her in his arms before she could take her next breath. He held her tight. "That was how a warrior princess saves her man. Hello, beautiful. That was a hell of a shot."

She let the gun drop to the desk beside her and wrapped him up in her arms. He was warm and safe and alive. It was more than she could have asked for. He was here. "I love you."

"I love you, baby." He held her close.

"That was a freaking shame," Big Tag complained as he stood over the body. "You couldn't have clipped her, Argent? I was planning on getting my torture on. In a nasty way, not a happy, fun way."

It had been too easy, but nothing would have stopped her from saving Theo. "She died knowing who won. I'll take it."

The door came open and Case and Michael Malone rushed in.

"You're too late, boys," Big Tag said with a sigh.

Case nodded. "Yeah, that's obvious. There's like twelve dead guys out here. I thought we were trying to keep the body count down."

Big Tag shrugged. "I said I'd try. And hey, I think we managed to not kill the lost boys, so I'm calling it a win."

Hutch looked at Big Tag, his cool finally vanishing. "Can I come home now, Ian?"

Ian stood in front of Hutch, putting his hand on the back of his head like she'd seen him do with his brothers whenever he wanted to get a point across. "We're all going home, brother. It's time to come home and let your family take care of you. You have no idea how proud I am of you."

He hugged Hutch, doing that manly back-pounding thing.

"He's getting hormonal in his old age," Theo whispered.

"It's manopause," Case agreed.

Ian stepped back. "I can still shoot the two of you. Are we clear?"

Michael nodded. "We are. Case and I have made sure we

cleaned every drive in the building and we destroyed the drug. We can call in Ten and Ezra and get these boys back to the States. Try to figure out where they belong."

It would be a long road for those men, but McKay-Taggart would do everything they could to help them.

Theo took her hand. "You ready?"

She was ready for anything as long as he was by her side.

EPILOGUE

Loa Mali
Six months later

Theo let his head drop back, the sun warming his face.

"Daddy! Daddy, play!"

He couldn't help but smile as he opened his eyes and his world was filled with grubby kiddos. He sank down to the sand beside his son. "Hey, buddy. You ready to build some sandcastles? How about the rest of you?"

Kenzie jumped up and down, the ruffles on the back of her bathing suit bouncing. Kala stared up at her sister like she didn't quite understand the exuberance. Aidan and Tristan were busy trying to get Carys's attention. The younger kids were all inside the main house, taking naps.

Faith and Ten were up there, too, looking after the babies, preparing for their own. He thought Faith found some solace in rocking the babies. Though she didn't talk about it, he was sure her sister's death had made her emotional. It didn't matter that she'd been evil. They'd shared a good portion of their lives and Faith would miss the good times she'd had. Still, she seemed to find comfort and joy in the child growing inside her.

Kenzie went straight for the pink buckets, but she seemed more interested in throwing the sand around than anything else.

Kala had picked up a small plastic shovel, considering it carefully, as though trying to decide what kind of damage she could do with it.

Yep, that was Ian Taggart's daughter. Kala was as serious as her sister was fluffy. Theo was eager to see what their new baby brother would be like. Seth Taggart was eight weeks old and already looked like his father.

TJ came over and plopped down on Theo's lap as the other kids began digging and filling buckets with sand.

He could hear Li and Avery splashing around a few yards away. God only knew what they were doing under the cover of the waves, but it had put a smile on Avery's face. Ian and Charlotte were lying under an umbrella, sipping drinks with Simon and Chelsea.

Tomorrow he and his brothers would get on a boat and take the boys out for their first fishing expedition. The king of Loa Mali, who was happily hosting the party, had promised them great fishing off the coast.

Of course, Theo would be the guest of honor. After all, he had hauled all these people on his honeymoon.

Three days before, he'd watched as the most beautiful woman in the world had walked up this beach in a white wedding dress, escorted down the aisle by Liam O'Donnell. He'd stood there with his brothers and his best man. TJ had been adorable as he'd watched his mom and dad get married.

It was one memory he would never have to fight for.

Jesse Murdoch strode up. "Hey, Theo, Robert's heading out. I thought you might want to say good-bye. Besides, I totally want to build sandcastles with these monsters."

Theo got up, shifting TJ off his lap. He kissed his son's head. "I'll be right back, buddy. You guys don't go too hard on Uncle Jesse. He's a delicate flower."

He took off toward the main house before Jesse could get him for that bit of snark.

Robert stood on the massive porch that overlooked the water. He stared out over the Arabian Sea, his focus clearly not on his immediate surroundings.

Robert still remembered only flashes of his past. He'd described them to Theo as murky and dream-like. None of them had led him to information about himself. Was he staring out and wondering if there was anyone in the world who missed him? Who longed for him?

Theo hoped not because it was obvious Robert had a thing for the London team's therapist. He lit up when Ariel Adisa walked into a room.

"Hey," he said quietly.

Robert turned and smiled. "Hey. I can't tell you how much fun I've had, but I've got to get back to London."

"I thought you were coming back to the States with us?"

"Change of plans," he said. "I'm going to work with the boys in London. Ezra's worried the Agency is getting a little too interested in them. They show no signs of memory. Not even Owen. The doc was right. She found a way to do it with one dose."

And wouldn't the Agency love to figure that out. Since the files had been destroyed, the six men who'd been in the building that day were all that was left of McDonald's research. Taking them into custody might be a good way to study them. "You should follow Ezra's lead. He's a good man."

Ezra and Ten had helped them bring down The Collective. When the story had broken, they'd been the one who put pressure on their bosses and people they knew inside the government to take it seriously.

The trials would begin soon, but Theo had no doubt justice would be served. The group itself had already fragmented and started making deals. They would no longer be effective as an entity.

The Collective was done.

"We're setting up at The Garden," Robert explained. "It's going to be our base for now. Ariel thinks she might be able to reach them with some pointed therapy and hypnosis. We'll work some jobs for McKay-Taggart and other agencies to earn our keep. If the heat gets too much, we'll reconsider."

He put a hand out. "Anything you need, brother."

Robert shook it before he looked behind Theo, his brows rising and lips curling in a smile. "I think I need something like that. Hello, Mrs. Taggart."

He let go of Robert's hand and turned. Damn but that was a beautiful sight. The latest Mrs. Taggart walked toward him, her hair spilling around her shoulders and that gorgeous body in an emerald green bikini. He didn't mind Robert's appreciation. She was all his. Everyone else could look. Hell, she was a damn work of art, but she belonged to him.

She gave him that smile that lit up his world. "Where's TJ?"

Theo glanced down to the beach. The kids seemed to have given up on building sandcastles in favor of crawling all over their Uncle Jesse. "They're busy burying Jesse in the sand. We'll have to dig him out later. I think some of the London contingent is leaving."

A brow arched over Erin's left eye as she looked at Robert. "Ariel told me she was heading out today. She thought she was going alone."

Robert managed to go only the slightest shade of pink. "It's a long flight. She shouldn't be alone. Besides, I do need to get back to the guys. They're adjusting to the real world. It can be hard."

Didn't he know it. Luckily, he'd had a goddess to show him the way. "I'm going to miss having you around, but I wish you all the best."

"We'll miss you," Erin corrected. "And please let us know if you need anything. Tell Nick hello for me. I wish he could have come."

"I think a wedding was hard for him to attend," Robert explained, picking up his bag. "Someone had to stay behind and watch over the boys. Nick pretty much insisted it be him. I also worry he's feeling guilty about what happened to Owen. He thinks he should have seen it."

"He couldn't possibly have known," Erin replied.

She'd done something shocking a few days after they'd gotten back to London. He'd worried she might seek some revenge against the Scot, but he'd found her in Owen's room, feeding him soup when he was too weak to feed himself. His body had a particularly bad reaction to the drug. It had taken his strength and his memory. He was only now starting to walk and move with purpose again.

"You're far more forgiving than I expected you to be," Robert said, taking her hand in his. "I thank you for not making this harder."

Erin shook her head. "No, I wouldn't do that. Owen did something terrible, but I understand why he did it. And he's paid a terrible price. I don't hate him. That surprises me, too, but I have to say it's so freeing to forgive him. I hope he recovers, though I don't know if I hope he remembers. It might be too painful."

Because he'd lost the very things he'd sold his soul to protect. That whole group had a hard journey ahead, but they had a great leader. They had Robert, and he wouldn't give up on any of them.

After all, Robert hadn't given up on him.

Robert waved as Ariel appeared. He rushed to grab her suitcase and they walked off toward the front of the house where the car would pick them up.

Erin slipped her hand into his. "So, Mr. Taggart, I think we should go and check out the hot tub. It looks like Adam and Jake are helping Jesse with the kids. Everyone else is out on the beach. We'd have it all to ourselves."

She winked his way and started toward the decadent frothing tub.

Theo followed because he was a man who knew never to turn down a good offer. "I think we can find something to do, Mrs. Taggart."

She laughed as he started to chase her.

He would never stop. She was worth the work.

* * * *

London, England
The Garden

Nick sat down in front of his laptop, calling up the files on the men McDonald had experimented on. The men she'd ruined. He glanced at the coffee mug Teresa had left for him when she'd brought in the morning mail. The sub was one of the few in The Garden he hadn't fucked. Not because she wasn't pretty enough. He actually had different ideas of pretty than most men. He liked a woman with personality. Her smile was more important than her breasts, and damn a woman who could hold her own intellectually did something for him.

Teresa was lovely, but he tried not to screw anyone he had to work with.

Not anymore.

The coffee smelled rich and inviting, and he was still thinking about the vodka bottle at the bottom of his desk.

Damn it. He was drinking far too much lately. He thought Damon was starting to notice. His boss had told him they would have a talk when the team got back from Loa Mali.

Was he going to lose his job? Owen had been his closest friend on the team. He hadn't seen what he was going through and it had almost cost Theo and Erin Taggart their lives. It wouldn't surprise him if Damon had thought about it and decided to cut him loose.

He would take it. He deserved it.

He fucking deserved all of it.

Like he'd deserved to lose Des.

The words flowed in front of him, everything they'd been able to record on the man they'd codenamed Tucker. Nick was supposed to be compiling all the data for Ariel, but he couldn't quite concentrate.

That bottle was calling him.

Maybe if he drank it, he could forget he'd lost her, forget he'd chosen her over the girl he'd been too afraid to really love. Forget he was the shit who'd watched her die and couldn't get another woman out of his head.

He said it was all about Des and it was, damn it. Des had been the siren calling him away from everything else.

Calling him away from the woman he'd nearly walked away from everything for.

Yes, all he had to do was take that first drink and not stop. When Damon returned he could turn in his access cards and go back to Russia where he could become what everyone always thought he would be. A feckless drunk with a meaningless life. A thug who worked for mobsters because no one else would have him.

That was what he deserved.

He started to open the drawer to his desk when there was a knock.

"Mr. Markovic?" Owen opened the door. He was a shadow of his former self. He'd lost a ton of weight, but sometimes when he smiled, Nick could see a hint of his old friend. "I'm sorry to bother you. I'm helping Teresa manage the front office."

He was nosing around Teresa was what he was doing. Despite the fact that the man had been wretchedly sick, he perked up around the sub.

He didn't remember that he'd already screwed the poor girl over and she'd likely never give him the time of day.

What would it be like to forget all his sins?

"It's all right. What do you need?" Ariel had told him it would be good for the men to have something to do. He'd arranged for them to handle some small jobs around The Garden. He'd also begun training for their Master rights. Well, he'd begun Master training for the ones who identified as Dominants, and sub training for the one who had admitted he needed to submit.

So far things had been quiet. Too quiet.

"There's someone here to see you."

That had Nick sitting up. No one knew where he worked. Unless it was someone Damon sent. He relaxed a bit. "Is Ezra back from wherever he's been?"

Owen shook his head. "No. It's a woman. Pretty thing, too. Says she knows you. Quite insistent."

"Yes, I am. Could you please move? I'm not leaving until I see him."

Nick froze at the sound of that husky American accent. It couldn't be. He hadn't seen her since the day of Desiree's funeral, and even then it had been from a distance because the family wouldn't let him in. He'd watched her, remembering the way she looked when she'd clung to him, wrapping her body around him while he drove into her.

And he'd remembered the way she looked when he'd told her he still wasn't leaving her cousin.

Hayley Dalton pushed past Owen, barging into his office. She looked every bit as delicious and curvy as she had that night they'd spent together five years before when she'd found him after a nasty fight with Des. She'd offered him comfort and he'd taken her up on it.

He hadn't taken her up on her proposal of marriage the next morning.

She'd been the funny, sweet, smart girl he'd enjoyed talking to when he was forced to spend time with Des's horrible family. He'd liked her and he would never, ever tell her how close he came to walking away with her.

Especially not when she despised him. Not when she blamed him for her cousin's death.

"You owe me, Nick. You owe me and I've come to collect."

He forgot about the vodka. It looked like his trouble was just beginning.

Nick and the entire McKay-Taggart group will return in *For His Eyes Only*, coming in February 2017.

AUTHOR'S NOTE

I'm often asked by generous readers how they can help get the word out about a book they enjoyed. There are so many ways to help an author you like. Leave a review. If your e-reader allows you to lend a book to a friend, please share it. Go to Goodreads and connect with others. Recommend the books you love because stories are meant to be shared. Thank you so much for reading this book and for supporting all the authors you love!

Sign up for Lexi Blake's newsletter
and be entered to win a $25 gift certificate
to the bookseller of your choice.

Join us for news, fun, and exclusive content
including free short stories.

There's a new contest every month!

Go to www.LexiBlake.net to subscribe.

MASTER BITS AND MERCENARY BITES
The Secret Recipes of Topped
By Lexi Blake and Suzanne M. Johnson
Coming November 1, 2016

Top restaurant has become the hot spot in Dallas for elevated comfort food—and a side of spicy romance. Run by executive chef Sean Taggart, Top is the premiere fictional destination for gourmet food. Join creator, *New York Times* bestselling author Lexi Blake, and Southern food expert Suzanne Johnson as they guide you through the world of Masters and Mercenaries via the secret recipes behind the food served in Top.

But what would a gourmet meal be without some company? Spend an evening with your favorite characters from McKay-Taggart as they celebrate the special moments that make up their happily ever afters. Learn how to make Sean's specialty dishes and Macon's desserts while exploring the private lives of the characters who make up the world. From Charlie and Ian's next demon spawn to a change in path for Simon and Chelsea, these are the times that bind us together, the moments that make us a family.

Good meals, good times, good friends.

Bon appétit!

PERFECTLY PAIRED

Masters and Mercenaries: Topped, Book 3
By Lexi Blake
Coming November 29, 2016

A table for two

Waitress Tiffany Hayes knows what she wants and she wants
Sebastian. Top's grumpy sommelier calls to her in a way no man has
before. She simply needs to show him that they belong together.
Finding an opportunity to spend some quality time with him turns
out to be the easy part. Convincing Sebastian to look beyond his
damaged heart and soul is far more difficult.

A thirst he can't deny

After losing everything he held dear, Sebastian Lowe has finally
rebuilt his life and the walls around his heart. Tiffany is a sweet
temptation he struggles to resist. She's bright and complex, but he's
sure she can't handle his dark desires. When they're thrown together
on an assignment, he can't help himself.

A perfect pairing

As passion builds, the new lovers are both forced to face their
pasts. To have a future, they must find a way to heal the wounds
they thought would haunt them forever.

* * * *

"I thought you just liked European wines."

Everyone thought he was a snob. "Not at all. I appreciate many
different types of wine and the places the grapes are grown. I love an
Argentine Malbec and a French Bordeaux. One of my favorite wines
to drink is a shitass strawberry wine sold in boxes in convenience
stores around Southern Georgia. It costs seven dollars a box, and
that's a big box."

"Seriously? I would not have taken you for a lover of cheap

hooch. I've never even seen you drink a beer."

"I wasn't surrounded by beer in my youth. My father loved wine. He sampled it and appreciated it, and when I was a teenager and couldn't get my hands on anything good, my best friend and I found a man who would buy us strawberry wine as long as we paid for a pack of cigarettes. We would take it out to the beach and we were the heroes of the high school. When I drink that wine, I am young again. I am sitting on the beach looking out over the Gulf with my feet in the sand and a whole life ahead of me."

"I would like to try that wine sometime," she said wistfully.

He couldn't help but wince. "It tastes like hell, but it's important to me. My point is that wine isn't something to be snobbish about. It's something to love. It's something that brings people together and it's been doing it for thousands of years. What I love about Riesling is it's a transparent wine."

She held the glass up again. "Not entirely."

She'd likely slept through his entire wine for beginners course he'd given for all the servers. She'd probably memorized the pairings list he'd given her and picked up no theory at all. "I wasn't talking about how it looks. I'm talking about the grapes and how Riesling grapes tend to embody the region they were grown in. It's why Rieslings vary pretty wildly. An Alsace Riesling is higher in alcohol. It's got more mineral notes and it's full bodied while German Rieslings can be quite sweet and fruity. There's a vineyard in Australia that produces Rieslings that zip with lime and citrus tones. Every Riesling is different and the wine's taste comes from the earth it was grown in, from the air it breathed and the rainfall that nourished the vines. It's a little like people. It's all about where it came from. That is why I love Riesling."

"Okay." Tiffany held the glass up to the light. "I like the color. It's a pretty yellow when sunlight filters in and turns a room bright. I don't think my sense of smell is anywhere near as good as yours though. I mostly smell wine."

"It's all right," he replied. "I just wanted you to think about it before you drank it."

"Because it's meaningful to you." She took a slow swallow this time as though truly considering the taste. "It isn't as sweet as some of the Rieslings I've tried. I like it."

"Good." He took a sip himself, letting the notes flow. Broad. Dry. Citrus and green apple. "It's quite a nice wine for the price. It's why I put it on the menu. It's going to pair with the pork dishes and some of the fish."

"I will make note of that." She sat back.

Damn but she was a beautiful woman. She was also something he needed to keep his hands off of. No matter what Big Tag said, he did not date women he worked with.

He didn't really date anyone anymore. He played with subs. When the need got too great, he found a partner for a brief time. He didn't sleep with anyone. He fucked and that was starting to get very old. Empty.

No one had seen him naked for years with the exception of doctors and nurses. He hadn't been skin to skin with a woman since before he'd lost his legs.

"So you said something about house rules?" Tiffany leaned forward, her elbows on the bar. "Are these housekeeping rules or like big bad Dom rules?"

"I don't suppose I differentiate." He couldn't let those big eyes of hers soften him up. It had almost happened back at her apartment. When she'd stood back up after he'd spanked her and there had been tears running down her face, his impulse had been to reach for her. He'd wanted to draw her in the way he had that night when she was drunk and she'd cried on his shoulder. He'd wanted to smooth back her hair and promise her everything was going to be all right, that he could fix things for her. It was a path that was sure to lead to discomfort for her and humiliation for him. "I prefer a clean living space. I don't like for things to be messy. I expect that you will keep your things in their proper place."

Because no matter how hard he tried, he could still trip. The legs he now walked on were only a year old. He'd spent the first two in a wheelchair.

The Garden's Wheelchair Dom.

He still wasn't completely comfortable in the prosthetics.

"I can try," she said with a frown. "I'll be honest, I'm not the world's biggest neat freak."

He'd been able to tell that from the state of her apartment. It had been cluttered, a bit dusty. With the exception of her easel. That had been perfectly taken care of. He rather wished he'd taken the time to ask to see her art.

He'd seen one painting that night he'd taken her home. It had been a painting of three laughing girls, the swirling colors so vibrant he could hear them giggling as they splashed in a puddle on a rainy day. The figures had been more impressions than photographic reality, but he'd known what she was trying to convey.

"If you cook I'll clean and the other way around." He'd started a list in his head on the long drive. The drive that would have been considerably shorter had they left at the proper time. As she'd sung along to sugary pop songs after she'd changed his radio, he'd sat and considered how to proceed.

With caution. Lots and lots of caution.

"I'm not the best cook in the world," he continued, "but I can manage. Most nights, of course, we'll be eating at Top as our training sessions for the new restaurant will last long hours, but I would prefer to eat breakfast here rather than skipping the meal or picking up fast food. Eric made sure the fridge was stocked with a few items I requested."

"Breakfast." She gave him a little salute with her free hand. "I can manage that."

"In addition to our duties at Top, we will now be taking on the additional task of appearing to be a long-term D/s couple and we need to talk about what that should look like." Another thing he'd been thinking about ever since that moment the trap had closed around him. "You know you probably could have gotten us out of this assignment. It's much more difficult for the Dom to say no. The sub always holds the power. Is there a reason you didn't use yours today?"

"I didn't want to," she replied simply. "I don't have a full-time Dom and I thought it would be interesting to see what that's like."

"You know nothing about how I function as a dominant partner."

"And now I do. You like rules and schedules and you tend to be very fair."

"I can be quite exacting in my standards."

"I can be quite flexible," she shot back as the sexiest smile crossed her face. "I'm serious about that. I can still do the splits and everything."

"You're far too reckless, Tiffany."

"You're far too uptight, Sebastian."

"Well, I've found being reckless and following an emotional path tends to lead a man into trouble."

"Sometimes trouble can be fun."

"And sometimes it can lead to tragedy."

She sobered a bit, leaning toward him. Her voice softened. "Yes, but anything can lead to tragedy, Sebastian. You can do absolutely nothing wrong, make all the right moves, and still have things end in tragedy. But real happiness and joy, those don't tend to come along without some risk. Those things are worth it."

BOUND TO SUBMIT
Blasphemy Book 1
By Laura Kaye

12 Masters.
Infinite Fantasies.
Welcome to Blasphemy…

He thinks he caused her pain, but she knows he's the only one who can heal her…

Kenna Sloane lost her career and her arm in the Marines, and now she feels like she's losing herself. Submission is the only thing that ever freed her from pain and made her feel secure, and Kenna needs to serve again. Bad. The only problem is the Dom she wants once refused her submission and broke her heart, but, scarred on the inside and out, she's not looking for love this time. She's not even sure she's capable.

Griffin Hudson is haunted by the mistakes that cost him the only woman he ever loved. Now she's back at his BDSM club, Blasphemy, and more beautiful than ever, and she's asking for his help with the pain he knows he caused. Even though he's scared to hurt her again, he can't refuse her, because he'd give anything to earn a second chance. And this time, he'll hold on forever.

* * * *

By the time Griffin was done tying the knots on Kenna's ankles, adrenaline was flooding through him, gathering force and picking up steam. The rigor, tightness, and demanding positions of Shibari alone could put a submissive into subspace, but it could also give the Rigger an adrenaline rush of his own. Both sides could experience a euphoric response. And he was definitely feeling that just then.

From the position on his knees, he peered up at Kenna's face and knew immediately—so was she. Her eyelids appeared heavy and her muscles relaxed, almost like she was in a trance-like state. She was swaying just the littlest bit, which meant she was starting to lose touch with the physical reality around her.

All of which was fucking perfect.

He rose and grasped her cheeks. And then he kissed her. Because he couldn't *not* kiss her. He needed to taste her beauty and her submission right from her lips. And the moan she unleashed, like his kiss had plugged her back into her body, was so desperate that his cock jerked. "Tell me how bad you want it," he rasped.

"God, please," she said.

"Tell me how bad you need it," he said, forehead pressed to hers.

Her gray eyes pleaded. "My pussy is aching so bad, Master."

Fuck, there was that name again. "Tell me you want *me* to take care of you, to give you everything you need."

"Yes. God, yes, Sir. You. I want you."

Christ. He couldn't wait another second. Without warning, he scooped her into his arms and gently laid her on the mat. When she cried out in surprise, he chuckled. "This is only the beginning, little one."

He left her there, needing a moment to center himself. Because he was about to suspend her from the ceiling, and that meant he needed to make sure he was following every step and procedure. Using a switch on the wall, he lowered two chains attached to a spreader bar using a motorized pulley system in the ceiling until the bar reached the floor.

Even from where he stood ten feet away, he could see Kenna's chest rising and falling faster, so she was aware of what was about to happen.

Kneeling at her feet again, he used high-capacity carabiner clips to secure the spreader bar to the knots. And then he crawled up her body, exploring her along the way with his tongue. Against the insides of her knees. The insides of her thighs. Along the ropes between her legs that pushed her lips together.

He paused there, helpless to resist, and plunged his tongue between her folds, teasing her clit and tasting her slick arousal over and over. Kenna cried out and tried to arch, but the ropes were so intricate upon her body that they held her prisoner.

And, God, he fucking liked that. He liked it a lot.

But he also knew that lying on the knots he'd tied all across her back would quickly become uncomfortable, and that he didn't want. He crawled up further to place a soft kiss on her mouth. "Slow and steady, little one. Ready?"

"Yes, Sir," she whispered.

He stepped away from her and pulled a remote control from his back pocket, and then the low *whirr* of the motor sounded out and slowly lifted Kenna's legs into the air. And then her torso. And then her head and shoulders. Until she was hanging upside down by the spreader bar, her head maybe three feet off the ground.

Coming up behind her, he collected the length of her hair into his fist and then wrapped it in a hair band to keep it from falling in her face.

"Christ, you are a *vision*," he said, walking around her as she slowly spun. "I've got half a mind to photograph you like this. Are you okay?"

"Yes, Sir. Green. It's really intense...after so long," she said.

Which was why he was diving right in. "I know, Kenna," he said, unzipping his pants as he came to stand in front of her. "But I'll take care of you. If you start to have concerns, speak freely or hum three times if your mouth isn't free. Understood?"

"Yes, Sir."

"Good. Then suck my cock." He freed his erection, aligned perfectly with her face, and pushed his jeans down past his hips. With a moan, she opened her mouth and sucked him in. He had to grit his teeth to keep from shouting out, because being inside her after all this time was blowing his mind—and reducing his restraint. "That's it. Move your head. Suck me good."

She did. Damnit all to hell, but she did.

It was so good that he couldn't hold himself still. He grasped the ropes near her breasts to leverage their movements as his hips started to move. And then he was fucking her mouth, sinking deep, making demands of her that she was meeting like a champ.

"God, Kenna. Take me. Take all of me," he ground out as he buried himself in her throat and grasped the back of her head to stay there. "Hold it. That's it. Hold it, baby."

Finally, he pulled out, and she gasped for air, but she was also smiling and licking her lips. "More, please."

"Okay, I'll give you more. But don't you fucking come until I do. Got it?"

"Yes, Sir. Please, Sir."

He got up close and penetrated her mouth again, and she immediately swallowed him down, and then he embraced her body and planted his mouth between her legs. Licking, rubbing, sucking. She screamed around his thrusting cock as he plundered her pussy with his lips and tongue and teeth. Wrapping his arms around the backs of her thighs, he added his fingers to the sensual torture, holding her open with one hand and fingering her with the other. When his fingers were slick with her arousal, he moved to her rear opening and pressed in.

She unleashed another garbled scream.

"Don't you fucking come, Kenna. Not before you drink mine down. Do you hear me?" he growled, his finger sinking deep into her ass.

She moaned in response. It was all she could do.

All she could do except suck him for all she was worth. Which she did until he was squeezing his eyes shut and thinking about every unsexy thing he could just to hold back.

But, *fuck*, he'd never been good at resisting her ability to deep throat. And she kept impaling the back of her throat on the head of his cock and holding herself there.

He was a goner.

On a shout, he came. He came so hard that his grip on the rope might've been all that was keeping him on his feet.

"Swallow, baby. Take everything I give you," he rasped. When the most intense part of his orgasm ended, he withdrew from her mouth and said one word, "*Come.*"

He went at her ferociously again, sucking her clit into his mouth, strumming it with his tongue, and finger-fucking her tight hole. Kenna came almost instantly, gasping and then crying out, her muscles clenching around his thrusting finger. Her whole body seemed to spasm, making the suspension spin. Griffin wiped his face and tucked his semi-hard cock away. "Yes, Kenna. Yes. I'm gonna need more of that from you, little one."

And he knew just how to get more, too.

DANGEROUS PROTECTOR
Aegis Group Book 5
By Sidney Bristol

Retired Navy SEAL Marco Benally knows the cost of right and wrong, and he's willing to pay the price. After his family's home is stolen out from under them by a company covering up their illegal activities, Marco takes matters into his own hands. No cost is too great to reclaim the generational homestead. Even if that means someone else has to take the fall. Or that's what he tells himself until he meets her. The woman with the tight skirt, tall heels and darkness in her eyes. One night, one lie to get the evidence he needs and then it's over. Or at least that's what he tells himself.

Fiona Goero survives by following very careful rules. She's lived more of her life in Witness Protection than out of it. As one of the Internet's Most Wanted for helping the FBI put away a group of hackers, she is never safe. She's the traitor. The hacker who turned against her own. For one night she wants to indulge her every desire. To be held. To feel again. What should have been a passionate encounter becomes a snarled mess of lies and spies. Someone close to her is not only using her, they're trying to kill her. Her one-night-stand might be the only thing between her and being six foot under.

Marco is a man on a mission to set things right before Fiona discovers that not all of the danger can be laid at her enemies' feet. The greatest danger Fiona faces just might be from Marco—the man she's falling for.

Warning: Stubborn heroes fall the hardest.

* * * *

Marco Benally swirled the ice cubes in his glass, each clink ratcheting up the tension coiled between his shoulder blades.

She should have been here already.

His source had put his mark here every Friday at five, like clockwork.

So where the hell was she?

The downtown Denver bar was full of the young, trendy office crowd. They didn't need shit on them to smell. Most of the ones clustered around the bar worked for NueEnergy, a company that touted themselves as the second coming for green electric alternatives.

NueEnergy was about as green as what came out the back end of his Harley.

He turned, surveying the happy hour crowd in their designer suits and fashionable hoopla.

When sludge started coming up out of the ground a couple acres from his parent's place in Moab, they'd trusted the authorities to get to the bottom of it and fix things.

That was nearly four years ago.

The sludge was still there, and his family had been forced off the property they'd owned for generations.

Life had taught Marco one very important rule, something the SEALs had instilled in him: if he wanted a job done right, he had to do it himself.

It was time to take matters into his own hands.

Which brought him back to his—

There.

She paused in the entry, her gaze traveling over the bar, no doubt looking for any one of her co-workers.

He shouldn't stare, but fuck.

The pictures his partner had scrounged up hadn't done her justice.

Her gaze slid over his, then snapped back, their eyes locking. He took a slow sip of his drink, simply enjoying looking at her.

Fiona Goero.

At least that was what she wanted her co-workers to call her.

It'd taken Marco's guy quite a while to find the loose link in NueEnergy's armor, and it was just his luck it wore sky-high heels and a tight skirt.

She turned her head, breaking their momentary contact, and strode around the bar.

Fiona's real name was a mystery. Even Marco's contact hadn't been able to find anything on her dating farther back than fifteen years. It was as though she'd simply been breathed to life as a perfectly formed, twenty-year-old girl.

And man, oh man, was she a woman now.

Marco knew everything there was to know about Fiona. And that wasn't a lot. She didn't have so much as a parking ticket to mar her good name. She'd either remade herself into Fiona, or she was some sort of espionage plant. The ultimate Trojan horse.

Either way, she was his mark, his way into NueEnergy, and he had one shot of hooking her tonight. How, exactly, he wasn't so sure.

Maybe he should have paid extra to get Ghost in on the ground floor. This was exactly the sort of thing that crazy fuck got off on.

Marco watched Fiona approach a thick knot of people, noted the weary smile, how she smoothed her hair and clothes perfectly into place. At exactly three paces, she flipped some sort of switch and the lights went on. She…beamed. The group parted, accepting her into their midst and closing ranks around her.

Well, hell.

Either he went into the fashion show after her, or he waited for her to come out.

The minutes ticked by and he watched her reflection in the bar mirror. She spoke with everyone, soft smiles, slight nods. More accurately, everyone spoke at her and she listened. Not many gave her a chance to speak.

There was a hunger…a deep longing staring out of her eyes that unsettled Marco, because he understood it. What it was like to be on the outside…looking in.

Fuck.

He downed the rest of his glass and tossed a few bills onto the bar. If he was going there, if that's where his head was, he had no business being in the field right now. He had time. Tonight was shitty anyway. His cousin should be released from prison any minute now and Marco needed to be on pick-up duty for his aunt's sake.

"One, please." Fiona leaned past his stool and rested her elbows against the bar. She'd shed her suit jacket, though it did nothing to detract from her buttoned-up appearance.

She glanced over her shoulder at him, plump lips slightly parted. Her brown hair was pulled up into a sleek bun he wanted to…mess up.

"This seat taken?" she asked.

"It is now." Marco nodded at the bartender and added a few more bills to the pile. When opportunity knocked, he sat his ass down and paid attention.

"This doesn't exactly look like your kind of place." She slid onto the stool, knees tilted toward him. Prim and proper.

"What kind of place should I be at?"

"Hm." Fiona cocked her head to the side. Her eyes were a little blood-shot and there was something...tense...about her posture. Yet she pursued him for a moment. "A biker bar?"

"Bike's outside. This," he spread his hands, "is now a biker bar."

"Thanks." She took the pint of beer the bartender slid her way with a smile. "I've never been to a biker bar before."

Marco watched her, not entirely sure what to do with that piece of information. Was it a hint? He accepted his second drink and left it on the bar with no intention of drinking it. He had a full night ahead of him, and one drink was his self-imposed max.

"Biker bar's just like any other bar, I guess. Just more noise." He shrugged and leaned back on the stool.

What game was she playing at? He knew what *he* was here for, but what was she doing? Fiona had come to him, but why?

Fiona bit her lip and looked at him. The gaze was full of questions.

"You're looking at me like you want to fuck me." Marco lifted his glass to his lips, more for show than an actual drink.

A red blush tinged Fiona's cheeks and her gaze went back to the bar top.

"Sorry, was that too crass?"

"You aren't sorry." She drew in the condensation clinging to her pint glass.

"Not really."

"What's it like?"

"What?"

"Always saying what you think?"

"I just open my mouth." Marco shrugged. She was getting at something, he just had to give her a little time to get there.

"I couldn't imagine saying what I think half the time."

"Sure you can. Try it." He turned his chair, his knees capturing

414

hers, forcing her to face him. "Tell me what you're thinking, right now."

Fiona's lips worked soundlessly, her hazel eyes going dark.

She had his curiosity piqued now. Just what was it the pretty lady wanted to say?

ABOUT LEXI BLAKE

Lexi Blake lives in North Texas with her husband, three kids, and the laziest rescue dog in the world. She began writing at a young age, concentrating on plays and journalism. It wasn't until she started writing romance that she found success. She likes to find humor in the strangest places. Lexi believes in happy endings no matter how odd the couple, threesome or foursome may seem. She also writes contemporary Western ménage as Sophie Oak.

Connect with Lexi online:

Facebook: Lexi Blake
Twitter: https://twitter.com/authorlexiblake
Website: www.LexiBlake.net

Sign up for Lexi's free newsletter at www.LexiBlake.net.

Made in the USA
Middletown, DE
18 October 2016